1936

A NOVEL

NFB
Buffalo, New York

1936

John H. Grandits

Copyright © 2025 by John H. Grandits

Printed in the United States of America

1936/ Grandits—1st Edition

ISBN: 979-8-9922001-6-4

Fiction> Historical Fiction
Fiction> World War II
Fiction> Thriller> Suspense
Fiction> Social Commentary

This is a work of fiction. All characters are fictitious. Any resemblance to actual events or locations, unless specified, or persons, living or dead is entirely coincidental.

No part of this book may be reproduced or transmitted in any form by any means, electronic or mechanical, including photocopying, recording, or by any information storage and retrieval system without permission in writing by the author.

Note on Cover Images:

"German American Bund Parade New York City 86th St. 1937," Courtesy of the Library of Congress.

Band image, federal stage shows div. of W.P.A.: "A sparkling musical revue 'Gaieties of 1936,'" Federal Art Project 1936, Courtesy of the Library of Congress.

"Curtiss P-36 Hawk", in flight, (U.S. Air Force photo), Courtesy of the National Museum of the United States Air Force. Disclaimer: "The appearance of U.S. Department of Defense (DoD) visual information does not imply or constitute DoD endorsement."

NFB Publishing
119 Dorchester Road
Buffalo, New York 14213
For more information visit Nfbpublishing.com

To Maura

Also by John H. Grandits

Canalside Tale

Official corruption, labor unrest, crime in the streets, waves of immigration, the chasm between rich and poor: these are issues that surface throughout American history—and still resonate today. Canalside Tale, an intense new novel set in the year 1880, brings to life the human drama behind these issues. Detective Danny "Brick Fist" Doyle polices one of most crime-ridden precincts in the world, the notorious Canal District of Buffalo. Despite a fearsome, and oftentimes wayward reputation, he is viewed as a useful tool by the department. However, when investigating a society murder and industrial disaster, he resists a rush to judgment as demanded by his superiors. Instead, he embarks upon a redemptive quest for the truth that leads him into conflicts with crime lords, corrupt officials and a bigoted tycoon. Set against the backdrop of powerful elites and struggling masses, Canalside Tale takes the reader on an exciting journey through Irish Hoolies, Victorian mansions, forbidden affairs, pestilent sweatshops, elegant receptions, clandestine union meetings and torch-lit political rallies. After winding through a world of colorful and unforgettable characters, the story leads to a surprising yet stirring conclusion.

Wayfarer's Passage

Steve Henson, a successful lobbyist and former high-ranking political figure, finds himself losing much of what he values most in life. In the course of trying to unravel the intrigues behind the collapse of his business, he forges new relationships with a beautiful woman harboring a terrible secret, and a mysterious old man whose dramatic life offers important lessons.

Eventually, the lives of unforgettable characters intersect to create an exciting and moving tale of love, loss, and redemption.

Before the story reaches its stirring conclusion, the reader gets to experience the glamour of urban night-life, cut-throat political wheeling and dealing, a dying rust belt city, powerful interests, distant lands, and other eras.

I

Even with the doors flung open, the air inside the Al Hambra Road-house was growing increasingly hot; yet rather than feeling stifling, the atmosphere in the hall was charged, as patrons eagerly waited for Hal Houston and his Uptown Orchestra to take the stage. Earlier, caravans of revelers had made the fifty minute trek from Buffalo to this popular lakeside resort. The eclectic mix ranged from young professionals to sales clerks, and factory workers. Primed for a good time, they were eager to hear some "hot" swing music—a recent craze that exploded onto the national scene the previous summer of '35, after Benny Goodman's land-mark performance at the Palomar Ballroom in Los Angeles.

As daytime began to ease into twilight, they continued to arrive at the club, which sat atop a small bluff overlooking the Lake Erie shoreline. With the ballroom quickly filling-up, couples began to stake out coveted spots on the dance floor, while others made their way to the bar, which stretched along a side of the cavernous hall.

The master of ceremonies on this night was Ernie Rodgers, the host of the Curtiss Wright sponsored radio program, "Skyboat: A mystical flight into the realm of popular music." Since it first aired a year earlier, it had gained a huge audience throughout much of the Northeast. Ernie's appearance at the Al Hambra was no coincidence, since this was Curtiss Wright Employee Night, when workers could enter admission-free, courtesy of the Buffalo-based aircraft giant.

By now, there was a buzz in the air as Ernie popped onto the stage followed by a dozen band members, nattily clad in white tuxedos. As he called out their names to loud applause, the musicians settled behind music stands adorned with the art deco monogram "HH." After waiting for the excitement to build, he finally shouted out, "Hey cats, are you ready for some music… some hot, hot music?"

The crowd responded with a roar of approval, as the orchestra launched into Benny Goodman's rousing hit, "Sing, Sing Sing." The raucous, opening strains, with its riveting drum solo followed by a chorus of blaring horns, seemed to light a fire under the crowd. As the infectious chords echoed off the rafters and rolled across the vast hall, the dance floor was transformed into a turbulent mass of bodies. Soon, arms were flailing, skirts were flying and bottoms shaking as the dancers lost themselves in the joyous rhythms of the music. Even the bystanders were tapping their feet and swaying their hips as they reveled in the excitement.

Outside, Alex Wagner parked his uncle's prized Pierce Arrow away from the chaos of the parking lot, before making his way to the roadhouse entrance. Standing in line beneath the building's gaudy neon sign and counterfeit minaret, he took a moment to shake the sand from his new white bucks.

Within a few minutes, he arrived at the door, where he shelled out the fifty cent admission. Despite being the scion of a wealthy family, he had a mere three bucks in his wallet. His current choice of jobs, reporting for a German community newspaper, was largely responsible for his limited resources.

Eager to quench his thirst after the hot ride down the turnpike, he made a beeline to the bar. He settled into a space along the corner rail, where he ordered his favorite lager. Drawing on his beer, he surveyed the dance floor, now awash with couples performing all manner of Lindy Hops, Balboas, and Collegiate Shags. One dancer instantly caught his eye, a tall red- haired beauty, whose powerful grace reflected her lithe, athletic frame. Nicely filling out a clingy silk dress, she shimmied to the beat of a tom-tom solo that filled the air. With her blue eyes beaming, she flashed a dazzling yet unassuming smile, as she and her female partner cut a fevered Lindy Hop. An infectious enthusiasm along with an apparent lack of pretense, served to underscore her beauty. Such an appealing portrait proved irresistible to Alex.

Despite the teeming crowd separating them, he was determined to meet this woman. Using his height to his advantage, he kept her firmly in his sight, and after a series of stops and shifts, he arrived at his destination, just as the final notes were fading.

The redhead was now standing next to the stage, catching her breath after the spirited dance. A rosy glow graced her cheeks as she shook her thick mane of hair in response to the heat. That, combined with a dress that now appeared even more clingy, only added to her appeal.

The break in the music, offered Alex his chance. Ignoring the inhibitions that often arise at such moments, he walked up to the girl.

"You look like a couple of professionals out there …er … dance professionals, of course," he smiled sheepishly.

"Yikes, for a second there I thought, that's an interesting way to meet new friends," she laughed in return.

"Shook our bottoms pretty good, didn't we," her pretty, dark-haired partner shot back with an exaggerated leer.

"Well, I suppose I can't argue with that, but first chance I get, and I flub it," he laughed. "But seriously, you dance great… and I have to say that you're not hard to look at either."

"Thanks for the compliments, and ignore some of the things she says. She always tries to be so sassy. And by the way, you're not too shabby looking yourself, Mister…"

"Thanks, Alex, Alex Wagner, and to whom do I owe the pleasure?"

"Maureen Costello. You're probably shocked that I'm Irish."

"And I'm Lisa Mangini, a little pisana caught between two giants."

"What do they say about good things and small packages…"

"You got that right, Al," Lisa giggled suggestively.

"I guess the red hair, fair skin, and blue eyes might be a tip off. And it works well. I can see why Tarzan fell for that Irish girl… what's her name… Maureen O'Sullivan?"

"Handsome and charming… nice," Maureen replied as a blush crossed her face.

"Charm, didn't't the Irish invent it? And I bet you have a ton of it."

After waiting for the emcee to announce the evening's sponsors, the band began to pump out another high octane number, Benny Goodman's, *King Porter Stomp*.

"Watch out, let's not get stomped ourselves." After gesturing that they move to the sideline, Maureen continued, "Another hot one. I say, let's sit this one out. Besides, I'd like to get to know our new friend, Alex, a little better."

"With all the complements flyin' around, something tells me you two wanna talk. As for me, I spotted that cutie from the wing line… you know, Frank Nowak—the one who's always eyeing me up in the lunchroom. He's standin' over there near the bar, and I'm sure he'll wanna toss me around out there," Lisa winked.

"Catch ya later and be careful."

"Okay, Ma; toot a loo."

Once more turning to Alex, Maureen said, "Speaking of Irish actors, you remind me of a blonde Errol Flynn, that new Hollywood star. You sure you're not Irish, or half Irish?"

"Thanks, I heard of him, that pirate movie guy, but no, I'm all German. That's not a problem, like with your folks, is it?"

"Oh, god no, Although, maybe, whether you're Catholic," she chuckled.

"Gee, Catholic, sounds like my mother," he smiled in return.

"Yet, you should know I live in the First Ward—you know, territorial. But, the neighborhood boys know better than to pull any of that baloney with me. I'm tough. Daddy and Gramps were cops."

"No big deal, you get that ethnic stuff everywhere: Polish, on the Eastside; Italians, Westside; Germans, Kensington-Bailey. One of these days they'll realize it's nineteen thirty-six, modern times."

"And then there's our group, tall people."

"Yeah, we should stick together. So let me guess, five-ten?"

"Uncanny! As for you… um, you're six-four?"

"About six-three. Is that okay?"

"Of course. The broad shoulders threw me off. Well, so far I know your height, I know you're German and Catholic, I know you're excellent at measuring, and you like dance. You must be graceful, since you look like an athlete. So, fill me in some more."

"Yeah, I played some college football. I suppose I'm okay at dancing, but one of my great passions is music, especially jazz."

"Music, you must have an artist's soul. That's good."

"Unfortunately I have my struggles at piano, but I sure love to listen to jazz, and follow it, and just be taken away by it. Now, as for you, you're a wonderful dancer, of course, and you work at an aircraft plant, if I'm not mistaken, and you're educated. It certainly comes across."

"Thanks, and I do work at an aircraft plant, Curtiss Wright. I work on the cockpit control panels, going on two years now, ever since I graduated from State Teachers College. Yeah, I'm trained as an English teacher. You see, Curtiss pays a lot more than high school, much to the chagrin of my grandparents. And what do you do?"

"Since I got out of Canisius in '32, BA in history, I tried a few jobs, much to the chagrin of my parents who want me in the family business. Right now, I'm working as a reporter."

"I bet it's sports or business. Where, the *News*, or the *Courier*?"

"Actually, the *Advocate*, largest German community paper in the country. I report everything. My editor says that's the best way to learn the craft. It pays the bills, I'm liking it, and I'm still shooting for a Pulitzer," he laughed

"Not only are we tall but we're both 'chagrinners,' rebels that we are. Oh, and let's not forget we're smart. I feel you were more than an athlete in school."

"Yeah, I loved football, but I loved class more. I'm curious, and like to find answers. My folks encouraged that."

"So did my grandparents."

"And your parents?"

"Sadly, I lost my parents when I was a little girl during the flu epidemic in eighteen. My brother and I also got sick, but I think Gram and Gramps willed us to survive. They raised us."

"I'm sorry. That had to be so terrible at such a young age. I can't imagine."

"We were blessed with my parents, and I remember them with all my heart. And we're blessed with my grandparents who made sure we had all the love and support we could want."

"Yes, we're so lucky to have our families. And from what I can see, your grand-folks have a wonderful granddaughter."

As the final chords of the "King Porter Stomp" faded away, the emcee mounted the stage to introduce the lead vocalist. Slowing things down, the band eased into the Dorsey Brothers' hit, "Chasing Shadows."

"I like this tune. Tommy Dorsey's trombone lick is really sweet."

"You and me both."

"Would you like to dance. I promise I won't break your toes."

"I'd love to, and I know it will be nice."

They quickly made their way to the far end of the ballroom, which offered not only room but a small measure of privacy. Maureen cast a striking image, in her pink floral dress that swayed with each step she took. For his part, Alex looked equally impressive, sporting a coral silk shirt and white cotton slacks. His thick blonde hair swept back on top, coupled with his cool blue eyes, made for a compelling look.

Taking her in his arms, he stepped into a sweeping fox-trot. With a grace that belied his size, he led her through a series of deft moves that caught the attention of those around them.

As the singer crooned out the lyrics, "chasing shadows, just a dreamer am I," Maureen leaned in and smiled, "I can see some dreamer in you, with that search for a career and all."

"Don't forget, I'm German," he chuckled, "you know, practical. But yeah, I want to test the waters before settling in—like you, I would guess."

"I like my job but I need the money. So, I suppose I'm practical. Still I have my dreams."

As the music ended with a flourish, the couple glided to a finish. Standing back, Maureen exclaimed, "I must say, Mister Wagner, quite a performance. Where did that come from?"

"Thank my mother. She believed dance classes were important for children."

"You must have looked cute in your little suit at Miss Whomever's dance academy; but, weren't you ribbed by your pals?"

"I have to admit it came in handy tonight," he winked. "It was 'Miss Kay's' and a lot of the other boys in my family's circle went. Still, maybe it forced my brother and I to handle ourselves at school. You know how that goes."

"Sure, and don't forget I grew up in the Ward. That can be a tough crowd."

"Hey, speaking of crowds, whaddya say we head out to the patio. It's beautiful, the sun's beginning to set. Plus, it's easier to talk out there—and get a drink."

As the singer began belting out another "killer-diller" number, the pair nimbly sliced their way through the throng. Once they arrived outside, the sky was beginning to fill with stars while strings of Chinese lanterns cast a warm glow to the courtyard below.

After Alex grabbed a couple of drinks from the patio bar, the couple made their way to the stone wall overlooking the beach. From their perch atop the lakeside bluff, they could look out at the vast shoreline that stretched back to the twinkling lights of downtown Buffalo. For the next half hour, they spent their time getting to know each other, while enjoying the atmosphere outside. They even discovered a mutual interest in baseball. In the midst of a playful debate about the Yankees and Cardinals, they were interrupted by the arrival of Lisa and some friends.

"Finally, there you are. Thought ya mighta headed to the beach, the way you were so goo-goo eyed over each other."

"Lisa, be nice."

"Okay, just jokin'. Anyway, I was dancing my brains out, so I'm a little bushed…" whereupon one of the men let out a snicker, to which she replied, "I said, a little bushed, ya pervert!"

Shaking her head, she went on to introduce her friends to Alex: Frank Nowak, the earlier object of her attention, and a couple of boys from Maureen's neighborhood, Danny Egan, who also worked at Curtiss, and his cousin Patrick, the source of the snicker. Lastly, there was Gina, who had grown up with Lisa on the Westside.

As the little group engaged in typical introductory banter, Patrick kept a quizzical eye fixed on Alex. Finally he spoke up, "Say, I know you. I've seen you with your brother. He fired me from Alpine Machine last year."

"Pat!" Maureen scolded.

Although confident he could handle the situation, Alex wasn't inclined to back away from his family. "That's all right, Maureen. Listen, I'm sorry, but I'm sure my brother did what he thought was right."

"Canned me, 'cause I was passing out those football parlay cards. Wasn't hurtin' nothin' or nobody."

"Not too many work places would let that go."

"Still, that was a bastard move." Alex felt his patience ebb, before the man continued, "And I got a little kid with my ex. So, that didn't just screw me."

Suddenly, Alex eased off. Perhaps it was the man's cheap wardrobe or the pain in his eyes when he mentioned his child. Or maybe it was the thought of Maureen watching him, but in any case, he couldn't bring himself to pile on. "Yeah, that was a tough break, Pat. Mistakes happen, but listen, I know some people who may be hiring. I could put in a good word."

"That's okay, Al. Sorry, I just got a sore spot, but I ain't so innocent either… besides, my uncle got me into the city, throwin' cans."

"Pat, you know my cousin Sean Shea, he loves his job on the trucks. He just bought a little cottage on Kentucky Street," Maureen said, as she cast an admiring glance at Alex.

"Throwin' cans musta helped ya toss me. You do a snazzy Lindy— especially for a Mick!"

"Hold on, Lisa, when I took step dancing as a little girl, the boys in class were really good, so *ixnay* on the Mick talk."

"So whaddaya think of this palooka out there?"

"He's hardly a palooka. In fact, Alex is quite a dancer. I was thoroughly impressed."

"Actually, I did watch him. Not bad at all," Lisa winked.

Her playful flirting drew a quick yet icy look from Frank as he stood by her side.

"So what's up? Are we stayin' or goin'?" Gina asked, while barely missing a snap of her gum.

"Yeah Maureen, the dance floor's getting too crowded. We're thinking about makin' tracks to Sugar's down at Point Breeze. You guys can tag along, if ya want. Whaddaya think?"

"Gee Lisa, I don't know. It's nice out here, and we can still hear the music. And what about the plant bus?"

"Danny's got a car. He'd be happy to take us home if we miss the bus. And what about Alex? He sure doesn't look like he took a bus."

"Yeah, I drove, but I can't be out here too long. I have some things I have to do,"

"Same here. I have to take my Gram out tomorrow morning. Besides, Sugar's not really my cup of tea, a little too rowdy, Lisa."

"Sure, it's a little whacky but it's fun and it's got a great jukebox,"

"Thanks, but like I said, I'm really enjoying it out here. The other kids from the shift must be around, but I don't want to leave you."

"No problem, Mo, I'll be fine. If it's dead, we'll shake a leg back here, otherwise don't wait up," Lisa said before adding, "And I can tell Alex ain't no cad. He'll take ya home."

'You bet," Alex smiled.

"Okay, but be safe. The roads are dark and watch the drinking, Danny!"

"Don't worry, Maureen, I ain't drinkin' tonight. My brother, Bobby's doin' me a favor, lettin' me use his car. He'd kick my butt if he heard I was hittin' 'em."

Just then, a busboy from the nearby Seneca Reservation knocked over a beer bottle while leaning over to retrieve it from the stone wall.

"Hey, Sitting Bull, what's wrong with you?" Frank snapped.

"Sorry, sir. I'll go get a broom and bucket."

"Listen you Injun moron, you'll pick it up now—by hand! The girls could get cut."

"Cut it out," Alex shot back. Directing his attention to the boy he added, "That's all right buddy, accidents happen. Go get your broom, we'll be careful."

"Mind your own business, Kraut," Frank sneered.

This time, Alex was not so patient. Raising himself from where he was leaning against the wall, he loomed over his adversary. "So, should I respond with what, Polak? Come on, the kid's just trying to do his job. Let's not have a problem…"

As Frank continued to strike a menacing pose, his co-worker Danny, was quick to intervene. Leaning in, he whispered, "Frank, have you gone bats. He was a Little All-American in football. I saw him play, he could run through a brick wall."

Despite his hair trigger temper, Frank finally realized his precarious position. "I suppose I'd prefer, Bohunk," he chuckled awkwardly in an attempt to save face. "Sorry, but I didn't want the girls to get cut."

"Good, no sweat. He'll take care of it. Just watch your step, ladies"

Trying to break any remaining tension, Lisa announced, "Well that's just peachy. Now that we got all the fun and games outta the way, maybe we can head over to Sugar's."

"Have a good time…and try to behave yourself," Maureen reminded her friend.

"Maybe… and you two have fun mooning over each other."

After Maureen once more rolled her eyes in feigned exasperation, everyone took a moment to exchange farewells. No sooner had they left than she turned to Alex, "I was so proud of how you handled Pat and then how you defended that Indian boy. He didn't deserve that humiliation. Still, I apologize that you had to put up with all that."

"And here I thought I was going out for a relaxing evening of music," he chuckled. "But really, no big deal, and more importantly, I met this wonderful girl."

"That's sweet, and I feel the same way about you. And yes, it was a big deal. You put that jerk Frank in his place. I don't like him, and I don't like him around Lisa, but she's a big girl."

"Sometimes you have to remind a bully to knock it off. The other guy Pat, he was just letting off steam, so you cut him slack."

"Not everyone would, but you were understanding of him. A lot of people don't care, or are mean and prejudiced like that bum Frank."

"Well, everyone deserves a fair shake."

"Like our President is trying to do. But, I won't hit you with that tonight."

"Hey, I like him too. I'm not a big political type, but he's good."

"Whew, that's good. One more thing I like about you."

"You're spoiling me," he smiled, before turning more serious,

"And I'm having the best time with you tonight … but …I have to leave here pretty soon."

"That's right, you said you had something to do later on. Is it work?"

"Yeah, I have to cover a story."

"Sounds important."

"A big deal for sure, the inaugural convention of the Bund at the Statler."

"Oh yeah, I read about them, and heard about that rally on the radio. Sounds like a nasty bunch of Nazis. And what's with that name, the Bund—German, I assume?"

"It's the *Amerikadeutscher Bund*, that is, the German American Federation, or Bund for short—and I agree they're bad They say their purpose is to promote a better understanding between Germany and America; but as you probably know, most observers think it's just a front for the Nazis. My editor and I share serious concerns about this, not the least of which is identifying all German Americans with this group. Knowing these people and their beliefs, we're going to make sure we give our readers a critical assessment."

"Seeing what's going on in Germany, especially the treatment of the Jews, I'm terrified of those Nazis getting a toehold here."

"That's why it's important that we cover this story—expose them for what they are. Still, I'm disappointed that I have to head out."

"I completely understand," she said with a reassuring smile.

"And didn't you say that you have to get home early. If that's still the case, like I told Lisa, I'd be more than happy to drive you back."

"That would be great!"

"Listen… it just struck me that since we're both headed to the city, why don't you join me on assignment?"

"Really?"

"It'll be interesting! You could act like a fellow reporter. You're smart. You can pull it off!"

"Interesting to say the least! I would love to see for myself what's going on there," she said, as she paused to ponder his offer.

"So whaddaya think? You in?"

"Well, Gramps always said I was his plucky little dare-devil … But just one thing, given who they are, do you expect any trouble?"

"I spoke to cops that I know, and they insist they're gonna keep a lid on things."

"Still, I'm sure my grandparents would be just thrilled, if I got rounded up in some sort of riot," she chuckled.

"It'll be fine. There'll be protests, but mainly from clergy, American Légionnaires, and Jewish War Vets— hardly a riotous mob."

"How can I resist? I'm all in!"

"And now, can you please spoil me some more, by joining me for one last dance?"

"I'd love to."

"Yes, right near the door, so I can look at you and still feel this beautiful evening."

"That will work for me too!"

II

His small, flinty eyes darted back and forth, scanning the room for any hint of danger. Although most diners fail to inspire that sort of reaction, in the case of Karl Braun it made sense. For him, life was a battlefield charged with all manner of menace. Jews, Blacks, homosexuals, and government, were just some of the malevolent forces at work against his world.

He was native born, but had little love for America, seeing it as corrupt and decaying from the weight of diversity, permissiveness and crass democracy. A measured and almost scholarly demeanor masked the hatred that filled his soul, and while he was adept at projecting a benign image when needed, his true nature was just beneath the surface.

On this night, Karl sat in a quiet corner of Ollie's Lunch Box, waiting for the last member of his group to arrive. Ollie's was an ideal site for this clandestine rendezvous, isolated, and a mere three blocks from their objective, the Grand Ballroom of the Statler Hotel. As the clock approached 7:45, the diner was a forlorn place. Besides Braun and his party, the only other patrons were a couple of aged regulars, seated at the counter, sipping their coffee while leafing through the well-worn pages of the morning paper, no doubt, in an effort to make the lonely night pass faster.

Outside, the glow from the restaurant windows was the only source of light on this desolate end of the block. Even the faded Coca Cola sign above the doorway, was obscured by the encroaching darkness. Once a bustling little commercial strip, Mohawk Street was now littered with boarded-up businesses. Besides Ollie's, only a used clothing store and a tiny cobbler shop managed to hang on.

Inside, Bennie, the night cook and waiter, was busy mopping the tile floor near a silent jukebox. A beat-up radio propped atop the cup shelf was crackling out a Buffalo Bisons baseball game. The sportscaster's ticker-tape recreation of an away game managed to smother the murmur coming from the back booth.

"I told everyone to be here by 7:30. This is inexcusable, and won't be tolerated anymore," Karl spit-out with a menacing glare.

Braun was a natural fit as group leader. He had been identified as such by higher-ups, before assembling a small band of like-minded thinkers over the last two years. He possessed a native intelligence that had been obvious to all throughout his life. More importantly for the purposes of the group, he had an unwavering commitment to the Nazi cause.

His American-born father died from the effects of alcoholism when Karl was a child. Thereafter, the boy spent every summer of his youth with his mother's relatives in Germany. It was there that he became enamored with the Nazi movement that was building at the time. Eventually, he went on to join the Hitler Youth. His admiration was inspired by the Nazi's bullying displays of strength and nationalistic pride, that appealed to his sense of a superior German heritage. It was an identity that his cold, yet influential mother took pain to infuse in him from an early age. Still, his embrace of Nazism was mainly a response to a wellspring of anger that was fueled by a sense of alienation and social isolation. Although always insistent on blaming others, he ignored the role that his caustic disposition and condescending attitude played in the barren nature of his schoolboy life.

It was no surprise then that a toxic ideology steeped in victimhood, scapegoating, racial superiority and violence, would prove irresistible to the young Karl Braun. Yet, while it became a belief system central to his core, he kept it largely hidden when in the States. Eventually, as he settled into his adult life as a master machinist, the unmarried loner found comradeship within a small circle of fellow Nazi sympathizers.

Confident in his role as team leader, Braun sat at the center of the group, beneath a yellowing, White Owl Cigar poster. "I suggest we get going. She can catch up later."

"Ya sure it's safe here, Karl?" Martin Hoffman asked. Hoffman was a handsome, thirty year old factory mechanic who worked with Braun over the years. Even within the group, the former soccer star was known for the intensity of his Nazi beliefs. A true fanatic, he self-inflicted a *"schmisse,"* or dueling scar down his cheek. It was in homage to the nineteenth century Prussian military practice that had resurfaced as a badge of honor among the most extreme Nazis.

"We'll keep it down, but don't worry, I know this place. Those two old coots at the end of the counter are as deaf as doornails. As for the cook, he's a slap happy ex-boxer who can barely make change."

"Yeah, look at that oaf! Probably a dumb Polak," Martin snickered

"Lucky for us, he's always listening to those infernal ball games. But even if they seem to pick up on anything, we can revert to German. Given all that, and it's location, this is perfect for tonight."

"I can always pump some nickels into the jukebox, if needed," piped in Kurt Metzger, a bald, mustachioed beer salesman in his early fifties. A former college wrestler and son of a Franco-Prussian War veteran, he belonged to the same *"Sangerbund"*, singing society as Braun.

Eager to get moving, Braun pressed on, "First, let's go over tonight. Then I want to report on some important new business. Plus, I have some ideas I know you'll like."

"So, as ya mentioned last week, we're just supposed to observe tonight, right?" the ever-eager Martin noted.

"Yes, that's what the bosses want," Karl replied, sticking to the veiled reference he used in regard to his contacts, both here and abroad. "But I want to go over things again to be sure."

"But this is our movement, these are our people, our *Volk*. Shouldn't we be involved and lend our support to the Bund?" asked Eric Bachman, a fat, German-born member of the group, and the owner of a small plumbing business. He knew the others mainly as a result of his constant presence at local German restaurants and bars.

"For now, we must continue to stay undercover. You may remember that Berlin pulled back on appearing to support the old 'Friends of New Germany.' Most members were German resident aliens, and that Jew Congressman, Dickstein, went after them as foreign agents…"

"And now the new German American Bund emphasizes its American face. Only American citizens can join. So, doesn't that solve the problem?" Kurt chimed in.

"Listen, tonight's the Bund's inaugural convention, and sure they share our beliefs, but the Bosses are being cautious. That's where we come in, to observe and report. I already met tonight's probable victor, Fritz Kuhn, a couple of times in Chicago."

"So how did that go?" Eric asked.

"I wasn't impressed. He does a lot of strutting around and not much else. He fancies himself an American Fuhrer, if you can believe that."

"And at our last meeting you said that me, Kurt and Martin are to just roam the floor, listening and takin' notes,"

"Mental notes only, and don't go signing up for anything. Remember, we're keeping it low key. The Bosses gave us passes. Hans and I will be wandering outside and in the lobby and gallery. We'll be listening to the scuttlebutt, along with watching the press and demonstrators, and of course, the cops."

"Yeah, it's important to check on these Jews, Communists, n*****s, and n****r lovers who hate us. You must know your enemies, so you can crush them," snarled the man at Karl's elbow, Hans Krueger.

As second in command, Krueger knew some of the strategic and tactical details kept from the others. Despite the lack of a high school education, he had cunning smarts, and with his wolf-like features, he had the look of a man willing to answer any offense with violence. During prohibition, he worked as a "strong arm" and truck driver for notorious local rum-runners. Upon the repeal of the Volstead Act in '33, except for an occasional debt collection for his old boss, he embarked on a new career. Expanding on his hobby, photography, he managed to make a living; nonetheless, his main source of revenue came from taking pictures of children using a borrowed pony as a prop. This constantly grated on his overblown ego. Still, he saw himself as an outstanding, if unrecognized artist, much like his idol, the failed painter, Adolph Hitler.

In addition to his ferocious devotion to the Nazi cause, his other great passion was gymnastics. A one-time vaulting champion, he worked as a part time coach at the local German Turner's Club.

Krueger also fancied himself as a ladies' man. Yet his temper and pervasive misogyny would eventually surface, precluding any normal, long term romantic relationships. Instead, he found relief in the company of prostitutes, or others surviving on the fringes of society.

"Yes, Hans, they hate us for our purity of blood, our superior culture, our history and industry," Karl said, always intent on trumpeting and re-enforcing their beliefs.

"And look what we brought to America, our great numbers who built things. Successful people like Rockefeller, Singer, Heinz…" added Kurt, eager to echo his leader.

"And don't forget the great Gehrig and Ruth," chimed in Martin.

"*Ach du lieber*," Eric shot back, rolling his eyes. "Ruth's a light skinned n****r, you *dummkopf*! Look at his nose and lips. He hid it, so he could play."

"That's right," Kurt laughed. "Ty Cobb wouldn't share a hunting cabin with'im. Said he never bedded down with a n****r before, and ain't gonna start now!"

"And never forget what we lived through during the War," Hans fumed, his eyes ablaze. "Our families always suspect; and humiliated. And the lynchings! Like with that man Prager in Illinois, who they marched through the streets and hung."

"Never again," hissed Martin.

"Even now, look how they framed and killed Bruno Hauptman, when in fact the Jews and British murdered the child, because of the Aryan hero, Lindbergh's isolationist beliefs."

"Yes, our enemies must be destroyed, and any uninformed idiots in this country—and they are many because of the Jew and British press—must be dragged to their senses," Karl said.

"With the German people at the dawn of a new age, under the brilliant leadership of Adolph Hitler, we must not fail to bring this to America!" Kurt vowed, caught up in the frenzy.

"No matter the cost, I pledge my life, everything, to my Fuhrer and Volk," Hans snarled.

"Make no mistake, my friends, our people will prevail. This is, and always will be an Aryan nation. For the sake of civilization, we must crush the degenerate, mongrel forces. They'll be gone or be back as slaves where they belong." Braun crowed.

"And don't forget all that perverted n****r records that the Jews sell, or play in their clubs. Or the Jew movies, that make our White women look like whores." Eric, added, keen to show his fealty to the cause.

"And not just the Jews and n****s, but the f****ts, and all the weaklings, right!" Martin proclaimed, perhaps a little too loudly, as Bennie the cook turned towards the noise.

Just then, they were interrupted by the arrival of the last member of the group, Britta Voight. Taking advantage of a work-break, she hurried over from one of her jobs, in this case as a cigarette girl at a popular bar and dime-a-dance club a couple blocks away.

In her mid-twenties, she was a shapely, handsome woman whose jet black hair framed a dimpled, apple-cheeked face. Her usual, sunny disposition was oftentimes suppressed by a darker impulse to blame others for her own failures. Despite lacking in confidence and having a pliant personality, she possessed a great singing talent. As a featured soprano, she achieved some renown as a member of the city's top Sangerbund, where she had met Karl Braun years earlier. Ignoring the warnings of others, she recently embarked on a budding relationship with Hans Krueger.

"Sorry I'm late. I just couldn't get enough of all those loser dancers and their creepy customers. And then, I hadda flirt with my boss to get out for an errand."

"What?" Hans snapped.

"No big deal. Thinks he's Clarke Gable, the little, guinea greaseball … Yuk!"

"You should get out of there," Kurt Metzger, the father of five suggested.

"Yeah, but I'm makin' some good money on tips."

"Well, don't be late again!" Braun snorted. "But enough of this, let's get down to brass tacks. I already went over their roles tonight," Braun said before turning to Britta. "As for you, you keep your eyes and ears open at the club tonight. I figure a lot of people from all sides of the convention will be stopping there later. They may be shooting off their mouths, especially if they're drunk."

Once again, they were interrupted, this time by Bennie the cook, who came to check on the pretty new arrival. Despite the intimidating look of matching tiger tattoos on his massive forearms, he was a gentle soul, who always sported a smile beneath a crisp white sailor cap, the type he wore to work since his days in the navy. Oblivious to the abrupt end to their conversation, he asked, "Is there anything I can get ya, Miss?"

"Thanks, honey, but I just ate," she replied with a smile.

Blushing at her use of the term "honey," he continued, "Well, you just give me a wave if you change your mind and want some coffee. I'll make it fresh for ya."

"Oh, you're so sweet."

"Ah, anything for such a pretty lady," he gushed awkwardly.

As the gentle giant made his way back to his stool beside the radio, Braun snapped, "Christ, enough of that idiot." Ignoring a quick look of reproach from Britta, he went on, "And remember, after the events wind down tonight, us fellas will rendezvous at the alley behind the Statler. "

"Is it what I think it is?" Martin asked, excitedly.

"I'll address that later, but for now, I have some good news to announce. First, I want to say a few things," Braun said with an air of pride. "We've known each other for quite a while, and shared our beliefs. These last two years we've forged ourselves into a strong unit. We've met and studied, and strengthened our beliefs and pledged ourselves to this noble cause…"

"And we have become onc, as comrades!" Hans proclaimed.

"That is right, my friends, and it has been observed, by important people," Karl, reported with a smile. "As you know, for many years, going back to my days in the Hitler Youth, I've developed relationships and contacts with people of influence in the movement."

"So, is that here or back in the fatherland?" Eric asked.

"I don't want to go too deep into that. We've talked about the need-to-know basis of information. We can't be too careful with all our enemies out there."

"As loyal Nazis, shouldn't we trust each other," Martin questioned.

"It's German iron discipline," Krueger snapped. "We follow orders, period. The tighter the circle, the better the chance of success. I learned that during my rum-running days."

"Believe me, our friends are aware of what we've become, of our commitment, of our skills. Our plans for tonight are an example of this. And now, I am proud to say they are entrusting us with a very important mission to help our Volk."

"Can you tell us any details about it?" Eric inquired.

"Only the barest, but I can say we have bosses who will provide guidance and financial support for this mission."

"Will they lead us directly?" Kurt asked.

"No, indirectly through me, and with my input. I am the sole point of contact with them, and will continue as your tactical leader. I can tell you this much: We have our superiors in Berlin, of course, and they're hands-on. Then there's my contact, who has official cover here. Finally, there's a person over here. I don't know him, but apparently, he has influence along with standing and money. Between you and me, he sounds arrogant, but that's immaterial."

"Can you give us some details about our roles?" Martin inquired.

"Hans, as my lieutenant knows some of the details. He, Britta and I will perform the initial tactical operations. You all will provide logistical support, at least for the time being. That's all I want to say about that, at this point."

"When will we start?" Kurt asked.

"Now. I'll get messages to you about meetings and about the time, place and nature of your particular tasks. The most important thing to remember, is that we must be deliberate and cautious. It's very sensitive and we must try to do everything right, according to plan. I know I've been sketchy and I can't say more, but I know we're good soldiers, ready to do our duty."

"We are strong, and will triumph!" Hans smiled, as the others voiced their approval.

"And what do you want us to do, when we rendezvous later, Karl?" Eric asked.

"On this, I didn't tell the bosses. I often read our Fuhrer's *Mein Kampf* to give me guidance and inspiration. As I said before, I keep returning to the thought of how Adolph Hitler has always been bold, and that if we are to succeed as a group, and contribute to the Nazi cause, we should emulate him!"

"Yes, yes, whether it was the Beer Hall Putsch, or seizing the Chancellorship under Hindenburg, our Fuhrer has always struck with resolve," Kurt beamed.

"Or leading the Brown Shirts into street battles with communists or other enemies!" Krueger roared, once more momentarily rousing Bennie from his focus on the ballgame.

"Is it that time for us to act boldly?" Martin asked, eagerly.

"Yes, indeed! As you know, we've identified possible targets, and Hans and I have cased them out. We've chosen the one on Huron near the hotel, and we'll do it tonight. You know the plans for that, and your roles in it, of course. I have the supplies in the trunk, so we're ready to go!"

"Yes, action," Eric smiled as he pumped his fist.

"This country is ripe for the message we bring," Braun asserted. "And a cause needs a dedicated cadre to inspire and educate the people. You can't lead from behind, and this is our's alone—no bosses to answer to. This is a role we must play to serve our cause and our Fuhrer."

"We must be at the front, exposing the vermin, so that this country can destroy the infestation," Krueger seethed, his veins popping from his neck.

"And we have allies, like our race brothers in the KKK. They're standing up for the White people in this country," Britta said as she looked for approval from Hans.

"Yes, the embers are smoldering, Braun beamed. It's time we whip the flames. Whether it's the corruption and degeneracy of the Jews and n****rs, or the despoiling of our women, we'll show them! Tonight, after we perform our duties at the convention, we'll make a statement announcing that a new era is dawning!"

"One People, one Reich, one Fuhrer," Hans proclaimed.

"*Heil Hitler*, blood and soil," they nodded among themselves.

III

With its bow drawn, the chrome archer atop the hood seemed to be pointing the way for the red convertible speeding down Lakeshore Road. As the Pierce Arrow 1601 sliced through the night air, light from a Strawberry Moon shimmered off its lacquer finish. Inside, the dashboard lights cast a warm glow throughout its leather upholstered cockpit, while Duke Ellington's "Take the 'A' Train" played on the radio.

By now, the beachside cottages had given way to the stone walls and ornate gates that guarded the summertime retreats of Buffalo's elite. Turning around a bend, the car approached a stretch of highway that looked out over the moonlit lake, sparkling beneath a blanket of stars.

"That's so pretty, Alex. And not a bad way to drive back to the city," Maureen said as she savored her surroundings.

"Top down is the only way to go on a warm summer night."

"Not to mention sitting in a Pierce Arrow, which I'm glad you explained to me. I got panicky when I first saw it in the lot. I thought it might be hot," she teased with a smile.

"Sorry about that. We were having such a good time at the club, I didn't want to get into all that family business stuff, right off the bat.

There's a lot to it, and I don't want to come off as having airs. Bad enough I'm driving my uncle's Pierce"

"Don't worry, I understand. I think you're nice. That's all that counts. And no, you don't have airs. That wouldn't work with me."

"And don't think I didn't want you to know about the business. I just wanted you to know me a little bit first. Don't get me wrong, I'm proud of what three generations of my family have built. But right now, I'm trying to figure out where I want to go with my life. Who knows, maybe I'll still join the business, someday."

"And what a company it is! Our plant gets a lot of its parts from Alpine Machine. When it came up earlier, I thought your brother was a boss there. I never figured your family owned the place," she chuckled.

"My dad and uncle do a great job running it, just like my late grandpa, who founded it sixty years ago. My brother, who's already heavily involved, is doing good."

"That's quite a family legacy."

"Yeah, over six hundred employees and millions in revenue each year, in addition to their other, smaller businesses. But I'm still not sure it's for me," he smiled with a hint of unease.

"It must have been interesting growing up in such a successful family. And they certainly seem to have done a good job raising you."

"Thanks. I'm very lucky with my family. My folks are really big on character and hard work. And of course, they loved us, just like yours, from what I can see."

"For sure, and we go back generations, too. My great grandfather owned the biggest tavern in the Ward, Blinky Shea's, and was a long-time power in Democratic politics."

"And you said your grandfather is a former Police Commissioner."

"Yeah, Hugh Costello, and still a legend in police circles. And my grandma, she's something. College educated back in the 1870s when it was rare for a woman. Ran her dad's business and was a well-known

Suffragette. She raised two families and is still involved in social issues. I feel totally loved, so I'm blessed like you."

"Speaking of families, maybe we'll run into my Uncle Max when we change cars at his place, down the road a bit."

"Just when I was getting used to riding in a car that costs more than most houses," she grumbled, feigning disappointment.

Arriving at his destination, Alex turned the car towards the stone pillars that marked the entrance to his uncle's summertime villa. Stepping up to the wrought iron gate, he dialed the phone in the call box, before the groundskeeper came and let them in.

Alex followed the beams of his headlights until he reached a brick paved plaza, fronting a Tudor styled mansion. Behind the house was a stunning, lakeside vista, highlighted by the city lights looming in the distance.

Finally, he eased the car next to his Chevy coupe parked in front of the carriage house. Sliding out of the car, she stood wide-eyed, beneath the glow of the antique street lamps lining the plaza. "Gee, and here I thought the car was impressive…"

"Yeah, nice digs, all right, but Uncle Max works hard. He's a big part of the most recent success, even during the worst days of the depression. He's very smart and always thinking ahead."

"Looks like his hard work paid off!"

"Believe it or not, he isn't here much. He's either away on business, or at his townhouse in the city. He lets me use the car when I'm out this way, and I sure get a kick outta drivin' it."

"Sounds like you're close, and you admire him a lot."

"Yeah, he's close to me and my brother. And he's especially close with Freddie the last few years, given their work at the company. I guess we're like his kids, since he had none of his own. He's always been a ladies man."

"He must be handsome like his nephew," she winked.

"Thanks! If I'm as handsome as you are pretty, that's a great compliment. But, yeah, he's an interesting guy. Quite the athlete—baseball and gymnastics. Signed with the old Boston Americans right out of college, as a third baseman. He played minor league ball a couple of years, before he realized he wasn't gonna unseat the great Jimmy Collins."

"Shows he is smart. Jimmy Collins was the greatest third baseman ever."

"He's from Buffalo you know. Went to Saint Joe's."

"Yeah, he's a good friend of Gramps. Lives over off Seneca Street. But wow, your uncle seems to be accomplished at everything, and by the way, thank you for that nice compliment."

"Easy compliment," he smiled. "And you're right, Max even manages to be involved with a lot of civic and cultural organizations, and he sits on a number of boards."

"Now I remember, Max Wagner… 'business leader and philanthropist.' I think I read he might run for governor. He sounds interesting for sure, and I can tell you're proud."

Just then, they were approached by the groundskeeper. "If you're lookin' for your uncle, ya just missed'im. He was out on Mister Klein's boat all day."

"That's right, there is a Sangerbund meeting at the country club, tonight. Yeah, Walt's on the board too." Turning to Maureen, he whispered, "Max's friend Walter Klein, is always arguing politics. He hates Roosevelt and thinks the New Deal was dreamed up by Stalin."

"I'm sure he'd love me and my family," she snickered.

After introducing the groundskeeper, Alex led her to the back of the carriage house. "I gotta show you something." There, on a patio overlooking the water, they were greeted by the sight of a boat gantry standing next to the stairs leading to the beach. Sitting in its cradle was a twenty-five foot, mahogany-hulled speed boat waiting to be lowered to the dock below.

"Chris-Craft, triple cockpit and eight hundred horse power. If I didn't know prohibition was over, I'd be worrying that Uncle Max had taken up rum running."

"Looks like a piece of art, so beautiful," Maureen sighed.

"Might have to work on Uncle Max to let me take that one out."

"I'd be too afraid. It would probably take me twenty years to pay it off."

"Probably take me thirty years at the newspaper," he laughed in return.

After heading back to the plaza, they jumped into Alex's '36 Chevy convertible coupe that sported a rumble seat in the rear.

"Your Uncle's car is amazing but this ain't too shabby, Mr. Wagner."

"My one indulgence, thanks to financing and my budgeting—mainly keeping the rent down..."

"For whatever reason, I thought you lived with your folks. Sounded too good to refuse."

"God, no! We're close, but I need elbow room. As it turned out, I'm not too far away, down Humboldt Parkway ..."

"Nice area."

"Thanks. One of our family friends had a vacant flat above their garage. They couldn't afford a handyman anymore, and I needed a place. So, it worked out, and I got a great deal on the rent."

They drove down the highway until the shoreline villas were slowly replaced by commercial strips and a sprawling steel plant complex. After arriving at the city's outer harbor, they crossed the Ohio Street Bridge and carved a path beneath the massive grain elevators before turning towards the lights of downtown.

"You know, since we're near your house, I can still drop you off, if you changed your mind about coming along with me."

"No way, I want to see this! Besides, I feel responsible for making you late."

"We're fine. The first couple hours is just resolutions and platform business."

Eager to get working, he raced past blocks of office buildings before arriving at Niagara Square, the city's hub. Once there, police were directing traffic away from the hubbub around the Statler Hotel, the site of the Nazi gathering.

Alex parked his car behind the square's other iconic structure, the twenty-nine story, art deco, City Hall. After a brief walk, they took up position across the street from the hotel. Standing beneath a theater marquee that trumpeted an upcoming appearance by Eddie Cantor, they watched as a steady stream of picketers circled the hotel. The demonstrators, a mix of veterans, clergy, NAACP activists, and members of the Jewish community, carried placards proclaiming "Nazis Not Welcome," "Boycott Germany" and "To Hell with Hitler." Chants of "No Nazis," filled the air, as scores of police ringed the building, determined to keep order.

After surveying the scene, Alex nodded towards the picket line, "Whaddah ya say we dive-in, and get some reactions—and feel free to join in."

"You don't have to ask me twice!"

They were barely half way across the street when their path was blocked by an officer from the mounted unit. "Hey, you know the rules: marchers on the sidewalk. Now get over there!"

"I'm with the press, officer. Here are my credentials."

Leaning down from the saddle, the cop took a quick look at the outstretched ID before giving a begrudging wave; but not without barking, "And what's with her."

"She's a new reporter. I'm bringing her along."

"Geez, a woman reporter. Listen, this ain't no place for a lady. You should be coverin' weddings."

"Or maybe I could write an article about coppers shielding Nazis from reporters," she shot back with a no nonsense look on her face.

Taken aback, he sputtered, "Well … okay, but watch your step, and don't go interferin' with police work!"

"Gee, maybe we should switch jobs. That was great," Alex smiled as they pressed forward.

"There's no pushing me around! I'm Irish, and my Daddy and Gramps were cops!"

Resuming their trek, they made their way towards a line of picketers. Grabbing a pencil and notepad from his pocket, Alex approached one of the marchers, who appeared particularly agitated as he pumped his fist and shouted slogans. "I'm a reporter with the *Advocate*, do you want to tell me what you feel about this Bund rally tonight?"

"The *Advocate*, ain't that that Kraut paper. Hey, they're your people. I fought you Germans back in '18, so you tell me, Mister Frankfurter"

"My name is Alex Wagner and I'm a fourth generation American of German descent. Our editor and staff want to provide our readers with a sense of whats going on here. If that's your answer, fine."

"Sorry, pal, and I get it, not all of ya are Nazis, but you go tell your readers this crap ain't comin' over here. Too many of our brothers are buried over there to allow this kinda bullshit. We'll fight these traitors and anyone else that supports 'em." As Alex scribbled his notes, the man went on, "And the name's Whitey Gallagher, formerly of the 5th Regiment, 3rd Division, veteran of the Marne." Eying up the couple, he cracked, "I can tell you're Irish, too, and I hope you're not with them."

"Yeah, I'm Irish American," Maureen shot back before adding, "And by the way, I'm concerned about Nazis, not German Americans."

As the man rejoined his fellow Legionnaires, Alex turned his attention to an oncoming group of picketers, whose signs identified them as belonging to a group called "Concerned Rabbis." Marching alongside them were ministers and priests from congregations in the area.

After introducing himself, Alex expected a skeptical response when he mentioned his newspaper. Instead, the spokesman for the groups, a Rabbi Levy, was eager to share his views with a German-American audience. He was joined by a Reverend Hill from Saint Luke's Episcopal, and a Pastor Johnson from Shiloh AME Church.

"So, why have you come out here in such numbers tonight?" he asked.

"We're anxious to remind your readers, and the other good people in the area, about the evil taking place in Nazi Germany, and to warn them of the growing threat here, as we can see tonight." Interrupted by a barrage of catcalls as police escorted some late arriving Bundists through a side entrance, the Rabbi continued, "It's terrible to think that the land of your readers' forebears, a culture that's produced the likes, Goethe, Beethoven, Heine and Leibniz…"

"Not to mention the great Martin Luther…" Reverend Hill joined-in.

"…yes, that great country is being led down the path of barbarism by Adolph Hitler. Daily, Jews are being beaten in the streets. Their homes and businesses are being terrorized…"

"And the Nazis try to cover their crimes by saying it's individual acts of, quote, 'retaliation'." Maureen broke-in, unable to hold back.

"That's right, young lady, the party line uses excuses like, 'provoked,'" Rabbi Levy nodded before adding, "They're enacting laws that bar Jews from government jobs, academia and the professions. Just last year, the regime revoked the citizenship of Jews, making them subjects to the state, robbing them of the rights enjoyed by other Germans. Their so-called "Racial Purity Laws," make intimate relations between Gentiles and Jews a crime."

"Christianity is also under attack," Reverend Hill declared. "They want to nationalize and 'Nazify' churches, that will promote dogmas that fits their 'master race' beliefs. Priests and ministers are being arrested and interred. That is what awaits our German brethren."

"Yes, and there are rumors of internment camps for their enemies being built around the country," the rabbi insisted.

"And their creed of hate extends to Gypsies, Slavs, homosexuals, Jehovah Witnesses, and my own Negro race. They call us, *untermenschen'* Perhaps you know what that means in German, Mister Wagner," Pastor Johnson added.

"Yes, it's translated as 'sub-humans,'"

"And sadly, they use America's treatment of its Negro citizens as an excuse for their horrors," the pastor observed with an air of irony.

Taking a break from his writing, Alex said, "As you know, a number of American reporters over there dismiss much of this as hyperbole, or a passing phase, that Hitler is merely playing to his craziest supporters. And some editors are wary of anti-German stories like the one about the so-called "Huns" bayonetting babies during the Great War. Yet, others, like Edgar Mower of the Chicago Daily News, and Dorothy Thompson, the foreign correspondent from Buffalo, have been sounding an alarm."

"And they were kicked out of Germany for their writings," Maureen piped-in.

"Yet, it's all out there," Rabbi Levy noted. "Hitler spells it out in 'Mein Kampf.' His toxic words are seared in my mind. In it, he calls for the elimination of Jews, which I quote, 'must necessarily be bloody.' He states that the German People will triumph, and I quote again, 'when their international poisoners,' meaning 'Jews,' 'will be exterminated,'"

"The book is a monstrous vision," Pastor Johnson proclaimed. Hitler describes his dreams for world domination. He goes on at some length about his plans for *"Lebensraum."*

"Living space," Alex replied.

"Yes, conquering land in Eastern Europe for the German people. As with all these things, believe him when he says it," the Rabbi said, while shaking his head.

"And hasn't Hitler started a rearmament program in violation of the Versailles Treaty, which so many Americans died for," Maureen interjected.

"Indeed," Reverend Hill answered.

"So, what do you want to see from this country, Rabbi, especially in light of the isolationist movement? You must read the letters to the editor— 'stay out of Europe's problems'."

"It's been less than twenty years since the War. We understand the mood of the country, especially since the passage of the Neutrality Act. Still, there are many good Americans raising their voices against this evil.

And we must stand with them, including by boycotting German goods, if that's what it takes."

"And what about measures our government should take?"

"Make every possible diplomatic effort, any leverage, to induce the German Government to end this madness. Beyond that, we must adjust our immigration laws to allow refuge to people fleeing the Nazi terror. Congressman Celler of New York is fighting to change the restrictive quota limitations of the Immigration Act of 1924."

As the Rabbi was saying this, an uneasy look crossed the face of his colleague, Reverend Hill. Picking up on his reaction, Alex asked, "And is that achievable, Rabbi? Polls show that Americans, by a wide margin, oppose changes to the quota system—even for refugees fleeing Hitler."

"I understand their fears: economic insecurities with the depression; national security concerns about foreign agents; but I'm not so naive as to be unaware that much of the motivation behind the national origin quotas, was to keep out Eastern and Southern Europeans, Asians, and Jews. Still, Americans are a good people. This is the land of Lady Liberty, the land that welcomed so many of our own families and forebears to its shores. We must now welcome those fleeing terror, and we have to ring the alarm!"

"We have to remember the slaughter of a million Armenians by the Turks during the War. It could happen again," Maureen said.

"But for the here and now," Reverend Hill added, "we must expose these Bundists for what they are: Nazi crusaders, eager to spread their dogma of hate and violence to these shores."

Satisfied that he captured the clergymen's arguments, Alex thanked them, before heading with Maureen to the entrance of the grand hotel. Once there, they waited beneath an elaborate metalwork canopy as police checked the credentials of those attempting to get in.

After a squad of cops whisked away a well-dressed man who began to shout socialist slogans, a weary looking sergeant kept waving along the line. "Have your tickets, hotel keys, or IDs ready. We ain't gonna have no trouble."

As the couple approached the glass doors, a flash of blue came rushing over. "Maureen Costello, you don't have anything to do with these bums, do you?" the cop asked while fixing a wary eye on Alex.

"For the life of me, no, Lieutenant Broderick! My friend Alex is a reporter and I'm here to help him."

He continued to cast a skeptical look, as he checked Alex's identification. Finally satisfied, he let them proceed, but not before adding, "You keep an eye on her in case there's trouble, got it, Wagner!"

"Don't worry," Alex replied with an edge.

Once through the doors, she turned to Alex, "Don't be offended. Bobby Broderick is always looking out for me. He was my dad's best friend growing up, and to this day Gramps treats him like a second son."

"With all these cops in your life, maybe you should be keeping an eye out for me."

"Speaking of which, I'm sure Gramps will be hearing about my latest adventure from Bobby."

After leading the way into the cavernous marble lobby. Alex stopped to take measure of the terrain, "So let's dive into this freak-show."

"Editorializing, Mr. Hearst," she teased.

"How could you not," he answered, while gesturing towards a group of overweight, middle-aged men. They were festooned in pseudo-military garb, consisting of black jodhpurs, riding boots, khaki shirts with various insignia, along with black ties and Sam Browne belts. It was all topped off with red armbands featuring a Nazi crest. Standing sentry outside the columned entrance to the Grand Ballroom, they tried to strike a menacing pose, with chests puffed out and hands planted on their hips.

Passing a group of reporters gathered at the rail of the lobby-bar, they couldn't help but hear a muffled quip, "Christ, the '*Advocate*', shouldn't he be covering some oom pah pah competition? This is for real reporters."

Alex ignored the insult, and instead hurried towards a trio of delegates headed for the convention floor. He was quick to pick out one of the group, a grandfatherly type in a baggy suit, who seemed to command the respect of the others. Catching him at the stairs to the ballroom, Alex lost no time in introducing himself and the newspaper. For his part, the man said his name was Conrad Schneider, and he was an insurance man from Cincinnati. He had a quick smile and friendly manner, that no doubt served him well as a salesman. He sported a cardboard hat and various buttons bearing the likeness of Fritz Kuhn, the night's expected victor. As such, he looked much like a typical party stalwart at any legitimate political convention.

Yet, any such resemblance quickly vanished when Alex asked him to describe what led him to the Bund. With the casual ease of a man talking about his favorite ball team, he launched into a deluge of his toxic beliefs. Revealing a consuming hatred that festered beneath an otherwise placid surface, he condemned all non-Aryans; however, he reserved his greatest vitriol for Jews, reviling them as vermin, and the source of all of society ills. Barely pausing to catch his breath, he went on to describe his draconian vision, where White men ran a terrorist regime with an iron fist. "Undesirables" would be "dealt with" or treated as nothing less than slaves, while women would be relegated to matronly roles, and subject to the will of their husbands or fathers. Any resistance wouldn't be tolerated; nonetheless, he heralded this Nazi world as a utopian paradise.

Straining to contain his shock and disgust in the face of the man's repulsive manifesto, Alex instead focused on scribbling his notes in an effort to capture every sinister detail for the benefit of his readers.

Maureen showed no such restraint, "What kind of depraved soul has such hatred for people and such a grotesque vision for the world."

"I'll excuse your rude, unmannerly remarks to being spoiled and naive, young lady."

"Manners! When you just outlined such monstrous beliefs! No, I just scratched the surface of my revulsion. And I'm not so naive as to believe the overwhelmingly decent people of this country won't totally reject this Nazi poison; or, abandon our hard fought freedoms and rights—for all!"

"You'll find out soon enough, when the Aryan race retakes this country from the mongrels, degenerates and traitors," he snickered with his friends. "You better see the light; and if not, you better watch yourself in the future."

Before Maureen had a chance to lay into the man, Alex intervened, "I suggest you watch your step." Feeling his anger rising, he snarled, "I'm not going to have any threats against my friend! Got it, Mister!"

"Okay, I get it. Although I'm surprised at this coming from such a fine example of Aryan manhood, there's always been race traitors. I just expect that you will report honestly. I'm sure your readers, our German brothers, will see the truth of my words."

"I don't care what you think of me. I'm a professional, and don't worry, I'll be reporting every syllable. And don't bet on our readers buying into your message. They're decent, loyal Americans who believe in the country's values. In any case, interview's over, thanks."

"Good bye, Herr Wagner, destiny calls," Schneider shot back before snapping, "Heil Hitler!"

As the delegates marched through the ballroom doors, Alex and Maureen retreated to a nearby corner. "Thanks for standing up for me. That was unbelievable, the evil he was spewing. It really hit a nerve. My family always taught me to stand up to injustice, but wow…"

"Don't worry, I wasn't gonna let that crazy little man threaten you."

"I'm fine, but thanks. Fortunately they're the lunatic fringe, but we can't ignore them—too dangerous."

"That's why I want to get this story out. The threat is real."

"I feel I should be scraping myself clean, but what's next on your agenda?"

"I wanna see what's up on the convention floor; but stay close by. These are sick people."

Unbeknownst to the couple, they were being observed at that very moment. Looking down from the gallery that circled the lobby, Karl Braun had spotted them the instant they entered the hotel. He was well aware of Alex, having seen him over the years when he would stop by the family business, Alpine Machine—where Braun worked. Despite having never met, he despised the young man. His hatred was fueled by resentment. He saw Alex as the spoiled son of privilege, a dilettante able to pursue a cupcake job, while reaping the benefits of generational wealth. It didn't help that Alex was not only tall and handsome, but was always charming to the girls in the plant, unlike the sullen and graceless Braun. His disdain was further fueled by Alex's writing. He felt that although reporting for a German community paper, Alex showed no appreciation for the Aryan Volk, and expressed nothing but skepticism, if not ill will, towards Hitler and the Nazis. As he watched the reporter scrawling into his notebook, he was certain it would be a hit job on tonight's events. As such, he felt that Alex Wagner was a perfect example of an aristocratic parasite that the movement was determined to crush.

Bringing his anger to boil was the sight of the woman at Alex's arm. She was the personification of Aryan beauty; yet, while the statuesque Valkyrie aroused him to his core, he was forced to concede that she was probably a whore, willing to sell herself for Alex's money and status. Consequently, in Braun's eyes, she was irreparably damaged.

Down below, Alex was eager to finish up, "Well, part two of the freak-show?"

"Lead on. This time I'll try to keep a lid on it," she chuckled, "no use starting a riot."

After reviewing his credentials, the Bundist guards at the door let them pass into the ballroom, owing in no small part to her red-haired beauty, as well as his German air. By now, the nomination roll call was well along. Each announcement of votes for the expected winner, was met by chants of, "Blood and Soil," "One Volk, One Reich, One Fuhrer," or "Jews Out."

The couple moved to a spot near a placard belonging to the Pennsylvania delegation. As the crowd began to spill out into the aisles in anticipation of the vote putting Fritz Kuhn over the top, Alex managed to corral two of the group. "So now that you're organized with your new leader, what do you see for the Bund?"

"I want to see us promote better relations between the US and Germany," the younger man with the Swastika tie-pin answered.

"And we want to point-out some of the great advances Germany is making as an example to this country," the little man with a mustache much like Hitler's, added with an affable air.

When Alex pressed them about treatment of Jews and Hitler's vision for an expanded Germany, any affability disappeared.

"Most of those are lies, concocted by the Jew press to smear the German Nation," the younger man snapped.

"Before you bash the land of your people," the little man shot back with a glare, "take a look at the way America treats its n****rs, thank god."

Just then, the hall erupted as Kuhn was proclaimed the victor. Not waiting for the cheers to subside, the new leader raced onto the stage. Dressed in the garish uniform of a Bund commander, he strutted up to the mic and launched into a speech extolling Nazi beliefs.

Mimicking the grandiose gestures of his idol, Hitler, he lost no time in ranting about Jews and other perceived enemies of the Aryan race. The harangue lasted another twenty minutes as he stood beneath a towering portrait of George Washington that was flanked on each side by Swastika banners and American flags. At the end of the speech he folded his arms and thrust out his chin to a rapturous chorus of "Seig Heils."

Alex was satisfied that he had gotten all that he needed, while Maureen simply had enough. Eager to escape, they quickly made their way to the rear exit. Once outside, in an effort to avoid the tumult of the demonstrations, they decided to cut through an alley, back to the car.

"Hopefully my story will show the readers what these people are all about."

"Yeah, they're crazy, but they're evil and dangerous. I worry that with that depth of hatred, we're in for real trouble."

IV

Huddled around the doorway of a shuttered bakery, they displayed the tense energy of a pack of jackals waiting to strike their prey. The five plotters were going over the details of their mission, anxious that it proceed without a hitch.

The bakery sat adjacent to a back alley, and provided an ideal vantage point for watching a newsstand, a block down the street. With a bank of clouds providing a convenient cover of darkness, the scene along Huron Street was forlorn, as all the businesses were closed for the night, and only an occasional car or pedestrian would be passing by at this late hour.

"Tonight, we take the first steps of action," Braun proclaimed, before spotting a nervous look on Eric's face. "What's wrong?"

"Just a little worried that the risk is worth it, especially for the first step,"

"There'll be no wavering," he snapped. "We've all agreed and we've planned and practiced. Besides, the cops are all at the hotel and we'll move fast,"

"And don't forget, we're German, efficient," Kurt chuckled.

"It's a small target, but it's the perfect time, with all the attention on the convention. It's time we show not just the Jews, but everyone that the defenders of the Aryan Race are here," Karl declared.

"We ain't no *hosenscheissers*. I'm eager to strike a blow! No more just talking, like at the convention, AKTION," Hans snarled.

"It will show Jews and our other enemies that terror can strike at any time," Karl smiled. "So, let's get going. Now, Kurt, one last time, you'll do the paint job, then help Hans and Martin with their little chore, right?"

"Yeah, got the can and brush from the trunk. I hope the swine will appreciate a beautiful swastika on the side of that shit-hole shack," he smirked.

"Eric, stay here and keep a look out. And remember, blow the whistle if you see any trouble coming."

"Sure, Karl, and when I see ya flash the rear lights, it's finished and I run to the car."

"Yes, I'll have the motor running. It will be over quickly, then everyone jump in the car, head up Delaware to Bryant to Best, then right into the garage I rent."

"And I switched the plates I stole from the junk yard, like you said," Hans added.

"Good work, Hans, and it looks like you and Martin are gonna have the most fun."

"Ya, Martin showed me some soccer kicks, and I showed him some boxing moves. That Jew scum is gonna regret that poster mocking the Fuhrer."

"With his mug all busted up, he won't be flirtin' with the Aryan girls, like I saw him doin' when I stopped for a paper," Karl sneered.

"Yeah, I saw it too, when I was casin' it out," Hans added.

"Last but not least, everybody, watch caps and bandanas! Now, let's move fast, before any do-gooders come down the street!"

With the precision of a well-drilled team, the gang flew into motion. Pulling his scarf over his face, Kurt rushed to the side of the shanty and began slapping a crude swastika onto the rag-tag clapboards.

Hearing a noise against the wall, Jake Bloom got up from the stool where he'd been counting the night's receipts. He was barely out of his seat when two masked men leapt over the counter. Soon, the smaller man began tossing newspapers and magazines in all directions, while the other delivered a haymaker to the face of the stunned vendor, dropping him to his knees. This was followed by a barrage of kicks and a slew of anti-Semitic slurs that filled the air. Fighting for his life, Bloom somehow managed to crawl through the gate to the street outside.

After smashing through shelves and emptying the contents of a cigar box into a bag on his belt, the smaller man, Hoffman, joined his partner in pursuing the victim to the curb. Yet his plans were interrupted by the blare of a whistle. Before he had a chance to react, he felt a powerful hand grab him by the nape of his neck, pulling off his mask, and hurling him backwards.

As Maureen screamed for help in the background, Alex turned his attention to the chief tormentor, who continued to rain a hail of blows onto the helpless victim. Without breaking stride, the former football star launched a right cross that sent Krueger flying.

Just then, Kurt emerged from the shadow of his swastika, brandishing a board he pulled from the shanty. As Alex bent over to help the victim, the old wrestler unleashed the weapon across Alex's back, sending him to the pavement. Seeing the attack on her friend, Maureen rushed to his side. Nonetheless, she was stopped in her tracks, when the lookout, Bachman, grabbed her from behind and tried to cover her mouth. Soon his cries eclipsed her's, as she sunk her teeth deep into his hand. Upon delivering a sharp elbow to his ribs that released her from his grip, Maureen looked on in horror as Kurt prepared to strike another blow onto Alex.

Yet, no sooner had he reared back, than a blur of a man came soaring into the picture. Leading with a massive, cocked forearm, the stranger sent the Nazi thug crashing into the newsstand.

Ignoring Kurt, who lost his cap, and was wobbling to his knees while using his mask to stanch his bloody nose, the Black rescuer turned his attention to Bloom. Fearing the worst, he tended to the groggy huckster, while Alex rolled back up to help.

By now, Braun was blasting his horn, while screaming for his broken comrades to get into the car. Licking their wounds, the erstwhile warriors stumbled into the welcoming embrace of the waiting beige Chrysler, which spun-off in a cloud of burnt rubber. Once on Delaware, Braun eased up on the throttle so as not to attract attention, but with every passing street light, he cursed the very existence of his boss's son.

Having escaped from her attacker, Maureen arrived at the site of the carnage, but not before taking note of the plate number, as the getaway car sped into the night. She also saw that it looked much like her granduncle Johnny's big, beige Chrysler, a fact she'd be sure to report to the police.

"Alex, are you all right; are you hurt," she pleaded as she stood by his side.

"Thanks, but I'm okay. Didn't see the third one. Got the wind knocked outta me—couldn't breath," he coughed before turning towards Bloom. "You okay? Can you tell us your name?"

"Jake Bloom," he rasped as he tried to raise himself up.

"Don't push it Jake, rest a little," Maureen advised, as she bent down to help.

"Jake, can you wiggle your fingers and toes?" the stranger asked. "Good, I see your fingers movin'. Can you feel you wigglin' your shoes?"

"Yeah, everything's working, cause I'm hurtin' all over."

"Now lemme check your eyes. Close 'em for a bit, then open 'em looking up at that street light. Then follow my finger."

The man did as he was told, and after the stranger checked for any breaks, he observed, "Good pupil response, eye movement in all directions, and no eye malposition. Noggin seems okay, and didn't feel any breaks. And what about you," he asked while turning to Alex.

"Ribs are a little sore, but I've had worse."

"You sure look like you know what you're doing Mister…" Maureen said.

"Jefferson, Jim Jefferson, ma'am. Well, they trained me as a medic in the War; 369th Infantry Regiment—the Harlem Hellfighters—assigned to the French 16th Division."

"The French?" Alex asked.

"Yeah, those southern cracker doughboys didn't want us anywhere near 'em, but those Frenchies treated us good, like equals. I was a fightin' medic, not one of those pacifists. I shot them Hun bastards because they were killin' my boys. Got this 'Croix de Guerr' See, I still wear it, along with an old cross my momma gave me."

"You're still a hero, Mister Jefferson," Maureen smiled.

"Yes, indeed, and thank you, Mister Jefferson. You saved Mister Bloom and myself from disaster," Alex said before introducing himself and Maureen.

"Well, you folks too. You went after those boys like bobcats. No tellin' what those punks woulda done, if not for you."

"Thank you all, for saving my life," Bloom winced, as he propped himself up with their help. "I was sure they wanted to kill me, yellin' k..e, and Jew scum, and shoutin' Heil Hitler.'"

"Probably some of that riffraff from the Bund convention," Maureen said.

"I know they had masks, but could you recognize any of their voices," Alex asked.

"Naw, but I'll never forget their vicious voices now."

"I think I can identify the first one. When I pulled off his mask as I flipped him, he had a big scar on his cheek."

"Yeah, I got a look at that big bald son of a bitch with the handlebar stash, tendin' to his busted up beezer usin' his mask," Jefferson said, before adding, "Lucky that's all he got, after I sent his punk-ass flyin' into that shed."

By now, a couple of passersby had arrived, before hurrying off to find a cop at the hotel down the street. Feeling better, Bloom asked for help in getting up, and as they steadied him onto his feet, he turned and saw the full measure of the ruin that was once his newsstand. "Oh no, our business," he cried before choking up.

"I understand," Maureen soothed. "But you're alive. Still, do you want us to get you an ambulance, just to make sure everything is all right?"

"I'm okay. I couldn't afford a hospital anyway, especially now," he chuckled sardonically.

"Well, the police are going to find those thugs, I got their plate number."

"I wouldn't be so sure. They've been doing this for centuries and they want to bring their hate here. Our poor people over there. The Nazis encourage this," he sighed, sadly.

"They ain't too big on my folks either, but I'll tell ya, they try this shit with me, I'll kick their Nazi asses," Jim snarled. "I don't take shit like that no more, from them or their mothafucka KKK friends—sorry ma'am"

"I get it, Jim," she said, before turning to Bloom, "Do you want us to clean up a bit."

"Naw, you've done enough; besides the cops should see what these animals did." Once more choking up, he continued, "My poor brother, he worked the morning shift. He should be here soon to pick me up, now that the late edition is sold out. And not a penny to show. Look at this mess. He'll be crushed"

"Do you need some cash to hold you over," Alex asked as he remembered the ten bucks he kept in his wallet for emergencies.

"That's kind, but no thanks. Our suppliers are friends, and Adam and me will be here later with hammers and nails. They ain't gonna shut us down."

Just then a squad car pulled to the curb, and a couple of patrolmen stepped out. A gray haired veteran who identified himself as Officer Walters, surveyed the destruction. Upon learning the victim wanted no further medical attention, he launched into questions about what happened. The cop listened as Bloom described the attack, including his insistence that it was Nazi inspired. Taking the others aside, his young partner took down witness statements, along with Maureen's description of the car and its plate number. Ignoring the call box a few yard away, neither cop called-in on the car.

After recapping their statements, Walters advised them that they would be contacted as the investigation unfolded; however, he wasn't finished. Instead, he turned his attention to Jim. "So what were you doing down here, before… 'stumbling'… over this robbery?"

"Whaddya mean," Jim snapped.

"Don't go getting uppity with me, if you know what's good for ya!"

Seeing Maureen's look to stay calm, he replied, "As I told your partner, before, I was on my way to play at the Starlite Club. That's my guitar sitting next to the garage over there."

"Ah, one of those colored musicians. You better not be carrying any reefers on you. Let's empty out…"

"We're not the criminals here, officer. Meanwhile, those thugs are probably safe in their beds by now," Maureen steamed, ignoring her own advice.

"I'm in charge here! So watch it, lady, or I'll be haulin' you in! And what's your name?"

"As I told your partner, Maureen Costello. You probably know my grandfather, former Commissioner Hugh Costello, or my brother, Lieutenant Danny Costello or maybe the rest of my Costello, or Shea relatives on the force."

Ah… ah… there's been some Negro crime down here lately. I wanna check things out but since ya say, ah…"

"…that he risked his neck to help strangers, his integrity is established…"

"In any case, we wanna get back to the precinct house and get this report out. Like I said, there's been some crime down here, lately, so I suggest you don't stay down here."

No sooner had the cruiser pulled away, than Bloom's brother arrived to pick him up. Seeing the mayhem, he rushed over to check on Jake. When told what happened, he broke down; yet, he quickly regained his composure, vowing not to bend to evil, and insisting they'd re-open in the morning. After battening down what remained of the shanty, he thanked the strangers for their help, before leading his brother back to the old jalopy waiting at the curb.

After gathering up some stray papers left adrift on the sidewalk, Alex and Maureen joined Jefferson as he went back for his guitar.

"Thanks again, Jim! They could've done some real damage to us. I owe you, my friend."

"Hey, that's okay, man."

"At least let me give you a ride to the Starlite."

"Thanks, but I wanna walk off some steam after dealing with those Nazis and that honky cop."

"No doubt," Maureen added as she shook her head.

"We'll have to catch you at the club. I love that place."

"That'd be cool, but it's sorta hit or miss when I play—depends if there's an opening."

"Well, we'll have to grab some beers somewhere. Besides, I want to pick your brain on music. How do I get in touch with you?"

"Sorry, Alex, I ain't got a phone. You see, I live down in the Hobo Jungle."

"The Hobo Jungle?"

Sensing Jim's unease, Maureen spoke up, "It's a camp called the Hobo Jungle. I know about it because Gramma ministers down there with other volunteers from Saint Ann's. It's on some scrub land on the other side of the Buffalo River. Several hundred transient men live there."

"I don't plan on being there long. I came up from down south when I heard some of the plants here might be hirin'. No luck so far, but I keep tryin'!"

"Listen, maybe I can help with that," Alex suggested.

"I'm cool with that. I ain't too proud for help with a job."

"I'll give you my card with my phone number. Maybe I can pick you up at the camp."

"First, ya gotta walk across the train bridge dodging railroad dicks. Then, it's okay for church folks bringin' stuff, and knowin' cops are looking out for them; but, even for a guy as rugged as you, there's some badass punks who'd jump ya, and slit your throat for a nickel. Then there's some Dixie crackers who still got their hoods and are lookin' for trouble."

"That's too bad, Gram say most of the fellas are good men. Just down on their luck."

"Sure, most the fellas there rode the rails looking for work after losin' their jobs, or homes, or leaving their family—they call it a poor man's divorce—but ya gotta watch your step and learn your way."

"Even with the police watching over the volunteers, Gramps says it can be dangerous."

"Well, no one messes with me. I don't take no shit—excuse me ma'am—not for a long time. Not since I was back in Tulsa after the War."

"Oklahoma, that's not like the deep south where it's so bad for Negroes, is it?" Maureen asked.

"White folks around the country never heard what happened there. People in charge, bankers, oilmen, politicians covered it up. None of the whites down there will talk about it. You see, back in twenty-one a Negro boy was accused of attacking a White girl. Even though he was innocent, they were gonna string him up. The sheriff knew it and tried to protect him. The folks in the Negro part of town, Greenwood—they called it 'The Black Wall Street'—Some of 'em got their guns and were gonna protect that boy. Soon, all hell broke loose. Whites, and most of the cops went on a rampage, burning down Greenwood."

"I can't believe I never heard of this," Alex said.

"Like I said, they covered it up real good. Twenty Whites were killed and hundreds of Negroes. They burned down my garage, and I was doing real good at the time… well, I've been moving around ever since."

"That's horrifying, that things like that could happen here, in this country, and you had to live through it—you and your family and neighbors," Maureen lamented.

"I don't like to talk about it, but all this stuff tonight brought it back. Life is what it is, and I just keep going."

"I'm sorry, Jim. This country has a long way to go," Maureen said.

"Well, I better get goin' if I wanna keep my gig tonight."

With that, they once more thanked Jim, before heading back to Alex's car, shocked by the turn of events, yet relieved for having dodged a bullet.

As she sat in the car, passing by the warm and modest homes of her First Ward neighborhood, Maureen was determined to protect her world and stand against any evil that could threaten it. For his part, Alex saw the Nazis as an aberration that had somehow taken hold in the land of his forebears. And he saw Hitler as a horrible, yet passing abomination. More importantly, he was certain that the Nazis didn't reflect the values of Buffalo's German American community, a community of good people, in which generations of his family had been prominent. As such, he was determined to use his reporting to expose the Bundist menace that threatened their reputation.

Upon arriving outside of her house, the couple took time to share their happiness in having met, along with expressing amazement over their night of adventure. They vowed to see each other again, before exchanging phone numbers. With that, they walked up to the porch, whose light had been kept on by her grandparents. Happy in its warm glow, they sealed their night with a long and passionate kiss.

V

$\mathbf{A}$s they strolled beneath the leafy canopy along the bridle path, the old man longed for the days when he could ride his horse down the two-mile mall that connected Delaware and Humboldt Parks. Yet given his back, he was now content to take his evening walk along an abbreviated loop from his home.

On this day, he was joined by his son Alex, as he made his way back to his brick colonial on Agassiz Circle. Although the house was grand by most any standards, it was relatively modest in light of its owners' wealth. As such, it reflected the unassuming natures of Rudy Wagner and his wife Anna.

No sooner had they passed through the foyer than they were met by the housekeeper Trudy, who quickly ushered them to the dining room where the guests were beginning to assemble. Soon, everyone was taking their seats around an elaborately carved table that had been handed down from Rudy's grandfather.

The Sunday dinner with family and friends was a tradition started by the former Anna Schultz from the time her children were young. As was her custom, she was assisted by Trudy in preparing a feast of German favorites, featuring the main course of sauerbraten.

After welcoming her guests to the table, she turned her attention to her husband, "My handsome *bärchen*, were you competing with Alex? Is that why you're late?"

"Thanks to your wonderful food, I better take longer walks, if you don't want me to be a big, fat bear!"

"Now don't go blaming my food; although, I am happy you're walking more to stay healthy." Turning to her friends, she beamed, "As you may know, our dear Rudy marches off to the dawn mass at Canisius every day, and now he's added a walk before dinner!"

"Thank god for my beautiful sister-in-law. Before he met her, I used to worry the Jesuits were gonna sign him up," Rudy's younger brother Max snickered.

"Well, somebody had to take up the slack for my playboy brother," Rudy dead-panned.

"Ah, those girls at Crescent Beach before the War; Those were the days, Max!"

"Victor, save that for the billiard room, later," Anna playfully scolded.

Victor Lange had known the Wagner brothers since childhood, as their families were close. The youngest son of a real estate baron, he was highly educated, yet largely aimless in his years after college at Cornell. That quickly changed after America's entry into the Great War. Always patriotic, he enlisted into the army at the ripe age of thirty; yet, after experiencing the horrors of the trenches as a front line officer, he was a changed man. Returning home, he was determined to have a positive impact on society. As such, he bought a small German language newspaper, changed it to an English format, and soon turned it into the largest community daily in the country. He served as both publisher and chief editor in the years that followed.

A childless widower, Victor had known Alex since the time of his birth. When the young man expressed an interest in journalism, Victor offered him a job as a reporter, and served as his professional mentor ever since.

"Oh, Anna, we just liked chasing the girls," Victor winked.

"And catching a lot of them, I might add," Rudy chuckled.

"Okay, so we weren't choirboys or as straitlaced as Rudy, but we turned out okay."

"Come on Max, you make me sound like a stuffed shirt. I can be frisky. In fact, I just might join Alex at one of those dance halls. See, I can swing." With that, he got up from his chair and did a quick shimmy to a chorus of laughs.

"Please don't. Remember your back," Anna teased.

"I just might take you up on that, Pop; but first we better work on that Lindy Hop!"

"No way! We love our fuddy-duddy just the way you are, *mein schatz*." she said before planting a kiss on his cheek.

"That's right, Anna! All kidding aside, we need more men like Rudy—steadfast, hard-working and great businessmen. Not like those crazy New Dealers, with their unions and so-called social programs that the government has no business financing. They want to turn us into Bolsheviks," the heavy set man at the end of the table bellowed.

Walter Klein was never short of opinions, particularly when it involved Roosevelt and his policies. A self-made millionaire, he started out as an auto mechanic before branching into used car sales. Eventually the hard bitten businessman opened a chain of new car dealerships throughout Western New York. Anticipating the end of prohibition, he purchased a number of successful restaurants, including the Tiergarten, a legendary German gathering spot. Ever savvy, he also bought a huge soft drink distributorship that he later converted to alcohol sales. He was an avid yachtsman, who met his future wife, Freida at a race.

"While I don't agree with everything Roosevelt has done, things are getting better, and we're doing better than ever these last two years,"

"That's because you and Max are great businessmen…"

"And don't forget our boy, Freddie, who's doing so well at the company," Anna gushed.

"I'm not surprised, look at his bloodlines," Klein roared as he turned and slapped young Freddie on the back. "Now Roosevelt on the other hand, has never had to work a real job all his life, yet him and his cabal want to give away all our hard earned money."

"At least there's no more Hoovervilles or bread lines," Anna said.

"Sure, he's taking care of all those lazy, shiftless freeloaders, and we pay for it!"

"Like old people and children, really, Walter," she answered back.

"Not the dole, but hard work and initiative! Like us and our families! German discipline and enterprise are what's needed. Strong leadership, not this coddling socialism."

"Roosevelt's been very effective. Things would be a lot worse if we still had Hoover and his policies of benign neglect. Without the New Deal, you'd really be looking at a Bolshevik revolt." Victor countered.

"I worry about the bills coming in for all of this, and the economy blowing up again," warned Peter Becker. Becker, whose somber personality was matched by his gaunt features, was the heir to the area's premier meat packing business. He was a mainstay of the local German-American community, sitting on the boards of the Sangerbund Singing Society, the Turner Gymnastics Club and Camp Reichsadler. His family had been friends of the Wagners for three generations.

"Be careful with Roosevelt," Becker's equally solemn wife, Hilda, cautioned. "He's totally in league with the unions, who want to run the show."

"Hell, I get along with the trade unions," Max calmly insisted. "Of course, we run the show, but I make sure we both get something."

"We just can't have any of that radical CIO industrial union nonsense," Rudy exhorted. "We pay our unskilled labor force well. But if they want trade union wages, let them learn a trade to better themselves."

"Unions, bah! Soon you'll be trading in your suits for overalls, but listen, it's not just about business, but look how Roosevelt and his Jewish allies are lining up against Germany!"

"Walter, you've been listening to that crazy Father Coughlin radio show, with all that Jewish conspiracy business," Anna said.

"That socialist agitator—no way," Klein continued. "But don't be so naive about the Jews. They control the banks, the press and now Hollywood with all its propaganda. They hate Germany and will push for war, eventually."

"That's old country talk, and don't even mention war," Anna shot back.

"I deal with Jewish businessmen," Rudy recounted. "They can be tough to bargain with, but I have no problem with that. At times, I've run into them around town and shared a drink. As for all this Jewish banker and press talk, I have no time for that. We do our banking with John Dorn at Buffalo Commercial. He's a fellow Knight."

"And perhaps you've forgotten, Walter, I own a paper," Victor teased.

"Don't worry, this country is far from war," Max reassured his sister-in law. "It's had its fill. Besides, FDR is too adept to go down that path."

"Speaking of politics, I hear talk you might be running for office, Max," Becker asked.

"Only if it's big enough for my old friend," Victor smiled.

"Listen, the idea of running for office has piqued my interest. I like the challenge that it represents—you know, making government more effective. I look around and see that there's not enough strong leadership in public life today, and I think I can bring a strong, clean, non-politician business voice to the table."

"Sounds like an announcement speech, to me," Freida Klein smiled.

"I'm at the earliest stages of weighing such a move. Obviously, there's a lot to consider, not the least of which, I have a pretty good life right now. So don't bet the house on it."

"So what office are you thinking about," Peter asked.

"Mayor, is up next year, but there's other offices—like governor. I like the administrative end. I like to see things run right."

"Have you been brushing up on your history, Max," Victor asked with a grin. "Like with Grover Cleveland going from Mayor of Buffalo to Governor to President in four years."

"Listen, my brother is capable and confident, but let's not go overboard. Besides, he has a business to help run."

Max Wagner was anything but lacking in confidence. Throughout his life, he was always the star, whether it be in the classroom, on the athletic field, or in the business world. As the scion of a wealthy family he lacked for nothing, especially in terms of education, having attended the finest schools in the country.

After graduating from Cornell with honors, he spent a couple years playing ball in the Boston system. Unable to crack the majors, he changed course and earned a master's in business from Harvard. Back in Buffalo, he joined the family business, learning the ropes from his father and brother, and over the next five years, he rose to the position of Executive Vice President. Faced with the prospect of the draft when America entered the World War, he ignored his college roommate's advice to join the army. Instead, he enlisted as an officer in he Navy, indulging his passion for all things nautical.

At the signing of the armistice, he took leave from Alpine Machine and headed off to Europe. There he pursued a life of adventure, while at the same time accruing a small fortune investing in real estate and start-up businesses. He returned home upon the death of his father, shortly before the market crash in '29. In the years afterward, he and his brother took the company to new heights of success, despite the challenges of the Great Depression.

Tall and ruggedly handsome, his chiseled features were underscored by his cool blue eyes and framed by a thick mane of salt and pepper hair. He had a gregarious personality and as such, always seemed to dominate his surroundings. Given his talents, things always came easy for him; however, it also left him with a tendency for dismissive impatience towards anyone who failed to meet his standards.

"Indeed, I'm not ready to plan an Inaugural," Max chuckled.

"I'd vote for you tomorrow, over that traitor Roosevelt," Klein bellowed.

"Even as a Democrat?" Max replied.

"What? You're kidding!"

"Not at all, Walter. As I said, there are things I don't like about Democrats … or, for that matter Republicans, but at least things are getting done."

"But Max, we build, they sponge," Klein grumbled.

"Listen, FDR has his policy issues, but, he knows how to lead. I admire leadership. Besides, if you want to advance politically in this town, the Democratic Party is the means for the foreseeable future."

"Well, you'd be great and I'm sure you'll have all our support, anyway. Besides, you'd be the handsomest politician around," the ever flirtatious Freida Klein said with a wink.

"Enough of all this political talk. We want to relax now that we're ready to eat," Anna declared as she and Trudy began to bring out the salads.

"Ah, I don't buy any of it. Max, my friend, I know you. You like the business action too much to let mere politics get in the way."

"You're right, Peter, I love it; however, although I like to think of myself as indispensable, Freddie has been taking on more responsibilities and doing a great job of it."

"Yes, my star, Friedrich is following his father's footsteps and making us proud … and Alex too," Anna gushed.

"Still, I can't picture you leaving, especially now," Becker continued. "I've been hearing rumors about the factory expanding and that another big contract with Curtiss is in the wind."

"Now Peter, we can't acknowledge any such thing," Rudy cautioned.

"Yes, Max you can't go anywhere. You're too important to the community, helping to lead the Sangerbund and the other organizations," Missus Becker added.

"Please, Hilda, Peter and Walter do more than me at the Sangerbund. As for the Turners, I just try to make sure Freddie has a place to continue to win championships."

"Yes, congratulations, I heard you had a great tournament in Milwaukee!"

"Thanks Walter, the club won seven championships," Freddie beamed.

"And you?"

"A gold in the rings and the all-around. As the team Captain, I'm proud to say we continue to dominate."

Friedrich, "Freddie" Wagner was always an overachiever. He worked harder than the rest to produce the most and reap its rewards. More forceful than his younger brother, he always knew what he wanted: success and recognition.

His dark, solid features reflected a conservative nature, while his wiry athletic frame suggested an underlying intensity. Opinionated, he had a definite sense of how things should be.

He married Mitzi Rath, the daughter of family friends, right out of college—which was quickly followed by the arrival of twin sons. The young family lived a quiet, yet affluent lifestyle, punctuated by his avid participation in the Turners, and her volunteer work with the Sangerbund. Nonetheless, eager to make his mark in the world, Freddie threw himself into helping to run the family business.

"Yes, we're vey proud of Freddie's gymnastics achievements. He's a fine athlete, like Alex and my brother."

"Thanks, Dad, and speaking of achievements, I hear that you really improved things at Reichsadler during your term as president, Walter."

"They needed a strong hand to get things fixed." Klein proclaimed with a martial air.

"*Jawohl, mein kommandant,*" Alex snickered, which drew some chuckles from the others.

"Alex, don't be smart," Anna scolded, as her son shot her back a wink.

"Oh, I can take a joke, Anna." Turning to Alex, he asked, "So how is your journalism career going, my boy?"

"Outstanding," Anna interrupted.

"Please Momma. Actually, it's been going really well."

"Right from the start, I saw that he had good writing skills," Victor added.

"The product of a Jesuit education," the father beamed.

"So what are some of the stories you're writing on," Freida Klein asked.

"I started out doing community oriented and human interest stories, before working my way up to meatier issues that are of interest to our readers."

"Like what," she continued.

"Well, I just covered that Bund Convention at the Statler the other day."

"That's meaty all right," Becker observed.

Just then Trudy began bringing out steaming platters of the main course. Nonetheless, the arrival of the savory fare failed to stem the talk at the table.

"Sensitive to say the least, especially for German Americans," his wife added.

"Sensitive? Jesus, I'll say! Just know that our enemies will twist every word to make us look bad," Walter Klein grumbled.

"Let's be clear, it was my call. It's an important story," Victor was quick to state.

"But 'The *Advocate*?'" Peter Becker wondered.

"What better than a German community paper to air it out," Victor replied.

"But with such a young reporter, with all due respect to Alex." Walter declared.

"Listen, Alex has become a good reporter, with a nose for the news. He's smart, studies the issues and works to gather the facts. More importantly, I trust his integrity and judgement. And remember, as editor, it's my job to supervise the process and decide what to print—and that goes for any of my reporters. Still, I know Alex will do a good job."

"Let's just be careful not to sensationalize this Bund business," Klein insisted.

"We cant forget the harassment, bigotry and even the lynchings during the War. I don't want to see that being dredged up again," Freida cautioned.

"It's no secret that we want Alex in the family business, but we support him following his dreams. I have no doubt he'll do a good and honest job. Still, I don't want him to be the source of any community resentment. He's a precious member of this family, a family that been a bedrock of Buffalo's German population for generations."

"You know me better than that, Rudy, and I have Alex's best interests at heart," Victor added. "This is my community too, but we best serve it by reporting the truth."

"Everybody just relax," Max broke-in. "These Bundists are just a bunch of crack pots marching around in their Boy Scout outfits. Reasonable people know they don't represent us."

"Still, no matter what we do, our enemies are gonna play this up," Klein growled. "And think of your political future, Max."

"Very little of that bad stuff happened here," Max replied. "We've been the most prominent ethnic group in this area for a long time. Look who's in power: Mayor Zimmerman, Sheriff Eberhart, Congressman Beiter, and the list goes on. Don't worry."

"It's not just Germans here, but nationally and in Germany. Communists and their allies are looking for any opening to exploit. They don't just want Russia, but the world, and Hitler's a bulwark against them," Klein proclaimed with an air of triumph.

"Russia's a medieval society and it's a continent and ocean away. We're a modern industrialized democracy," Victor replied.

"Worry about their Bolshevik followers here, along with their Jew allies. Go pooh-pooh about their control of the banks and press, but Henry Ford wrote about it. He's a brilliant man, and he'll open your eyes."

Unable to hold back, Anna broke in. "I grew up in North Buffalo and knew Jewish girls and boys in school. They were my playmates and their families were nice. All this evil Jewish conspiracy talk is crazy, Walter!"

"Well, all I got to say is I hope they feel the same about you. They hate all things German."

"A lot of Americans are concerned about Germany right now," Alex spoke up.

"You mean with the order and prosperity?"

"No, with the oppression, racism, and resurgent militarism," Victor interrupted.

"Anti-German propaganda! At the least, those stories are overblown. Don't forget, all countries have some bigotry. Just look at how they treat the coloreds down south."

"Well, I suspect there's still some Anti-German bias by the press remaining from the War; but, there's little doubt there's been some regrettable excesses by fringe elements over there. Still, I'm confident the military and businessmen—sober, successful men like my brother—will reign-in Hitler and some of his hooligan supporters. We Germans are a practical people."

"Enough of this talk," Anna scolded. "It's going to give us indigestion."

"Indeed, let's enjoy this glorious sauerbraten," Hilda smiled between bites.

"By the way, I was listening to the 'Magic Key of RCA,' last night and heard that rising young opera star from Buffalo, Rosa Brampton,"

"Me too! Isn't she wonderful," Anna gushed. "I hear she's singing at the Music Hall this fall. We must have the boys take us!"

"And maybe Max can charm her to come to the Sangerbund," Freida giggled.

"I'll be happy to get all the tickets—for good music—not like that crazy music the young people like,"

"Don't be such an old crank, Walter. Besides, Alex likes that music, don't you dear?"

"I've seen those newsreels. Those swing dances look like a real romp," Hilda observed. "Do you go?"

"Sure do, great music and a lot of fun, but my real passion is Jazz."

"I get the fun with the girls, but what's with those discordant so-called melodies. It's African based, right?" Becker asked.

"Yes, it has African roots and it's great art, with incredible virtuosity."

"You better get back to the Sangerbund and straighten out your ears, Alex," Klein scoffed.

"Well, I'd listen when Alex would play his records here, and it grew on me. It would get my foot tapping," Rudy smiled.

"You Too!"

"You know, Anna's right. You're becoming an old crank," Rudy shot back.

"I'll tell you what I won't do: fatten the coffers of those Jew businessmen who publish the music and own the clubs for all that colored tribal music!"

"Ugh! There you go again with that talk. We're cutting off the schnapps, Walter! You're getting whacky," Anna said, shaking her head.

Taking the cue, Hilda turned toward Freddie, "Now, I hear you're building a new house."

"Yeah, up in Snyder. I wanna get away from the city, it's getting too… complicated. A lot of work, but I'm leaving most of the furnishings to Mitzi. She could tell you more, but she's at home with the kids, who are sick."

"They're so cute and getting so big. They'll have a lot of room to play up there,"

"And what about Alex? When will he settle down with a nice fraulein?" Freida asked.

"My sweetie has met a nice girl, a nice Irish girl."

"Mom, please! I just met her. Now you've got me married!"

"I'm your mother, and I can tell. You're smitten."

"An Irish girl, interesting…" Hilda mused.

"Better watch yourself in that neighborhood," Walter said. "All they want to do is drink and fight. I know."

"For god's sake, stereotypes. I'm sure somebody in the Ward right now is bringing up how Germans are all cold, humorless and fat," Victor exclaimed.

"Well, lucky Alex isn't bringing home a Negress or Jewess, given all the time he spends in those Jazz clubs."

"Freddie, I won't have you talk like that. I raised you different," Anna chided.

"Just a joke, in light of what Uncle Vic said about stereotypes, Mom."

"All I know is that the Irish are good Catholics," she declared.

"Ya, if they're not cops, firemen or party workers, they're priests," Max chuckled.

"Speaking of which, when we're done cleaning up, we girls can head to the parlor for the 'Catholic Hour.' I love to listen to that young Monsignor, Fulton Sheen. He's so smart and insightful about life."

"Have you seen his picture? Very handsome with riveting blue eyes," Freida swooned.

"The boys can go off to the billiard room to smoke their cigars and talk about business or politics or whatever," Anna added.

With that, the women tended to the table, while the men, lured by the prospect of a rare bottle of single malt scotch, proceeded to the library which doubled as the billiard room. Upon entering the mahogany framed sanctuary, they were met by walls of shelving that contained Rudy's extensive collection of books. At the far end of the room, a massive antique desk sat beneath an art glass window, depicting a panorama of the Bavarian Alps. A nine foot billiard table stood at the other end, under the light of a brass chandelier.

Rudy fetched the bottle and tumblers from the wet bar, as Klein and Becker were helping themselves to a couple of Cubans from the humidor next to the door. Meanwhile, Freddie and Max were about to square off for a game of eight-ball, as Vic racked the balls. While this was going on, Alex nervously stood by, hoping for a private moment with his father. He saw his chance, when Rudy began pouring out servings of the whisky. "I should have brought this up earlier Pop, but I didn't want to interfere with your dinner. I know how much it means to you."

"What's going on, son, is anything wrong?"

"Oh, no, nothing's like that, I just want to run something by you."

"So, how can I help?"

"Well, as you know, I had that dust-up at the news shanty when I was covering that Bund Convention the other night."

"Your mother and I thank God nothing worse happened to you. Like I said, helping a person in trouble is good, but in the future run to the cops or try anything to avoid that."

"I understand Pop, but at the time I thought it was the only thing to do. And like I said, a big reason nothing worse happened was when that Negro man, Jim Jefferson helped me."

"Yes, we're very grateful, but when I mentioned some sort of reward, you said he didn't want anything."

"Yeah, I told 'im I wanted to repay him, but he insisted it wasn't necessary."

"Very noble and upright, and something I admire, but I'd still like to show my gratitude."

"And that's what I want to talk about. You see, we got to talking that night—you know, introduce ourselves after what happened. Well, he's a jazz musician but he's looking for something more steady and practical…"

"I think I see where this is going…"

"Yeah, Pop, I know how you feel about using the business for favors, so I didn't offer him anything. But I did say I might have some connections that I could check, and I did call some pals whose families own businesses, but nothing came up."

"I see, and you're right, I don't like to use the business to offer jobs to friends or associates or politicians or whoever. I have strict rules on hiring."

"From what I learned, he's a hard worker, with skills. He had some bad breaks, owned his own garage that was burned down in a race riot—plus he's a war hero."

"That's impressive, but, it's not that simple, son. We're not missionaries. Our first responsibility is to the business my grandfather founded. An important part of that is having a harmonious workplace and good relations with our workers."

"Still, I think he fits the rules as a good hire. I'm not so naive to believe his color won't be a problem for some on the floor; but that shouldn't dictate things, should it?"

"Alex, a large portion of our workforce are tradesmen, and they only allow who they want in their unions—so that's that. And that attitude filters down to the laborers."

"But don't we have some Negro workers already?"

"Indeed. I try to give Negroes a chance to show they're capable, to show they can handle things and prove themselves. I've brought them in after I've seen them work in our other businesses, like Ralph Brown who worked as a janitor in the apartments and is now doing the same at the plant; or Lincoln Sims, our old delivery man, is now working in the cafeteria."

"Well, I got a good impression of the guy and I owe him."

"Son, nobody is owed anything in this life."

"I know. You've told me that all my life, but didn't you say you wanted to reward him. It's not like you'd be handing him a check. He has a trade. He just needs a shot."

"Alex, you have a sympathetic heart like your mother. So, maybe we can find something to phase him in. He said he had a garage, so maybe he can work on our cars at home, and since he's a mechanic, we can have him do repairs at some of the other properties. If that all works out, maybe we can put him on the shop floor."

Off to the side, Freddie was into his match with Max. Despite the whirl of the overhead fan, he was able to make out what was going on with his father and Alex, "Really, are you kidding?"

"What's wrong? "Alex asked.

"I can't believe it. Who is this mystery man? What was he doing down there that night in the first place? Just saying."

"Actually, he was on his way to a jazz gig. He's a musician."

"Ah, a 'gig'. Boy, you're really getting into that jazz scene. What's next, reefers?"

"Freddie, watch your tone," the old man cautioned.

"Sorry, Alex, I'm sure he's okay, if you say so. Look, you're my brother, but you don't have the business experience, especially for something as sensitive as this."

"I'm just making a suggestion about a good hire, a good guy. What's so sensitive about that?"

"We're no settlement house. We're running a business, Jesus, these Coloreds were pickin' cotton down south, before coming up here. They've got to prove themselves, first. Just cause some banjo player helped Alex in a fight, doesn't mean we hand him a job."

"I appreciate what that man did, and I've listened to what Alex had to say, so I've decided to give him a chance."

"But gee, dad, you know those laborers' unions are banging on the door to get in. We don't need a race problem to cause workers to go scurrying off in that direction."

"Let's first see how he works. If he ends up at the plant, our managers better make sure there's no problems."

"Let's hope so," Freddie sighed.

"That's what we pay them for. More importantly, maybe all this will get Alex thinking about a return to the business. He can bring value, because he's good with people. That's important. Running a business isn't just finances and ledgers, but it requires people skills whether it's sales, personnel, management, or marketing. Max has that."

"Well, maybe after I win my Pulitzer," Alex smiled.

"And don't forget engineering," Freddie shot back. "We still gotta build things."

"Both of my boys have wonderful talents, whether my engineering and business wunderkind, or my ace reporter, for now. But enough of all this talk. We have to test that scotch and then see who's champ."

"Yeah, I got winners," Alex said, as he slapped his brother on the back.

VI

As they approached the entrance to the club, Alex paused to look at the Auburn 852 SC parked in the small lot off to the side. While taking time to admire the streamlined design of the green, two-passenger speedster, he caught sight of scratches that marred the otherwise gleaming fender.

"My buddy, Sid's. Gotta be a story behind that. He treats his new car like a baby."

"I can see why," Maureen said, "it's so beautiful. Those futuristic lines look like something out of a Buck Rogers strip."

Eager to get in and enjoy the music, they headed to the door just as a line was beginning to form. The Starlite Grille was the premier jazz venue along Buffalo's renowned Michigan Avenue Strip, that included its chief rival the Rhythm Cafe and a bevy of other entertainment destinations within a four block area. The Grille was especially popular on Sunday afternoons, when the house band would be joined by local jazz luminaries and even national stars, who would sometimes arrive early for performances booked for later in the week. Its owner was Manny Cohen, a long-time restauranteur and impresario whose love for the music dated back to the days of his youth in New Orleans. He was one of the first to introduce Black artists to White audiences, which caused no small controversy among some of the locals. However, any such feelings had no effect on the ever growing number of jazz fans of all races who frequented the club.

Upon passing through the doors, they entered the Ebony Lounge, which featured a chrome framed bar, backed by a lengthy mirror, etched with an art deco motif. Pink neon lights ran along the edges of its ceiling, and as its name would suggest, black was the prevailing color throughout the room.

No sooner had their eyes adjusted to the subdued light, than Alex spotted his friend Sid Cohen standing at the bar, clad in his usual tuxedo.

"Hey, Sid, big crowd! I heard Benny Carter might be showin' up."

"Ain't about to ruin any surprises, but don't worry, I got a table up front for you and this beautiful lady."

"Thanks, and yeah, Maureen Costello, Sid Cohen. We've been pals since our first days in high school."

"But Alex, you went to Canisius, right?" she said with a puzzled look.

"Ya see, my folks didn't want me in any more trouble. And it worked, thanks to the good Fathers," he smiled, always amused by the curious reactions.

After the usual introductory banter, Alex asked, "So how's your dad?"

"Doin' okay. But that heart attack was quite a scare. He was lucky."

"Hope he rests up and mends."

"Hard for him to sit still, but I think he's realizing that even he has limits."

"I can only imagine all the work that goes into a place like this," Maureen observed.

"Not just his businesses, but all the other organizations he's involved with, like the Red Cross and the Anti Defamation League."

"That's right, didn't I read an article in the 'Courier' where he was speaking for the ADL about the German Boycott?"

"And shortly afterward he started getting hate mail and hang-up calls. Listen, he's always gotten the occasional n****r-lover letter over the club, which he just shrugs off as crazy. But lately, he's been getting a lot of Christ killer, and k**e messages, along with warnings and threats. He won't say, but I'm sure it added to his strain."

"That's terrible and I…"

"…And I think I got a taste of it last night," Sid interrupted.

"The scrapes on the car? I was gonna ask you about that."

"Yeah, slept over at the folks, after I got into the bourbon too much last night. When I got up this morning, there were the scratches and a brick from the garden lying next to the tire."

"Too much of a coincidence to blame on neighborhood brats."

"That's what I figure too."

"As I was going to say, Maureen and I had a run-in with some Nazi thugs the other night when I was reporting on the Bund convention for the paper."

"Wait, our Rabbi told us about being interviewed by the '*Advocate*,' and about an attack on one of his congregants who owns a newsstand near the Statler. So, that was you who helped the man. Well done, my friend!"

Alex went into more details about the incident, including the critical role paled by Jim Jefferson. After revealing Jim was going to play at the club on the night of the attack, Maureen added, "And he's over there, setting up with the band. I spotted him when we first came in."

"Okay, the new guy near the back of the stage. Doc said he likes his sound and is trying him out for a while."

"Yeah, that's him."

"Listen, I don't like to interfere with the music side of things, but as far as I'm concerned he's got a gig for as long as he wants. Besides, like I said, Doc likes his sound," he smiled.

"From what he said, he has quite a music resumé."

"Sid, did your Rabbi say how Mister Bloom was doing," Maureen asked.

"He's okay except for some bump and bruises, and he had to fix up the place. Now what about those thugs? You said, Maureen got the plate number. Did the cops track 'em down?"

"I stopped by Headquarters the next day to follow up. They said they traced the plate and discovered it was stolen."

"Could you I-D 'em if you had the chance?"

"They all had knit caps and masks, but I tore the mask off the one I tossed, and I'd recognize him again."

"The bastards musta had 'im staked out. I don't like seeing it here. Bad enough in Germany!"

"I'll drop off my article. I want you to read it. These people are a lunatic fringe, but as we know, they can be dangerous. I don't think they're a long term threat like the Reds, but you can't ignore them."

"Sure, just look at Hitler, but enough of this depressing talk. There's some great music in store this afternoon. But first, let's get you some drinks before I take you over to the table. And of course, I wanna meet this Jefferson fella."

Meanwhile, as Sid turned to greet a group of regulars, another couple of patrons were busy talking at an isolated table at the far end of the concert room. Yet, the men showed no interest in the band, as it went about the task of setting up. Instead, they leaned close-in, while constantly casting their eyes for any hint of eavesdropping.

"So what did you learn casing the outside," Braun asked his lieutenant, Hans Krueger.

"There's a little alley behind the ballroom where the n****r musicians and waiters come out to smoke their fags or reefers. They're all laughin' and jivin' and they got a bench. It's like their own little club."

"While I was snooping around inside, I noticed a busboy taking some trash out the stage door... "

"Yeah, there's a bin in the alley…"

"And behind the curtain there's a store room where I saw a bar-back carryin' out bottles of whiskey. It must be where they store the liquor." Braun whispered.

"Gotta be. When they were passin' around some hooch, outside, one of 'em says that he'd like to get his hands on some of that good stuff, pointing towards an extension, sorta like a shed. Must be that storage room you saw… are you thinking what I'm thinking?"

"Sure, get some alcohol soaked rags, stuff 'em against the liquor shed, and poof!"

"Pin it on the n*****s; throw the cops off our tail," Krueger smiled.

"At first, but later, we'll call Cohen, and let 'im know it's us Nazis who did it, and to lay off the boycott, k**e scum!"

"See how he likes losing some of those shekels. I think of it as our own boycott bonfire," Krueger sneered.

"More importantly, all the Jews, mongrels and their degenerate allies will learn the Aryan People are making themselves heard."

"And last night was a good hello."

"Ha, that J*****y's flashy car isn't so flashy this morning! And Martin said he would've done even more, if it wan't for some neighbor walking his dog at that crazy hour."

"Do ya think the bosses will have any trouble with this stuff?" Hans asked

"The bosses don't need to know about our other activities. Like I said, the American sounds a little too smart, and remember, we agreed we would be bold like the Fuhrer."

"Still, didn't they want us to concentrate on our main mission?"

"Don't worry, we're going to accomplish our main mission, and we'll lay low, like a lion stalking its prey. And just like it's a lion's nature to hunt the weak and inferior, it's our nature to attack and be bold!"

"Like our Fuhrer!"

As the two plotters toasted to their success, a small party arrived at the back of the stage, where Jim Jefferson was taking the last steps in tuning his guitar.

"Hey, Jim, told ya we were going to catch your act," Alex piped up.

"Glad you could make it, my friend! Gonna be a good session."

"Yeah, we got a table up front, thanks to our friend, Sid, here."

"Sid Cohen," he said, as he thrust out his hand, "my father owns this place. Doc Jones tells me how much he likes your sound, so when Alex said he knows you, I figured it's a good time to finally meet."

"Jim Jefferson, good to meet you, Sid. Your father has a nice place here."

"More enjoyable circumstances than the last time we got together," Maureen said.

"Listen, I love playin' here tonight, but I gotta admit, it made my day helpin' out, and sending them crackers scurryin' like rats."

"Like I was saying, Sid, Jim saved the day during that melee the other night."

"Hell, my man here flipped one cat like a pinwheel and nailed another with a right cross that would do James J. Braddock proud. And this pretty lady nearly bit through some punk's hand. So I just sorta mopped up."

"From what Alex told me, you're being too modest, Jim. In any case, it's great to meet someone so good at kicking Nazi ass. So, thanks from this Jew."

"My pleasure, and don't forget, those Nazis ain't big on my folks either."

"Our enemies' enemy is our friend. So, you got a regular gig here for as long as you like, Jim."

"Thanks, a lot, man!"

When the maitre d' came over to speak to Sid, Alex saw his opportunity to take Jim aside. "My co-worker left a note saying you called me. Since I couldn't call back, I figured this would be a good way to talk—along with hearing you play of course."

"Not too many phones down the Jungle," he smiled. "I probably shoulda called more, but I didn't want to pester you at work."

"That's no problem. So how's this working out?"

"The band leader, likes my sound and so now, it's a regular gig. But it's not every night, so it's not gonna pay the rent. You got anything?"

"Like I told ya the other night, I was gonna check out some possibilities with some of my connections, but nobody was hiring right now."

"I appreciate you tryin', man. It still ain't flush out there."

"Well, hold on. I wanted to check with my connections first, then with my family."

"Sure, I can dig that. I like to do things my way first."

"Well, my father, who owns a machine factory, has a very set system for hiring. In fact, he never lets us take care of friends or court politicians or whoever by offering jobs at the plant."

"I got the skills to work in a factory, and I'm willin' to apply, and compete with anybody."

"It's not quite that simple…"

"Ya, I know how that works, I've been dealin' with that all my life," he said with an air of resignation, as he turned his attention to the sheet music in his hand."

"No, wait, Jim. My father isn't like that. He's a fair man, but he does have his ways of doing things that have served him well."

"Like I said, I appreciate you tryin'."

"Although he isn't able to offer you a job at the plant right now, he did say he could hire you to work on the family cars and do some repair and fix-up projects at some of the properties the family owns around town. It's steady and pays well, and maybe it can work better with your schedule here."

Despite the skeptical look that crossed his face, Jim couldn't ignore that this was the best offer he had in some time. Besides, he liked Alex and sensed he could trust him.

"It sounds good, but do you think I can get into the plant at some time?"

"I cant say for sure, but like I said, my father's fair."

"Well, I can sure work on cars, and I can fix anything, and I can sure use the money, so yeah. What do you want me to do?"

"Here's my father's card with his secretary's number. She'll know the situation and can tell you what to do."

Just then, after ordering a couple of beers from the waitress, Braun and Krueger turned their attention to the stage. What they saw left them stunned. Braun was the first to digest the scene, "Jesus, Hans, it's that *schwein* Wagner and his *miststück* woman! And they're with that n****r who jumped us the other night!"

"And that j****y owner's son!"

"I shouldda known that n****r was a degenerate musician."

"Now that's a cozy little group. Maybe they'll enjoy each other's company in an internment camp when things change."

Meanwhile, Sid lead his friends back to their prize table next to the stage, while Jim joined the rest of the band, who were going over their final preparations for the show. As Maureen settled into her seat, the warm glow from the candle on the table underscored the depth of her beauty.

Across the room, Braun sat transfixed by the sight of this Aryan vision. Yet, despite once more feeling a rush of desire, he was consumed with thoughts of jealousy and revenge, knowing she was beyond his reach, and with a man he had grown to hate. Watching the couple as they touched and whispered, only served to further inflame his anger.

"Still, that's gotta be one fine Aryan piece of ass," Krueger leered.

"I wouldn't lower myself," he replied with a shake of his head. "She's with a race traitor, and the *schlampe* probably even fucked n*****s and k***s."

"Ach, you're right. Too bad she ruined herself with such scum."

Elsewhere in the room, most of the patrons were now at their tables, and an excited buzz was filling the air. Before assuming his role as emcee for the afternoon's performance, Sid brought over Benny Carter, to meet his friends. The presence of the rising young saxophone star caused a minor ruckus, as a group of fans rushed over for autographs. Sensing a chance to gather some dope, Braun made his way towards the scene.

"I didn't want to ruin the surprise," Sid announced to the couple.

"Not exactly the best kept secret," Alex interrupted with a chuckle.

"I know, but Benny got in early for a gig at Richardson's, so he wanted to sit-in with the fellas this afternoon. Benny Carter, my friends: Maureen Costello and Alex Wagner."

"Love your music, Benny! Saw your show at Richardson's last year, and before that at the Rhythm Cafe." Sensing a possible faux pas, Alex was quick to add, "But of course, the Starlite's the best. I should know, I go to 'em all, being a big fan of jazz."

After some friendly small talk, Benny turned his attention to the fans seeking autographs, while Alex and Maureen turned their attention to each other.

At the same time, satisfied he had accomplished his mission, Braun rejoined Krueger.

"So, you pick up anything?" Hans asked.

"Yeah, he goes to all these jazz clubs."

"It figures, he likes that jungle noise. Christ, how can he be German? What garbage!"

"History is full of those who betray their people, but this time, they'll answer."

"What else ya got?"

"Yeah, the girl's name is Costello. Maureen Costello."

"Ah, a d**o, makes sense. They're just one step removed from Africa."

"Naw, it's Irish. I went to school with a Costello, always goin' on about the Irish. They're Aryans, but not pure Nordics. They're a shiftless, drunken people always wrangling for government jobs. Figures she'd latch onto a rich boy."

"Low-class brawlers. I won't forget that b***h nearly bitin' offf Eric's thumb!"

"Don't worry, they're gonna pay! I'm startin' to think up some plans for these two. It'll fit right into our strategy for action."

"Count me in," Krueger cackled.

"We'll start by tailin 'em when they leave. It's important that we I-D his car and where he lives. And with her name and address, we can check out her, too"

"Good thing we came in my uncle's car, they might recognize yours."

"Too bad we have to stay for this *scheisse* music."

"Well, for Reich und Volk."

Off to the side, a much different atmosphere prevailed. Once the band launched into their opening number, Alex leaned over and kissed Maureen. This inspired an exchange of smiles, and an effort to snuggle even closer.

Not wavering as he cast a hateful glare in their direction, Braun snarled, "…and what better way to exact vengeance than by achieving our aims through their pain."

VII

Standing on the porch of the gray shingled bungalow, they could hear the sounds of laughter drift through the windows. The sun was just beginning to set as Maureen fumbled with her keys and Alex surveyed the street-scape of a neighborhood that was largely foreign to him.

"You're right, the grain elevators lend an impressive panorama to the area."

"Yeah, like our own little mountain range."

"Hey, did you catch that. A car just slowed down and then sped off when I gave it a closer look."

"Oh god…"

"So, the Micks already sense a Kraut in the neighborhood?" he laughed.

"We're not that tribal, I hope. No, it's probably Terry Sullivan. He's had a crush on me… forever. Maybe one of his pal's cars—trying to be sly"

"Should I be jealous? I suppose I'd be jealous too, seeing the way I kissed you a minute ago."

"And a wonderful kiss it was," she winked. "But don't worry, he's harmless. All five feet two and a hundred ten pounds of him. He's sweet, but relentless. You try to be nice, and it just encourages him. Good God, I have to find a girl for that boy."

Triumphantly waving her keys, she unlocked the door and yelled, "I'm home." After passing through the hall they entered the parlor that had a warm, domestic feel, with creamy yellow walls and old-fashioned, floral print draperies. Oriental carpets covered oak floors and a brocade couch sat off to the side, where a contented tabby rested against a pillow embroidered with the Gaelic greeting, *"Dia is Muire Duit,"* or "God and Mary bless you." A china cabinet filled with generations of family photographs, stood next to a tile framed fireplace.

Across from the sofa, an elderly couple sat alongside a Philco console tuned to the popular "Fibber McGee and Molly" comedy program. Upon spotting the couple, the old lady piped up, "Oh, dear, Gramps had the radio turned up so high, we didn't hear you come in. Here, let me turn it off."

Before the couple had a chance to advance, the man shot up from his chair, "First, I want to hug my sweetie. Then I want to meet this young gentleman I've heard so much about."

"Now Gramps, don't go embarrassing me, but before I forget, you have to be more careful with the radio. Someone could sneak in without you hearing."

"Did you forget, I'm a cop," he said with a smile. "And honey, these are our neighbors and this is our home. Keena's lived here all her life. Only manners prevent me from saying how long," he said with a mischievous wink.

"Eighty-one and proud of it," she teased back. "But your Grandpa's right, we couldn't be safer. He's still a cop, whether it's lunch with his retired buddies, huddling with the current brass, or keeping up with all the new trends. Did you see the book he just put down, 'The Future of Forensic Criminal Analysis'."

"Well, I guess once a cop, always a cop."

"Oh, you're more than that Gramps." Turning to Alex, she added. "Him and Gram share an interest in history, social justice, the outdoors and of course, exercise, just to name a few."

"We better be in shape, raising this dynamo and her brother," the wife smiled.

"Besides, I want to make sure I get my moneys worth with the gym at the Knights. But enough of this, let's get down to proper introductions," he said, while thrusting out his hand. "Hugh Costello here, and this is my beautiful wife, Keena."

Alex was quick to return the gesture, before noting what a lovely house they had.

Despite having lived over eight decades, the Costellos were still a handsome pair, as each looked years younger than their age. Friends ascribed this to their unremitting love for each other, and their family, along with an ever-present lust for life.

Remarkably, Keena sported a thick bun of auburn hair, with only small swaths of gray betraying her years. She was tall like Maureen, and no doubt possessed an equally beguiling figure in her time. Her graceful, patrician features easily embraced the lines that came with age, and her probing blue eyes would light up, whenever she'd break into a smile.

Hugh Costello still possessed a raw-boned ranginess that belied his years. Tall with a shock of white hair, he had pale blue eyes that always seemed to twinkle when engaged in conversation. Friends on the force sometimes called him, "Little Brick." Most assumed it was in reference to the solid build of his youth, but in fact, it was an homage to his long-dead, partner and mentor, who went by the nickname, "Brick Fist."

Still, the Costellos were not immune to the passage of time, as each would laugh that they moved more slowly, or were often forced to write things down.

"Sorry we missed you when you picked up Maureen, but we were at a baked goods sale after mass."

"Keena contributed her signature soda bread," he said with an air of pride.

After another a round of introductory banter, Alex and Maureen made for the sofa. "Beans, I know you have the run of the place, but could you please make a little room for us," she chided the cat, before he reluctantly yielded, and sauntered to a corner.

"So, Alex, Maureen tells me you're a Canisius man."

"Yes, Mister Costello, both high school and college."

"Likewise, class of eighty-six, for college, Took me ten years," he said sheepishly before adding, "my family and police job came first."

"And our son and grandson followed suit. The Jesuits know how to educate and mold young men."

"My mother says the same thing, Missus Costello. And like your family, my father and grandfather went there too."

"That's right. Maureen tells me your family are the Wagners from Alpine Machine. I met your grandfather a number of times, and I know your father, Rudy—a fine man and outstanding business leader. In fact, I just read that his company was awarded additional contracts for the planes that Curtiss is building for the army."

"Yeah, he's very happy about that."

"And those additional planes are keeping Curtiss humming. I'm bringing in some serious money with all the added overtime."

"Just don't forget, money isn't everything, honey. And as I said before, you can do anything, medicine, law, academia, whatever. Always at the top of your class, and *summa cum laude* at State," her grandmother said with a look of pride.

"And as you know, I'm still searching and keeping my options open. Maybe teaching in some capacity, or maybe I'll save up and start my own business and run it just like Gram did with her father's place."

"You can be a ground breaker, but whatever you do, you'll have our support."

"You're smart and strong, maybe a little too strong willed at times," the old man added with a chuckle. "And you always make us happy and proud."

"Thanks, I'm the most blessed person in the world to have you, and Danny."

"And thank you for the kind words about my father, Mister Costello. And funny, he said similar things about you when I brought you up—especially about your distinguished police career. And of course, Maureen has such wonderful things to say about you two."

"Well, as you can tell, she and her brother are the centerpieces of our lives."

"Indeed, family is everything," the old man nodded. "And thank you for those kind words, but I have to say that Keena is the real star around here. Still, I was blessed to be a policeman. Rewarding work, solving crimes and helping people. But enough accolades about us old coots, let's hear more about you."

"Yes, Maureen tells us you're a reporter."

"Yes, for The *Advocate*. Are you familiar with it?"

"Of course, a fine publication."

"I try to read most of the papers, especially when I was Commissioner. Gives me a good sense of what's going on in the community. Besides, I'm friends with Victor Lange, a good fella."

"And he's a great person to work for. He's taught me a lot. I'm working my way up and he's got me doing some interesting assignments, like the Bund story last wee… uh… Listen, I know Maureen told you what happened. So, I want to say right off the bat that I'm sorry she ended up in a bad situation. I'm not reckless or irresponsible, and I'll always be careful when she's with me."

There was a brief pause as the grandparents cast knowing looks towards each other. "Thank you, Alex for bringing it up. Obviously, our granddaughter's welfare always comes first," Keena said.

"And don't forget, Alex didn't twist my arm to go. It sounded interesting and it was. I always felt safe, and despite the surprise at the end, it all worked out."

"Don't worry, dear, like grandpa said, you can be a little headstrong, but you always show good sense, and we trust you."

"And don't feel bad, Alex. We realize nobody could have predicted what happened, and you did the right thing helping that man. We trust Maureen, and I'm sure Victor wouldn't keep a reporter with bad judgement. Of course on the other hand, these Nazi types shouldn't be dismissed as mere crackpots. They can be dangerous, and have to be treated as such."

"I know, I still have bruises on my back to remind me."

"When I first heard what happened, I got in touch with Captain Duggan of the Gang Squad. After finding out the plates were stolen, he had his boys go over everything again, but they couldn't come up with anything more."

"I'm not surprised. This was planned, a quick in and out."

"You're right, son. The plates, the masks, the paint can, the choreographed moves, all point to that."

"Yeah, they wanted to make a statement," Maureen said. "The Swastika, anti-Semitic slurs, and the beating of Mister Bloom, a Jew, are proof of that."

"But there may be more than meets the eye here. Captain Duggan—by the way, a good cop—started out with your dad and worked with Danny and me…"

"Yeah, my older brother Danny, I told you he's a cop. And we recently found out he made lieutenant. We're all so proud."

"Indeed," added Keena.

"I'm overjoyed of course, but I can brag some other time. In the meantime, Duggan tells me that there's been cases of anti-Semitic flyers being left around town. More importantly, there's been incidences of vandalism of Jewish stores, and some random attacks against Jews and Negroes."

"Can't be coincidence. Sounds like it could be a clandestine group out for violence and intimidation," Alex replied.

"And advancing their warped cause with those flyers," Maureen added.

"Exactly! Duggan says they haven't come up with any connections or solid evidence, but they're keeping an open investigation. He promised to keep me posted."

"I'm surprised there hasn't been much from the city or the papers on this."

"You're right, Gram. I suspect somebody figures this gives the city a black eye and hurts business, so they want to keep a lid on it,"

"And of course, there's always plain ol' bigotry. I'm sure there's people who don't give a damn what happens to Negroes or Jews. They may even think they deserve it," Keena replied.

"That's troubling, but I still know a lot of the fellas on the force, like Duggan. I'm sure most of 'em want to pursue this sort of case. Still, there's bigotry in a lot of places."

"My father told me you took a stand over Anti-German harassment during the War."

"Everyone deserves the protection of the law. That was my job. We went after any acts of harassment and kept the press informed. In fact, your grandfather came to me about some vandalism at the plant. We put a quick end to it."

"Still, as much as you keep your irons in the fire, honey, there's been at lot of changes since you were there. I know you don't like this current Commissioner."

"Yes, Henry Wilson, highly political and curries up to the power brokers. Not much of a cop when I had 'im—shifty and a real operator."

"Let's hope he doesn't interfere on this," Keena observed.

"I'll keep an eye on things. I trust my friends, but I don't want anyone dismissing this attack on my granddaughter and her friends. This sort of hate has no place in our community."

"Thanks, Gramps, you and Gram always preached tolerance and goodwill."

"We try to live our faith," the grandmother answered with a smile.

"Like you said, the major papers aren't really picking up on this story," Alex interjected, "Sure, they ran with the news on the Bund Convention, but the *Advocate* is following up and addressing this Nazi issue. The Bund convention put a spotlight on things."

"So are you still involved with that story, Alex?" the old man asked.

"Yes, Mister Lange has me taking the lead in a multipart series. He liked my report on the convention—and the attack—so we're taking a broader look at the issue."

"Interesting, a German community paper taking a lead on this. Speaks well of Victor."

"Makes sense, in light of what's going on in Europe and now here. It has to have an impact on our community. We'll see what's going on in the community, and how people feel about all this."

"It has to be controversial. Knowing Victor, he won't hold back. But what does your family think of your involvement. After all, they're prominent in the Buffalo German community."

"They've expressed their caution. They remember the War years, as do I, so we don't want to see that rear its head again. But they trust and support me, like with you and Maureen. Besides, Victor is one of our family's closest friends. He respects the community's concerns, but he'll follow the facts. I tend to agree with my family that Hitler will be brought under control by other German interests. As for all this Bund business, those people don't reflect our German American values, and I'm sure our report will reflect this."

"How did your report on the Bund go over in the local community, so far?" Kenna asked.

"There was some negative feed-back for even bringing it up, while others said they were happy to see this extremism exposed. Some letters said they worried about anti-German backlash. Still others believe the conditions in Germany were being embellished by the press because of bias over the War."

"Some of my German American friends feel the same as you, and believe that things will settle down in Germany" Hugh observed.

"Hopefully, that's the case. We don't need any more European crises. The world is just getting back on its feet."

"I hope that's true, but I worry." Hugh responded, "I believe Nazism is a genuine threat to the world. I'm sure that Hitler, like any tyrant once he has secured his power, crushes any opposition, and expands that power."

"And his ideology of hate is like an infection that can spread. Especially in times of economic uncertainty, demagogues exploit fear of others. And we're still not out of the woods with the depression. We have to stand against such evil," Keena added.

"My darling wife doesn't abide injustice. She's my justice warrior and it's filtered down to our granddaughter."

"Your whole life has been devoted to the pursuit of justice, Gramps. I have to follow in both your steps," Maureen said with an air of pride.

"I try. But even at my age, I shudder at what the future may bring; especially with Hitler's recent rearming. Still, I pray I'm wrong."

"Time will tell, and hopefully, I'll find the truth with my reporting."

"I'm sure you will, Alex. You strike me as earnest, and eager to do a good job."

"You're right Gramps, I've read some of Alex's work. He's a good reporter and writes beautifully."

"I'm also looking forward to reading Alex's articles, but listen, all this Nazi talk is getting me too riled up," Keena sighed. "I want to hear about your concert today, honey. How was it?"

"It was Great! Sunday afternoons are the big draw for jazz fans at the Starlite over on Michigan."

"Today they had Benny Carter. He's a saxophonist—a national act—and was terrific!"

"We're music fans too, although hardly experts. We like Bing Crosby. Isn't he jazzy, if that's a word?" Hugh asked.

"We listen to him on Thursday nights when he hosts the Kraft Music Hall,"

"Yeah, he once sang with Paul Whiteman, and he's been known to bend a note and use off-tune phrasing. He was also influenced by his friend, the great jazzman Louis Armstrong. So yeah, he's like you say, jazzy, but his style is more conventional now."

"You got me on that, Alex, so I'll take your word for it," the old man smiled. "And by the way, Bing's a Jesuit graduate too; Gonzaga University, out there in the Northwest."

"I figured we had something in common," Alex chuckled.

"And we also got to see Jim Jefferson perform. He's the man who helped us the night we were attacked."

"Of course, and how's he doing. I'm sure you expressed our appreciation to him."

"Indeed, Gram, and he seems to be doing okay."

"Fortunately, he didn't suffer any damage that night, but he's had financial struggles."

"Up to now, he's been working odd jobs and living down in the Hobo Jungle."

"Honey, don't fall into that trap and call it a jungle. Jungles suggest animals, not human beings." Turning toward Alex, she continued, "If you don't know, it's a camp for itinerant men located on scrub land across the Buffalo River. For whatever reason, the men who find themselves down there are homeless and on the road."

"You're right, Gram, it could be any of us."

"And it wasn't that long ago when we worried we could end up in a soup line," the old man said, shaking his head.

"Alex, I don't know if Maureen told you I'm part of a group that volunteers at the camp. We try to help with food and clothing and provide job advice and leads. Our priest, Father Martin, and Sister Genevieve also minister to their spiritual needs."

"That's awful nice of you, Missus Costello, but, I hope you're careful. Jim tells me that it can be dangerous down there."

"Don't worry, we're not naive. There's some bad apples and troublemakers, especially some K-K-K types from down south, who showed up after riding the rails. Still, most are decent men, just looking for work so they can help their families back home."

"Captain Plunkett over at precinct eight put out word there'll be no nonsense when it comes to these volunteers, and oftentimes, a couple of his men show up when they're there."

"The good news is that Alex's friend offered Jim a regular stint at the Starlite, and more importantly, Alex arranged with his family for some full time work."

"Well, he's an interesting guy. Besides being a musician, he's a mechanic and once owned his own shop"

"I imagine there may be opportunities, given the work these army contracts must be generating," Hugh observed.

"It might not be right away at the plant. Most of the jobs there are for the trade unions. Plus, my dad has specific rules for filling positions. So, at least for now, he'll be working at other properties and on company cars,"

"I see… In any case, I'm sure they appreciate what he did for you as well."

"They do. And hopefully, it will work out for him and he can get out of that camp."

"Speaking of work, I better start getting ready for tomorrow. I've got the seven o'clock shift and it's going to be crazy. They got some dog and pony show set up announcing the new order for planes."

"That's right, I'll be covering it."

"Gee, I hope you aren't disappointed, in case you see me in work overalls," Maureen laughed.

"Fat chance of that!"

"I suppose us old folks should be getting ready to hit the hay too, but not before our cup of chamomile tea," Keena announced.

As Maureen joined her grandmother in the kitchen, the old man took Alex aside. "I'm sure my idealistic granddaughter will want to get involved with your series on the Nazis. She's smart and strong, but of course, she has no experience in investigative stories; especially when it may involve criminality. So be careful about bringing her into these things. Try to keep it to advice—if that's possible with my headstrong angel. And being cautious doesn't just apply to Maureen, you have to watch out for yourself too. This group or groups are violent, fanatical people. Perhaps the worst kind of criminals to go up against, even for the police. I'm sure your German background won't make a lick of difference to them. You're the enemy, a threat. I imagine even Victor has never dealt with this type before."

"Which brings me to this point. You may need a veteran police hand to advise you when looking into these sorts of criminal matters. I've spent a career in investigations, especially dealing with criminal minds. So please, I'd be more than happy to help you in any way with this assignment of yours."

"I'll be very careful with Maureen, Mister Costello, and try to keep it to advice. Most of my work will be with members of the community, but, when I get into any of this gang business, I'd love to have your expertise and help."

"That's great, Alex! I'm sure I can be of assistance."

"I look forward to getting your input, so I'll be in touch." With that, the old man broke into a smile and slapped him on the back.

Just then, Maureen returned with Keena, who was carrying a tea set. As the old couple prepared to enjoy their nighttime ritual, Alex thanked them for their warm reception. Soon everyone was expressing their pleasure in having gotten together. After bidding his farewell, he headed with Maureen to the privacy of the porch. There, away from the glare of the door light, they fell into a long and passionate embrace. Finally, after sharing one last kiss, Alex jumped into his car for a satisfied ride home.

Across the way, on the now desolate O'Connell Street, two shadowy figures sat in a car, taking note of what was happening. Under the cover of a sprawling oak, they were largely invisible. Inside, neither man spoke, as Karl Braun watched with a cold-eyed stare. As Alex pulled out, they turned the corner and followed, intent on discovering where he lived, too.

VIII

The metal skins of aircraft glistened under beams of sunlight pouring down through banks of skylights. Inside Curtiss Wright's sprawling Plant #1, scores of planes sat cradled along a factory floor that teemed with energy.

Tow carts criss-crossed the landscape, ferrying dollies to assembly stations throughout the plant. Each was loaded with all manner of bulkheads, struts, and other components destined for a range of aircraft.

The sound of rivet guns, grinders and drills filled the air as an army of workers swarmed over planes in various stages of construction. Meanwhile, cascades of sparks, and the glow from a bevy of welding arcs provided a luminous backdrop to the vast industrial panorama.

Most of the factory was devoted to the manufacture of military aircraft for the US government. Yet, some were destined for export, when permitted under the Neutrality Act, which outlawed the trading of arms with countries at war, and reflected American isolationist concerns.

Areas of the plant were sectioned off for the production of the Model 77 Helldiver, a bi-plane naval dive bomber, and the A-12 Shrike, an Army Air Corp ground attack aircraft.

A tract at the far end of the building was reserved for the Model 75A, Hawk fighter. As part of the work group assigned to the project, Maureen Costello was crouched in a cockpit, busily connecting gauges to an instrument panel. Her friend, Lisa Mangini stood atop a wing, trying to coax a stubborn belt onto the pilot's seat frame.

Off to the side, a podium had been set up in anticipation of a press conference set for later that morning. Those slated to attend included, Curtis officials, military brass, political dignitaries, representatives from subcontractors, and members of the press.

Curtiss designed the Hawk to be the most advanced military air-craft in the world, at the cutting edge of aeronautical engineering. Some of its innovations included all metal construction, mono wing design, re-tractable landing gears, and an enclosed cockpit.

The company invited those in attendance to a plant tour prior to the news conference. As a major subcontractor, Alpine Machine sent a sizable delegation to the event. Besides Max and Freddie Wagner, the group included sales personnel, members of the engineering staff, along with the firm's chief machinist and his two assistants, one of whom was Karl Braun. Alex Wagner was also there, as a member of the press.

By now, the tour had arrived at the factory's machine shop. As guides ushered the group around the worksite, the Alpine contingent paused to talk among themselves.

"Interesting work flow process," Freddie observed.

"Designed to get the most out of the workforce," Max agreed.

"And it's good to see all of us interacting. Like I said earlier, let's take this as an opportunity to learn things."

"Especially those affecting the bottom line," Max chuckled. "But seriously, as we always stress, we're committed to manufacture the best products at the best prices in the industry."

"Dave Zack, Curtiss' Director of Purchasing pointed out that they never had one of our parts fail," Chuck Cooper, the chief engineer added.

"And we never will," Freddie nodded to the others in the circle. "So, let's keep buttton-holing our counterparts."

Braun needed no such prodding. After all, the Curtiss Hawk was the subject of the special operation that his handlers had assigned to his group.

As a long-time party loyalist, who had shown himself to be smart and capable, Braun had been groomed for years as a potential asset by Nazi intelligence. Yet, it was his job at Alpine that ultimately brought him to this sensitive mission. Given his work for an important Curtiss subcontractor, he was in an ideal position to gather information for the German military.

Braun was determined to carry out what he saw as his sacred duty, and he viewed today's event as an important step in that endeavor. As he set off on his mission, he was amused by the easy access and relative lack of security surrounding the Curtiss facility. He attributed this to America's decadent pre-occupation with promoting any money-making enterprise, and he felt proud that this could never happen in Germany.

The early part of the tour, focusing on the Helldiver and the Shrike, held marginal value for the spy. Although important to America's aerial arsenal, the planes were of conventional design, and since they were active components of the military's fleet, much information was already available to the public through sources like *Jane's All the Worlds Aircraft*, and other military journals.

On the other hand, Germany's interest in the Hawk was well placed. For some time, Curtiss had been alluding to its revolutionary design, and although details were still under wraps, rumors of its significant innovations were rampant within the world of aeronautics. In light of the Nazi's fevered program of rearmament—in violation of the Versailles Treaty—Hitler's military was determined to use any means possible to acquire this information.

As the plant visitors listened to a spokesman describe the operations of the machine shop, Braun spotted a counterpart he had met in the past. After re-introducing himself with some small talk, he turned the conversation to professional matters.

"Yeah, Tom, as you probably know from your work here, Alpine is also always lookin' for better quality at lower prices per unit."

"Don't I know, Karl!"

"Yeah, any bonus I get depends on my team's piece work."

"Same here."

"So, I'm always lookin' for better equipment to suggest to 'em. Now, what's with that? It looks new…"

"Sure, it's a continuous band saw—produces much better units. Eliminates much of the extra machining afterwards."

"So who makes it?"

"International Machine, outta Saint Paul; but, that's not my real baby. That's over there behind that rack."

"Oh, yeah, Benjamin Machine. Looks like a boring machine."

"It's a honing unit that makes much finer engine cylinder bores."

"Who's the guy who repped it?"

"Bob Templeton. He's one of their sales reps but also a former machinist, so he knows his stuff. Great guy, I'm sure he'll shoot you out some brochures with the tech data on it."

Braun kept up with his questions as he moved from station to station. At each stop, he would innocently finger a handful of machine shavings before sliding them into his pockets when no one was watching.

While Braun continued to probe and observe, company staffers were applying the finishing touches to the site of the upcoming news conference. With the plant tour drawing to a close, workers assigned to the Hawk were excused from their duties and shuffled off to a spot away from the seating area. Meanwhile, maintenance personnel quickly draped tarps onto the aircraft, thus revealing only the bare outlines of the three planes.

A large billboard featuring an array of images from Curtiss Wright's past was rolled out, while crews arranged rows of seats for the invited guests. Even though the Hawk line had been shut down, factory sounds continued to reverberate from elsewhere in the building. In response, stands of speakers were placed along the edge of the staging area.

Despite being clad in her blue overalls, Maureen still managed to strike a beguiling figure as she stood with her co-workers waiting for the proceedings to begin. That didn't escape Alex's attention when he finally spotted her as he neared the scene. Likewise, she was quick to recognize him. Upon locking eyes, the couple lost no time in exchanging smiles and eager waves.

As the audience began to take their seats, staff directed dignitaries to chairs behind the lectern. Once the crowd settled in, Curtiss's PR Director stepped to the mike and welcomed the guests, before introducing company officials and various public figures. "And of course, I would be totally remiss in failing to acknowledge our legendary Design Chief, Dave Borne, Principle Engineer, Bill Evans, his deputy, Jeff Gates, and one of his assistants, Peter Meyer, and our amazing lead test pilot, Eddie Jackson." Each introduction was met with a chorus of applause.

"Now, before I go on, I must stress again, no pictures regarding the Hawk. The shrouds to your left should be a remainder of that," he added with a smile. "As you know, it's a work in progress, and hasn't yet been formally launched."

"Now, the purpose of our presentation today, is threefold: One: update you on our vision and progress in regard to the Hawk. Two: announce, in conjunction with the War Department, local manufacturers who have been awarded additional subcontracts to produce components for not only the Hawk, but for parts reflecting some refinements to the Helldiver and Shrike. And Three: highlight the effect our business is having on the local economy."

"With the Hawk, our goal is to produce the most modern military aircraft in the world. Without going into restricted details, it will have the most innovative features of any plane in the air today. As such, we're confident the Army Air Corp will ultimately agree with our assessment and procure substantial numbers of the Hawk, an aircraft designed to play an important role in our national security. Given our successful history in military sales, we can deliver abundant numbers of this incredible plane in a timely, and cost effective manner."

Finally, he introduced officials from companies awarded subcontracts, before inviting Max Wagner to speak for the group.

"Thanks for the kind words and opportunity to speak, Rich, but you're always a tough act to follow," he chuckled to the audience. "First of all, I want to say that Alpine Machine has worked with Curtiss since their start here, and we know first hand, their commitment to excellence—a quality that serves this country well. And I'm proud to say, we at Alpine Machine share these same values. As for this diverse group of suppliers, I know most of them professionally and some of them personally, and I am aware of their reputation for making quality products at a fair price. What Curtiss and all these companies are trying to accomplish here, is important not only to our country, but especially for the fine people of this area. "

With that, he launched into a bevy of statistics focusing on how these military contracts were impacting the local economy. He eagerly cited the rising employment figures for Curtiss and its suppliers, before pointing out how their worker's wages were fueling sales for all manner of local business.

Carrying himself much like a candidate on the stump, he ended his speech with a rousing declaration, "Having spent all my adult life in commerce and civic involvement, I firmly believe that business can lead the way in securing a better and more prosperous future for all the citizens of this great community, this great country!"

Lighting up the hall with his smiling good looks and infectious charisma, Max reveled in the applause of the energized audience.

Despite wanting to maintain his journalistic distance, Alex couldn't help but feel a rush of pride, as he watched his uncle glad handing listeners on his way back to his seat. He was reminded of Max's repeated refrain that his family were achievers, who had a responsibility to set an example and lead. They could never join the ranks of the passive and mediocre. Alex was still trying to find himself; yet, having been raised in an atmosphere that preached excellence, he couldn't help but feel special.

Sitting three rows back, Karl Braun was busy taking notes; yet, he kept returning to the sight of Alex, whom he had seen interviewing Curtiss officials and other dignitaries since the start of the tour. By now, his hatred for the Wagner scion was palpable; yet his focus was interrupted upon the introduction of the Chief Engineer of the Hawk Project. Braun immediately recognized the man's assistant, Peter Meyer, whom he had seen at various choral events in his role as the youth chorus master for the First Evangelical Lutheran Church.

At the close of the program, Braun wove his way through the crowd, and approached Meyer, who was about to return to his office. "Great presentation on the Hawk. Sounds incredible! And congratulations, you must be proud of your work on it."

"Thanks. Still a work in progress, but we believe it's gonna be even better than advertised, Mister…"

"No doubt. And yeah, Karl Braun here, assistant chief machinist over at Alpine. I guess we're both assistants to the boss—as much as a machinist can compare to you engineers."

"Hey, you're bein' too modest. We're both professionals and speak the same language. Besides, pretty hard doin' this without the help of you machinists," He said pointing to the draped figures off to the side. "We need the help from below."

"Any way we can help," Braun said, adopting a fawning tone.

"So, glad to meet you, Karl… it's Karl, right? And call me Pete. And while I got ya here, those Alpine parts of yours are A-one."

"Thanks, Pete, and yeah, it's Karl," he replied, already resenting his condescending attitude. "Yeah, like you, I take pride in our products, not that the big shots reward our efforts, for bustin' our tails."

"You got that right, same here," he snapped with a shake of his head.

"Listen, as much as I'd like to pick your brain about your work— I'm sure I could learn a lot," he said as Meyer flashed a look of self-satisfaction, "I figure you've been button-holed all morning. Besides, I gotta say, I recognize you from some of the *Sangerfests*. First Evangelical Lutheran, right?"

"I'm the youth chorus master. It's my passion, along with aircraft … and other things," he smirked while nodding towards a shapely young secretary bending over at the lectern. His darting eyes lent a hungry, grasping sheen to the otherwise nondescript little man. "And you? Are you a singer?"

"Sure," he replied, while casting a knowing leer towards the woman. "I can see … and yeah, second tenor for the *Steinadler* Sangerbund."

"Oh, wow, I'm impressed! We're not in your league."

"I'm flattered, but from what I've heard, you folks are beginning to make your presence known. You must be doin' a great job."

Once more, Meyer couldn't hide the look of satisfaction on his face. "My turn to be flattered, especially coming from a singer with Steinadler."

With introductions out of the way, the pair engaged in some easy banter about their experiences in the world of chorus.

Finally, Meyer revealed he was late for a meeting, before adding that the session was sure to be a cavalcade of ass-kissing and bullshit.

"Been there myself," Braun was quick to offer with a look of frustration. "But listen, this has been great, we should get together."

"Yeah, manufacturing pros and chorus lovers, makes sense. We got the Sanferfest next week at the Music Hall. I'm sure you'll be there, so drop over to where we are, Karl."

"Absolutely, Pete! Look forward to it!"

As he watched the engineer march off to his appointment, Braun couldn't believe his good fortune. Besides having picked up on Meyer's disgruntled attitude, he was aware of a significant chink in the man's armor.

Although having crossed paths in singing circles, Karl never had any desire to know anything about him, particularly his job. Sure, he was aware of his mediocrity as a chorus master, but he was also aware of rumors that the man had unseemly interests in some of the adolescent girls in his charge.

Up until now, Braun couldn't care less. After all, Meyer was a *"weichei"*, or a soft egg and a deviant to boot, while the girls were probably little tarts, the products of a decadent society. But that all changed the moment he saw the engineer at the dais. His predatory instincts now fully engaged, he realized such knowledge could prove invaluable in the future.

As the Alpine entourage gathered to leave, Braun had a smug look on his face. Given what he had learned, it was no wonder he considered the day a stunning success.

Meanwhile, Alex saw his chance to steal a moment with Maureen as she waited for the crowd to disperse. Bursting into a welcoming smile as he approached, she teased, "You're not gonna run off now that you see me in my work duds?"

"You kiddin'? You look great. Whaddah say we play a little hooky," he said with a playful leer.

"Don't tempt me. I have to be responsible."

"Ahem… didn't you forget to tell me how nicely I fill my overalls," Maureen's friend Lisa interrupted as she walked by with a provocative wiggle.

"Ah, I only have eyes for this beautiful lady."

"Good answer, for your sake; but, I figure the rest of these fellas are checking me out when I bend over that cockpit, " she giggled before joining a group heading back towards the planes.

"She's incorrigible, but I adore her. She's such a good friend."

"And speaking of friends, you probably didn't hear, but Sid's place caught fire last night."

"What! We were just there yesterday. God, anybody hurt?"

"Fortunately, no, but it's pretty badly damaged. I'm really upset for my friend. The clubs not totaled, but it's probably gonna be down for some time."

"Any idea what happened?"

"Spoke to Sid on the phone this morning. As you can imagine he's devastated. He was told it might have been a cigarette in the back trash bin; but, he said the fire investigator acted funny, like he was figuring, it musta been so-called, 'Jewish lightening.' You know, arson. That's bullshit!"

"That's terrible! Hard enough dealing with something like that, without that kind of bigotry."

"Ridiculous! Besides being good people who wouldn't do anything like that, the place is a gold mine. And remember, Sid told us his father was getting hate calls for his work with the ADL."

"And don't forget what Gramps said about Nazi vandalism and gang assaults. Sounds like there could be a connection."

"Yeah, I mentioned it to Sid. I also let Victor know at the paper. He agrees: more to be aware of and to look into for the series."

"And I'll bring it up to Gramps. Hopefully the club will be back up and running sooner rather than later."

"Yeah, it's a real musical institution, besides being my friend's place."

"He's got a good friend in you."

"Thanks, and what about your day. I hope it's better."

"Just another day keeping our nations skies safe," she chuckled. "And what about you? So how do you like all this?"

"Pretty amazing. Got a lot of background for a good story."

"Had to be fun running into your family on a professional level."

"Sure, I get to report on Max's remarks."

"My bosses were quite complimentary about Alpine; and by the way, your uncle is almost as handsome as you. And was that your brother seated next to him?"

"Thanks! And yeah, that's Freddie. I'm sure they appreciate the praise—and they deserve it."

"And who was that odd little man who appeared to be with your family's party, seated right behind Freddie. He was either scribbling like crazy or else just gazing up in the air. But the weird part was that every so often, he'd turn towards you with like an angry glare. I managed to catch it, and I wondered what that was all about. Any idea who he was? Had kind of a thin, sneaky face.”

“Beats me. Besides Max and Freddie, the only people I know are the Chief Engineer and the Sales Manager. The rest, I think we’re just a bunch of nonentities, salesmen and machinists and the like. Oh, wait, I seem to remember some strange little man, maybe a machinist. Maybe that’s it. Well, whatever. The guy you saw was probably just some odd-ball.”

“Oh, Alex, ‘nonentities,’ that isn’t you. They’re somebodies; someone whom somebody loves, who contribute to your family’s business. You’re too nice to use that term.”

“I suppose I coulda put it better, but still, nobody forced ‘em not to go to college. Sometimes, I think a lot of people want to just cruise through life. They lack motivation.”

“Most people are just struggling to keep up. They’ve never had the means for college,” she said with an air of rebuke before adding with a chuckle, “Looks like I might have my work cut out for me, showing you the other side of life.”

“Hey, I try to be open minded,” he said, before smiling, “And I can be a star pupil when it comes to you. Listen, I can see your point, but on the other hand, I gotta say, I came from a background where effort and achievement are expected. So, it’s sometimes hard to identify with what might be a contented lack of motivation”

“My family has been successful too, but I’ve been raised to understand that it’s not easy for people to rise above their circumstances. All sorts of things can intervene—kids, unemployment, illness, whatever. Well, maybe you’re not where I am on some things, but I know you have a good heart. Besides, all of us learn new things along the way… if we’re smart.”

By now, a guard arrived to advise Alex that he’d have to move on with the other guests, as operations were soon to resume. After exchanging cheery goodbyes, the couple prepared to go their separate ways.

Just then, as the Alpine group began to exit the door, Braun turned for one last look, only to be met by the sight of Alex and Maureen in the distance. The surprise sighting of the woman, once more set his mind in motion.

IX

Alex slowly pressed the brake as he approached his destination. Turning down the access road, he spotted the familiar wooden sign hanging above the gate. Carved into its surface were the words, "Camp Reichsadler, members only."

After driving up a wooded hill that obscured the campgrounds from the highway, he continued on, as the road dropped and entered into an open field. There, he was greeted by the sight of teams of bowmen practicing at an archery range. At the far end of the meadow, an imposing lodge sat before a forested terrain that stretched across the nearby hills. Off to its side was a large, open-air, beer garden that looked out over a parade ground that included a ball diamond, soccer field, and swimming pool, which by now was alive with bathers.

The chalet looked as if it was plucked straight from the pages of a German travel magazine. Built in the style of a Bavarian alpine retreat, it featured a gabled roof with wide eaves, exposed beams, wooden balconies, and a bright stucco facade. A dozen baskets, overflowing with flowers were strung across the top of its lower terrace.

Camp Reichsadler, named after the German Imperial Coat-of-Arms, was a popular, yet exclusive destination for the local German-American gentry. Its grounds boasted scores of hiking and riding trails, along with numerous remote campsites.

Pulling into the gravel lot off to its side, Alex walked up to the entrance, whose doors were flung wide open. Above the doorway, a sign proclaimed, *"Willkommen Daheim,"* or "Welcome Home," in Gothic font. He had been coming here for as long as he could remember, as his family had been members for generations. Yet today, he was here for business rather than pleasure.

Inside, the walls were decorated with flags and crests from the various German states, along with murals depicting idealized nature scenes from German life. Overhead, a large American flag was suspended from the ceiling.

A spacious fireplace stood at the opposite end of the great hall, flanked by a bar, stage, and dance floor on one side, while across the way were a kitchen, along with men's and women's locker rooms.

A host of tables took up much of the floor, with most of them filled with lunchtime diners. On stage, an accordion player was serenading the crowd with traditional German tunes.

Hoping to interview some members for his series on events in Germany, and their impact here, Alex made his way toward a seat at the bar. He realized the controversial nature of his report; nonetheless, he was sure he could gain cooperation.

As he wound his way around the edge of the tables, he spied Walter Klein sitting with a group of other local German luminaries, all of whom were dressed in traditional *lederhosen* and *dirndls*. Trying to avoid an encounter, he ducked, before being spotted by the family friend.

Waging his finger in a manner of an exaggerated rebuke, Klein came rushing up. "Alex, my boy, good to see you, but I haven't seen you here all summer. When you were a *junge*, your parents couldn't keep you out of the pool, off the field, or away from the trails for that matter."

"That's for sure, and it's always good to get out here, but today, it's business, not pleasure."

A quizzical look suddenly crossed Klein's face, "What to you mean, business, Alex? Is it something with your newspaper?"

"Yes, I'm going to interview some people around here for the series I'm doing for the *Advocate*."

"Now wait a minute. You mean it's about that story you're doing on this Bund, Nazi business?"

"That's right, remember I told you about it at my folk's house. Like I said, it's multipart. Have you read any of it?"

Instantly the businessman's cordial expression turned cold. "Indeed, I have, and I have some serious reservations about opening that can of worms. I was going to talk to your dad about it."

"It's my story," he said with a hint of an edge. "It's an important subject and I'm proud of it."

"Yes, I understand, but like I told you before, it's a sensitive subject, and you have to be cautious. You should have talked to your father, first."

"Victor Lange edits my work, and he's satisfied," he answered as his frustration grew. "We're getting both positive and negative reactions from the readers, which is good."

Getting more agitated, Klein snapped, "And what about these interviews? Our members expect privacy. We can't allow this!"

"Victor and I are committed to approaching this subject sensitively. Besides, Victor talked to Mister Kissel and the other board members, and they're okay with it."

"Oh, really? I know my term as President is over, but Leo should have asked me about this."

"I'm sorry you're upset about this," Alex replied, hoping to calm the waters.

"That's all right, Alex, you're a good boy. I'll take this whole thing up with Victor. As for you, son, you can't forget you represent your family and all the leading families of our community."

"This isn't about my family, Mister Klein."

"But you have to know who you are. We're proud Germans, with a great history and culture! Remember this, and don't disappoint us, Alex."

"I respect all that, believe, me; but, I've got to do my job," he smiled awkwardly.

"That's right! We work hard, not like other, low-class people in this country. So go on son, I guess you got permission, but be careful." With that, he shook his hand before heading back to the table, where he immediately launched into a spirited conversation with the others.

Meanwhile, Alex hurried-on to get to his task. Yet, as headed to the bar, he couldn't help but notice some of Klein's friends had kept their eyes fixed on him. He recognized most of those at the table, but some were well-heeled strangers, decked out in expensive watches and jewelry.

Taking one of the stools, Alex ordered a cold lager from his friend, the camp's main bartender, Ol' George. Soon, he began to scan the surroundings in an effort to pick out some prospects for his piece. Wanting a representative sample of the crowd, he spotted a middle-aged couple sending boys out onto the ball field; an old man reading the paper after lunch, and a young woman fresh off a dip in the pool.

After explaining his mission, he was surprised that they were all willing to respond; yet, the couple asked that their names be withheld.

For the most part, Alex found their responses to be what he expected. All were native born, and expressed a loyalty and love for their country, along with a pride in their German heritage. To a person, they insisted that America should make every effort to stay out of Europe's problems.

None claimed to know any Bundists, except the old man who owned an electrical supply company. He confessed to hearing of a couple of "low class underlings," in his employ, who were members. Still, he cautioned it was none of his business, this being a free country. The others were quick to dismiss the group as being a bunch of crackpots.

The two men voiced concerns over what was going on in Germany, but were skeptical about the extreme nature of some of the reports coming out. They both suggested that acts of violence directed against Jews and other minorities were perpetrated by rouge gangs of thugs. They stressed that the German people as a whole, with their great history and culture, should not be painted with the same brush as those hoodlums.

The mother of the ballplayers, added that Hitler was a passing aberration not reflecting German values, and if he continued to pursue a controversial path, the military and business would eventually find a way to replace him. She went on to state that the German people only picked him in the first place, because of the chaos and privation of the Weimar Republic, and the onerous demands of the Versailles Treaty.

The young woman expressed growing distress over what was alleged to be taking place, and feared its spread. Still, she was confident German values would prevail.

All agreed that American Democracy was strong and resilient, and none were familiar with any Nazi threats here. Finally, the old man was quick to remind Alex that German-Americans must be vigilant about any repeat of the hostilities directed toward their community during the Great War.

Although for the most part satisfied with the information he gathered, Alex was eager to get a different, more critical perspective for his story. Looking around the room for another source, his search was answered in the form of a waitress who had just finished her shift.

In her late forties, she had a beautiful yet world-weary face, that reflected decades of tending to the needs and demands of her restaurant clientele. Taking the initiative, she approached the reporter. "Excuse me, but I couldn't help but hear what you were up to while I was waiting on these tables."

"Well… ah… I wasn't up to anything. I was just asking people some questions for a newspaper story I'm doing."

"Don't worry, I wasn't knockin' ya. In fact, I read your article in the *Advocate*, and I thought it was good.

"Thank you, I'm flattered. Ah, I assume it's the one about the Bund activity?" he asked, a little surprised at being recognized.

"Yeah, that's the one. I've seen you here when you're with your family, nice people."

"Thanks again, and Alex Wagner, here… well, I guess you know my name already, and yours is… Marsha…" he said, taking note of her name plate.

"Marsha, Marsha Andrews."

"Gosh, one of the few non-Germans around here," he chuckled.

"Not so fast," she laughed in return. "My maiden name is Eckert. The family's been here since fleein' the German Revolution that failed, last century. We've always been rabble rousers. My grandpa and pa were both railroad men—and union organizers!"

"Maybe you're a person I need to talk to. Something tells me you may have a different angle on things."

"Damn straight I do! I'm not about to pussy-foot about Hitler and white-wash what those Nazis have been doin' like those folks you were talkin' to."

"So tell me more."

"Sure, but first you gotta promise me you won't use my name."

"Will do, but at least, can I refer to you as a staff member?"

"Listen, I need this job, along with doin' special events at the Music Hall. Your friend, Mister Klein over there, I'm sure he'd sack the whole bunch of us, if ya call me staff and write about what I'm gonna tell ya."

"He's my family's friend, and yeah, I see your point, Marsha. So I'll just say you're another person here, and leave it at that. You have my professional word on it. So, what do you say we go out to a corner of the beer garden, away from prying eyes?"

"Good idea, and yeah, I trust ya. Like I said, your family is nice and your boss, Mister Lange, he's the best!"

After they took different paths to an isolated corner of the beer garden, he asked, "So what do you think of what's going on here and abroad. Is Hitler a threat?"

"Of course he's a threat. He's a power-mad dictator. First thing he did was break up the unions, strangle the press, and go after political opponents. Then, he terrorizes the Jews. Now, he's re-arming, and it's only gonna get worse."

"Many people argue he's a passing aberration, a reaction to the chaos of the Weimar."

"My father, he ain't educated, but he reads a lot. He says, people like that don't let power slip through their hands once they seize it."

"They also say that German institutions and laws will prevail; that the military and business will step in if things get any more extreme."

"Really? Tyrants don't give a damn. Institutions are like ants to be stepped on. As for business, all they're interested in is money, period; and the military, just give 'em their toys and soldiers, and they're happy. They're rearming aren't they?"

"These reports of violence and abuse of Jews and other minorities, just exaggerations?"

"Exaggeration, my… ah… foot! Oh, yeah, I heard them goin' on about questioning those reports. Oh, sure, I bet you and your fellow reporters lie all the time," she said shaking her head. "What about all those American students, tourists, and businessmen seein' stuff."

"Some people insist it's rogue gangs."

"Are you kiddin' me? People don't sneeze over there without his secret police knowin' about it."

"A lot of isolationists suggest that the German people with their great history and culture, and Christian values will eventually intervene, if things get even worse."

"Listen, like I said, I'm proud of my German heritage; but where were those Christian values when our German cousins sank neutral, civilian ships or gassed my German American brother, who's been in and out of veterans hospitals since the Great War."

"Sorry to hear that about your brother."

"He's tough. He's hangin' in there."

"So do you worry about Nazi beliefs spreading here?"

"I'm a patriotic American who has faith in this country; but people can be used and manipulated. In tough times, a strong-man can sell easy answers and scapegoats. It's a credit to this country, that we held it together during the worst of the Depression."

"Did this recent Bund convention concern you?"

"Ya can't ignore it! When hundreds of Nazis show up for a gathering, something's out there. It just didn't happen outta nothin'."

"Have you heard any support for Nazis among friends or neighbors where you live?"

"I'm near Saint Boniface, close to Emslie, so, yeah, a lotta Germans. And by the way, please don't mention the area."

"Sure thing."

"But unlike those folks ya talked to, who know nothin' or nobody, I've heard some rumblings from a few neighbors. Not actual support, but things like he's brought order and prosperity. That sorta thing."

"So, no overt pro-Nazi sentiments."

"Not among my friends or neighbors, but I have seen some things around here."

"What?" he asked, stunned at the thought it could happen at the idyllic playground of his youth. "Are you saying, here at Camp Reichsadler, pro-Nazis?"

"Oh, yeah, I've seen 'em carryin' on, right on these grounds."

"Can you describe for me what you witnessed?"

"I'll tell ya about it, but you can't go writin' about what I saw. They could somehow track me down. These ain't Boy Scouts. I'd be scared for my safety."

"I understand your concerns, and I won't write about it. I'll just use it for my background information when I dig deeper into any Nazi activity here."

"Good, like I said, I trust you, and Mister Lange."

"So what was it? Was it out in the open? Did management know?"

"It's not like that. So first, lemme tell ya how it all sorta came about. I noticed three of these fellas started showin' up here once the weather began gettin' better."

"Did you recognize any of them? Were they members, or relatives of members?"

"I suppose they coulda been members, but they were low-key, keep to themselves, and only occasionally talked to other people. Although, I heard that one of 'em said he was a musician or something. But what really caught my attention, was they didn't seem to belong here."

"How's that?"

"Well, as you know, this place is sorta exclusive, finest families and all that; and while they didn't look low-class, they just kinda didn't seem to fit. Plus, they were an odd mix, a couple guys—looked in their fifties, one of 'em a baldy sour—and the other guy in his twenties, who had a nasty scar."

"A scar… on his face?"

"Yeah, why's that…"

"Nothing important, but go on."

"Anyway, they musta been friends with somebody who could pull strings. That happens sometimes."

"Any idea who may have pulled strings for these strangers?"

"Who knows, maybe another member or upper staff. And they weren't all strangers. At one point, they were joined by a woman I know, Britta Voight. She worked as a barmaid at the Statler when I was there. She was a rising star in those choral competitions."

"Sangerfests?"

"Yeah, but I later heard she was wasting her talents—liked the social life a little too much. She even got members' tongues waggin'. She's rather shapely, if ya know what I mean. Another waitress here said she heard that she had a boyfriend, an athlete of some sort."

"So what did this group do to make you think they were Nazis or whatever."

"Nothing at first, but lemme get back to the story. I usually work the evening shift, and whenever they let us out early, me and another waitress, my friend, Mary, we take a hike through the trails to exercise and relax a little before headin' home. This one night, we're pretty deep into the woods when we hear some ruckus coming from an outta the way campsite. Being the nosy type," she chuckled, "I sneaked closer to see what was up. What I saw nearly knocked my socks off. Outside of where the tents were pitched, were some banners and other Nazi regalia. Around five or six people were sittin' around a fire, including Britta and some of the guys from the little group I saw."

"Did you stick around long enough to see or hear what they were up to?"

"Sure. It was scary lookin', and Mary wanted to get the hell outta there, but I shushed her up and calmed her down. No use rushin' outta there, causing a racket and bein' heard. But I was curious, and besides, we were far enough away and behind some thick brush to be safe. And yeah, believe me, I heard a lot."

"Like what?"

"They were carryin' on about how great Hitler is, or boasting to each other about bringin' the cause here; like makin' trouble for the Jews and coloreds and inspirin' others to follow. With each boast, somebody would break into a *'sieg heil,* 'or a 'blood and soil,' which made your skin crawl. So not wantin' to press our luck, we high tailed it back to the lot where her car was."

"Did you tell anyone about this?"

"No way, especially management! Besides, I'm sure these people are dangerous. So, me and Mary told each other we'd keep a lid on it; but, when I saw what you were doin' today, I figured you should know what's goin' on out there. Maybe knowin' all this can help ya find out and warn people that this stuff is here."

"Other than Britta, you say you didn't know any others in the group; but if you saw them again, could you identify them?"

"Britta of course, and maybe those three guys I saw around—especially the one with the scar—but it was dark, and their backs were to us, so I know I couldn't I-D those other guys."

"And Britta, can you tell me anything more about her?"

"I pretty much only knew her through work. Like I said, she was a big-time party girl, and that can get crazy. One day she even showed up with a shiner."

"Gee, that's bad."

"Got that right, but I've seen it before. That's why I wasn't surprised to hear that she was squandering her talent and dropped outta the music scene. Still, from what I heard about her ability, I hope she's back at it."

"Do you know if she's still at the Statler?"

"Naw; heard the new boyfriend was showin' up and hasslin' customers who were friendly to her. Rather than have those kinda problems, they canned her. Somebody told me she was working at that airplane bar out near the airpark… ah…"

"Barnstormers?"

"Yeah, that's it. And that could be trouble, her and all them red-blooded flyboys who I hear hang around there."

"Interesting… and can you think of anything more that can help me with all this?"

"That's about it."

"And if this group shows up again, and you find out who they are, would you be willing to share that with me? The same confidentiality rules would apply."

"Sure. Can I have a card or something, so I can contact you?"

"Here, and thanks! I appreciate you trusting me with all this. This business about that group is scary stuff, like you said, and it took guts to tell me. And you're right. It will help me find out more about secret Nazi groups and activities."

"Glad to help. I love my country and I'm a loyal American."

"Which reminds, me, a lot of German-Americans worry about a repeat of the anti-German hysteria that surfaced during the Great War. Do you have any fears that bringing up this Nazi business could help lead to that again?"

"Maybe, but I think the country eventually saw how loyal we were, and I'm sure this will always be the case. But, we gotta be careful with this Nazi stuff. I want German Americans to know what could be going on. Just because our German cousins share our blood, doesn't give 'em a free pass on what's goin' on over there. What's wrong and evil, is wrong and evil—period!"

With that, he thanked her once more, before she left with a co-worker who was giving her a ride home.

As Alex walked over to the bar to sample some Pilsners with his friend, Ol' George, he wondered if this group was connected to the Bund or to the gang that jumped him and terrorized Bloom.

He was eager to get to the office tomorrow and discuss the matter with Victor. He knew there'd be a lot more digging around as he delved further into the story. He was also happy that he could tap into help from Commissioner Costello, and his lifetime of investigative experience. But first, he wanted to grab his drink and head back to the beer garden, where he could relax while watching the nearby ballgame.

X

There was little talking as Karl Braun guided his car up Ontario Street. Instead, both he and his passenger, Hans Krueger, focused on the respective roles each would play tonight.

As dusk began to settle in, the modest working class homes of the city's Riverside neighborhood started to give way to an industrial landscape to its north. The area reflected Buffalo's ever growing manufacturing footprint into the surrounding countryside. The expansion was first spurred by the arrival of manufacturing powerhouses such as DuPont and Dunlap, and gained momentum when Curtiss-Wright built its massive Plant, #1, a few years later.

Slowing down, Braun pulled into the parking lot of Wally's Tavern, an old stagecoach inn that had been converted into a working-man's bar in response to the nearby industrial building boom. Sitting next to a railroad overpass, it looked out upon a panorama of factories, their skylights and windows aglow, while clusters of smokestacks spewed out plumes of soot.

After passing through the doors, they saddled up to an antique bar that had seen better days. Once there, they found a spot conveniently removed from a trio of workers still holding court since the three o'clock shift change. Ignoring the pair, the barroom regulars were fully engaged in a beer fueled debate about the Bisons.

Off to the side was a small dining room. Above its entrance was a faded advertising placard from the Blackrock Seafood Market, which featured a splashing yellow pike, the staple of Wally's Friday night fish fry. An elderly couple sat at one of the tables, enjoying the night's special of pierogis, cabbage and pork chops.

Working the taps, Wally, the tavern's namesake and owner, stood before a mirror covered with posters and flyers announcing all manner of church lawn fetes, union picnics and fund raiser's for sick neighbors. Just as he was finishing an order for the workers in the corner, a train came lumbering onto the adjacent overpass, which sent a shudder through the ancient building.

Once the clang of the locomotive bell had faded, Braun quickly ordered a couple of drafts. He was anxious to reach the privacy of a nearby booth, and once more go over the details of tonight's mission. They had been planning the operation since first receiving their assignment from Braun's contact weeks earlier. Nonetheless, he took a moment to engage Wally in some friendly banter. Since he began surveilling the area, Braun had come to realize the gregarious barkeep seemed to know all the neighborhood scuttlebutt, especially in terms of the surrounding factories, whose workers formed the core of his bar's business. As such, he made sure to touch base at this critical juncture, before heading to the booth.

"Anything new from that dim-wit blabbermouth," Krueger asked, as Karl crunched into a corner of the booth.

"Lucky for us, he's a busy-body and wind bag. Otherwise, we wouldn't know what we do about the railroad dicks. And that train that just came by was right on time. Like clockwork—just as he said."

"Yeah, but he's still a dumb Polak!"

"Those Slavs will make good beasts of burden in the new order," Braun chuckled. "But, let's get to work and do a last check down before we move. You got all the camera equipment, right?"

"Yeah, the Leica and that Gossen meter are in the sack in the trunk. Only the latest and best German camera equipment. Thank you Mister Bank Roll," he said with an exaggerated air of reverence.

"And I'm sure the American will try to take the credit for this," Braun sneered. "But I'll make sure we get our glory with headquarters. It's our operation!"

"You getting all that information and the metal shavings during the plant tour was excellent, my friend!"

"Thanks, but let's get back to business. The other equipment?"

"Sure, I got that clamp contraption you made for me to prop and steady the camera. All the stuff's in the bindle sack. Just in case some worker spots me, he'll think I'm just a bum ridin' the rails."

"Good!"

"And I got the remote release cord and light meter in my pocket, but I'm pretty sure on the aperture and shutter speed. Like I told you, I've been testin' out shots through a skylight onto a lit stairwell in my cousin's apartment building."

"You know what you're doing. And the bandanna, and cap and gloves? Any cover helps, even on a moonless night."

"Got 'em in the sack. And I got a blackjack and knife in my back pocket just in case. Nobody's gonna take me."

"Damn it, no! That's why we planned this so well—no problems. And that's why we have a backup getaway plan as well!"

"Yeah, they're no match for our plan. Still, my little sidekicks make me feel I got an edge. I always carried a roscoe when I ran booze for Mitch Murphy."

"Well, just watch your … edge … Anyway, getting back to the plan, we know from Martin keeping tabs, that after this last train, the next won't cross til after ten-thirty. So the track's clear. Now, let's go over the main points."

"The railroad dicks get here about eight twenty-five."

"Right. As you know, Wally blabbed it, and both Martin and I

have seen them a number of times. They're here forty-five to fifty minutes."

"Lucky for us they're lazy *scheisse*—fifty minutes for dinner! I
want that job," he laughed.

"Let's keep it serious. What's next, Hans?"

"We head out to the car."

"No, we wait a couple minutes to finish our beers. We don't want
to arouse suspicion."

"Right, then we walk out to the car where I grab the bag and head
over to the bushes next to the overpass like I'm takin' a piss. If all's clear,
I scramble up the hill and follow the tracks towards the train yard. And
you pull out and ride around til the pickup.

"Don't forget to follow the lone track to the left, the others lead
into the yard. From the city map and my walking surveillance along Ken-
more Avenue, that lone track runs alongside the fence surrounding the
Curtiss property."

"Will do! And good thing havin' Eric pretend to get lost driving
into the rail yard."

"Yeah, said the grounds narrow as you get past the parking lot, to
where it's like an alley when you get behind our target, the north side of
Building A, the final assembly site."

"And he told us there's a lotta brush along the fence; I can duck in
if it gets dicey."

"You don't want the wire cutters I got, right."

"The fence ain't much higher than the parallel bars—no problem."

"And don't forget, he said there were two large trash bins right
next to Building A."

"Yeah, it should gimme cover and a leg up on climbin' to the
roof."

"Now you're sure you don't need a rope? I got one in the trunk."

"No way! Too much stuff to carry and tossin' up a hook would
cause noise; I'll shimmy up some pipes and ductwork that's always on

these buildings. Besides, you forget I'm a champion," he noted with an air of mock indignation.

"Hardly, that's why you're perfect for the job, my friend," Braun said, before stressing, "And remember your time."

"Don't worry, I got a stopwatch from the gym; big white face, easy to see."

"And once you got the pictures, don't waste time gettin' outta there."

"Yeah, I'll scurry down, head toward the overpass, but this time, before I get to the bridge, I cross the tracks and head north. After goin' through a couple hundred yards of scrub land—keepin' low all the time— I'll see the street lights at the dead end of Kingsley Street on the right..."

"There's only an abandoned garage and a machine shop on Kingsley, and that's closed for the night. Remember, don't walk down the street, but make your way behind the buildings."

"Until I reach the abandoned garage at the corner where you swing in, and I jump into the car. Mission accomplished."

Moments after the conspirators offered a toast to their success, a couple of burly men came walking through the door. Despite the heat, they both wore suit coats in an effort to conceal the shoulder holsters underneath. Sweating profusely, the pair ordered a couple of cold beers from Wally, before heading to the dining room.

"Careful turning around, they just walked in," Braun cautioned.

Slowly looking over his shoulder as the men paused to read the specials on the chalkboard, Hans sneered, "Fat *schweine*! Lucky for us, they couldn't catch a milk cow."

After waiting for the railroad cops to take their table, the Nazis executed a brisk exit from the bar. Once at the car, they exchanged quick thumbs up, before Krueger grabbed his bag and entered the brush. Satisfied that all was clear, he hurried up the hill and followed the tracks. He cautiously made his way along the fence, constantly looking out for any sign of danger.

Arriving alongside the back of Building A, he launched himself over the fence with a gymnast's ease. He then took a moment to collect himself, before jumping on a dumpster, and scurrying up the utility pipes to the roof. There, he scampered low, along the edge while peering through the skylights and observing a landscape of Helldivers and Shrikes that he knew from various magazine articles. He quickly made his way to the corner of the building, where Braun said the Hawks were located. Peeking through the window, he was greeted by the sight of modern-looking aircraft in various stages of construction. Of the original six prototypes, two had already been shipped off to Curtiss' test site—located at a secure, remote corner of the municipal airfield—to soon begin vigorous, in-flight trials, while another was sitting next to a custom trailer, ready to be tarped for its ride to the airport. Certain that this was his target, he carefully mounted the camera and its clamp onto the window frame. He then checked the meter, aperture opening and shutter speed, before peering through the lens to confirm the shot. Rolling onto his back, he grabbed the remote cord and hit the shutter release. Anxious for more, he adjusted the camera from another angle, and repeated the exercise two more times.

After checking his stopwatch, he realized time was now becoming an issue. Satisfied he had gotten what he wanted, he began to remove the camera assembly from the skylight; however, in his haste, he managed to dislodge a strip of glazing from the window frame. As he looked on in horror, the caulking tumbled down, narrowly missing a worker who was exiting an aircraft.

Startled by the material smashing at her feet, Lisa Mangini looked up to see an obscured face looking down from a skylight.

"Hey there's somebody up there!"

Unable to be heard in the din of the factory, she rushed over to her co-worker, Maureen Costello, who was descending a ladder after applying a final polish to the plane's instrument panel.

"What's going on, Lisa, you look frazzled?"

"Nearly got conked by some shit fallin' down from up there."

"This stuff? Looks like caulking from one of the skylights."

"Scared the piss outta me. Then looked up and saw some guy starin' down from that window…" she said, while pointing towards the skylight directly above.

"Nothing up there now."

"I'm sure it was a face; like he was watchin' us. And I think I saw a camera."

"Could it be a maintenance worker? But with a camera? And they wouldn't be doing any repairs up there at this hour."

"Naw, and I ain't batty. I'm sure I saw some guy."

"I believe you. Plus, there's this," she said, as she picked up a piece of dried putty from the floor.

"Watch it! I see that jerk, Meyer, eye-ballin' your ass when ya bent down."

"I swear he spends half the day standing at his office window watching the girls on the floor."

"Always calling me his little doll. Gives me the creeps. I'm sure he's a weirdo pervert."

"A creep all right! If he isn't leering at the girls or making off-color remarks, he's trying to bust unions."

"Don't I know! Remember when he sent me home for a day, when one of his ass-kissin' flunkies overheard me talkin' about the machinists' union."

"I wouldn't put it past him putting a spy up there to see who's talking to the union activists. Actually, that could be it," Maureen said, while looking up at the roof.

By now, the commotion had drawn the attention of the other crew members, including Frank Nowak, who was checking air pressure on the tires. "Hey, if it's about me, take it outside, ladies," he crooned, as he puffed out his chest.

"Put a plug in it, Romeo," Lisa snapped back.

"Better yet, keep it in here, if it's a cat fight," the little engine mechanic laughed.

"Don't be an idiot, Tommy."

"Just havin' a little fun, Mo," he answered awkwardly.

"You know I don't find that funny. And knowin' your wife, Maggie, she wouldn't either. But I won't tell," Maureen teased.

"Just for your information, boys, I saw some guy lookin' down from the skylight. We figure it's probably one of Meyer's flunky, scab spies keepin' tabs on us."

"Christ, Lisa! Have you gone bonkers? Probably some pigeon or cat. They're all over the place catchin' mice," Frank scoffed.

"I suppose that glazing he knocked down over there, is a product of our imaginations. Hysterical women, right?" Maureen replied sarcastically.

Just then, Meyer showed up after watching events unfold from his perch in his office. "What are you up to? Goofing off? You know I want this thing sparkling for Colonel Gerard tomorrow! I came in special tonight to make sure."

"We don't goof off, Pete. You know better than that," Maureen said with an edge.

"We were just tryin' to calm the girls down, Mister Meyer..." Tommy piped up.

"Whaddah mean, calm 'em down. What's going on?"

"I saw some guy up at the skylight. Looked like he was watchin' us."

"Come on, that's what you're upset about?"

"Wouldn't be the first time people around here were watching their co-workers and blowing them in." Maureen shot back.

Although taken aback by her abruptness, Meyer knew he had to tread lightly with Maureen. Besides harboring a romantic fantasy for the beautiful subordinate, he also knew that her sponsor was Bob Kane, Curtiss' security chief and good friend and golfing partner of the plant manager. And while not carrying a flame for Lisa, as he did with Maureen, he was aroused and obsessed with her small, yet shapely figure. Still, despite all this, he couldn't resist the urge to condescend and demonstrate the power he had.

"Believe me, ladies, there's no boogie man out there. And spies! That's another fairy tale!"

"What about Lisa's time on the beach a couple months back, after some nice snitch reported on her?"

"Listen, that was just a co-worker coming on their own, and telling me about subversive union activity. They love their jobs and know how bad unions are. This company puts a lot of responsibility in my hands, and I'll always protect its interests."

"Yeah, like a company's interest in worker morale. Snitches are so good for that," Lisa sneered.

"Careful, dolly! Any other manager would send you home for that crack, but I like you, and Maureen too. Besides, I know you're a little emotional with all this boogie-man stuff, so I'll cut ya slack."

"We told 'em it was just a pigeon or cat or somethin'," the kow-towing mechanic was happy to say.

Ignoring the toady, Maureen cracked back, "Well, if some phantom managed to loosen a window pane that falls on this beautiful plane tonight, I'm sure you'll explain to the army that it was just the product of overly emotional female imaginations,"

Wanting to save face, and hoping to show he could fix things, he answered, "I'm just trying to reassure Lisa that there's nothing out there. As for that skylight, rest assured, I'll be all over that window contractor tomorrow."

"Sure. Okay if we get back to work now, Pete?" Maureen smirked.

The pompous engineer always bristled at her refusal to call him Mister Meyer; nonetheless, wishing to demonstrate a grace he didn't possess, he let it pass with a nod and a smile.

Meanwhile, Krueger was on the ground, kneeling next to the dumpster, hoping to escape detection. In his haste to get off the roof, he awkwardly slid down the utility pipe, nearly breaking his camera and turning his ankle upon landing. He tried to brush it off; yet, if anything, it was more a blow to his ego as a champion gymnast.

After checking the camera in the sack, he waited another moment to see if the coast was clear. He then made a beeline for the fence; however, given his injury, he failed to launch himself with his earlier ease, thus putting additional strain on his foot. After once more shaking it off, he rushed as best he could along the solitary track towards the overpass. He paused at a clump of bushes, not only to make sure all was safe, but also to rest his foot. His caution was rewarded upon seeing headlights rising up a ramp next to the bridge. Hitting the ground beneath the brush, he watched as the unmarked patrol car aimed its spotlight on the main track leading to the yard. Fearing they would turn the lamp in his direction, he lay motionless as they cut off the engine. Instead, he looked on as they trained their light on a row of boxcars sitting along a rail spur. He now saw his chance when the railroad cops grabbed their flashlights and headed towards their target. Wasting no time, he made a hobbled dash to a nearby creek bed, his alternate escape route. Pressing against the bank, he could almost make out their muffled conversation as the cops checked out the inside of the car.

The sudden appearance of a muskrat sliding into the water, nearly brought out a yelp that would have easily exposed his position; yet after collecting himself, he waited for the cops to move on. Upon hearing the car doors slam, he crouched down and followed the creek a couple hundred yards to the nearest street light, which signaled the dead end of Kingsley Street. Peering over the edge of the shallow gully, he once more surveyed the scene to see if all was safe. Satisfied, he slowly climbed out, taking care to protect his tender foot. He tried to avoid the glow of the lamp, before awkwardly scaling the last strip of fence in his path.

Picking his way along the back edge of the closed machine shop, he was determined to stay in the shadows. Startled by a family of wandering raccoons, he warily approached the rear of the garage. After catching his breath and dusting himself off, he calmly sauntered out towards the front of the building. As if on cue, Braun wheeled around the corner and pulled into the littered driveway. Krueger barely waited for the car to stop, before jumping into the front passenger's seat. With the camera now stuffed safely onto the floor in the back, his partner wasted no time in turning the car onto the street.

"Mission accomplished!"

"Great! Heil Hitler, *mein freund*! But is everything all right? You're limping."

"Just a little hiccup; twisted my ankle; no problem."

"And no trouble, right?"

"Well… not exactly. Taking down the camera, I knocked off some glazing. Some bitch worker looked up and saw me. That's why I haddah hustle outta there."

"Ya had the bandanna on, right?"

"It got wet from my breathin' so I pulled it off before I shot. I din't want the lens steamiin'. But for Christ's sake it was dark."

"Let's hope she couldn't make ya out; but ya got the pictures, didn't ya?"

"Should be good shots! Can't wait to get back and develop them."

Shortly after they turned onto Ontario Street, they were greeted by the sound of a police siren. Pulling to the curb, Braun sat stone faced, while Krueger nervously fingered the knife in his pocket.

"Your driver's license, please."

"Yes, sir," the Nazi smiled. "Is there anything wrong, officer?"

Ignoring the question, the policeman aimed his flashlight at the license, before stating, "I was driving up Ontario when I saw your buddy getting into the car at that old gas station on Kingsley, so I circled back down. So, what were you guys doing over there?"

"My friend haddah take a leak. We were down at Wally's earlier; had a few beers and he couldn't hold off til I get'im home."

"Is that so? So, were you outta the car too," he asked Braun with an air of suspicion, as he leaned in and trained his flashlight at the passenger.

"Christ, I haddah go bad, couldn't just hang it out on Ontario," Krueger snapped back, which turned Braun's face a couple shades paler.

"Hey, I recognize you. You're Hans Krueger. I competed against you. I'm with the South Buffalo 'Y'. "

"Yeah, you look familiar. So, now ya know we ain't burglars, or worse yet trespassers," Krueger said with a forced laugh.

"Oh… ah… sorry. Listen, they got me keepin' an eye out for h***s doin' their perversions down these dead end streets at night. There's been complaints, so I haddah check it out. The Captain gave me this shitty assignment just because I put in for downtown."

"Well, we ain't no degenerate f*****s," Krueger snapped.

"Sure… ah… of course. And yeah, I seen you with that dark-haired girl at the meets. If ya don't mind me sayin', she's quite a number," before adding awkwardly, "she's your gal, right?"

"Yeah, and I'll take that as a compliment, officer…"

"Fitzgerald, but call me, Rick. After all, we're both gymnasts, which reminds me, you got hurt lately? I saw you limpin' over there."

"Just twisted my ankle doin' a dismount off the pommel horse the other day. Must be gettin' old."

"Geez, ain't we all. But you're still great!"

"Thanks."

"So, we good to go, officer? I don't want it to be my turn pissin' outside, after all this," Braun said with a calculated chuckle.

"Sure. Don't wanna hold ya up any longer. But be careful, like ya said, you've been drnkin'."

"Sure, thing, Rick!"

Pulling away, they both breathed a deep sigh of relief.

"Fucker, that was close."

"Well, he was right on one thing, let's get straight home," Braun added.

"Shit, I thought the idiot was gonna check out the sack in the back."

"Lucky for us, he knew you."

"I sure didn't remember him. Gymnast, my ass; looked like a skinny klutz. And thinkin' we were h***s."

"Show's ya, decent people like us getting harassed because of those degenerate scum."

"Well, the Fuhrer has an answer for that! Those f*****s won't be a problem in the future."

"*Jawohl, mein bruder*! And we sure served our noble cause, to-night!"

"*Die fahne hoch*! One Volk, one Reich!"

XI

The wing of a War-era Jenny hung from the rafters of the converted barn, its Air Corps insignias looking down upon walls covered with all manner of photographs and flight-related memorabilia.

Barnstormer's, as its name would suggest, was a popular aircraft-themed bar located next to Buffalo's municipal airfield. Among its clientele were airport workers, along with flyers and flight aficionados from around the area. However, its most prominent patrons were the test pilots, who enjoyed the status of sports heroes or movie stars within the local flying community. Eddie Jackson, chief test pilot for Curtiss Wright, topped the list of these celebrity flyers. At the moment, he was holding court at his usual spot at the end of the bar, surrounded by a bevy of friends and admirers.

Alex was here to dig around for his story. Thanks to the tip from the waitress at Camp Reichsadler, he hoped to connect with the barmaid, Britta Voight, who appeared to be involved with a band of Nazi sympathizers. That morning, he had laid out his plans with his editor, before leaving the office.

Earlier in the week, Victor had published another installment of

Alex's series on the Bund, which addressed the upswing in anti-Semitic and racist incidents in the area. Much of its content came from an interview with Captain Duggan, the head of the Buffalo Police Gang Squad, which had been arranged by Maureen's grandfather.

As the young reporter approached the rail, he spotted a heavyset man who fit the description of the tavern's owner, Jim Newton. The Air Corps veteran and retired cop was working the taps in front of a gleaming propeller mounted on the back bar. Pulling out his card, Alex introduced himself.

"Oh, yeah, my old friend Victor Lange called and said you were coming to talk to me. So what's up, Mister Wagner?"

"Please, call me Alex, and as he probably mentioned…"

"We didn't really have a chance to talk, I was busy. Lunch gets a little crazy around here. But he did say you were workin' on some story."

"Yeah, I'm doing some stories of interest to the area's German community."

"Sure a German paper, but how can I be of help?"

"Well, you see, I'd like to talk to one of your workers, Britta Voight. She's a talented singer in the local choral and Sangerfest movements, which is a big deal among us Germans."

Casting the skeptical eye of a long-time cop, Newton asked, "Listen, I trust Victor, but just to make sure, you ain't some jilted boyfriend pokin' around on her, are ya?"

"Oh, no, Mister Newton, never. I go out with Commissioner Costello's granddaughter. As a matter of fact, when I told him I was coming here, he made me promise to pass on his greetings."

"That's good for me, son. Hugh Costello was the best man I ever worked for, and be sure to say hello for me. But listen, I can't be of much help, she up and quit a couple weeks ago."

"What happened, if I can ask."

Once more, the barkeep hesitated.

"Don't worry, Mister Newton, I won't write on this, but I can always use a little background for a story."

"Well, as a favor to you and Victor, if you're plannin' on doing a tribute about this canary, you might wanna be careful, she ain't no Girl Scout."

"What do you mean?"

"Well, for starters, she was gettin' way too friendly with the customers."

"I thought a little flirting worked in this business."

"Don't get me wrong. Flirtin' does bring in more bucks movin' drinks, especially with a stacked dish like her, but it became a problem."

"Not like pulling tricks or anything like that?"

"I wouldn't stand for anything like that. At first, it was no big deal. I figured she had a thing for flyboys—like a lotta girls—you know, those dashing pilots. Anyway, she especially came on strong with Eddie Jackson over there."

"Sorry, I don't know him. Can you fill me in?"

"Well, Eddie's quite famous in flying circles, not to mention he was an Ace during the War. He's the chief test pilot for Curtiss. They got a test facility over in the far corner of the airpark—you know, away from pryin' eyes."

"Sure, and oh, that's right, I remember hearing Victor, another vet, talk about him."

"Anyway, she was all over him, but he wasn't havin' any of it. Christ, he's got more tail than you can shake a stick at. And he brings half of 'em in here. So he ain't about to pitch tent with her in this place. And by this point, it was beginnin' to affect things. Other customers couldn't get drinks. So I hadda step in."

"Is that when you had a falling-out?"

"No. Listen, despite all this, she still helped business and worked hard, besides bein' a nice kid. So after our talk, I came away thinkin' she understood. She toned it down, especially with Eddie. Musta got the message that it was goin' nowhere anyway. Still, she had her fans at the bar who hung around her station during her shift, carryin' on and such, like that string bean with the ball cap next to Eddie over there. Mickey Mullaney, kinda an odd bird …"

"How's that?"

"He's kinda Eddie's little puppy. Idolizes 'im. Eddie even joked that he worried he'd wake up one morning with Mickey standin' by the bed holdin his toothbrush. Works as a supply clerk in the shop over at the Curtiss Hangar, where they test out the planes."

"Basking in the glow…" Alex observed with a wry chuckle.

"And he even fancies himself a flight expert, always carryin' on about how much he knows about aircraft, and flyin'. I think he even wanted to fill Eddie's shoes with Britta."

"From the looks of it, he strikes me as a little awkward for that."

"You got that right. Was battin' way outta his league with a hot number like that."

"In any case, he's her friend?"

"Yeah, when things would slow down, they'd spend time talking. I figured she was just bein' friendly with the runt of the litter, or trying to get back into the game with Eddie. Who knows for sure, but that's when things got to be a problem again."

"Like how?"

"One morning, I'm in here cleanin' up when Mullaney's ol'lady comes stormin' in, yellin' about how I was harborin' hussies that break up marriages. She said she found a bill from a florist for some flowers sent to a woman on the East Side, along with a note with a telephone number with the name Britta, and a perfumed thank you card from this same woman, who she heard works here."

"An affair? A little far-fetched, huh."

"Ya think! Anyway, she demanded I fire that, quote, 'whore,' and threatened to call the cops on our Monday night card games. I was quick to cover my ass, and calmed her down by comin' up with a story that Britta's mom died. I went on to promise to fire her and ban him if I ever got wind of any hanky-panky."

"So what happened next?"

"Well, I wasn't gonna send her packin' over some guy moonin' over her, or his crazy wife, without hearing her side."

"How did that work out?"

"She laughed it off, calling it a misplaced schoolboy crush, and promised to set him straight. I was fine with that. Like I said, I liked her."

"But you said there was more than all that, that led to her leaving."

"Yeah, even after all this, she couldn't keep outta trouble. I started hearin' from customers that she was spoutin' off about how great Germany was, and other pro-Kraut crap." Realizing who he was talking to, Newton was quick to add, "And I mean over there, of course."

"No offense. I know us German Americans are among the most loyal citizens of this country."

"Absolutely, I agree. So many of my friends and customers are Germans and great Americans. But getting back to her, a lotta guys here are vets, including myself. Hell, it ain't that long ago we were gettin' shot at by those Heinies. So any pro-German talk, even if its about makin' the trains run on time, ain't gonna sit well here …"

"No doubt."

"Listen, I'm a proud isolationist, but I ain't naive. I know Hitler's no fuckin' good. But that's their problem over there, and we gotta keep it there. So, I didn't wanna deal with that sorta stuff."

"I can understand that."

"Still, bein' a softie, I was gonna give her one more chance if she could keep her yap shut. But when I pulled her aside, I didn't get ten words in, before she calmly says that it was time for her to move on, no hard feelings, and offered to finish her shift. Go figure. Well, she may be a great singer, good worker, and a real looker, but she can be a pain in the ass. So that's the deal with Britta Voight," he said with a sardonic laugh.

"Hmm… interesting; but listen, do you know where she moved on to, or have her number or know where she's living?"

"Don't know where she was gonna work, just wished her luck.

And I don't give out any personal stuff on employees, unless my brother cops wanted it. But off the record, she never gave me a number, and only gave me a P-O box for any official stuff."

"Suppose that Mullaney fella over there might be able to help me get in touch with her?"

"Yeah, or else his ol'lady, who seems pretty good at tracking things down," he chuckled, before turning serious. "Listen, ya work for my friend Victor, and, it's a free country if lover boy wants to talk to you, but I just ask you not to press'im. He's a good customer, and he's got friends here."

"Sure thing," Alex answered before thanking his host and heading with a beer to a stool down the bar. There he waited for his break, watching as Eddie and Mickey sat with their friends a few seats down. Alex was close enough to hear snippets of conversation, as Eddie shared details of his wartime exploits. The test pilot certainly looked the part, dressed in a worn leather jacket, with a checkerboard scarf draped over his shoulders and aviator goggles hanging from his neck. A pencil-thin mustache and slicked-back hair, imparted a swashbuckling look that only added to his image.

A trio of office girls, were eagerly listening to his heroic tales. A blonde, looking as if she was fresh out of secretarial school, sat transfixed at his elbow. Already, his hand had made its way to her stockinged knee, while nearby, a couple of his pals shot knowing looks to each other.

Mickey Mullaney sat at his other side, and although having no doubt heard the story many times before, listened with a similar expression of reverential awe. It was obvious for anyone to see, that the man was happy in his role as Jackson's Sancho Panza.

Alex's chance finally arrived when Mickey walked over to the Wurlitzer, that was sitting along the opposite wall. After strolling up beside him, the reporter lost no time in handing him his card and explaining his paper's interest in doing a story on the singer Britta Voight. "And I heard you're a friend, who could help us get in touch with her."

Turning from the glow of the juke-box, the man looked at Alex with an air of suspicion. "What's the big deal with your paper's interest in her, and how'd ya know about us bein' friends?"

"Like, I said, our paper carries stories of interest to the German American community, and singing societies and their singers are a big deal to our readers. She's not in the phone book but a friend told me she worked here. I was out this way, so I figured this would be a convenient way to interview her. When I checked in with Jimmy, he said she no longer worked here and didn't know how to contact her. That's when he said you might know because you're friends."

Slowly easing off from his wary attitude, Mickey gestured that Alex join him at a nearby table. "That's fine. Maybe a nice story will help with her career. She said she was takin' a break from singin'. Still, I gotta be careful 'cause people were sayin' stuff about us 'cause we were close."

"Don't worry. We're not interested in any sort of things like that."

"I wish I could help you but she left so fast. So, I never was able to find out where she was goin' or how to keep in touch. I once had her address, somewhere on the east side, but… ah… I lost it…"

"Too bad, since you were good friends."

"You betcha! Besides being so pretty, she's great. Was always listening to me and we had a lot in common. She loved planes and flight, and wanted to know everything she could about it. She even said she wished she could be another Amelia Earhart. And me, I know my stuff about flyin'. Ya see, I work over at the Curtiss testing hangar, where I've learned so much about those planes. And bein' so tight with Eddie Jackson—you musta heard of him…"

"The war Ace and test pilot, yeah."

"Next to Lindbergh, the best pilot in the world! And us bein' so tight, he gives me all the scoop on performance. Hell, I sometimes think I could be an aircraft engineer," he smiled before turning dark. "But then those damn waggin' tongues had to ruin all that!"

"But wasn't there talk about her praising Nazis, that got her in a jam with some of the people around here?"

"Jimmy shouldn't be repeatin' any of that crap. But listen, she's a true blue American. Her dad fought with TR down in Cuba and her brother's a cook in the Navy. She said she loved singin' the national anthem at a Bisons game, so she's a patriot…"

"But that doesn't seem to jibe with this Nazi talk."

"Well, ya see, some of the gals around here are jealous of her and some of the guys don't like her 'cause they couldn't get to first base with her. So, they exaggerate things…"

"Did they make it up?"

"Listen, she might have been yankin' their tails, because they were always teasin' her with *'fraulein'* or 'milk maid' because of her name and lookin' so German."

"So no talking-up the Nazis?"

"A couple of Legion guys said she said something about Hitler bein' great."

"You think they lied…"

"I know her, she ain't that way. She was probably just sayin' he was makin' things better for the people over there, after all their sufferin' after the War."

"Did you, yourself, hear anything that people might think was pro-Nazi?"

"No, she only said that now that Germany was back on its feet, it was once again taking its rightful place in the world."

"Did she criticize the US?"

"So what's with all this third degree on Britta's politics?"

"We're not going to do a featured piece on a person who might turn out to be an Anti-American Nazi."

"Okay, I see, and no, she only said we got to preserve our Anglo-Saxon identity. And I get it, with all these immigrants with their foreign ways comin' into this country. And now we got all these Negroes coming up from down south. Listen, I don't have a problem with those folks, as long as they don't wanna take over. This always gotta be a country of White Christian values."

"Did she talk about Jews?"

"About the only thing she mentioned about the Jews was that Jewish bankers and businesses took advantage of the German people during the War and afterwards, and that Hitler's government made reforms so that wouldn't happen again."

"And Negroes?"

"She just felt like a lotta people that people should keep to their own—you know, no mixin' or anything like that, which I agree."

"Did she call for persecuting Jews or Negroes?"

"She ain't like that. She's just big on White Heritage."

"As friends, you seem to agree on some political and social issues. Did she ever ask you, or anyone else to join any groups that shared her beliefs?"

"She may love her German background, but no way. Don't get me wrong, I'm Mister USA. My two older brothers fought in the War. I still don't trust those Germans over there."

"Do you know if anyone else around here might know how to contact her?"

"Naw, these people aren't her real friends. And that's why she left so quickly. She was hurt. When I heard she quit, I rushed out to say goodbye, but she was already takin' off in her brother's car. Her brother was always protective, pickin' her up after every shift in his big Chrysler."

"A beige Chrysler?"

"I dunno. I think it was light colored. It was always dark out. Why's that?"

"Ah ... not important, just curious. In any case, I'm sure I'll get in touch with her eventually."

"Yeah, and I've been thinkin' when we've been talkin' here, when you do get a hold of her, maybe you can put a word in for me. Tell her to contact me. I wanna tell her I'm sorry how it worked out here. Just kinda straighten things out between us."

"I'm sorry, Mickey, but the business doesn't work that way. Still, I wish you luck on that."

After offering him thanks for his time, Alex watched as Mullaney returned to his station at his chief's side. Taking a seat beneath a panoramic painting of a squadron of Jennys flying off to a dogfight, he was content to finish his beer while mulling over what had just transpired.

Although frustrated in failing to meet with Britta, or to get her address, he felt his efforts were not wasted. He discovered that she did in fact harbor pro-Nazi beliefs, despite Mickey's attempts to paper them over.

He dismissed the thought that her purpose was to proselytize or recruit, especially with a war hero like Eddie Jackson. Of course Mullaney was holding back, as evidenced in his failure to mention his gift of flowers and his wife's subsequent fury. Moreover, he didn't believe the man's love-struck fantasy that Britta's driver was her brother.

Perhaps most importantly, Mullaney's mention of a light colored Chrysler, made Alex think of the getaway car on the night of Bloom's attack. It opened the possibility that Britta could be connected to that band of Nazis. And in light of Marsha's reference to a scar-faced man, they could be the group in question at Camp Reichsadler. All of this gave him fuel for thought as he pondered his next moves.

XII

$\mathbf{I}$t was two hours before showtime, yet excited crowds were already streaming into the concert hall for the fifty-third annual Sangerfest of Buffalo. Many were decked-out in the traditional garb of their ancestral homeland, while others were dressed in their Sunday best, reflecting the auspicious nature of the evening's events for the local German community.

All manner of cars were lined-up behind the main portico, waiting to deliver their cargo. Meanwhile, a squadron of buses were dropping off various choral groups along the side entrance of the building.

The Elmwood Music Hall, the city's premier concert venue, was a converted armory. It was built at the height of the gilded age, when such imposing structures were meant to convey a sense of military power, so as to discourage labor unrest and other upheavals among the urban masses.

Maureen and her grandparents sat beside the elaborate fountain of the former parade ground, as they waited for Alex to park the car. Upon his return, they made their way through the turnstiles and into the cavern-ous foyer. As with the other patrons, they were dressed for the occasion. Maureen, her red hair cascading over her shoulders, wore a fitted, floral print day-dress, that underscored her lithe, athletic figure. Alex donned a cream colored suit with a mint shirt and champaign tie. Coupled with his sun bleached hair, it was a look that proclaimed wealth.

Looking for a place to relax before the show, the ladies found a bench at the far end of the lobby. As the women went over the evening's program, Alex took the opportunity to brief Mister Costello on the status of his investigative series on the Bund.

"… and I see you cited Captain Duggan extensively. He tells me he was impressed by you."

"And thanks for opening that door for me. As the head of the gang squad, his knowledge lent credence to the story."

"Well, you did good investigative work finding that witness to that gang out at Camp Reichsadler, and learning about that Britta girl at Barnstormers."

"I promised my source from the camp, Marsha, I would only use her testimony about the Nazi activity at the camp as background information for my investigation. Victor says we're on the right track, when it comes to this gang business."

"So you think this Britta woman may be here… and even some of her friends."

"Yeah, at least one of them may also be a musician of some sort, and given the scar-faced guy she saw at the camp, like I said, I have a feeling they may be the same bunch that attacked Bloom. As you know, one of the attackers at the newsstand had a scar on his face. And I'm pretty sure Marsha is here tonight and can I-D Britta. She told me she works special events here… and as luck would have it, I think I just spotted her at the cloak room."

Wasting no time, the pair made their way through the crowd. They didn't go far before running into Uncle Max, who at the moment was surrounded by his typical entourage, consisting of friends, businessmen and civic leaders, along with a sprinkling of strangers eager to make his acquaintance. Sporting a deep tan from a recent trip to Bermuda, and dressed in a tailored tuxedo, the business magnet looked like he just stepped off the set of a Thin Man movie. His friend Walter Klein stood at his side. Upon spotting Alex, Klein couldn't resist casting a critical eye toward the young journalist.

After an exchange of greetings, Max and Costello expressed their mutual admiration. On the other hand, Klein replied with an unmistakable air of rebuke when addressing Alex, which didn't go unnoticed by his uncle. Pulling him over, he said, "Listen, pay no attention to Walter. He's had a bug up his ass about the latest article, but you're not alone. He's even more pissed off at Victor."

"I think I'm professional and measured, but I'm not gonna downplay the seriousness of things."

"Hell, you know Walter, he loves anything German and is real defensive about it. Don't take his cold shoulder seriously. He's cranky about losing his boat race today."

"What about you, Uncle Max, what do you feel about the articles."

"Well-written and interesting. Like I said before, be careful, and don't generalize. Besides, Victor's on top of it."

"I've put a lot of work into it, and Commissioner Costello provided some advice. I hope it opens up eyes about Hitler and how it could spread here."

"I'm sure Hugh suggests being careful too; but listen, FDR's smart. He'll be able to deal with Hitler. As for these extremists, fringe elements can pop up at any time, any where."

"I just think the people have to be aware and vigilant. Look how the KKK terrorizes, especially down south."

"Strong leadership is needed! Although, I'm not saying whom…" he smiled slyly.

"So you're running?"

"Not quite there yet, but if I do, I'll be all in; hitting it hard! But enough of this political talk. And it's nice to see you covering a cultural event. You know I'm always proud of you! We're here to enjoy the music and our friends!"

As he watched his uncle return to the warm embrace of his audience, he felt a rush of pride.

Once more eager to meet up with his information source, Alex and
the old man headed towards the coat check.

"Hey, Marsha, I remember you telling me you sometimes worked
here."

"Well, other than being bored stiff and bringing-in all of fifty cents
in tips, I'm doing just peachy," she replied with a wide grin.

"In that case, let me throw in a tip in advance for a cold or rainy
day," he joked while tossing a half dollar into the jar.

"Oh, that's not necessary, Alex."

"No, I insist. The next time I might be broke," he chuckled.

"So what brings you tonight, business or pleasure."

"A little of both, but first let me introduce my friend's grandfather.
Marsha, this is Mister Costello."

"Nice to meet you, sir."

"And please, I may be an old man, but call me, Hugh."

"Thanks, Hugh, and I recognize you. You're the former police
commissioner."

"Hope you were satisfied with my work," he smiled.

"In the papers, you always seemed to be in command, making
sure the streets were safe, which was reassuring to a lady who had to wait
for the bus at night after her shift."

"Why thanks, Marsha. That's very kind."

Taking Marsha aside, Alex whispered, "I asked the Commissioner
to help me on the Bund matter. Would you have any problem talking about
it in front of him. With all those years running the force, he's professional
and discreet, and would never divulge a source."

"That's fine." Turning back toward 'Little Brick,' she added,
"And how great it must be, having an advisor like Hugh, especially knowin' what you're writin' about."

"You got that right, Marsha. But cutting to the chase, have you run into any of that bunch from the camp that we talked about, especially Britta. I looked her up at Barnstormers, but she quit. I figure with her being a top singer, she might be here tonight.”

“None of those men, but she’s here. I just spotted her a couple of minutes ago…”

“Can you point her out?” the old cop was quick to ask.

“Sure, she’s over in that corner, near the backstage entrance.”

Scanning the landscape, Alex observed, “That dark-haired… ah… impressive looking woman?”

“Yeah, the one who’s stacked,” she laughed.

As Alex acknowledged the sighting, he was unaware that another set of eyes was bearing down on him. Karl Braun was standing with a group from the Sangerbund and Turners Club, which included Freddie Wagner. He suddenly ignored the conversation around him, as he fixated on the man across the room. Given the hatred he’d developed for Alex, it was no wonder that an angry look erupted on the Nazi’s face

His fuming was interrupted upon seeing Pete Meyer, the Curtiss engineer leading a couple of singers from his youth chorus toward the backstage entrance. Reminded of his purpose, Braun seized the opportunity and followed.

Meanwhile, after thanking Marsha for her help, Alex quickly set his sights on his target. The old man wished him luck; yet, still urged caution, given the menace of her comrades.

By now, Britta was alone, as a soprano from the Steinadler Sangerbund bid her adieu and headed backstage. Seeing his chance, Alex made a b-line in her direction, “Britta, Britta Voight?”

“Ah… yes…. do I know you?” she asked with a smile, flattered by the attention of the handsome stranger.

“Oh, no, but I do recognize you from earlier competitions. That’s why I’m here, I’m a reporter doing a series on some of the more prominent Sangerfest singers.”

“Gee, I’m flattered, but I’m not singing tonight. I’m taking a break for a while.”

"That's okay, we're still interested in your perspectives. I'm with the *Advocate*, Alex Wagner. Here's my card."

Realizing who he was, her mood instantly changed. "Wait! Wagner! Didn't you write that trash about our people!"

"I thought I was objective and fair, but I'm here about music. Still, I'd be happy to hear your…"

"Get out of my way! You're smearing Germans everywhere," she snarled as she brushed him aside.

Across the room, Hans Krueger was unaware of what was happening with Britta. With his camera slung across his neck, he was waiting for a signal from Braun to begin his assignment. In the meantime, he was talking to other members of the Turners when one of his friends began to tease him about the handsome stranger with his girl. Seeing it was Alex, he rushed over, and after stopping to check on Britta, he confronted the reporter, "Hey, pal, what ya doin' upsetting my girlfriend."

Alex immediately recognized Krueger as a champion and coach at the Turner club. In an attempt to calm the situation, he struck a conciliatory tone, "Sorry, I was just doing a story on singers for The *Advocate*…

Incensed, the volatile fanatic growled, "Listen, you fucking, lying excuse for a reporter, you stay away from her, or I'll take that hack newspaper of yours and shove it up your ass!"

Not one to be intimidated, or insulted by anyone—especially by someone he suddenly realized was a Nazi gangster—Alex quickly changed his tune. Leaning his powerful frame toward the smaller man, he shot back, "I don't skip around on mats, so don't ever threaten me again, punk. Got it!"

Krueger's bravado was just that. Realizing he bit off more than he could chew, he backed off without a word; but not before shooting a hateful smirk towards his nemesis.

By now, 'Little Brick'had arrived with drinks for his wife and granddaughter. No sooner had Alex returned, than the old man observed, "I saw the reaction by that woman Britta, and I assume that man was her friend."

Since all were aware of his plans, Alex sat down and explained what happened.

"She sure had problems with your article," Missus Costello said.

"Which seems to confirm her attitude about Nazis, and like you said, her charming beau might well be part of the Nazi gang." Maureen added.

"It all seems to tie-in with what you learned at the camp and at that bar Barnstormers, and of course from Captain Duggan."

"Don't forget the attack at the newsstand and the beige Chrysler, Gramps."

"And Britta's friend at Barnstormers, Mullaney, said her quote, 'brother,' would pick her up in a light colored Chrysler—could be connected," Alex said.

"And we can't forget that guy at Reichsadler with the scar. Like we know, one of the Bloom attackers had a scar," Maureen added

"And this boyfriend of her's, could he be one of those men at Reichsadler that your witness spotted?" Kenna asked.

"Well, he doesn't have a facial scar and he isn't in his fifties, so there's no ID there; but there were other men at the campsite where they were having their little Nazi party. And like I said, Krueger's a big deal at the Turners, and Marsha said that Britta's boyfriend was an athlete of some sort."

"And didn't you say that Marsha mentioned one of the camp Nazis was a musician—who knows, maybe a singer," Maureen added.

"Yeah. And if Britta's involved, and I'm pretty sure she is, some of her buddies, besides Krueger, may be running around here tonight. We'll keep our eyes peeled and I'll check with Marsha later, to see if she spotted any of them."

"I don't want to wield a broad brush," Mister Costello observed, "but it sounds like some of this group could be associated with groups, like the Turners or the Sangerbund."

"I don't want to think they could be breeding grounds for any extremist groups like this, but I got to go where things take me, so I'll keep digging."

"And Alex, you might want to touch base with Captain Duggan to see if he has anything on this fella, Krueger."

"Don't worry, I will; and thanks again for introducing me to him"

"And like Gramps said before, these are dangerous people, as you know firsthand. And that especially applies to you too, young lady." Keena was quick to add.

"I know, and Alex will keep me safe, but I'm all in on helping him. It's really caught my interest,"

With that, at the behest of Missus Costello, the little party changed the subject, and began to discuss their anticipation for the evening's events.

By now, Karl Braun, dressed in his choral attire, stood anxiously waiting outside one of the backstage offices. A strip of tape, noting, "First Evangelical Youth Chorus" was slapped on the door. Just minutes before, he signaled to Krueger to take his place outside the window, and earlier that morning, he had jimmied the doorknob, so that the lock wouldn't work. Trying to gauge his timing, he edged closer to the frame, hoping to listen to the goings-on inside. Upon hearing the faint murmur of moans, he burst through the door, announcing, "Pete, you said to drop by…" He was immediately met by the sight of Meyer's back with what appeared to be a figure knelling before him. In an instant, Meyer pulled the figure to its feet, before adjusting his pants.

Acting as if nothing was wrong, Braun calmly stated, "Oh, I didn't know you had a meeting. I can come back in a bit."

Left reeling, yet anxious to establish a cover, Meyer tried to affect a calm facade to mask his inner panic, "Yeah… ah, that's all right, we were just going over some concert details." Turning to the teenage girl, he added, "So remember, stand straight and keep your shoulders relaxed." Blushing profusely, the adolescent awkwardly wiped her mouth, as she rushed by Braun and out the door; but not before the Nazi made sure he could identify her.

Braun was eager to affect a light and supportive tone in an effort to ease Meyer's fears. Nonchalantly leaning against a nearby desk, he said, "Pete, I hope I didn't bother ya with my bungling entrance just now."

"No, no, I was just wrapping up with one of my singers. Ah… it wasn't like it looked…"

"Hey, come on," he smiled with knowing leer, "You're my friend, and if anything, I must say, I'm impressed."

Sensing an ally, he let down his guard, "Well, let's just say, one of the perks of the job."

"Who's about to turn that down, little Miss…"

"Suzy."

"Ah, Suzy, charming little fraulein…"

"Yeah, blonde, blue-eyed, German fraulein, Suzy Kurtz."

"And back in the old country, she'd already be gettin' married off. Here, these girls are slutty little tarts. Still, you gotta be good at charming the ladies," he said, while making sure to take note of her name.

Reassured, Meyer couldn't resist the urge to crow. "Well, ya gotta have some savior faire," he smirked, "And know how to finesse 'em— sense their doubts, gain their trust, and flatter 'em."

"Whatever it is, it must be workin'," he said, trying to keep him going.

"Hell, I got another one, even cuter! Her younger cousin!"

"Two of 'em! Cousins! Christ, howd'ya find the time?"

"Hey, I got appetites," he chuckled. "Every Tuesday, one before practice, one after!"

Grinning while shaking his head, Braun, satisfied with what he confirmed, shifted gears, "Listen, speaking of appetites, I came over here in the first place to invite you to join me for a cigar and a drink before the competition. I've got a great scotch whisky and a couple Cubans in the car. Cigars, not girls," the humorless, Nazi awkwardly winked.

The Curtiss engineer needed no coaxing, being eager to relax after having just dodged a bullet on being discovered. For Braun, it was a critical component of a plan he'd been working on since the Curtiss tour. Wasting no time, he led his target out the rear utility door to the far edge of the lot where he parked the car.

"Wow," Meyer blurted out as they approached the gleaming Chrysler. "I like that low streamlined look—and some grille!"

"Yeah, thirty-six Chrysler Airflow. Eight cylinder, one-hundred thirty horsepower and a three hundred forty cubic inch engine. Beauty and power. Whaddya say we pop inside."

As they slid into the car, Braun continued, "There's a bottle of Balvenie single malt and a box of Partagas under your seat, and some glasses in the glove compartment."

"Sweet treat! And this car, even more snazzy on the inside—all this leather, wood grained dash … and a radio!"

"And the ladies love it!"

"I guess so! I wouldn't mind something like this!"

"Yeah, I can see you like your tail," he nodded suggestively.

"Sure! And I do pretty good, if I say so myself," he boasted before pouring the drinks.

"No doubt, and there must be some nice pickings at the factory."

"You bet, my friend," he crowed as he continued with his fable.

"Must be nice, and ya know, speaking of women, when I was on the plant tour, I spotted a tall, good looking redhead workin' on the Hawk line. What's the deal with her, assuming she's not in your sights…"

"Ah… that gotta be Maureen Costello, and ah… yeah… she's a real looker, but good luck with that. She's snobby and cocky. Probably gold diggin' for some big shot. I even heard she might have some rich guy…"

Sensing a resentment, yet a desire for a woman far outside his league, Braun continued to play him, "Hey, nothing serious here, I'm looking for a good German girl, not some Irish floozie. Still, I could use a little diversion. You ever see her around. Who knows, maybe I'd get lucky with a quick roll in the hay. Ya see, I know how to handle those snooty types, starting with this," he said, as he motioned around the car.

"Typical money hungry bitch… anyway, if you wanna go that route, I know she attends all the Curtiss socials at various clubs. She always meets up with a cute little dago canary from work, who I got an eye on. They're dance maniacs, who cut up a rug together at those Curtiss parties."

"You go to those things too?"

"Yeah, a lotta times."

"Ya know, we think alike. We gotta get together! When's the next one of these parties? Maybe we can put a make on both those canaries!"

"Yeah, next Thursday at the Richardson Hotel down near the Central Terminal."

"Shit, isn't that owned by that n****r, Dan Richardson?" He asked, before firing up a Cuban

"I know, but even though all the acts and help are n*****s, it's a popular place with Whites. That ol' Dan's one smart n****r."

Although consumed by his race hatred, Braun realized he had to stick with his plan, and put his loathing aside for the moment. "He's just fuckin' lucky, or in the rackets. Still, I suppose any n*****s that might go in there, know their places. So, I'm willing to hold my nose to have some fun."

Despite a reluctance to expose his social ineptitude to his new friend, Meyer was eager to join him, figuring that some of Braun's confidence could rub off on him. "Sounds good, besides, everyone from Curtiss will be White."

"Great! I can pick you up. You don't have to use your car…"

"Ah, actually, I don't have a car. I can't afford one right now."

"Gee, excuse me. I didn't mean…"

"That's okay, but how do you pull this off? Your folks got money?"

Braun took a long draw on his cigar, before casting a crafty look towards the engineer, "Let's just say I augment my earnings."

"How's that? You gotta work a lotta extra hours to afford this. Howd'ya pay the rent?"

Failing to mention that the funds for the car and other expenses had been funneled through Deutsche Bank courtesy of the *Abwehr* Intelligence Service, Braun launched into his ruse. "Listen, I like good things, like this car, this watch and these hand stitched imported shoes. I work hard and I think I deserve them. But as you know, our big shot bosses don't pay us what we're worth. Let's just say I discovered a way to correct this unjust situation." Seeing an uncomfortable yet curious look cross Meyer's face, Braun adjusted his course. "Before I go on, what I'm gonna tell ya is harmless. Still, some people might take it the wrong way. But I know I can trust you, just as you know you can trust me."

Reminded of Braun's earlier show of support and discretion, and given his resentment over his salary, Meyer was quick to respond, "Hey I got your back, and yeah, we get scraps."

Confident he had the man's fealty, Braun continued, "A while back, I got together with a former co-worker, who was in town for a visit. This old friend had taken a job with Consolidated Aircraft where he's moved pretty high up the ladder. Anyway, one night we got talking about the industry, our jobs and what's going on at the companies where we work. When I mentioned some of the things I was familiar with, it caught his interest. He eventually found the information helpful, and as a show of thanks, rewarded me—and rather handsomely, I should add. We've kept up our little arrangement the last couple years. You can see the results for yourself," he smiled, as he once more gestured around him.

A look of concern crossed the engineer's face, as he whispered, "But… ah… isn't that industrial espionage?"

"That's an unfortunate term, and a tired old argument used by the tycoons to corner markets and stifle competition."

"And you make many of our parts."

"We make a lotta parts for the whole industry, and for a lotta companies. But that's beside the point. Listen, keep in mind the old expression, 'high tides lift all boats.' That's what happens when you share ideas, everybody benefits. As my friend pointed out, everybody improves.

Everybody ups the ante with competitive innovation, which means more work and more money all the way around.”

“But I know how much effort Curtiss puts into R and D…”

“Everybody does, and that’s good. Like I said, this is good for the aircraft industry and good for the country. That’s why I have no problem doing it. It’s not like I’m selling this to those slant-eyed j*p savages, the Jews, or to the Russians. Hell, I’m no communist,” he chuckled.

“But don’t you worry about getting caught?”

“Do the big shots worry about me makin’ crumbs? But more importantly for me, life is not without risk; but take it from me, I make sure I minimize any risk I take.”

“It sure seems to be working for you. And you’ve already been doing it for a couple years now, right?”

Satisfied he piqued his interest, Braun was convinced his plan was working, and could reel him in. “Yeah, with zero regrets. And ya know, as I’m telling you about all this, I realize this arrangement could work for you too. Hey, you know a lot more than me, and that can put you in the cat bird’s seat—very marketable!”

“Are you telling me, I can do better than this?”

“Of course! Why wouldn’t you?”

Seeing Braun’s lavish lifestyle and confident manner, left the awkward engineer feeling a similar arrangement might significantly change his fortunes—especially with women; yet, he still held back. “I like the idea, but I got a lot invested…”

Knowing his resentments, the Nazi moved in for the kill. “Do I have to remind you that you owe them nothing? You’re like I was, struggling and not getting what I deserved. Your boss—I saw’im at the plant tour—he’s a lot younger than you. And he didn’t strike me as being very sharp, unlike you; yet, they musta passed you over, and he got your job!”

“You got that right! He’s a dumb shit, but a real operator who made his way kissin’ ass.”

“And I betcha he feeds off your work, gets all the credit, and makes a whole lot more than you do! Am I right?”

"Damn right, the fucker. And damn right, I'm in!"

While marveling that the idiot Meyer couldn't grasp the irony that he was being played the same way he played his teenage victims, Braun exclaimed, "Good! You're doin' the right thing, my friend! You're gonna love it!"

"And you can set this up with minimal risk, like you said?"

"Listen, my friend doesn't even have to know who you are or what you do. He trusts my judgement. I'll just say that you're a person of influence at Curtiss, who has valuable information. I'll be the go-between, the conduit. Just you and me, and we trust each other. There'll be no paper trail to you. You identify important information, or I'll get requests from my buddy and will ask you. You can then just tell me, and show me paperwork and prints. I'll write things down, and then get it to him. Of course, he'll destroy any evidence. And everything is strictly cash, no trace. So, as long as we all use our heads, risk is miniscule. And you're a smart guy, Pete!"

"Sounds like a great plan, Karl! I'm already eager to get started. Hell, I can almost feel my ass in the seat of a new car!"

"Okay! I'll get in touch with my friend, then we'll get together at a little place that I know is safe, and we can go over things."

As he watched a self-satisfied smile spread across Meyer's face, the Nazi knew he owned his prey.

As Braun was wrapping up his plan, Alex was making one last trip to the bar, where he ran into his brother. After a little small talk, he got straight to the point. "I saw that coach, Krueger, from the Turners milling around with your friends. What's the deal with him?"

"Ah, somebody did point out you were making a new friend. Must be his girl. You should know not to make passes at girls you don't know."

"Come on Freddie, you know I'm with Maureen…"

"Doesn't hurt to sniff around the pasture once in a while, if ya know what I mean," he smirked.

"Yeah, I get it; but really Freddie, you still doin' that? You've got a beautiful and loving wife, who's given you wonderful children…"

"What can I say? I've got big appetites and like risks, little brother. Besides, Mitzi's happy, the family's happy, and I'm gonna be the head of a multi-million dollar company before I'm forty," he said with an air of superiority that suggested Alex posed no competition.

"And you know, Freddie, I'm happy too," he said, eager to change the subject. "I'm doing a story on Sangerfest singers. That woman is one of the more prominent ones."

"Oh, yeah, I have seen her at the competitions. She has an awesome body."

"Well, this Krueger's got a hair trigger."

"Don't worry, you could kick his ass, if he hurt your feelings …" he teased.

"That has nothing to do with it. Do you know anything about him, his politics?"

"His politics! What's with that?"

"It's just with all this Bund business…"

"Ah, the article. Listen, we don't talk politics at the club. Besides, I hardly know him, other than he's a fierce competitor. He's a loser. Takes pictures of kids on ponies for a living."

"Do you know anything about that group he was with, that was standing next to you guys?"

"Naw, maybe the usual gym rats or maybe some of those singers. I really didn't notice."

"One of that group—he was dressed like the rest of the Sangerbund singers—kinda weasely looking, does he work for us?"

"Weasely looking… ah… can't say. But he works for us?"

"Actually, I think I might have seen him at the Curtiss tour, I covered. I think he was part of our group."

"Our group? Where's the journalistic distance, my brother?" he joked.

"Cut the crap, Freddie. I think I saw him talking to Will Richter, a few minutes ago. I could ask him."

"Oh…wait… yeah, kinda weaseley looking… could be Karl Braun. He's a machinist at the plant, I think."

"Know anything about him? Is he friends with Krueger at the gym?"

"Like I said, I don't have much to do with Krueger other than compete."

"And what about this Karl Braun fella? Ya ever hear if he talks up politics at the plant, like with this Bund stuff?"

"Never heard anything, but I'm barely aware of the guy. I seem to remember I've seen him around the Sangerbund, and I recall one of my foremen pointing him out as a top machinist. So what's this all about, anyway?"

"Getting some background for the Bund series. I've heard this Krueger and his friends might know about some of this stuff."

"Be careful about accusing anybody of extremist activity, and don't go looking for Bundists under every rock. Just because somebody is proud of their German heritage, doesn't make them some kinda Nazi. Remember what happened during the War."

"Don't worry, I'm responsible. And of course, Victor's involved with it all."

"And watch yourself. These Bundists are a bunch of crackpots and it will all peter out after a while; but you never know, it just takes one to be trouble."

"Thanks, but I'm careful."

"Good! But enough of all this political stuff. I'm looking forward to the show tonight. Mitzi put in a lot of time organizing this. I'm sure it'll be great."

"Yeah, should be! Hey, did ma and pa get here yet?"

"No, you know pa, always last minute. Can't take standing around waiting."

"By the way, you see Uncle Max? He was around here earlier."

"Yeah, he was here with his latest squeeze. Some dish, I think she was younger than me. Anyway, he headed off to his seats. Probably want-ed to escape Walter Klein's bitchin' about being cheated out of his win at the boat races. I saw his anger first hand. I had Uncle Max's boat out this morning."

With that, the brothers caught up on some family news before bidding their farewells. Heading back to Maureen and her grandparents, Alex was not only eager to reveal what he learned, but more importantly, was eager to share and enjoy an event that was so important to his family and community.

XIII

Sitting in the shadow of the Central Terminal, a soaring, art deco masterpiece, the Richardson Hotel was fast becoming an entertainment mecca for the city's fun seekers. It was located at the edge of a tree lined neighborhood that surrounded the recently constructed rail hub.

Inside the hotel's lounge, the house band, The Rhythm Maniacs, was belting out a rousing hit, while a chorus line, aptly named the Rhythmettes, was high-kicking its way in front of a backdrop featuring the nighttime silhouette of the Buffalo skyline.

At the end of the opening number, and backed by a lively fanfare, the show's MC bounced onto the stage. Tornado Butler, whose furious energy matched her name, launched into a storm of bawdy jokes that left the audience roaring.

The adjacent tap room, with its polished mahogany bar, was packed with patrons. Many were well-heeled members of cafe society eager to be seen at an increasingly popular, if not "exotic" in-spot; yet, most just wanted to experience the kind of cabaret revue rarely seen outside cities like New York, followed by an evening of dance. On this night, the crowd included workers from Curtiss Wright, out for one of their regular company get-togethers.

The hotel's staff and entertainers were mostly Black, while the patrons were mainly White. As was the case with other jazz venues, its mixed clientele was the exception when it came to most Buffalo bars and restaurants. Its Black owner, Dan Richardson, was a successful business-man with a host of political, civic, and business friends. He oversaw a popular hospitality and entertainment chain that included two other hotels and restaurants. Seated at his usual spot at the corner of the bar, he was a hands-on manager, who loved to mingle with his many guests.

As Alex walked in, he took a moment to stop and say hello to the impresario, whom he had come to know not only through his interest in the local jazz scene, but also through his family's patronage of Richard-son's famous steakhouse, downtown. Afterward, he was quick to scan the room in an effort to spot his girlfriend.

While failing to find Maureen, he did manage to see Lisa Mangini sitting with friends at the end of the bar.

"Hey, Lisa, where's Maureen?"

"She's not here yet. Didn't she get hold of ya? Said she was gon-na call."

"Musta called when I was out getting groceries. Anything wrong?"

"Naw, don't think so. She just hadda drive her Gram over to a relative's at the last minute. As usual, I was in a hurry to get dancin'. I love the Rhythm Maniacs, so I took the company bus."

"You love that hot swing, don't ya," he smiled.

"You got that right! I'm gonna kick up a storm tonight!"

Just then, Maureen came rushing through the hotel doors. Look-ing a bit frazzled yet radiant with her dazzling smile on full display, she was quick to spy her friends.

"I'm so sorry for mucking up the plans, but my Gram had an emergency. Gramps wasn't there, so I hadda drive."

"Everything all right?"

"Is she okay?"

"She's fine, but her cousin, my great aunt, Kitty, who's in her nine-ties, had taken a spill."

"So how is she," Lisa asked.

"Actually, being the tough Irish gal that she is, Kitty's doing well, no breaks."

"Thank, God! That could've been bad," Alex added.

"I stayed to make sure everything was okay. My brother's going to pick her up, but still, I'm sorry for being late."

"Please, you're a good granddaughter," Alex beamed, which was quickly returned with a grateful smile from Maureen.

"Come on and relax on this," Lisa offered as she slid over a beer she just ordered.

After things settled down, Alex headed to the hostess station, where he arranged for a table in the ballroom when one became available. Upon his return, Maureen lost little time in introducing him to more of her co-workers. In the midst of this, Alex felt a tap on his shoulder.

"Jim Jefferson! Good to see you, my friend! How you doing?"

"Good seein' you too, Alex, and I'm doin' great!"

"Good to hear, Jim! And may I add, it shows. You're dressed rather snappy."

"Thanks, Miss Costello; and thanks to Alex, that job he set me up with is working out real good!"

"Yeah, Dad said it's working out well. He's impressed."

"And these threads are courtesy of Missus Wagner, nice lady that she is."

"She sure is a nice lady," Alex said as a quizzical look crossed his face. "Maybe I should sign up with the family business after-all," he chuckled. That looks like a Kleinhans Executive…"

"Yeah, she said it was your pa's, and it didn't fit'im any more. Ya see, when I told her about me hopin' for a gig here—with the Starlite burnn' down and all, which is why I'm here tonight—she said I better dress right for the occasion."

"Guess she's given up on Dad losing weight," he chuckled. "And good use of the suit."

"Yeah, looks like new and fits me to a T!"

"So, you auditioned," Alex asked.

"Actually tomorrow, when the band's practicing. Jimmy Smith, he's the talent manager for Mister Richardson—plus being a damn great drummer—he seemed impressed with my experience, and he wants me to meet with Dan after the show tonight. I've been practicin' all week, so I'm hopin' it goes well tonight and tomorrow. I could use the extra cash…"

"You'll get it," Maureen insisted. "We've heard you at Sid's, and you're great!"

"Thanks for the compliment, Miss Costello."

"Please, Jim. Like I said when we met, we're friends. Call me Maureen."

"Sure thing, Maureen. And like I said, I could use the money. I lined up a little flat, off Michigan Avenue."

"Great," Alex congratulated his friend.

"Where about on Michigan?" Maureen asked.

"Down near the Michigan Avenue Baptist Church."

"It should be easy to get around from there, plus, you'll be outta that camp," Alex said.

"That's for sure! I've been itchin' to get outta that Hobo Jungle. It's been gettin' bad. Those KKK, rail riders have been tryin' to rile things up down there. They even brought in some local honky supporters to cause trouble."

"Gee, that's interesting. Can you let me know if you see or hear any more of that?"

"I gotcha on that, Alex. I've been keepin' my eyes and ears open for that kinda bullshit, ever since that ruckus at the Jew's newsstand: but, I'll tell ya more later…"

Biting at the bit, Lisa couldn't hold back any longer, "So when's somebody gonna introduce me to 'Mister Tall, Dark and Handsome'…"

"Oh, sorry, Lisa, we were so busy catching up. Lisa Mangini, Jim Jefferson, a friend of ours. I told you how he saved our bacon during that newsstand attack," Maureen said.

"And a hero to boot. I'm impressed," she purred.

"My pleasure to meet such a pretty lady. And thank you, Lisa. I don't know about that other stuff, but I do know, I'm tall and dark," he chuckled.

Just then, the maitre d' arrived to tell Alex that a table was ready. Eager to take-in the floor show, the couple set off behind the hostess, but not before reminding Lisa there was a place for her and for anyone else she wished to invite. Yet, by now she was fully engaged with her new friend, and put it off for the time being. Soon, her conversation with Jim turned from introductions to discussions on music and dance, along with a dash of flirtation.

Meanwhile, the rolling chords of a ragtime march were an assault on Karl Braun's ears, as he passed through the taproom doors. Realizing that enduring such "garbage" was part of the price for a successful mission, he picked his way through the crowd with his new friend, Pete Meyer. He stopped long enough to spot his comrade, Eric Bachman sitting in a booth he secured earlier that night. Sliding onto the leather bench, Braun lost little time setting into motion his plan to establish a friendly rapport with his intelligence source, Meyer—along with exacting revenge on another target

"Hey, Eric, ready to chase the ladies!"

"Primed and ready to go, buddy. And who's your pal."

"Pete Meyer, Eric Bachman. Pete's a good guy and a top engineer at Curtiss, who just so happens to know a lot of the dolls floatin' around here tonight."

"Yeah, it's the Curtiss Night Out Party, so a lotta girls from the plant are here. Since I'm boss to some of them, I have to show up. Besides, I'm gonna steer one of those dishes from the rest of the flock, if you know what I mean," the engineer winked.

"Sure! I wanna grab a dame myself, but tell me, Pete, why this jungle village of all places?" Eric asked.

"It ain't my call, but they move it around. You know, east side this time, west side next; whatever. I guess they try to even it out for the workers."

"Gotcha, but this damn n****r music. Pain in the ass we gotta put up with this shit for a little tail."

"Whaddah gonna do. The thing's pretty much run by the girls. Those lame brains don't know any better."

"Ah, fuck it. Some hooch and snatch will get us through, "Bachman chuckled.

"Speakin' of which," Braun broke-in, "how about one of these black ass bitches, gettin' us some drinks. And where's, Kurt? He should be here by now."

Almost on cue, Kurt Metzger emerged from the foyer—now clean shaven after the Bloom attack—and using his muscular frame to his advantage, sliced his way through the crowd. Catching sight of Braun, he shot him a knowing nod, before arriving at the table.

After a quick introduction, and the usual small talk, Metzger settled into the booth. Once Meyer was distracted, in this case bombarding Bachman with self-promoting fables about his lady-killer prowess, Braun turned to Kurt and whispered, "So did you spot our target, and I-D the car?"

"Yeah, fortunately, just as we got here, and I waited a few minutes before leavin' Hans and coming in. He's on top of our plan and in a secure spot, keepin' an eye on things and ready to jump into action."

"Good! And we'll keep this chump happy, ply him with drinks, tell'im how great he is, and have Britta flirt with him…"

"Britta's not comin'. She got into a row with Hans."

"That idiot," Braun whispered, barely able to keep it low. "When's he gonna learn?"

"I guess it's okay now, but she's still upset. Probably got a shiner. Anyway, I got my cousin and her girlfriend coming. They don't know nothin' of course, but I told her we got a Mister Lonely Hearts here, who could use a little encouragement. Nothin' serious."

"I don't wanna bring anybody else in, even slightly. Listen, let's see how things are workin' before callin' in renforcements."

"Gotcha. Anyway, I'm sure once we're outta here tonight, you're gonna be his best friend ever!"

"That's the plan, *mein Kamerad*!"

With his team set, Braun ordered a round of drinks followed by a toast to their new friend. Ignoring Meyer's adolescent comments about the figure of a woman standing nearby, he began to scan the terrain in the hope of spotting the focus of his plot. Just as he was about to get up and scout the adjacent ballroom, under the guise of going to the head, something in the corner of the bar caught his eye.

"Pete, I thought you said the n*****s here would know their place. Look at that black a*e chattin' it up with that White girl over there."

Having been bragging about his quarry tonight—especially her youthful appearance and the certainty of her affections—Meyer was caught flat footed, "Oh, shit!"

"Yeah, disgusting isn't it?"

"No… No," he stammered. Unable to control his anger, he blurted out, "That… that's Li… ah… one of the girls on my line!"

Just then, the black man turned in his seat to order a drink. Upon recognizing his nemesis from the newsstand, Braun could hardly believe his good fortune. As such, he was more than willing to adjust his plan on the fly.

Despite his racist revulsion, Braun happily grabbed the opportunity before him. Suspecting that Jefferson's youthful looking friend was in fact Lisa, the object of Meyer's desire, he seized the chance to incite the engineer's racism and jealousy. Continuing his charade as an empathetic friend, he offered him a life-line. "Ya know though, I betcha that black savage has that poor little girl cowered, intimidating her to talk to him. No doubt, she's afraid."

"Who does that n****r think he is," Meyer snarled.

"Yeah, all uppity and thinkin' he can just march in here and push around innocent White women," Braun shot back.

"Somebody's gotta show that n****r bastard who's boss around here," Meyer bellowed.

"Right, kick his ass! We got your back," Kurt joined in.

Goading him on, Braun continued, "Yeah, he can't go fucking with one of your workers. And her friends from the plant can't be happy with that either." Which in one case was true, given that Frank Nowak, a riveter at Curtiss who was constantly badgering Lisa for another date, stood off to the side, seething.

Despite their prodding and offers of support, Meyer sat nailed to his seat. Although always one to boast of his toughness, he was paralyzed by the thought of physical confrontation. Sensing the man's false bravado, Braun nudged Kurt under the table, as he nodded to the corner of the bar.

Shooting up, the former wrestler roared, "Fuck that n****r! Pete's our pal!"

Elbowing their way through the crowd, with Meyer always taking up the rear, they headed towards the bar. As they approached, they stopped long enough for Meyer to enlist his subordinate, and known hothead, Frank Nowak into the posse.

Intent on trouble, the gang surrounded the couple. Taking the lead, Metzger snarled, "Yo, Sambo. Quit botherin' the lady!"

With eyes blazing and jaw set, Jim spun toward his abusers. Recognizing the situation, Lisa was quick to intervene. "Hey, that's not nice, Mister! I'm talking to my friend, so please, leave us alone!"

"He ain't no friend of yours, Lisa. He's just a shiftless n****r tryin' to get in your pants," Nowak broke in.

Once more Jim was about to get up, but was restrained by a look from Lisa, who shot back, "As I told you before, Frank, I ain't your girl, so mind your own business."

This only served to further incite the rejected suitor who refused to move on. No longer surrounded by friendly co-workers who knew her penchant for flirting, she knew they had to escape from Nowak and the menacing strangers. "Come on, Jim, let's join Alex and Maureen."

Itching for a fight, and confident that any altercation would be Jim's fault in the eyes of the police, Braun murmured to his henchmen, "Keep it up, boys. Don't let 'em go." Stepping back, he watched as his comrades pressed forward.

"You ain't goin' nowhere til we straighten things out," Kurt growled.

"What do you mean?" Lisa shot back as she once more tried to hold back her friend.

"I mean, we don't like seein' n*****s with White women," Kurt sneered.

"Yeah, you should be ashamed of yourself, lettin' that black m****y near you," Eric spouted off as the gang edged closer.

Hoping to protect Lisa, Jim mustered all his strength to stem his urge to fight. Still, he knew they had to get away. "We don't want any trouble, and we're leaving. Excuse us."

"Just try it," Kurt spit out.

Just then, Braun's voice rang out from the back, "Watch it! The Negro has a knife!"

With that, the former wrestler let loose with a haymaker that Jim managed to deflect, before following up with a right cross that split Metzger's chin. In an instant, the corner of the bar was a rolling mass of bodies, with arms flailing in all direction. While careful to avoid combat, Meyer stood at the edge of the melee, cheering on his comrades. For his part, Braun stood even further back.

As the outnumbered black man headed to the floor, a couple of bartenders leapt over the rail to help him. A tuxedo-clad bouncer, hearing the bedlam, quickly followed. The maitre d', versed in the "special rules" that applied to Black bars, quickly called the police.

By now, Alex and Maureen heard the uproar, and seeing where it came from, rushed towards the scene to check on their friends. Dan Richardson was already there, separating the last of the combatants, while trying to sort out what had happened. At his side was the bouncer, Eddie

"Boxcar" Brown, an ex-boxer who once challenged for the title but was denied matches because of his race. Urging calm, Dan asked patrons to return to their places in an effort to restore order; Boxcar's presence put an emphasis on it.

However, Jim would have none of it. After a vain attempt to speak to the talent manager, he made a quick exit toward the door. Being a veteran of the Black club scene, he knew the police were on the way. Besides wanting to spare Mister Richardson trouble, he had no illusions about how things would turn out. As a Black man involved in a scuffle with a group of Whites, he knew who the cops would believe. At best, he would expect to be hauled off to the precinct house, followed by a quick ride to the county lock-up. If however, he tried to defend himself too vigorously, this would be augmented with a beating in the shadows of the police station. Better to risk friendships and blow a chance for a job than to suffer the abuse reserved for Black men at the hands of authorities.

As Maureen rushed to Lisa's side, who sat stunned and upset at a table near the ballroom, Alex ran ahead to intercept Jim.

"Jim, Jim, wait!"

"Makin' tracks outta here, Alex. Cops are coming and that's trouble," Jim yelled while pausing barely long enough for his friend to catch up.

"What's going on? What happened?"

"Those motherfuckin' honkies yukkin' it up at the bar over there started hasslin' us for just talkin' to each other."

"I get the picture. And I recognize one of 'im. Works at the plant with the girls. Real trouble."

"They kept pushin'. Wouldn't leave us alone," he growled, as he stood there with his shirt torn and a sleeve from his prized suit hanging by threads.

"Did you try to move?"

"Fuck, why should I move. But yeah, we tried to get over to you, but they blocked the way, and then some bald prick threw a punch at me. That's why he's holdin' a towel to his chops."

"That's why you shouldn't go. You have to tell the police what you just told me."

"Sweet Jesus! You don't know nothin' about the street, do you, boy! Who them cops gonna believe? This n****r, who was talkin' to a White woman, or those White boys, one of 'em sportin' a bloody chin. My black ass will be thrown in the back of the wagon before I get four words out!"

"Listen, you're going to look guilty. Let me talk to Dan Richardson. He's a friend and he has a lot of connections. I'm sure when he hears this, he'll go to bat for ya."

"Alex, you don't know how this shit works around here. Sure, Dan knows a lot of those big shots, but his hands are tied. Ya know that fancy lounge over at the Terminal?"

"Sure, the Deco D'arte"

"Yeah, that's it. I hear from other musicians that the rich owners of that place feel Dan's hurtin' their business—bad. Word is, they paid off the Captain over on Broadway to find any excuse to shut'im down. Besides saving my black ass, I don't wanna hurt him either."

"I get it, but that's bullshit; corrupt bastards!"

"Aw, yeah! But that's what it's like for us Black folk all the time!"

"Yeah, I suppose you do have to take off, but listen, I'll hang around here and see what I can do for you …"

"Thanks, but lotsa luck on that. Time's wastin' so, so-long," he said as he dashed out the door.

Hans Krueger was tucked low in the seat of his beat up Ford, carefully watching every move outside the hotel entrance. He was parked along a dark street across from the nightclub, adjacent to a line of tracks leading to the Central Terminal. Nervously chewing on a cigar he refused to light in the fear of being spotted, he was poised to jump into action whenever the opportunity arose. Earlier, when once more going over the details of the plan with Metzger, he failed to notice Alex as he marched into the cabaret. However, not long afterwards, while still in the company of his accomplice, he watched with cunning satisfaction as Maureen arrived in her ancient Buick. This was shortly followed by Kurt's exit to the club.

Continuing with his surveillance, Hans spotted a number of local luminaries walking into the building. Letting out an oath, he quickly relegated the party to the status of degenerates, given his hatred of any kind of race mixing. As time passed, his eyes locked onto a lone figure rushing out from the building. Much to his surprise, he recognized his old nemesis from the newsstand attack, the Black musician. As with Braun, he immediately realized the ramifications of his presence as it applied to their plans. A wide smile crept across his face as he watched the man make his way towards the bus stop outside the Terminal. Nonetheless, this was not the time for action, that was reserved for the focus of their plot. Soon, his attention, if not his fear was aroused by the arrival of Buffalo police squad cars squealing up to the club exits.

Barging through the door, Captain Bill Barton cast a menacing glare that swept across the room. He carried himself with an arrogant air, secure in the knowledge that he was the law around here, but more importantly, was protected in his actions. He achieved this status having funneled a portion of his bribes to politicians and others of influence both within and outside the department. Wide, yet not imposing, he pushed his way through the crowd, until he arrived at the feet of the owner, who by now had calmed things down.

"What the hell is going on here, Richardson," he snarled. "More ni … ah, Negro problems," he stumbled, knowing the owner's popularity and connections.

As Richardson began to lay out some of the facts he had learned, Kurt Metzger shot up from his stool, "Some n****r attacked me."

"That's right! He went off on all of us like some violent animal," Eric chimed in.

Ignoring Richardson as he tried to explain the situation, Burton strode towards the group in the corner. "So some outta control Negro started fighting with patrons at the bar?"

"Yeah, for no reason," Eric pleaded.

"So where was security," Barton snapped as he turned toward the bouncer, Boxcar.

"I was at the door, and got there as quick as I could, plus the bartenders jumped in too."

"So, where's the Negro who started all this trouble, you got'im, right?"

"He musta took off," Boxcar admitted.

"That sure shows your fellow Negro's innocence," He bellowed sarcastically. "And by the way, crackerjack job on maintaining an orderly premises!"

Finally able to elbow her way to the bar, Lisa jumped in. "We were just talking and these guys came over and started harassing us."

"We was just seein' if she was all right. He seemed to be botherin' her," Nowak piped in.

"They were menacing us, and wouldn't let us leave."

"We couldn't get outta the way. He got all uppity and belligerent," Kurt insisted. "Then the next thing you know, he started throwin' punches."

As Nowak nodded in agreement, Lisa shot back, "You were jealous and just wanted trouble, Frank!"

"Wait, you know each other?" Barton asked.

"We both work at Curtiss," she answered.

"Well, it sounds like he was just trying to check up on you; no reason for a fight."

"No, they started it! Kept pushing!"

"Then why did he high-tail it outta here, something a guilty man would do," the cop sneered.

"Listen, officer, we were just having a drink, and asked how she was doin'. So this is my reward," Kurt stated as he pointed toward his battered chin.

"And not lookin' for any trouble," Eric nodded.

"You're all lying!" Lisa shouted.

"Now calm down, young lady. I'll cut ya some slack because of your youth. Which shows you're naive enough to think you met a new friend, when in fact he's just some shifty Negro trying to take advantage of an innocent White girl. These fellas were just looking out for you when that n****r starts throwin' punches!"

Off to the side, Braun sat back smiling with satisfaction at seeing his plan play out for a Black-White altercation, in addition to reveling in the good fortune of having damaged an enemy in the process. Still he was poised for more.

"No! That's just because he's a Negro!"

"Don't go thrown' that crap around here, sister or I'll toss your…"

By now, having managed to carve her way through the crowd and phalanx of police, Maureen tried to intervene, "Please Captain, I know Lisa and her friend, they wouldn't start a fight."

Spinning around, Barton snapped, "So, you're accusing these men. Did you happen to witness any of this?"

"Well no, I was sitting in the ballroom, but…"

"Well, unless you can see through walls, lady, I suggest you just turn around and stop interfering with police work."

A lieutenant at his side leaned over and whispered, "That's Little Brick's granddaughter, I know her from the Ward."

Delighted at the chance to insult his old tormentor in front of his granddaughter, Barton let out a stage whisper, "Well, thank god the dithering old codger ain't around anymore. As for young Costello, I booted his sorry ass outta the precinct years ago."

Enraged by the inflammatory lies about her family, Maureen charged towards Barton before being restrained by Alex, "We can't win this one, right now. Hold back, you'll have your day."

Leaving little doubt as to where he stood, Barton turned towards the surrounding patrons, "Anybody see these three gentlemen start a fight?"

Silence filled the air as most of the clientele didn't see the disturbance, while those in the corner who did, were reluctant to get involved, especially in light of the Captain's sentiments.

"Just as I thought." Turning towards Metzger, he continued, "Do you want to press charges for the assault?"

"Naw, that's all right, it's over," Metzger replied, knowing he didn't want to leave an official trail.

"Good, I don't want my boys wasting another minute chasin' some crazy ni… ah, Negro, but that's very generous of you, Mister…"

"Thanks, Kurt… ah… Kurt with a 'K'."

Once more turning toward his audience, Barton boomed, "Did ya hear that, he doesn't want to press charges. Now that's the action of an innocent man."

With that, Barton instructed one of his subordinates to gather information for the Liquor Board. Turning his attention to the owner, he strode over to where Richardson was seated.

"Listen, Richardson, you know the rules, especially about insuring a safe environment."

"You know damn well, those White boys were the instigators and we didn't do anything wrong. I'm sure this doesn't have anything to do with Deco D'Arte."

"Watch it, Richardson! If it wasn't for your connections, I'd be shutting your ass down tonight. But rest assured, I'll be reporting this to the Liquor Board for failing to maintain an orderly premises."

Satisfied that he demonstrated his power, Barton gathered his cohort and started to march out.

Seeing this, Alex decided to try one last time to help his friend—regardless how futile the odds. After waiting until the Captain neared the ballroom's side exit, away from his audience, Alex spoke up, "Captain, excuse me but I may have some information you should know."

"I already completed my inquiry!"

"But I talked to my friend Jim who was attacked by those men just because he was talking to his friend."

"Who the hell are you?"

"My name is Alex Wagner…"

"So what do you do? You a cop, a seasoned investigator?" he chuckled dismissively.

"No, I'm a reporter for the *Advocate*."

"Ah, the *Advocate*. Listen sonny, maybe you didn't hear me, but I got all the facts I need about this n****r causing a fight."

"But I talked to him, he didn't start…"

"Shut up and quit interfering, or I'll haul your ass in. And while I'm at it, tell that prick Lange to stop slingin' mud about me, if he knows what's good for him!" With his face glowing red, the corrupt cop waved to his crew and stormed out the door.

Angered and frustrated, but not surprised given the stories about Barton, Alex hurried back to the ballroom where Lisa had now joined Maureen at their table.

"You okay? Did any of those bums hurt you?"

"I wasn't hurt, just shaken up, as I was telling Maureen."

"Thug chivalry, according to those bums," he said sarcastically.

"No doubt on that, they glared at me like I was garbage, but Jim's the one I'm worried about. I yelled over to him as they were pullin' him off that guy. He managed to nod that he was okay, but he took some shots."

"I talked to him a couple of minutes ago and he didn't mention any injuries, but he was anxious to get out, figuring he didn't have a chance with the cops—which no doubt was true."

"Thank god he wasn't hurt," Lisa observed. "Good he got outta here before the cops. I got a taste of that racist cop's sense of justice. Treated me like shit while backing those punks!"

"I tried to explain Jim's side but he just brushed me off, before threatening me."

"Yeah, I had the pleasure of being introduced to Barton's idea of respect and fairness. Corrupt bastard! I remember Gramps talking about him—dirty as they come."

"Just so happens Jim mentioned rumors that he is on the take from competitors of Mister Richardson to harass him."

"It just shows you these bastards help each other in terrorizing people with their hateful bigotry," Maureen said.

"And those people who don't like Negroes and Whites socializing, particularly Black men and White women; but, even here at a jazz club," he said, shaking his head.

"Well, too fuckin' bad for those assholes!" Lisa snapped.

"There's still so much of this around. Damn, over seventy years after the Civil War and we have this Bund and KKK crap," Maureen said.

"Yeah, we got a taste of that at the newsstand."

"What really pissed me off was seeing all those fine folks who kept their yaps shut after seeing what happened," Lisa smirked.

"When we got near, I caught sight of Frank Nowak pushin' and shovin'. And were the others from Curtiss?" Maureen asked.

"Naw, I don't think I ever saw them around; but Pete Meyer was with 'em, off to the side, eggin 'em on! Lisa scoffed."

"Really, Frank's bad enough, being a jealous hot-head…"

"Meyer, now I remember him from the Curtiss tour. You later told me you didn't have much use for him. And yeah, Nowak, he's the one I had words with at the Al Hambra, when we first met." Alex broke in.

"That's right, but Meyer is just a creep; stalking Lisa and other girls at the plant when not busting unions!"

"Got that right, Mo," Lisa agreed. "And always telling me that I look like a cute little cheerleader. Gives me the heebie-jeebies."

"Yeah, I wouldn't want him anywhere near my daughter if I had a kid in that youth chorus he directs. Ugh!"

"And Frank's always got his head up Meyer's ass, suckin' up for overtime. And I saw him yukkin' it up with Meyer and the chief trouble-maker after Mister Richardson settled things down."

"Wait! Now I remember seeing Meyer with a group near the bar when we rushed up after hearing the bedlam. Was one of them the attack-er?" Maureen asked.

"Yeah, hold on, that's him over there, the baldy holdin' the towel to his face, and talkin' to that bastard Nowak. See 'em! He's the one who told the cops he was the victim. That prick Nowak better not get near me at work, if he don't want his balls stuck in his throat."

"Okay, I see them. They had their backs to me before, but where's Meyer? I don't see him."

"Knowing him, I betcha he skedaddled. Mister 'Cover-your-ass,' don't want any involvement in a brawl at a Curtiss social, followin'im back to the plant."

"Looks like they're heading towards those booths near the front of the bar. Good! I don't want to look at them, knowing what they did."

"Lisa, let me get you a drink." Alex added

"Gee, thanks, guys, but I'm not in the mood. I'm really shook up and angry about this."

"Listen, maybe the best medicine is to have a drink and relax with friends."

"Just lookin' at those punks…"

"Ignore them, like I am. Besides, you're too tough for them," Maureen said.

"Yeah, nobody fucks with me," she chuckled sardonically. "But I can't enjoy myself. I feel so bad about Jim. He was so nice and then got beat up just for talkin' to me and then hadda scram; and maybe even lost a job."

Pausing as she watched the pain in her friend's eyes, Maureen said, "I understand. That's fine, but I'm taking you home."

"No, I can take care of myself. You finish your meal and enjoy your date."

"But how will you get home? You took the company bus."

"I'll see if anybody with a car is leaving early. Otherwise, I'll catch the city bus. One stops at the Terminal every fifteen minutes."

"Well, I'm walking you over there,"

"Come on, Alex, you know that's not me."

"Wait… listen, Lisa, why can't you just take my old jalopy. Alex can take me home, and you can pick me up tomorrow. Simple. No problem."

"No problem from my end," Alex smiled.

Maureen continued trying to persuade Lisa to stay, before giving her the keys; and after declining Alex's repeated offers of an escort, Lisa headed to the door.

Watching the cop cars leave the scene, eased the tension Krueger always felt when dealing with the hated police. It wasn't long afterward, that the Nazi caught sight of a lone female figure leaving the club. His excitement grew to a fevered pitch as he saw the woman slowly approach the old Buick sitting in the far end of the parking lot.

Springing into action as she fumbled with her keys, he pulled out from his hidden perch, and pointed the car towards a dark spot near an abandoned line of tracks. Easing onto a gravel strip behind the Terminal, he jumped out of the car and popped open the hood. After stepping out into the street, he began to wave his arms as a lonely car began to approach. Sticking to his plan, he yanked down his cap and pulled up his collar, as the Buick came to a squeaking halt.

Leaning in as the woman rolled down her window, he pleaded, "Gee, lady, do you have a flashlight. I got a little problem with a hose that needs a quick fix."

No sooner had she turned toward the glove compartment, than he ripped open the door and flew in. With his excitement at a fever pitch, he struck her with a ferocity that sent her head bouncing off the dash. As she fought to cry out, he muffled her mouth with his free hand. It was then, that he realized this was not the tall red haired target of their plan; nonetheless, as was their contingency, he knew that ultimately, any girl would do. Focusing all his pent-up rage over women, he unleashed a lightning string of punches, as she struggled beneath his weight. Satisfied that she was unconscious, he put the car in gear and steered it deeper into the access road. After flipping up her dress, and pulling down her panties, he grabbed his belt, only to realize he had creamed his pants. This only served to further incite his fury. Screaming out, "No wonder, you dago n****r," he frantically searched for an object to substitute.

Just then, the darkness was pierced by the glare of a spotlight and a chorus of shouts coming from the adjacent train yard. Not waiting for the cavalry to arrive, Krueger leapt from the cab and raced down the access road and back to the street, where he jumped into his car and sped off into the night.

XIV

The crime scene rope bobbed steadily in the wind, as a late summer storm blew in off the lake. Meanwhile, as a train pulled into the back of the terminal, the forlorn sound of its bell, only added to the gloom of an overcast morning.

A team of detectives combed around the old Buick awkwardly sitting at the edge of the tracks, while two of their cohort carefully picked their way through its cabin. With his fedora pulled low, and his collar pulled up in response to the rain, the man in charge kept questioning his crew as he joined in their efforts.

Alex slowly steered his car past the police cars and investigators' black sedans that now filled the narrow confines of the utility road. After finally finding a parking space, he was quick to spot Mister Costello standing near the entrance of the station underpass. The old commissioner was in the company of two men, who judging by their bearing and dress, appeared to command some measure of authority. Yet, no sooner had the reporter set his course towards his friend, than he was greeted by a bark coming from behind, "Hey pal, where do you think you're goin'?"

Snapping to his right, he was met by a sentry, who was manning his post from the comfort of a nearby police car. "I'm here to meet Commissioner Costello, up there."

"Unless this is police business, this is a crime scene, off limits to civilians. So turn it around buddy."

Anxious to get on with his business, Alex finally conceded to reveal his press credentials.

"Ah, the *Advocate*," the old cop smirked before waving him past the wooden barricade.

He made his way past a group of reporters watching for the arrival of the department's spokesman from downtown. As he stood off to the side, waiting for the old man to be free, he began taking notes of the nearby crime site. In the midst of his writing, he was roused by the sound of a familiar voice, "I'm glad you made it Alex, although under terrible circumstances."

"Yeah, horrible, to say the least. And thanks for giving me a head's up on the press conference, Mister Costello. But more importantly, any more news on Lisa?"

"My Maureen's dear friend, Lisa, poor girl. These are times that you hate as a cop, or let alone as a grandfather. Her poor family... heartbreaking... So yes, she's in critical condition, but thankfully she's stabilized, and doctors are hopeful, according to Steve Donnelly, Chief of Detectives. He's the taller of the two fellows I was talking to over there. The other is Dick Gorski, head of security for the Central Terminal. Christ, she took a savage beating... among other things..." he sighed.

"God, I hope it's not..."

"I can't go into that, but I will say they now believe the attacker was scared off before he could do anything worse... thank God for the railroad swithchmen who chased him off," he added as he dabbed his eyes. "and then, I keep thinking that it could have been Maureen..."

"I know, but at least there's the good news, that she's stabilized. Last night was terrible. After leaving Dan's, we saw the commotion up here, and were horrified when we spotted Maureen's car. A cop friend of

Maureen told us what happened. We raced over to General, where all they would tell us was that she was alive, before asking us to leave—family only. So do you know if she's conscious, can she speak?"

"No, the doctors say that's the problem with head injuries, could be hours, could be days, could be…longer… they just don't know for sure."

"Let's pray for the best. But that's got to be tough for the police. Still, any leads? Any suspects?"

"Of course…you didn't hear, did you?"

"No… hear what?"

"They picked up your friend Jim Jefferson early this morning. They're going to charge him with first degree assault, for now."

"No, No that can't be…"

"I'm sorry, but I'm afraid so, son. They picked him up at that Hobo Camp. From what I hear, things got bad there. He resisted, shouting his innocence. His colored friends tried to help him, and then, some hoboes from down south, started calling him n*****, and shouting 'lynch him.' Nearly had a riot before they restored order. My grandson Danny was there, along with one of the units they called up."

"Listen, Mister Costello, he's innocent. He couldn't do something like that!"

"I understand your feelings, Alex. I'm conflicted myself. A man just doesn't go from risking his neck for strangers on one day, to brutally assaulting an innocent girl on another. It just makes no sense, and I was telling my old colleagues that, just now. But here's what they think they have: a solid case, with means, motive, opportunity and witnesses. Witnesses who say he was bothering Lisa. Apparently, some bystanders said they tried to help her, and he blew up and started a fight before taking off a few minutes prior to her leaving."

"Believe me, it's nothing like that! We were there. Maureen must have told you!"

"No, I didn't talk to her. After she called from the hospital, I rushed over here. By the time I got home this morning, both her and my wife were sleeping. Knowing how distraught they must have been, I couldn't bring myself to wake them."

"Ah, that's why the busy signal, phone off the hook. But sir, it's not like they said."

"That's all right, son. I believe you, but go on, tell me what you know."

Alex went on to describe what they witnessed, along with an account of their conversation with Lisa, and what he heard from Jim. He also detailed Lisa's argument with the corrupt precinct Captain, along with his and Maureen's interaction with Barton.

"Yeah, Barton's a bad apple all right. I wouldn't trust a word he says. Tried to drum him out before I left. He was a patrol sergeant on the take from whoever could pay, pimps, gamblers, rum-runners; but, he had some friends who dragged things out until I was gone. I'm sure he'll try to get Dan shut down, by pushing the bogus line that he failed to control violence."

"Yeah, and throw Jim to the wolves in the process."

"He wouldn't hesitate. Now, as for this Nowak fella who was part of this group harassing them, he worked at Curtiss, and Lisa rejected him after dating a little while?"

"Yeah, that's what Maureen told me. Apparently, he was real possessive even though they only went out a couple of times. She broke it off, real quick."

"Sure sounds like trouble," Little Brick said, while shaking his head.

"Yeah, a real hot-head. I had a run-in with him at the Al Hambra, when he was picking on an Indian busboy. Smoothed it over, but he has a hair trigger."

"That should arouse suspicion. One of Burton's men took his statement according to Chief Donnelly, who I pointed out earlier "

"Was undeniably truthful, no doubt."

"Right, hardly credible, but whatever the case, the time line of everyone's movements should be further looked into for starters. And then there's that fella you mentioned, Meyer, her boss."

"Yeah, like I said, Lisa believed he was part of the group egging them on. But unlike Nowak, the girls insisted he was more of a creep. He would lurk around saying suggestive, even weird things; asking Lisa about personal matters. That sorta stuff. They even mentioned rumors about him and young girls in the youth chorus he directs."

"That certainly deserves greater scrutiny."

"And Maureen insists he was nowhere to be seen after the ruckus."

"Another aggravating factor. At least on the surface, these two would seem to have a stronger motive than Jim. I'll have my friend and former deputy, Bob Kane, the security chief at Curtiss, look into these fellas, Meyer and Nowak. And those two other, so-called good Samaritans, did anybody recognize either of them?"

"Not Maureen or me. Lisa didn't mention she knew 'em, and neither did Jim. Yet he was in a hurry to take off, knowing the cops would never believe him…" Alex hesitated, realizing he was talking to a retired cop.

"No, I understand. Unfortunately, there's still so much of that on the force, and especially when it involves Barton's unit."

"Did your friend Donnelly have anything on the others?"

"Yeah," he said, "It's in my notes here… Apparently the guy with the banged up chops, quote, unquote, 'Kurt,' didn't press charges, and took a powder before they could question him further. Good police work there! The other guy named Bachmann, a plumber, lives on Goethe Street. Gave a statement that pretty much collaborates what Nowak says: Negro bothers the girl, starts a fight, takes off."

"Still, it certainly doesn't seem like enough to link Jim to the attack."

"Unfortunately, that's where the switchman comes in, when it comes to Jim and the police. You see, this fella was out checking switches when he heard someone shout 'n****r'."

"Coming from the car?"

"Well, the notes mention that he said it was coming from this direction. He was over there near that switch, what, maybe two hundred feet away… So then he shouts 'what's goin' on,' and starts pointing his lantern around. That's when he says he made out the car rockin'. So, he puts down the lantern and starts running toward it, when he sees a fella bolt…"

"So was he a Negro? What was he wearing?"

"Let's see… he said it was dark out. Thought he was wearing a newsboy cap. Yeah, he said the fella was dark, probably colored, and quote: 'had an athletic build and was fast as lightening.' He went on to say that he flew around the corner of the underpass and was gone by the time he got there."

"Yeah, no moon, two hundred feet away, athletic build and fast. Of course that nails it down. It musta been a Negro, and Jim specifically," Alex smirked, before adding, "And whom, incidentally, I didn't see wearing, or carrying a newsboy cap when he left Richardson's."

"Sure, that's the stereotype, but that's what the switchman said, and that's what the police went on."

"And I'm sure they didn't lead the witness. And how could he be sure what he heard coming from inside a car two hundred feet away? Muffled at best!"

"I know, son, especially after hearing what you told me today."

"And, besides, Lisa wouldn't use that term 'n****r.'"

"Although, if you're being attacked, well, no telling… but listen, Alex, we have a lot to work with, knowing what you and Maureen saw and heard. And I'll help. I want to get to the bottom of this as much as anyone, for obvious reasons."

"Yeah, our main concern is Lisa, of course, and I'm sure people will be all over this, given the race element."

"They are already. The gang unit is reporting that there's a flyer out on the streets trumpeting Negro rapists and calling for White revenge."

"What! How could they get it out so fast?"

"Well, it was out there already. Jake Connors, the night court reporter for the Courier, caught wind of the attack, and followed the units out to the Hobo Camp. He filed the story in the daybreak edition, front page."

"I'm not surprised in light of its sensational aspect, but even with that, to get a flyer out so quickly… It's like they knew. Could it be coincidence? And that third person harassing Lisa and Jim, what's his name… Bachman, German name, lives in a German neighborhood. I hate to stereotype my own people, but you have to wonder. Could he have any link to a Nazi gang? There's obviously a racist aspect to the attack in the bar."

"I've seen stranger coincidences turn out to be crimes in my years on the force, but for now, let's keep our eye on the ball and concentrate on what you and Maureen witnessed, along with looking more closely at these fellas, Nowak and Meyer, not to mention that main combatant who seems to have disappeared. And I'll relay all this to Donnelly."

"And I'll keep digging around and maybe some of my Sangerbund friends know more about this Meyer guy. I'm gonna try to see Jim, and I still want to check out if any Nazi gang fits into this somehow."

"I'm always here to help, and like I told you before, when it comes to these Nazis, be careful, they're dangerous. And as you know, any information on possible criminal activity has to be shared with the police."

"Don't worry, I'm with you on both counts."

"I have a big stake in this, so I'll be devoting whatever I can."

"I feel so lucky to have your help and expertise, and maybe I can help with Lisa."

"We make a good team, son. But listen, I've been here long enough. I've got to get home and tend to my wife and granddaughter."

"I'll keep you posted on anything that comes up in the press briefing. And of course, I'll be checking on Maureen, after she rests."

"Thanks, Alex," the old man smiled, as he headed off with an even more vigorous bounce to his step.

XV

The steady tap of a nightstick against the jailer's stool, was the only sound to be heard in the bleak, tight confines of the visitor's room. Alex could almost feel the intensity of the officer's glare, as he anxiously waited for Jim's arrival. He sat there nervously fingering the access pass that he secured through Little Brick's connections.

By now, his claustrophobia had already kicked-in, as he found himself surrounded by slits for windows, gray tile walls, and bars everywhere. It was a condition that plagued him since childhood, when, while exploring, he slid down a chute and into a coal bin, where he wailed for what seemed like hours, until rescued by his mother. He could only imagine his friend's suffering at being trapped in a cell for who knows how long.

Some measure of relief finally arrived, as Jim, shackled hand and foot, came shuffling in, flanked by a pair of burly guards. Shoving their charge onto a chair, the nastier of the two snapped, "Ya got thirty minutes, not a second more," before the two manned their posts beside the door.

Staring through the steel mesh, Jim sat in pained silence before Alex broke the ice, "Sorry you're here, Jim."

"I'm a Black man in America, so I"m always prepared for this," he said with an air of disgust, as the guard watched from his stool.

"Are you okay?"

"About as good as ya'd figure, for a Negro accused of attackin' a White girl: spit on; screamed at, you know, 'n****r,' 'savage,' 'monkey;' tripped down stairs, smashed against bars, you name it!"

"Good God! Be careful my friend—as best you can. And don't forget, we support you."

"Alex, you're a good man but you know shit about jails. You gotta know how to survive in here. This ain't my first visit to crowbar hotel."

"You never told me."

"A lot I didn't tell you, but listen, any Negro who's moved around this country as much as me, is gonna find his black ass in jail… you ever hear about sunset towns?"

"No, I haven't…"

"Didn't think so, so lemme tell ya. It's where lily White towns have signs sayin' ya better get your black asses outta here at sundown, if ya know what's good for ya, whether you're workin' or buyin' food, or just passin' through…"

"You gotta be kiddin' me!"

"You darken that tan, and dye 'n kink that hair, and you'll find out. Shit, I remember one time workin' at a garage down in Kentucky, where this cop had a dumb fuck brother who couldn't get a mechanic's job. He'd hide and wait in his car, until one day, I worked late, and sure 'nuff, he hauled my ass off to the pokey—for a week! Afterward, I high tailed it outta there, so I never found out if that dim-wit brother got my job—or killed anybody puttin' the brakes in backward," he chuckled, before continuing, "And then there was a time I was in some hick town at a grocery store buyin' a soda pop, where this lady was in line in front of me, and kept talkin' and talkin' to the sales clerk. After I got my coke and walked onto the porch, the lady was out there and started yellin', 'n****r after dark,' 'n****r after dark.' Three White men came runnin' up, and dragged my ass down to the sheriff's office."

"Damn, Down South!"

"Down South. Naw, that shit's all over, boy. When I first got here, I took a hike up to the Falls. On the way back, I was passin' by the lumber docks in North Tonawanda…"

"A Sunset Town? They pulled you in?"

"You got that right, brother! Same as Down South, and lemme tell ya, if they got them fuckin' laws hurtin' innocent colored people, ya gotta know they're gonna treat us like shit in jail. I figure I ate snot and drank piss in my food more than once in jail…"

"Good, god…"

"Yeah, brother, but if you're hungry or thirsty enough, you don't give a shit," he said before whispering, "This time though, I ain't goin' down without a fight. Some of my Black brothers are gettin' me a shiv to protect myself."

"Jim, it may be easy for me to say, but don't go there. You have people out here who know you're innocent, including Maureen's grandfather, the retired police commissioner. I'm sure he knows jail brass who can do something about the abuse."

"Tell 'im he's gotta. Otherwise, I swear I'm gonna stick that fat, cracker motherfucker if he starts whuppin' on me," he said, once more lowering his voice.

"Don't, then you are screwed. They'll beat you down even more or kill you. Dig-in and have your friends watch your back—whatever—until Mister Costello can help."

"I'll try, but I don't know how much longer I can take this shit."

"I know, but don't forget Lisa. Once she can talk, she'll let them know it wasn't you."

"What if that poor girl doesn't wake up, or does't remember anything. Don't forget, during the War I was a trained medic and treated head wounds. I know there ain't no guarantees…"

"Well, then we'll just have to plan for the long haul. Which reminds me, do you have a lawyer?"

"The bulls… er… the guards say they're gonna put me in front of a judge tomorrow—if ya can believe them. As for a lawyer, the brother in the cell next to me says they give us poor Black folks young lawyers just outta school."

"Maybe we can do something about that … but in the meantime, do you mind talking to me about it?"

"Sure, you're a friend who believes in me, and let's face it, folks ain't exactly lining up to support me."

After describing what he and Maureen witnessed at the nightclub, along with their discussions with Little Brick, Alex confided to Jim, "Both Maureen and I have since provided statements to the police, but up to now, they don't seem to have impacted the case; but listen, we're gonna keep pushing—including Commissioner Costello." Pressing him further, he asked, "So, did you see anyone lurking around, or sitting in a car. Anything like that?"

"Naw, I just wanted to get away from there. My plans for a job, ruined, my chance for a little enjoyment, shot, and my new suit tore up."

"Yeah, Mister Costello heard that you said you didn't take a bus."

"I just wanted to walk off the tension, forget everything and get home. And lucky I said so. They already checked with the bus drivers, and none of their riders that night fit my description."

"Well, that had to help your credibility."

"Don't I wish. No, they just used that against me, askin' if I was worked-up enough to hurt a girl."

"Which brings us back to the club. Like I said, judging from what I know, any of those punks who attacked you could have done this. Some guy named Nowak that Lisa worked with, along with a weird boss of her's named Meyers, both had a motive, if not an opportunity to do it—and Mister Costello agrees. Listen, think hard on this: did you by chance see any of the attackers outside or, even recognize any of them from before that night?"

"Yeah, I was just going to tell you. Ya see, I've been going over everything that happened at Richardson's—sitting in the slammer has a way of sharpenin' your thoughts—and I kept thinkin' that the bald prick who took a swing at me, looked familiar, but I couldn't pin'im down. Well, it finally hit me that he mighta been there at that attack on the Jew."

"What!"

"Yeah, if ya shaved the mustache from that punk-ass Nazi, who I dropped after he whacked you, I'm pretty sure he's the same guy. Mothafuckin' redneck!"

"Good god, did ya tell that to the cops?"

"I didn't realize it til later, after I kept rollin' it over. Like I said, sitting in a six by ten box all day gives ya time to think."

"I get it, but this could be an important lead; could be a break we need."

"I know cops. They'll say I can't be sure, and even so, so what!"

"Listen, it's a lead and it gives us something to go on. Something they can check out. You dig around enough, and you may find more leads, leads that can crack a case."

"Can you get Maureen's grandpa to talk to the cops, to look into things."

"Of course, and like I said, he sees the merit of your case. And I'm sure he'll bring up not just this bald guy, but these other two suspects, Nowak and Meyer, who, another friend of his, the security chief at the Curtiss plant is checking out."

"But what if the cops just say 'fuck it,' figurin' they already got their guy?"

"I promise you, we'll keep looking, both myself and Mister Costello. I also know I'll have the support of my editor Mister Lange, once I fill him in on what we know."

"I hope you're right, and thanks for your help. But that's a tall order, not just with the cops and D-A, but I betcha all them newspapers wanna nail my hide to the wall. I figure by now, most folks wanna fry me. That fat fuckin' guard said so, when he shoved a flyer in my face that screamed, 'n****r rapist.'"

"Those flyers were out within hours, which makes you wonder how anybody could get it out so fast. For my series, I learned about these inflammatory flyer campaigns, which the police gang squad say are sent out by Nazis. It makes you think that it's possible there's a common Nazi thread here."

"Listen, the night at Dan's, before you and Maureen headed off to your table, I was tellin' you I had some information…"

"Oh, yeah, I remember…"

"I was gonna tell ya later that night," he chuckled ironically, before continuing, "Anyway, ever since that night at the news shack, I kept an eye out for any of that Nazi shit; especially bein' a Negro and bein' a vet and all. I dunno if I told ya, but we got some good-ole-boy, KKK bitches from down south livin' at the camp. They don't try to fuck with us Black brothers, knowin' there's more of us than them. Still, they try to stir up shit between us and the other White boys in the camp. Most of the fellas didn't take the bait, figurin' we're all in the same boat, the same poor boat; so, no big problem; other than those crackers are mother fuckin' no good. But anyhow, lately, they brought a couple Nazis around."

"Nazis, you sure?"

"Fuck yeah! They were *'Seig heilin,'* yellin' 'Hitler's great,' and screamin' 'Jew scum,' and all that other Nazi bullshit, all over the place. But they knew better than bad mouth us brothers, seein' enough of our colored faces around. Still, we kept an eye on 'em, knowin' our black asses are right up there with the Jews, when it comes to their hatin' folks."

"So, were they just trying to cause trouble or were they trying to recruit too?"

"Both, I figure. But they didn't get far. A lot of the White boys are vets, and I can tell most of the others look at themselves as loyal Americans, despite everything. As a matter of fact, them Nazis hadda go through some shit gettin' outta there."

"Like I've been saying and writing about, these Nazis are popping up more often. But listen, did you recognize any of them, maybe even get their names or at least describe them?"

"Never saw 'em before and wasn't close enough to hear their names. The one who seemed to be the leader—him doin' all the talkin'— he was just a regular lookin' White guy, although sneaky lookin,' you know, like a rat. The other guy was kinda a good lookin' White boy, but with a bad scar down the side of his face…"

"Wait! A scar on his cheek? Blond hair? Probably in his late twenties?"

"Yeah, sounds right."

"Don't you remember, the night at the shanty when I tossed that guy and pulled off his mask. He had a long scar like that!"

"Naw… sorry, I was busy makin' sure that big fuck—who I now think is that instigatin' prick from Richardson's— wasn't gonna tee off on ya again with that two by four."

"And I'm sure glad ya did," Alex laughed, before once more turning serious, "But see, these Nazi could be part of that group who attacked us, and there's a thread that could lead to the attack on you and Lisa, and maybe even to the attack on Lisa in the car. It's something I want to dig into."

"I think you're onto something, but like I said, I dunno about the cops. A Black man or White boys, even if they're Nazis, don't go bettin' your life on that. I remember during the War, those Frenchies had a crazy sayin' *'ne pisse pas dans un violon.'* Do you know French?"

"No, can't say I do."

"When those Huns were shootin' at ya, you learn it pretty fast. It means 'don't piss in a violin.'"

"Uh, I'm not sure I get it…"

"It's just their way of sayin' don't waste your time.' I just hope it ain't the case with this stuff."

"I know Mister Costello will work on it, and try to convince the police, too. So, don't lose faith and you have to keep fighting," Alex said as he looked up only to see the last five minutes of their time, beginning to tick away.

"I've been fightin' all my life, Alex, and I'm damn tired of it..."

"I know, Jim, it's got to be hard being a Negro in America..."

"And not just talkin' about fightin' but it seems I've been fightin' for real all my life... Alex, did I ever tell you how I ended up in the Great Plains, the Great 'White' Plains."

"No, Jim, you didn't."

"Well, ya see, my ma, good woman that she was, God rest her soul, was widowed early on when my pa was killed tryin' to organize Porter Car workers."

"Gee, I'm sorry to hear that. It had to be horrible."

"It was. And it was never solved, but I'm proud of him to this day. Still, that left my ma alone with four kids. She worked hard as a housekeeper, and found us a run-down, one bedroom flat in the San Juan Hill section of New York. My older brother, Tommy, he was twelve, helped out as best he could cleanin' at a juke joint down the street. Still, my ma was desperate. That's when her boss, a White minister, persuaded her to send us two middle kids, me, nine, and my younger brother Ben, seven, to foster care at Christian farms out west. When we got off what was called an Orphan Train, we were hustled off to a pen, where this group of us were picked like prize cattle. Bein' colored, me and Ben were among the last. He was taken by some White lady and I was picked by an old White man. I never saw Ben again, and I ended up at a farm in Nebraska, where I worked like a dog and was beaten almost every day for not doin' enough to earn my keep."

"Still, it was where I learned the guitar from one of the hands who'd give me a few cents every time for helpin' 'im fix equipment. After years of savin' those pennies, I bought my own guitar. When the old farmer found out, he smashed it, sayin' it took away from my work. By now, I was big for my age—fifteen—so when I found him behind the barn, I whupped his rotten ass so bad, I kept runnin' and jumpin' trains til I found myself back in New York. There, I learned my ma, and little sister Flo, died of consumption, and Tommy had joined the Merchant Marine as a cook. I found a job helpin' a janitor fix things and lived in a settlement house until the War came, and I signed up with the Hellfighters."

"When I was part of that French unit, I was finally treated like a man, but when I got back home after fightin' for my country, it was the same old shit. I almost wished I was back in the trenches. That's when an army buddy of mine convinced me to head with him to the Greenwood section of Tulsa, which sounded to me like Heaven. And it was at first. I worked for a fine man, Lester Smith, who owned a garage. I fell in love with his beautiful daughter and my future wife, my dear Lucy, and after a year of saving, along with my army money, I bought into the garage. I told you about the riots, but I didn't tell you about Lucy and Lester, who died in the fires. I hardly tell anybody about it. I can barely say the words even now. I pretty much kicked around ever since. For years, I think I kept moving, just to keep from blowin' my brains out."

With that, Jim paused as neither man broke the silence until Alex finally said, "I can't tell you how sorry I am, Jim."

"So, like I said, I've been fightin' all my life, and I'm just tired of it. Still, I can't let 'em finish me off like this, after all these years.

"I understand, my friend, and I know you can do it, and I know I will try to help you any way I can."

"I gotta do it! Maybe fighting is my fate."

By now, the last seconds of their allotted time had ticked off. Eager to haul their unbroken prisoner back to his cell, the guards rushed over. "Okay, sweethearts, times up! Let's break up the pillow talk," the nastier of the guards snapped as he yanked Jim's shirt.

Perhaps it was the stupid, goading smirk on the jailer's face, or perhaps it was Jim's sad yet heroic tale, but whatever the case, Alex wasn't about to take any crap from this jailhouse bully. "Fuck you! You don't talk to us like that, pal!"

"Oh, this college boy thinks he's tough. Wanna take this outside, punk!"

"Any time, fat-boy! You name the time and place, as long as it's before I talk to my friend, Commissioner Costello about this shithole!"

After hearing Costello's name, and watching as his adversary lift his tall, athletic frame off the chair, the guard immediately had second thoughts. "Ah, I wouldn't wanna waste my time with a n****r lover."

By now, Alex regretted his abrupt actions, fearing that they would make things worse for Jim; yet, his regret was laid to rest as he turned and saw a reassuring smile sweep across his friend's face. He went on to watch in awe as Jim stood tall and unbent between his two jailers. He had come to know the man's compelling story, and how he had overcome so much. It was this strength of character that would lead his friend to do it again, and Alex knew he had to help.

XVI

The sound of Benny Goodman's "Goody, Goody" filled the air as the sultry figure turned from the Wurlitzer and began sashaying back to the table. By now, the lunchtime crowds were long gone, and only a lone patron sat at the counter sipping his soup. Off to the side, Benny, the night cook, was manning the grill while straining to hear the broadcast of the game. Arriving at their usual perch at the far end of the diner, Britta was greeted by the dour face of Karl Braun presiding over a gathering of his crew.

"Enough of that nonsense! We have business to take care of."

"Hey, I love music and there were a lotta choices. Besides, you wanted to drown out any nosy eavesdroppers," she said while languidly slipping into the booth.

"Music, yes, not that n****r, Jew *scheisse*. Anyway, let's get on with things."

"Yeah, an' puttin' on that little show," Hans sneered, "wigglin' your ass for that trucker at the counter."

"You love-birds can take that up at another time," Braun snapped. "We got a lotta ground to cover, and our guest will be here at seven-thirty."

"Why couldn't we meet at the Tiergarten? We should be celebrating the Nuremberg Rally which starts today," Martin chimed in.

"This is fine, low key. Certainly not the Tiergarten, too many people."

"We'll have plenty of time to celebrate, later," Hans agreed.

"Getting back to business, we should be proud of what we've done. As for our big assignment: Britta, you did good getting all that flight data from your source. And Hans and I couldn't have gotten those Curtiss pictures without Martin, Eric and Kurt scoutin' out the plant."

"And that was great, you getting those metal shavings from the factory," Kurt beamed.

"And used the *schwanz* engineer to get those plans," Britta added.

"And I assure you, we'll get even more, which is the other purpose for our being here tonight, and…"

"Yeah, be bold like the Fuhrer recently re-occupying the Rhineland with troops," Kurt blurted out, which seemed to rouse the trucker who was filling out his log.

"Keep it down," Karl warned as he nodded towards the counter. "And indeed, *meine Kameraden*, the Fuhrer is our inspiration!"

"*Sieg Heil*, fuck that treaty!" Martin exclaimed as he lowered his voice.

"Yes, yes, and like I was going to add, Hans did more great work with his camera, which should help with our guest tonight." Karl said.

"How's that, Hans?" Eric asked as he turned towards his friend.

"Let's just treat it as a surprise that we'll let you in on, later," Braun was quick to intervene.

"So, you don't want all of us here for this meeting with the engineer?" Martin asked.

"Right, I'm gonna meet him alone. I don't want to make him nervous, before I make things clear to him."

"What if he gets worked up over that, can you handle that by yourself?" Eric asked.

"That's where Hans comes in. Just before you leave, about ten minutes before he gets here—believe me, he's punctual—Hans will mosey over to the counter like he wants to listen to the game…"

"Perfect cover, it'll be in the middle of the game, and the Bisons have a chance to clinch the pennant tonight," Martin exclaimed.

"…and, I'll look like I'm reading the paper until Meyer arrives. When I get to the point where I want to stress the seriousness of things, I'll give a nod to Hans, who will come over and let him know in no uncertain terms that it's in his interest to play ball. As we all know, Hans is more than capable of handling any situation like this," he said with a sly smile.

Just then, Braun abruptly ended the discussion with a wave of his hand, as Benny approached the booth. Sporting his ubiquitous sailor cap, he carefully balanced a tray crammed with plates of Ollie's signature hotdogs, plus an assortment of fries and onion rings.

"Ah, here they come, the best franks in town," Eric—given his girth, an obvious connoisseur—marveled. "Klein's wieners, an old country recipe."

"No wonder you're fat. You oughta let me run ya through the paces at the gym," Hans smirked.

After passing out the orders, the smitten cook couldn't help but observe, "You look so pretty tonight, Miss, but did ya get hurt? Your cheek looks a little swollen."

"Why thank you! But no, I'm not hurt, I'm just clumsy. I was in a hurry and bumped into a closet door."

"You'll have to excuse us, ah… fella, we're busy. Here's three bucks, keep the change," Braun interrupted.

"Holy cow, thanks," Benny smiled, before adding, "that's awful nice of ya, Mister. Is there anything more I can help ya with? I'm brewin' a fresh pot of coffee."

"That's fine. Now leave us alone, buddy," Braun said as he shooed him away.

"Christ, I thought he was never gonna leave. And you," Hans snarled as he turned toward Britta, "do you really need to encourage the village idiot to flatter ya, like some trash floozy?"

"For god's sake, I didn't encourage nobody. He was just being sweet."

"How many times do I have to tell you two to knock it off," Karl snapped. "Now let's get back to business. Our propaganda and activism are really paying off. Those pamphlets are working well, especially after that n****r attacked that White girl," Braun added with a sly smile.

"Folks are really gettin' worked up over it. I even read this morning that some d**os on the West Side kicked the shit outta some n****r workin' on a coal truck. Probably egged on by our flyer," Hans boasted.

"It's good they know that there's people like us defending the White race against all the scum threatening us," Braun crowed.

" *Jawohl* ," Martin was about to shout before catching himself, and toning it down.

"And no small thanks to you, Eric, setting up that printer in the basement of your shop."

"Nice machine, thanks to the money from our friends. And easy to learn. A lot easier than plumbing," he laughed.

"And that piece of shit, hopped-up, black savage assaulting that poor White girl! And you guys were there that night, right?" Britta interrupted.

"Luckily, it dropped right into our laps," Kurt added as he cast a knowing look towards Braun.

"Yeah, it was a Curtiss social at that n****r lounge. We were plying the engineer with booze and building his trust," Braun answered.

"Too bad we couldn't save her," Kurt winked to Hans.

"She shoulda known enough to stay away from savages like that, until we finally put 'em in cages," Braun added.

"Yeah, don't go shedding any tears for her. She was playin' with an ape and got bit bad, and that should serve as a warning," Hans hissed.

"Still, to be beaten up like that…" Britta said with an air of sympathy.

"In any case, she's paying a price," Braun said. Trying to navigate the awkwardness of Britta being left in the dark, he quickly changed the subject. "And I want to congratulate some of our *kameraden* in mirroring the work of our brown shirt brothers…"

"Yeah, Martin and me, we went n****r huntin' last week," Kurt smirked. "We caught one of 'em staggerin' outta a juke joint over in the Fruit Belt late one night. We kicked his ass, and let'im know to tell his friends to start knowin' their place!"

"Nice goin'! Made it to the radio! It lets everybody know we're out there," Braun smiled as the others agreed.

"And then me and Kurt nabbed a couple k***s wandering outta that rats' nest of a Jew Center over on Jefferson, Sunday night. We laid a real beatin' on those two, before remindin' 'em that us Nazis are comin' after 'em all, pretty soon," Hans bragged.

"Well done! Yeah, that one made it to the newspapers," Braun gushed.

"And as you know, Karl, we answered that by puttin' out a pamphlet sayin' the Jews were printin' up counterfeit money in the Center, hopin' to flood some of the banks and cause a run."

"Yes, Eric! Propaganda!" Kurt proclaimed. "And don't forget, Reich Minister Goebbels says, 'repeat lies enough, and it becomes the truth.'"

"Like the *'Große Lüge,'* that the Fuhrer described in Mein Kampf," Braun added. "Come up with a big lie that people will think, no one could, quote: 'have the impudence to distort the truth so infamously.'"

"*Das ist wahr*," Kurt agreed while shaking his fist.

"That's all good news, but I have to report that despite the help of southern Klansmen, we didn't make much headway at the Hobo Jungle."

"That's too bad. There had to be a lot of discontent at that camp."

"Ah, too many veterans still fighting the War, Eric. They're too dumb to recognize the real enemies. Still, we strengthened our ties with the Klan," Braun replied

"That's why those bums are in that camp, *dummkopfs*," Eric laughed.

"Still, it should remind us that there are many enemies out there who want to thwart us," Braun stressed.

"Like that *schwein*, race traitor, Wagner, the reporter," Hans snarled.

"And his *zicke* whore," Braun growled, before gulping down the last of his fries.

"We're getting near the time of his arrival," Hans announced before whispering to Braun, "and I'd like to talk to you about the attack, after the others leave."

"Good, and I want to talk to you too, about certain things," Braun said, making sure the others didn't hear.

With that, Braun ordered Britta to have the cook clear the table. Eager to please her, the love-struck Benny quickly finished the task. Once he was gone, the four conspirators toasted the cause before saying their goodbyes and heading to the door.

"So what's on your mind, first, Hans?" Karl asked.

"I just didn't want the others hearing… Anyway, I was reading in the Evening News, that the car was registered to a Hugh Costello…"

"Sure, the old man she lives with. Her grandfather, I assume…"

"Yeah, her grandfather all right, and former police commissioner of the City of Buffalo."

"Fuck! That's not good! We better tighten security, especially until we wrap up this airplane work for Berlin."

"Speakin' of Berlin, I wanted to ask what they think of our outside activities?"

"They know about the flyers, and are okay with it; but the ones about the beatings, I tell 'em it's the Klan. They don't want us taking chances beyond our plane mission. Still, what they don't know won't hurt 'em."

"And the American, anything new with him? What's up there?"

"Apparently, he has input on things; I think they see him as a valuable asset and are careful and circumspect about him. From what I'm able to pick up, he sounds arrogant and too self-confident—the type who will claim all the credit for himself. But don't worry, I'll make sure they know we're the straw that stirs the drink."

"You'll always have my support, my friend!"

"Thanks. And now ya got me thinking about that old cop, and how his getting involved can be a problem… so, as I was gonna ask you away from the others, did the cops get Kurt or Eric's names?"

"Kurt told me he just gave his first name to that police captain, when he declined to press charges against the n****r."

"Why even use the first name; why not Mickey Mouse or better yet, *Michael Maus*!"

"I know, but he said he saw Meyer was close by at the time, and he remembered he'd been introduced as Kurt, earlier, so he didn't want to cause any suspicions."

"Okay, and what about Bachmann?"

"He said he just gave his name to a young cop taking down info for a Liquor Board complaint about the bar. He said he was sure we were long gone by the time the cops started investigating the attack."

"The idiot! Even if he isn't lying about only giving his name, his address will be simple to find out for the old cop. It's an opening that you can bet your ass he'll be checking out, since it was his granddaughter's car. In any case, we'll address any problems later on. In the meantime, tell those two to lay low, especially at German bars, and most of all at the Sangerbund for Kurt. As for Eric, we gotta be real careful with him, he's as dumb as he is fat."

"Sure, and I better get back to the game, he'll be here in a few minutes."

No sooner had he plopped down onto a stool at the counter, than he was set upon by the nearby trucker. "Hey, buddy, ya just missed Sparky Olson's homer for a three run lead. We're gonna clinch tonight!"

Hoping to remain nondescript, Hans muttered some measure of agreement while managing to avoid eye contact.

"I'm gonna race home, tell the little lady to turn off Jack Benny, and listen to us win the pennant."

"Sounds great," he replied, barely acknowledging the man's presence.

"Yeah, I gotta believe I'm the Bisons' number one fan. Joe Miller here," he said as he thrust out his hand.

Intent on cutting off the conversation, he snapped, "I just wanna concentrate on the game," He quickly turned toward the radio, ignoring his hand.

As a sense of unease filled the air, Benny arrived at the scene carrying a pot of coffee. Addressing Hans, he asked, "Ready for a refill, Mister?"

"Glad to meet you too," the trucker grumbled as he counted out his change while listening to the last out of the inning.

By now, Meyer was cautiously eyeing the landscape as he walked through the door. He was decked out in a new suit, topped off with a silk tie, matching pocket square and crisp dress shirt, that no doubt the sum total of which, cost more than all of his old outfits. No sooner had he spotted his host and settled into the booth, than he was greeted by the trucker who was headed to the exit for a rendezvous with his new Philco. "Say, I know you! You're the coach of the youth chorus at Evangelical Lutheran. You got those kids singin' like angels."

"Ah… why, thank you… "

"Yeah, you probably don't recognize me. I'm Joe Miller. I'm the part-time sexton for Pastor Lutz… and I'm sorry, but what's your name again?"

Glancing over to the stone-faced Braun, he replied, "Meyer, Pete Meyer. Nice to meet you."

"And by the way, is that your car out there? That's a real beauty. A new Packard, right? You gotta be doin' okay, huh?"

"Thanks again, but excuse me, I have to get back to my old friend here, and time is running short."

"Sure, yeah, and I gotta be gettin' home, but good seein' you again, Pete."

After waiting for his new pal to leave, Meyer chuckled, "Glad Mister Chatty is gone. Thought he was gonna start asking what I was doing in a joint like this."

"I chose this place because there's hardly anybody in here at this time; but, you hadda go knowing that big mouth," Braun grumbled.

"Well, at least he has good taste in cars," Meyer said, trying to make light of the situation.

"Not losing any time living it up, I see," Braun answered, once more failing to show any hint of humor.

"Ah… well, just following your suggestion about getting what I deserve," Meyer replied, picking up on Braun's disapproval.

"You dressing up for work like that?"

"Why… ah… no. This is just for goin' out. I'm headed to the Statler bar, later."

"And the car, you take it to the plant?"

"Why sure… that's why I… "

"…look suspicious, like you should be carrying a sign saying, 'I'm on the take.' Did anybody ask how you got it?"

"Well, no… I guess nobody noticed."

"Thank god for small miracles like the fact you're not exactly Mister Popular; but, if they do ask, come up with some bullshit, like you're maiden, great aunt died and left you money. And watch yourself at the clubs. Have the good sense to be sober and low-key."

"But… ah…, I have been careful," he stammered trying to appease his interrogator, "I haven't been out since that social at Richardson's. And I feel bad about what happened to Lisa."

"That's what happens when you play footsie with n*****s!"

"I know, but do you think it was that colored guy? She didn't seem to be afraid of him. Maybe she was just being friendly, before brushing him off."

"Just keep your mouth shut about the whole thing. You don't want to attract any more attention than you have already."

"But what if somebody, especially the authorities ask?"

"Listen, just do as I say, period!"

"Why are your speaking to me like this? I thought you were my friend."

"Because I can't afford mistakes! Now, let's get down to brass tacks. I don't want to be here any longer than necessary. So simply put, I want more information."

"But I got ya more on the ninety degree swivel for the landing gear…"

"Fine, and I paid you well for that information, but I want more information, like about the fifty caliber machine gun."

"But Karl, that's subcontracted through the Air Corps. They're very…"

"No! You just get it! Understand!"

"Wait, you can't talk to me like that!"

"I can and I will. Let's just say it's in your self-interest to do as I say. You see, I'm sure Curtiss would love to know one of their engineers is selling highly sensitive information."

"But… but… you can't prove that!"

"Really? All we have to do is send a letter mentioning your new car and citing some of the classified information you gave us; that you had access to."

"But you'd be in trouble too."

"Well, just between you and me, I have an exit strategy, and if the prospect of going to jail for industrial espionage doesn't incite fear, I want to show you something else." Smiling devilishly, he pulled out an envelope from his jacket pocket, and slid it across the table to his prey.

Viewing its contents, Meyer let out a wounded moan.

"I see you appreciate the gravity of those pictures. A little grainy, but thanks to a photographer I know, you can easily see what was going on."

"But she was willing and she's built like a woman," the chorus director quietly sobbed.

"Get a hold of yourself. You're causing a scene."

"But how could you do this? I trusted you."

"You believe a man giving you money to betray a trust, is someone to trust? Please! You only have yourself to blame. Blame your greed, your perversion. Besides, as any child rapist should know: One, there's no consent when it comes to sex with a minor. Two, if you're going to engage in these crimes, at least have the brains to draw the curtain all the way; Three: never announce the time and place of your degenerate activity. And finally, if by chance you find yourself in jail, and believe me, you certainly will if you don't obey my every word, you should know that child molesters have a very hard time in prison."

"You set me up, you bastard."

Eager to re-enforce his position of power, Braun quickly gestured to his accomplice at the counter, before snarling, "Just to make sure you recognize that I'm not fooling around, I'd like to introduce an associate of mine."

Not saying a word, Krueger slowly slid into the booth. Casting a cold glare, he opened his jacket to reveal a holstered pistol sitting at his waist.

"Just who are you? The people at Consolidated would never act like street thugs."

Exchanging a fiendish sneer with his Nazi comrade, Braun calmly announced, "That's really of no concern to you. But let me warn you in no uncertain terms, if in case you get cold feet, or if somehow, your so-called conscience gets the best of you and you decide to throw yourself at the mercy of the authorities, I'd like to let you know that my friend here used to be in the rackets. One of his jobs was to solve difficult problems for his boss, if you know what I mean."

Reeling from what had just transpired, Meyer silently sat in shocked disbelief for a number of moments as he tried to regain his bearings. By then, he could barely get the words out, as he whispered, "Am I free to go now?"

"Of course. We'll wait a couple of minutes to make sure you're gone. But mark my words, you better get me the information on the machine gun if you want to enjoy your new-found toys, money, and your very freedom, as I'm sure you know by now!"

With that, the broken and troubled figure slowly lifted himself up and limped out the door,

XVII

A festive air filled the stands as the crowd buzzed in anticipation of the opening ceremonies renaming Bison Stadium in honor of Frank Oberman, the late, popular owner of the team.

As the grounds crew were setting up the dais and microphones, players decked out in their crisp, white flannels, were shagging fly balls in the emerald expanse of the outfield. No sooner had they ended their pre-game work out, than "Big Ben" Brouthers, former major league slugger and current batting coach, decided to launch a ball over the right field wall. Much to the delight of the fans, the booming shot landed on the porch of one of the houses bordering the ballpark. This was followed by a chorus of cheers, and calls for him to take the field.

Seated in a box along the first base line, Alex, Maureen and her grandparents were no less vocal in cheering the second generation Bison hero.

"I remember his dad playing at old Riverside Park back in eighty-one, when the Bisons were in the National League. He was a big guy too, who could really smack the ball. He led the league in home runs that year, with all of eight; but that was when the ball was a lot less lively."

"Yeah, I'll say," Alex added. "Jimmy Fox, Mel Ott, and Lou Gehrig had almost a hundred home runs among them last year!"

"Danny Brouthers and a bunch of ol' Bisons like Pud Galvin and Jimmy O'Rourke used to frequent my dad's tavern, back in the day," Kenna chimed in.

"And your dad's place was where I first met Frank Oberman. His printing business was just taking off, and I was just promoted to Captain of the Seventh, in the Ward. Even back then, he was a human dynamo."

"And that was his undoing. Running his business, running the team, and then being elected Sheriff last year, how could anyone keep up that pace? Let that be a reminder to you, 'Mister I-can-do-anything,'"

"Oh, don't worry about me, sweetie! I keep in shape. But getting back to Frank, he always loved law enforcement. When he first bought the team, he allowed free admission to cops for weekday games, when they showed their badges."

"Yeah, my dad said he was generous to everybody. I guess that's why they're packed in here today."

"Speaking of pushing yourself too hard, what are you doing with your suit coat still on, Gramps?"

By now, with the temperatures reaching into the eighties, the men in the stands had largely abandoned their coats and rolled up their sleeves, while most of the women were clad in sun dresses and wide-brimmed hats in response to the sun and heat. Many had already discovered a more useful purpose for the programs, using them as fans in an attempt to get some relief.

Acting on his granddaughter's request, the ever-formal Hugh Costello doffed his linen suit-coat, and settled into the seat next to his wife.

"Thanks, Gramps, I've been worrying enough about Lisa, without worrying about you getting heat stroke."

"You're right, honey, but don't forget this is going to be a leisurely afternoon to enjoy the game. You need a break from your worrying about Lisa. Like I said before, she's in good hands at the hospital."

"And more importantly, God's looking out for her, sweetheart," Keena added.

"And I'll nix all the crime talk, despite being with such an expert as the Commissioner," Alex smiled.

"But let me get one thing in along those lines before the game starts, and while I have my husbands's attention; and that involves what happened at the Hobo Camp yesterday."

"So what happened?" the old man asked.

"As you know, and to bring Alex up to snuff on what I do, I was on our parish's regular monthly trip to distribute canned good and clothes that we collected after mass last Sunday, to the men down at the camp."

"That's awful nice of you, Missus Costello."

"Thanks, Alex, but it's just our duty, and it's enjoyable to boot. Anyway, this time it was just me, and Meg O'Connor, along with Jim the parish janitor in his rickety old pick-up. Meg and I were in the back when we neared the end of the railroad bridge. Just then, four or five men popped out of the scrub brush along the other side of the river. They waved us down, and one of them announced in what was an unmistakable southern accent, that they were with the Ku Klux Klan and that in the future we were to give out donations only to worthy White folks…"

"What!" Little Brick blurted out, barely able to contain himself.

"Wait, it only gets worse: and that, quote, 'you fish eaters'—I assume meaning, Catholics—were to abstain from, and I quote again, 'any of that anti-Christ, papist preachin'…"

"Oh, no they don't…" Maureen seethed.

"They then said that they were going to let us go through this time, because they were… get this, 'chivalrous gentlemen of the South;' but, they would be watching, to make sure we weren't donating to quote, —Oh, I can't say that horrible word for Negroes—since it would only encourage them…"

"So what happed next!" Hugh interrupted.

"We were just a couple of old ladies and a crippled janitor. But, needless to say, we ignored everything they said, and went to our regular spot just outside the camp, and gave to anyone who asked. Yet, I suspect the next time there'll be trouble."

"Why didn't you tell me last night or at breakfast, this morning?"

"Because when I came home last night, you were already sleeping on the couch during the 'Major Bowles' Show.' You've been pushing yourself all week, so you needed the rest, my hard-driving sweetheart. As for this morning, if I told you then, you and your pals would be there right now. I wasn't going to ruin this wonderful outing."

"Well, I'm going to have a talk with Gerry Ryan over at Seven, the first thing tomorrow morning. We'll put a quick end to that nonsense. So, now that we have that taken care of, can we go back to enjoying this beautiful event?"

With that, the little party resumed their light-hearted banter. During this time, Little Brick was constantly interrupted, exchanging greetings with a host of friends and former colleagues from the police department.

Finally, the Stadium announcer directed the crowd to turn their attention to the gathering at home plate. Surrounded by the Oberman family and a multitude of business and civic leaders, Mayor Zimmerman delivered a ringing testimonial about the late team owner, before unveiling the new sign that would soon grace the entrance to the ballpark.

As the celebration on the field was drawing to an end, Maureen spotted a familiar face in the stands. "Hey Gram, there's Danny and Karen; see 'em, about thirty rows up."

"Oh, Yeah, good, he made it after all!"

"Wonderful! He musta been able to trade shifts with one of the other officers." With that, noting that there were no vendors in sight, the old man suggested that he and Alex head up to the beer stand in the concourse.

Carving a path through a sea of boat hats and straw fedoras, they made their way to the beer taps along the back wall of the concrete mezzanine. The area was packed, as lines were already forming for the rest rooms, no doubt reflecting the increased consumption of cold brews in response to the heat.

No sooner were they heading back to the seats with their beers and hot dogs, than they were greeted by Little Brick's old friend, Bob Kane, Chief of Security at Curtiss, who was rushing up from the direction of the turnstiles.

"Hugh, good to catch ya. I figured you were here. Tommy Morton of the Bisons told me you were down behind their dugout."

"I thought you were here already, you being tight with Frank."

"Sure, planned on it, but I was workin' late on that matter you asked me to look into regarding that girl," Kane said, as he looked at Alex and back at his old friend.

"That's all right, Bob. He's in on everything. Bob Kane, Alex Wagner."

After a quick nod of acknowledgement, Kane returned to the matter at hand, "Yeah, I found out a lot the last couple days, and was gonna fill ya in on things after the game, but then I got a call about an hour ago."

"What happened?"

"I got a call from Bud Kowal over at precinct ten, telling me that Peter Meyer killed himself. Did the rope dance."

"What!"

"Yeah, they found him this morning. The brother, his point of contact in his file, he went down to his place after I called him to report Meyer was AWOL, not calling in the last couple days."

"Geez, what the hell could have happened? Here I was wondering how this guy could have fit into Lisa Mangini's case…"

"Well, lemme say there's something to your suspicions about the guy, Hugh."

"How's that," Alex anxiously piped in.

"I've been askin' around about the guy, especially the last couple of days with him bein' out; and I was discreet, and promisin' anonymity knowin' they worked with, or for the guy, but not lettin 'em know what was up. They hadda figure it was just some personnel matter."

"So, what did you hear," the former commissioner asked.

"I gotta tell ya, almost to a man, and especially the ladies, they said he was one weird bird; no real friends; creepy, kinda stalking some of the female workers. He seemed to target little, young looking ladies; sayin' off-color things, personal questions, that sorta stuff. A couple of 'em mentioned another, youthful lookin' gal who got this treatment, and ended up quittin'. And then, there were rumors about him being a little too friendly with girls he coached at his church's youth chorus."

"That's pretty much what we heard from Maureen; except for the girl who quit, Mister Kane."

"And there's more. Now remember, he was an awkward kinda guy, but they told me that lately, he started showin' up dressed to the nines, and talkin' about buyin' a bunch of things. He said a maiden aunt died and left him money. Somebody even heard he bought a fancy new Packard."

"Interesting how this could impact things…" Little Brick mused.

"Especially when you realize he might have been thinking of taking the pipe," Alex wondered out loud.

"Maybe blowing his wad one last time," the old man speculated.

"Of course, I didn't know he was gonna kill himself, but all this got my curiosity goin'. So, last night, after everybody was gone, I picked the lock on his desk."

"One of the tools of the trade," Hugh winked mischievously at Alex.

"And it didn't disappoint. Turns out your suspicions were right. There was definitely something going on with the guy. First, I found a key ring from Kaiser Packard. They don't sell Tin Lizzies over there. So the rumors of a new car might be true, but that ain't half of it. He had some of his workers' personnel folders in his one drawer. One of 'em was for that girl who quit including a news clipping from well after she left, that noted she won a bowling tournament. And right on top was Lisa Mangini's, with some crude comments scribbled on notepaper. I'm pretty sure it wasn't written by Missus Baker, the personnel chief."

"Highly unusual, and probably against company policy for him to have those files in the first place. And it certainly casts a credible light on another possible suspect in Lisa's case, who shows the characteristics of a sexual predator." Costello remarked.

"And adds credence to Jim's claim of innocence," Alex added.

"And if that ain't bad enough, look at these," Kane said as he pulled out a couple envelopes from his pocket and handed one to Hugh.

"Oh my God, he WAS a pedophile," Hugh exclaimed, as he passed the photos to Alex. "Probably girls from the youth chorus and no doubt taken without his knowledge."

"Blackmail!" Alex blurted out.

"Bingo! Yeah, and they were sitting right next to an envelope with two crisp fifty dollar bills, and a note which reads," he said, as he pulled out his reading glasses, "You're late! You did well with the fifty, but I want more, as we discussed. No excuses! Do it or else!"

"Blackmail, indeed." Little Brick agreed.

"The files and now this; certainly seems to be a deviant with a penchant for sex crimes," Alex insisted.

"And we have to get this information to the fellas working Lisa's case, for them to look at Meyer as a possible suspect."

"Assuming they want to reopen a case they think they have nailed down, Mister Costello."

"I'll talk to them and whatever the case, I'll keep digging." Turning towards Kane, he continued, "As you know, Bob, I have a lot at stake with this, considering it could have been Maureen. Not to mention it was her best friend."

"Don't worry, I'll make my pitch too, Hugh. But listen, Bud invited me to go down to Meyer's apartment over on Chester, which I'm taking him up on. I'm sure he won't have a problem with you coming down."

"I hate to leave the family and muck up our plans for a great day, but this is too important to pass on. Yeah, count us in," he said as Alex nodded in agreement. "And by the way, Bob, have you secured all that material in the desk?"

"Musta read my mind, Hugh. It's sitting in my office under lock and key, right now."

With that, Alex and Little Brick returned to their seats just as the Bisons were going into the second half of the opening inning. Already feeling contrite, the old man couldn't hide his feelings as he approached his wife. "Listen, honey, I'm so sorry. I know I promised a wonderful afternoon to be together and enjoy ourselves, but something's come up. I ran into Bob Kane and there's a new development in Lisa's case, and I've been invited to observe."

"Oh, Hugh, we've so looked forward to this. Couldn't it wait, dear?"

"I know, sweetheart, but we know how this has impacted poor Lisa, and of course Maureen, and all of us. And besides, the crime scene is only a couple blocks away, and we'll be back well before the game ends."

"If it involves Lisa, I'm coming too," Maureen insisted.

"But we can't leave Keena alone."

"Danny and Karen can come down and join me. But first, you're sitting down and having your lunch with us. Bob can wait."

Chastened, Hugh finished his hot dog and beer, before taking off with his two young assistants. After jumping into Alex's car, they left a prime parking spot next to the park, and headed to Meyer's residence. Pulling up to the address, a Craftsman, double decker house, they noticed a couple of patrolmen standing outside a garage apartment to the rear. The first officer immediately recognized the police legend, before he had a chance to flash his retired commissioner's shield.

"No need Commish, Captain Kowal said you'd be coming."

"Thanks, and good to see you, Doug. I hear you're getting ready to retire."

"Yeah, right after the new year. Forty years is enough. And who's the civilians?"

"The handsome young fella is Alex Wagner, a reporter, and this beautiful young woman is my granddaughter Maureen, and assistant, who's gonna take notes for this old codger."

"Hardly, sir," Doug smiled. "You look like you could run a marathon! And glad to meet you two."

"You might not wanna go in there, Miss" the other officer interrupted. "It ain't pretty."

"I'll be all right, officer," Maureen shot back, annoyed at being singled out; yet, no sooner had she walked through the door than she had second thoughts. Looking to her right, she was greeted by the sight of a coroner dutifully taking notes, as her boss hung from a rafter, his face discolored and distorted, with a swollen tongue pushing out from his mouth. Adding to the horror was the putrid odor drifting out from the bloated corpse.

Catching sight of his granddaughter, Little Brick was quick to intercede and grab her hand, "Just go upstairs with Alex, and wait with Bob Kane. I'm going to take a couple minutes down here."

The apartment upstairs was if anything, nondescript. The kitchen was equipped with the usual, table, chairs, range and ice-box, while the living room was furnished with a sofa, lounge chair, and coffee table. Sticking out was a brand new, polished rosewood, console radio.

Likewise, the bedroom was nothing out of the ordinary, except scattered throughout the space were a rainbow of dress shirts still in their packaging, unopened boxes of shoes, and a trio of suits, still hanging in their Kleinhans, garment bags.

"Looks like someone was on a spending spree," Alex observed, as a young detective was going through the dresser drawers.

"Yeah, and did ya see the new Packard, and the radio out there. That Zenith hadda cost at least fifty bucks," the investigator quipped as he continued with his search.

Soon, they were joined by Little Brick and Kane, who while his old friend was downstairs, had been looking at the contents of Meyer's bathroom medicine cabinet. Motioning for them to withdraw to the kitchen, in an effort to give the young cop some space, Hugh was eager to share some news. "According to Steve Tanner, the coroner, no evidence of foul play so far, and he said this young detective is sweeping through the place pretty good."

"Yeah, nothing jumped out up here, but quite a collection of goodies," Kane remarked before filling in his old boss about all the purchases.

"Sadly, it is looking like a suicide, all right. Steve shared with me the contents of a note he found in Meyer's shirt pocket. I wrote it down here…" Flipping open his dog eared notepad, the old investigator recited, "'Love my country, my work and my family. I'm sorry, but I can't take it anymore. God will punish lying, evil-doers. Goodbye."

"Tragic and heartbreaking," Maureen sniffled.

"The guy had his problems, but nobody should feel compelled to resort to this. Sad," Alex said.

"Sad indeed," Little Brick concurred. "The evidence here suggests that he died by his own hand. Nonetheless, there still seems to be a crime here that affected his death—extortion!"

"Gramps, those photos you told me about would surely seem to point to blackmail," Maureen agreed.

"And there's that note that would seem to be demanding further payment along with the two fifty dollar bills," Alex added.

"And how did that note go again, Mister Kane? Did you write it down," Maureen asked.

"Actually, I still have it here. I have to give it to the detective before I leave. Now, lemme see… okay, here it is, 'You're late! You did good on the fifty, but I want more, as we discussed. No excuses. Do it or else!'"

"No ambiguity there; extortion The question is who sent it." Little Brick announced.

"Hold on, I just thought of something," Maureen broke-in. "Could I see it, Mister Kane?"

"Sure," he said, as he handed over the note.

"Hey I recognize that paper!" Alex exclaimed as he looked over Maureen's shoulder. "The blue border; they use it at the Sangerbund. Sky blue is the color on the Bavarian flag. Old Mister Mueller, the long-time secretary of the society found it at Ulbrick's Stationers."

"Ulbrick's sells a lot of paper, or do you think that the old club secretary's blackmailing Meyer," Kane grinned, condescendingly.

"Well, at least there's a link to something," the old commissioner interrupted.

"Of course, Mister Mueller isn't involved, but he is always complaining about people constantly coming into his office when he's not there, and snatching office supplies. He complains about the expense."

"Still, it's a reach, and besides that, I don't think the department is gonna waste the man hours chasing this down a rabbit hole. Meyer is dead, and I'm sure the family doesn't want his proclivities being aired."

"I suppose somebody from the Sangerbund could have gotten wind of Meyer's… ah… aberrations, via the competitions or music community scuttlebutt, and decided to squeeze him for some money." Hugh speculated.

"Sure, it's possible; but, like I said, he's dead and besides his family, I gotta believe the families of these girls, his church, and the whole choral community would just as soon like to see this go away, " Kane answered.

"But what if we're missing something. What if there's something more to this; something more complicated," Maureen interjected.

"What do you mean?" Alex asked.

"Here, let's take a look at that note again. See, I noticed that there seems to be a little dot before the fifty numeral."

Leaning over, Kane observed, "I dunno. I can hardly see it. Could be a random mark on the paper. Or are you sayin' they were squeezin' him for fifty cents," he chuckled.

Ignoring his sarcasm, she responded, "No, not cents, caliber."

"A firearm? How's that?"

"Listen, a fifty caliber machine gun is the main weapon on the Hawk fighter plane. I should know, I work on that line, and Meyer, my boss, was an assistant engineer on the project."

"Sure, industrial espionage," Alex observed, "bribing him for information and blackmailing him for more. Could even be a foreign..."

"Jesus, Maureen," Kane interrupted, "that's classified information you can't..."

"Bob, come on. It's my granddaughter, for God's sake. She's responsible, and besides, you've known her all her life."

"I know, I know, Hugh. But you just can't blurt out stuff like that, people can misinterpret..."

"But he seems like an easy mark, and what if somebody wanted information about the Hawk..." Alex offered.

"Christ, you can't just bandy around terms like industrial espionage," Kane once more interrupted. "This is just a straight-out, sex crime case, closed-out with a suicide. Listen, this is my bailiwick, plant security. It would never happen on my watch."

"Of course not, Bob," Little Brick was quick to intervene.

"But what about..." Alex insisted.

"Listen, we know this fella, Meyer is a sex criminal, even taking his own life over it. And I'll talk to the boys workin' on Lisa's case. This new information will help, at least until she regains consciousness," Hugh stated.

"But... But..." Maureen stammered.

"But we learned a lot today. Our work here is done," the old cop observed.

"I'm glad, Hugh," Kane replied, happy to put to rest any talk of a security breech at Curtiss.

With that, the little party exchanged farewells with Kane before walking back to Alex's car.

Once away from the building, Hugh turned to the young couple.

"I know you're confused, but I'm with you on your thinking. I just didn't want us to get into a pissing match about espionage with Bob. He's an old friend, but he's ambitious, and loves all the amenities of his position. He's got his dream job, and he doesn't want anything mucking it up. Let's get our ducks in order before he gets wind of it and tries to undercut our suspicions."

"Yeah, and maybe we were looking at it backwards. Maybe Meyer was being bribed for information on the Hawk; and then, blackmailed for more. He was being sucked in, deeper and deeper over his actions. The photos were a coercive tool for his cooperation." Alex offered.

"That would explain all the goodies up there—and the car," Maureen added.

"Right off the bat, that was suspicious. I don't buy into that inheritance business," Little Brick said.

"That suicide note. Didn't you find that oddly worded," Alex suggested.

"Bringing up loving his country—in a suicide note. That's weird. And then 'evil liars.' What could that be all about?" Maureen said.

"Perhaps at first, he was told he was selling information to a business rival. Then, he finds out it's a foreign government. That's a whole different ballgame."

"Like Germany!" Maureen exclaimed.

"Interesting. They lied to him. And when he tries to end it, they were already aware of the skeleton in his closet," Little Brick mused.

"Like someone in the choral community who knew the gossip about this guy, and arranged a little photo shoot that would insure his further cooperation. Like someone at the Sangerbund with its blue bordered stationary," Alex brought up.

"Like Britta," Maureen stated.

"And her friends from the camp included a musician—maybe a singer. And remember, according to my brother Freddie, her boyfriend

Krueger, who he knows from the Turners, made his living taking children's pictures …"

"…and could be the source of the photos of Pete with a young singer," Little Brick observed.

"Right! And speaking of whom, as you suggested, I checked with Captain Duggan about Krueger. He told me he was a wheelman and some-time strong-arm for a rumrunner named Mitch Murphy."

"Ah, well that adds credence to our suspicions about Krueger," the old man nodded

"Speaking of photos," Maureen broke in, "a few weeks back—I remember it was the day before an Army inspection—Lisa and I were working a night shift on the Hawk line, when she spotted a face up in a skylight—maybe with a camera. She swore to it, and I believed her. Plus, I saw a fresh chunk of glazing lying on the floor that she insisted was dislodged by whoever was up there. A couple other workers saw the caulk too. When Meyer saw the hubbub, he came out, but pooh-poohed our concerns. At the time, Lisa and I figured it was a company spy looking for union activity. Until now, I didn't make much of it, but knowing all this, maybe it was someone taking pictures of the Hawk."

"It fits into what we've learned," Alex said.

"And Alex, that fella at Barnstormers who had a crush on Britta and worked at the Curtiss test hangar in the airpark. You said he was kinda a hanger-on to the chief test pilot for the company," Little Brick said

"Sure did! He told me him 'n her used to talk about planes all the time, and he bragged to me that he knew all the inside details on the plane ·I bet he tried to impress her with what he knew, and in light of this, I'm sure she was more than happy to hear all about it."

"And don't forget, those bums who were harassing Jim and Lisa the night at Richardson's, Didn't Jim tell you that he thought one of them might have part of the gang that attacked Bloom's' news shanty." Maureen said.

"Yeah, a big bald guy who instigated the fight at Richardson's, and threw a punch at Jim."

"I'll continue to address these things with my contacts on the force. Maybe, this new information could affect Jim's status, and proper justice for Lisa."

"Maureen, can you dig around at the factory—discreetly of course—to see if Meyer was requesting blue prints, plans, or even test reports that normally, he might not need." Alex asked.

"You have to be careful, honey, this is a sensitive subject," Little Brick cautioned.

"Don't worry, I have a friend in the blueprint office, and I'm pals with a secretary down at the airpark test facility. I'll just make small talk about whether Meyer spoke with them lately, and take it from there."

"Well, we discovered a lot today: mainly that Meyer was a sexual criminal, who could be a suspect in Lisa's attack. And the circumstances surrounding his death suggest the possibility of blackmail, and this blackmail could involve industrial espionage, perhaps even involving a foreign country."

"Indeed, Gramps!"

"And I would add," Alex continued, "in looking at all this, there could be a possible link to a local group of Nazi sympathizers—a fifth column! This group could be the same one that attacked Bloom, including that big bald guy who keeps popping up, and that fella with the scar, who may have been one of the Nazis that Marsha ID'd at Camp Reichsadler, and who Jim said was at the Hobo camp trying to stir things up, in the company of the KKK. They may be behind all this pamphleteering, too. And remember, those flyers on Lisa's attack were out before most of the papers."

"And don't forget the beige Chrysler that keeps showing up and could link these people together," Maureen added.

"We have more work to do on this, including our duty to inform the proper authorities about what we know."

"Sounds good, Mister Costello."

"So, I think it's time for me and my two, crime-fighting associates to head back to the ball park and enjoy what's left of the game with my beautiful bride."

XVIII

Franklin Roosevelt stared down with a capable and confident look from his perch upon the office wall.

As he gazed at the official portrait, it struck Alex that those same qualities, as reflected in the man's face, helped propel him to a resounding victory four years earlier, and would again help send him to an even greater landslide later this fall.

What he didn't understand, was why the President's picture was relegated to an obscure spot outside the office doors of the Special Agent-in-Charge of the Buffalo Field Office, for the newly re-christened Federal Bureau of Investigation. Adding to Alex's sense of irony was the fact that the President himself had cut the ribbon for the WPA-constructed Federal Courthouse earlier in the year. His curiosity was quickly answered in the form of a booming voice that roused him from his musings.

"Such an impressive looking man turns out to be a raging Bolshevik, huh…"

"Actually, I'm impressed enough to vote for him again," Alex shot back as he stood up with Mister Costello to exchange greetings with the local law enforcement bigwig.

"Ah, just joking. He's my boss after all," he said, as he waved them towards his office, before adding with a chuckle, "but did ya notice he's facing left!"

Although stunned by the disrespect displayed by the agent, Alex wasn't surprised given the heads-up he had received from Mister Costello.

Donald Perry was the third generation member of a family steeped in police work, and Little Brick was familiar with all three. 'Spit'n Polish 'Perry, the family's late patriarch, and a stickler for detail as his nickname would suggest, had ascended the career ladder to a Captaincy thanks to an unwavering history of kissing superiors' asses. Donald's father and namesake followed a similar trajectory, devoting all his efforts to performing tedious administrative tasks that were shunned by his bosses, at the expense of doing actual, hands-on police work. For his part, the youngest Perry managed to parley a lackluster crime fighting record into his current position, due to his willingness to perform all manner of favors for his political overlords.

After ushering them past his secretary, whose gum chewing seemed to compete with the speed of her typing, he swung open the door and welcomed them into a spacious chamber that overlooked the city's downtown hub, Niagara Square.

Grabbing a cigar from his desktop humidor, he asked his guests to take a seat before sliding into his plump leather chair. Aware of his forebears' resentment of Little Brick's legendary renown, he was determined to fully display the trappings of his office.

He was also eager to show who was now in charge. After scanning the contents of a report on his desk, he turned to his guests, "I got three bank robberies in two days. Christ, everybody wants to be Baby Face Nelson, but listen, knowin' your long-time police service, I wanna squeeze you in as best I can, Commissioner."

"Thanks, Agent Perry, I know how valuable your time is," he said as he noticed some nearby golf balls, and a putter leaning against the office fireplace.

"So, I'm told you have suspicions about some spy business that might be going around in these parts."

"Possible espionage. As I explained to your assistant on the phone, in the course of my inquiry involving the case of my granddaughter's friend, who was attacked outside the Richardson Hotel, I discovered her boss at Curtiss could be a person of interest…"

"Yeah, a pervert of some sort…"

"A possible sex criminal, but that's not why we're here, as you know. I discovered it was highly probable that he was being blackmailed, with photos and a note demanding cooperation. That, and a sudden increase in his finances and personal consumption, along with suspicious content in his suicide note, point to the possibility of his being extorted for classified information available to him in his job as an engineer—perhaps at the direction a foreign power."

"Right, right, Agent Guthrie filled me in on all that. On the surface, that sounds interesting; but being blackmailed and ending up with more money… I don't know about that. As for the suicide note and the note appearing to demand cooperation, they can be interpreted in all sorts of ways. And when it comes to his finances, maybe he came into some money or bought stuff on time for one last splurge before taking the pipe. Listen, as I see it, at worst, he's a pervert being squeezed. All that other stuff is a stretch. Simple extortion, a local matter."

"But the totality of all these pieces, and given the national security implications, I believe this deserves further scrutiny…"

"Believe me, with all due respect, national security has long been part of my duties…"

"I didn't mean to suggest, I know more…"

"And I know someone at Curtiss," Alex broke in, "who says they spotted someone observing the Hawk production line, and maybe taking pictures from a skylight one night."

"And who are you again?"

"Alex Wagner, as I said, a friend of Mister Costello, and a reporter for the *Advocate*."

"Well, Mister Wagner of the *Advocate*, I should remind you that the military equipment in question is classified, and any conversation you had about that with employees could put you in a jam."

"This was a confidential journalistic source, and as such, is protected under the First Amendment."

"Don, I don't think Alex had any intention of accessing sensitive..."

"No, no, I get it, and I don't wanna press the issue. So, let's get right to the meat of the matter. After Guthrie filled me in on all this, including spies in skylights, I contacted Bob Kane, who as we know, is the Chief of Security at Curtiss. Bob insisted there was nothing to this; that with the security measures they have in place, this spying story could never happen. It was nothing more than a tragic incident where an employee took his life due to personal problems outside of work."

"Still, there seems to be links to a subversive group or groups that are active in the area. There's incendiary flyers. There's attacks on Jews and Negroes. There's a witness who believes he saw a Nazi who attacked a Jewish news vendor, in the company of Meyer that night at Richardson's," Alex replied.

"And as the Commissioner told Guthrie, that witness is currently cooling his black ass in jail over the attack on the White girl. Hardly credible. As for the Nazi activists goose-steppin' around, they're no real threat. And don't forget those first amendment free-speech rights, and if they attacked people, that's assault, once again, a local police matter."

"We have knowledge, " Alex continued, "that a couple of those activists—let's call 'em what they are, gang members—they knew about Meyer's issues with young girls, via their involvement with the local choral community."

"Hell, a lotta folks hadda know about his perversions. And then there's guilt by association, through that German Sangerbund society or whatever? Do you hear yourself, 'Herr' Wagner? I've got the responsibility to insure that we don't have a repeat of bigotry against Germans Americans, like during the War."

"It's not bias, it's just a matter of motive and opportunity," Little Brick added.

"And one of those gang members is a former barmaid who used to pump information on military aircraft from a Curtiss employee at their airpark test facility, when she worked at Barnstormers," Alex added.

"Come on, if talking about airplanes at that gin mill was grounds for suspicion, we'd be haulin' in half the patrons over there."

"And we have a witness who saw this same woman taking part in some Nazi ceremony with four or five others at a remote site in Camp Reichsadler. And I can identify an individual who attacked the Jewish-owned newsstand that the Commissioner told your assistant about. This individual was also seen with the Nazi group at Reichsadler by the witness," Alex pressed on.

"And once again remember, guilt by association, but even if it did happen, sounds to me like a handful of crackpots dressin' up like Hitler. Harmless!"

"Unless they're dangerous and, unless they're being directed by a foreign power," Little Brick insisted.

Pausing to think as he slowly rolled his cigar and tapped the tip into the ashtray at his side, he sat up and announced, "Listen, these crazy Nazis are small potatoes. With all that had happened in the War, they ain't gonna catch-on here; and it's gonna blow itself out over there. So, I'm not gonna waste my valuable resources chasing phantom threats."

"There were hundreds of Bundists at the Statler, and I'm pretty sure the Nazis 'over there' are in it for the long term," Alex shot back.

"Don't just listen to me, take it from my boss, J. Edgar Hoover, who famously took out Dillinger..."

"I read that Chicago Agent Melvin Purvis took him out in that shoot-out at the Biograph Theater," Alex was quick to reply.

"Don't believe everything you read. The Director planned the whole operation based on scientific crime-fighting. Gangsters pay-off corrupt reporters to tarnish his reputation, because he's leading a successful war against the underworld."

"I would hope that he wants to exert the same kind of effort against foreign enemies."

"Listen, Commissioner, the Director knows who the real threats to this country are. And it isn't that tin-pot dictator or his tiny number of sympathizers here. Mister Hoover realizes, and I certainly agree, that the real enemy is Communism. They've infiltrated the unions, they're all over college campuses, and they're doin' all they can to rile up all those nig… ah, Negroes into an uprising through that Bolshevik cover group, the N, double A, C-P. And between you and me, a lot of those New Dealers are secret Communists. Throw in Hollywood, and all the Je… ah, and, especially that Red traitor, Charlie Chaplin, and you got big trouble. Believe me, they're all working to subvert this country from within, and impose a godless, socialist regime, unless we're vigilant and willing to fight for our way of life. And you can take it to the bank that the FBI is gonna root 'em out, and destroy their movement."

"That 'tin-pot' dictator is rapidly re-arming in violation of the Versailles treaty; and wouldn't he want a Berlin-directed, fifth column group of sympathizers over here, collecting sensitive military information that could help his build-up?" The old cop asked in reply.

"Like I said, Nazism has no legs here, and lemme tell ya, Hitler is in no position to match or threaten us. Those Krauts, are still pickin' themselves up after the ass kickin' we gave 'em in the War, and besides, our powerhouse military suppliers like Curtiss aren't stupid. They have great systems in place that prevent any possibility of spying. So, I'm not gonna go chasin' down your theories."

After listening to the agent's long-winded pronouncements, Little Brick saw the handwriting on the wall, and realized any further discussion was a waste of time. As such, he knew that he and Alex were largely on their own when it came to help from Perry's Office.

"Well, I hope you keep in mind what we told you, and we'll certainly forward to you any pertinent information that could change your mind, if we become aware of it."

"Good, and I know that I don't have to remind you about usurping proper authorities."

"Well, I'm going to continue with my series on Bund-related activities, and I'm well aware of my responsibilities," Alex shot back.

"And I'll continue to advise him, along with keeping in touch with the Department regarding Nazi gang activities," Hugh said, unwilling to acknowledge Perry's reminder.

"That's fine, and if by chance you find anything, feel free to contact this office."

"Well, thank you for your time," Hugh replied, curtly.

"Listen, I can't justify pursuing this, but as a professional courtesy to you and knowing your connection to my family, " he said as a sop to the old man, "I'll assign one of my boys, a new agent, B. J. Higgins, fresh outta college and from your neck of the woods. He'll be available to help you, if he thinks you're on to something."

Recognizing the gesture for what it was, little more than a toothless, condescending offer of support in the form of the most junior agent in the field office, the old cop refused to take the bait. "Thanks, Don. I know the family. I'm sure he's a fine young man," Little Brick smiled,

With that, they bid their adieus as the meeting broke-up; but not before Perry offered each of them one of his prized cigars, along with his business card, which contained more gold leaf than an Eastern icon.

No sooner had they left the suite of offices than Alex turned to the old man, "Not much there, huh! Lowest man on the totem pole. That is, if the kid deigns to hear us. What a joke."

"Judging from the top banana, we could've done worse," Hugh chuckled. "Besides, the greatest cop I've ever known, took a chance on me when I was starting out. So, you never know. His grandfather's a former fireman, and one of the finest men I know. Let's hope the apple doesn't fall far from the tree. Anyway, as I told you earlier, I wasn't expecting much, but we'll keep digging around. We still have Captain Duggan of the Gang Squad, and my other connections with the law enforcement community."

"Yeah, but this spying thing, that's Federal territory."

"Sure the FBI is the lead, but there's others who may be interested, particularly, the War Department. I may know someone who has connections to army intelligence."

"You know, besides my series and the case of Lisa and Jim, I really believe there's something to this spy story, and we've got an obligation, a duty on that."

"I'm glad you feel that way, Alex. It's how I feel too," the old cop smiled, as he slapped his young partner on the back, and headed towards the stairs.

XIX

$\mathbf{T}$he screams of riders faded in and out, as the roller coaster cars raced along the twisting wooden tracks that hugged Canada's Lake Erie shoreline. By now, as the sun made its descent, a pageant of multi-colored lights began to cast their glow, while the park's carousel calliope piped out melodies that filled the air.

Meanwhile, as two seagulls jousted over a discarded French fry, Alex and Maureen made their way down the busy Crystal Beach pier. The couple were heading toward the SS Canadiana, docked at the end of the promenade, where the excursion ship was boarding passengers eager for a moonlight dance cruise back to Buffalo. Strolling beneath a string of lights, Maureen redirected their path to a railing that looked out over the vast amusement park. Down below, the last of the beach goers were packing up their belongings. Across the seawall, a long line of music fans were filing into the Crystal Ballroom, which on this night, was featuring the premier Canadian swing band, The Harlem Dukes. With nearly forty minutes to kill before departure, they took time to enjoy the scenery.

"Everything seems even more exciting, once the lights come on."

"And pretty, with all the colors and the warm glow," she said, as she snuggled closer.

"Speaking of a warm glow, I hope you can stop at my place once we get back."

"Well, I do like your apartment," she smiled with a hint of blush and a wink.

"That's great! I'd love to have you over," he said as he smiled and returned the wink. "And ya know, looking out over this beautiful scene, I realize how much I love every minute with you."

"Back at you! And I want to drink in every one of these moments."

"We'll have a lot of wonderful times, I promise," he said as he drew her into a long kiss.

"Wonderful indeed," she whispered with another kiss. "And I want to make sure we seize every moment," she smiled, before pausing, "…because from a young age, I've been aware how quickly things can be taken away. And Lisa's been a reminder of that."

"Yeah, that's been so hard on you. Thank God she's out of the coma and appears to be on the road to recovery."

"Like I told you, I cried with joy when they said she could speak, move her limbs, and thank God, seems to have all her mental faculties."

"That's good news for sure!"

"God, I miss my pal so much! I want her all fixed up and back to her old self as soon as possible!"

"You said she's responding to physical therapy well, but she still doesn't remember that night?"

"I suppose it spares her in some way, but it's unfortunate for Jim."

"Yeah, I know."

"Still, the doctors think that should come back, too, with time."

"She sure is feisty and has pluck!"

"Yeah, that should serve her well, along with the love and support of family and friends"

"At times like this, you realize how important that is. And that goes for Jim as well. Rest assured I'm gonna do all I can to make sure he gets justice."

"So what's happening with finding him a better lawyer?"

"Well, I had dinner with Dad last night, and asked if our family's attorney could take a look at things, but he put the kibosh to that pretty quick…"

"But I thought he liked Jim and his work?"

"He does, and he believes in my take on the case, but he was adamant in saying he doesn't want our family or company publicly associated with such an explosive case."

"That's too bad, but…"

"I know. He's coming from a different place than you or me; but listen, he did say that behind the scenes he'll ask a lawyer friend to find, as he put it: 'some left-wing, Jewish lawyer, or a good colored attorney to take the case'—and he'll pay for it."

"Well I hope it works for Jim. I suppose it may be better than some high-priced, snooty lawyer, who doesn't care. He needs somebody who's committed!"

"Don't worry, I'm all in on Jim, and I'm gonna keep diggin' on this Nazi series. And your grandfather is on board on all this, too. That's invaluable!"

"I'm really glad you're working with Gramps. It's invigorated him—as if he needs it," she chuckled. "And I'm so proud of your reporting. You have a real gift for that."

"Thanks. You know, with all that's been happening lately, it's really focused my attention on what's important to me, my dreams, my vision for the future, which I hope includes you of course"

"Same here," she smiled back.

"And you know, up to now, I've been able to take things for granted … "

"But you're certainly not spoiled. Your parents raised a good son in my opinion."

"Thanks, and they're great, but my family and all that that entails—connections, safety net, or whatever—are always there. I've always looked at things through the lens of my family. Don't get me wrong, I'm blessed with that, but most people, like Bloom, or Jim or Lisa don't have those luxuries. They could never take so many things for granted, test so many jobs, and always have that safety net, like me. They have a lot of struggles just to get by."

"But it seems to me that you're beginning to carve out your own path."

"Yeah, and I really like what I'm doing, and I like being out there, depending on myself. You know, like paying the bills, maintaining my place."

"So, do you think you have a better idea on what you want for a career?"

"This series has been a turning point and eye-opener for me. I want to get to the truth of things. And I think whatever that truth is, it's important to people. It can help them understand things a little better, as these things affect their lives."

"Lofty ideals! So, do you think journalism is what you want to pursue?"

"Ideals, I don't know, there's enough room in life to get jaded, judging from what I've seen. Still, I think it might offer me a chance to feel good about what I do, which is what I want—along with paying the bills," he chuckled. "Or maybe, I could publish my own paper, or get into radio, like Walter Winchell. You can always dream!"

"Why not, you're so talented!"

"Thanks again. And then there's the law. Lately, I've come to realize justice is fragile, or for some people, always outside their grasp. It might be interesting working in the legal system."

"Maybe you could do both, write for the paper while going to law school."

"Or clerk, reading the law at some law firm to pass the bar. I know lawyers who could sponsor me. In any case, I want to do it myself, like you, working at the factory to set yourself up. I admire that about you."

"Like I told you, I really love my job at Curtiss, but I don't look at it as a career. I know some of my snooty classmates think it's beneath college grads to work in a plant, but that's phony elitism and just plain ignorant. I work with some great people, use skills, and contribute to society… "

"Which you should be proud of," he smiled.

"I am, and I make pretty good money, better than what a lot of those wannabe snobs make. But, I still want to teach; maybe go back to school part time and work my way up to teaching at a college, or administration."

"You can do anything, in my book!"

"I'm going to shoot high, no small thanks to my grandparents who besides loving us, made sure we were strong. I'm not going to be held back by what society thinks are traditional roles for women. I'm convinced education is the way to change things. Lately, seeing those Bund types and that gang, reminds me that education can help prevent that sort of hatred."

"That's why I admire you," he smiled. "The most important thing I learned this summer is what a remarkable woman you are, and how crazy I am about you."

"I know the feeling," she smiled back. "And today was so typical of our time together."

"I don't know what I enjoyed more, the rides or the arcade games; which reminds me, you're quite the sharpshooter. "

"Had to be the sugar waffles and the butterscotch suckers. But listen, you must have a spell on me, getting me on the 'Cyclone' three times."

"But the topper was kickin' off our shoes and walking along the beach…"

"Romantic, alone time is always good with you; but, say, did you notice those two creepy gawkers who were ogling me. Didn't get a good look, with them standin' a bit away; but a girl can feel those eyes. Yuk, older, and dressed weird, not for the beach!"

"What?'

"I figure you didn't, so I didn't want to tell you, knowing you would've told 'em off. Besides, I glared at them, and they slithered outta there. So, no big deal."

"My hero," he smiled.

"Well, I'm sure having my six foot three boyfriend next to me, tipped the scale."

"Goes to show nothing can ruin a day like today; and we still have our moonlight cruise."

"Yeah, and I can't wait to dance. It's been a wait. I couldn't even think of it while Lisa's condition was bad."

"Well, I'm gonna dazzle my sweetheart with some fancy footwork tonight."

Just then, a blast from the horn signaled that the cruise ship would be departing in twenty minutes. Eager to find a spot alongside the port-side rail of the ballroom deck, they headed down the pier towards the gangway.

Upon passing their tickets to the agent, they hurried up the carved oak staircase leading to the second deck. No sooner had the pair arrived, than they were greeted by three of Maureen's friends from her high school alma mater, Mount Mercy Academy. After a round of excited gasps over their chance encounter, the classmates settled into catching up on the latest news. For her part, Maureen lost little time in introducing her handsome boyfriend, while he was quick to take drink orders from the ladies.

Down below, crew members were finished lifting anchor. Then, with a blast of its horn, the ship slipped its moorings, and steamed out to open waters. Almost on cue, the chief steward jumped on stage and rattled off the safety instructions before introducing the evening's emcee.

Just as Alex arrived at the starboard side, he spotted his friend Sid Cohen's younger brother Lou, who was there with some of his old high school pals. After quick greetings and the usual small talk, he invited them to join his party. Eager for female company, they were quick to accept.

By now, the emcee had introduced the band, who launched into their opening number of the Albert Ammons hit, "Boogie Woogie Stomp."

With the help of his new friends, Alex grabbed his order and slowly carved his way through the twisting bodies on the dance floor. Yet, unbeknownst to him at that moment, he was being closely watched from among a throng near the stage.

By now, the crowd on the ballroom deck was alive with excitement. On the other hand, Braun and his crew were equally enthused, but for vastly different reasons. The gang's presence on this night, was no mere coincidence. For some time, they were aware that this date had been designated "Bennett High School Alumni Day" at the amusement park. They were also aware that many of the school's alumni were Jews. With that in mind, Braun saw a golden opportunity to incite an anti-Semitic incident. As he surveyed the scene, he felt a rush of pride in having devised such a scheme; yet, that was only half of it. Earlier that day, he spotted Alex and Maureen at the park, and ordered Kurt and Eric to keep an eye on them—at a distance of course. Now, seeing them onboard, he recognized the chance to finally exact revenge on his nemesis. Calling over Kurt and Eric, he quickly hatched a plot to square accounts with the couple.

While eager to set his plans in motion, Braun knew that timing was critical. As such, he was content to sit back and wait, despite his disdain for the music, and for what he saw as a largely Aryan crowd that seemed intent on rejecting their blood and culture.

As he waited, Braun reflected on his gang's successes. With a sense of pride, he went over a roll-call of actions that he believed mirrored the bold maneuvers of his idol, Hitler. Whether it was the beating of Blacks or vandalism of Jewish businesses, all were intended to proclaim a Nazi presence in the Buffalo area.

Still, their crowning achievement was gathering intelligence on the Curtiss fighter. And despite the suicide of the principal source, they amassed information that no doubt would prove to be invaluable.

They were now close to forwarding these findings to the Abwehr in Berlin, where they would be viewed as heroes—and, he would make damn sure that was the case.

Meanwhile, Alex and Maureen's friends had melded into one happy group. Couples were soon competing with dance moves, and vying for the chance to buy more drinks.

"Katie seems taken with your friend Lou," Maureen whispered as they waltzed to the Fred Astaire hit, 'The Way You Look Tonight.'"

"Maybe, but can't you women just enjoy the fun we're having, without playing matchmaker," Alex chuckled.

"I know, and that's how I usually feel, but Katie's such a good friend. I want her to find someone, like with you and me, or like Fred and Ginger in the movies," she smiled.

"That's right, 'Swing Time.' I remember you crying when he serenaded her while she was washing her hair. I was touched."

"Well, it was so romantic."

"No, I wasn't teasing, I was truly touched, and not just by the scene, but by you. You're not just beautiful, and smart, but you're sweet, kind and romantic, too."

"Now who's being sweet," she blushed.

"It's easy with you," he whispered as he glided her into a dip at the end of the song.

"I'd say we're getting pretty good at this, among other things," she sighed as she pulled his face closer and planted a kiss.

Just then, the band struck up the opening chords of Eddie Duchin's "Moon Over Miami."

"Speaking about romantic moons, whaddah say we sneak away for a little alone time," Alex suggested.

"Just what I was thinking. We can't waste that beautiful moon shimmering on the water."

Taking each other's hand, they slowly strolled along the deck rail to a secluded spot near the stern.

"You know, being out here tonight, being with you, having my life, I just feel so blessed!"

"Likewise! And that's another thing I love about you. You have wonderful values, and a beautiful faith."

"Why thank you, Alex," she sighed as she placed her hand bedside his face. "That means so much coming from you. My faith is a central part of my life, and I try to live it by my actions."

"And I hope that you can see those things in me."

"Indeed I do, and I love it."

"My turn to feel loved and thankful," he smiled. "As you know, my beliefs are important to me, but I suppose I keep it low key. I don't like it when people are too aggressive in pushing their religion, or more importantly, forcing it on others. That's not religious freedom. That's religious bullying, religious tyranny."

"I suppose if anyone asked, I'd be happy to say my Catholic faith brings joy, comfort and meaning to my life. Fortunately, my parents and grandparents helped teach me my faith, but they also taught me to be open, tolerant and respectful of others; that we don't have a monopoly on truth."

"Otherwise, when you think your way is the only way, that's when things can get corrupted—like with the Nazis."

"You're right! It's like a religion for them, the way they worship that… that despicable man, Hitler, and his toxic beliefs. An evil cult!"

"We've seen how that works, with our own eyes!"

"That's why I think education is so important. When I got to State Teachers, it really opened my world, even more."

"Yeah, when I got to college, like you, I started to see things differently."

"Funny how that works: you learn more, question more, and then you start to figure out answers."

"When I was younger, I just assumed I was going to meet a nice German girl, work in the family business, and settle into an appropriately big house among our people. But that's all changed now."

"I hope you have some of that out of your system," she giggled before adding, "Still, I know it's important to love one's family and honor one's roots, but one can't let that hem in your life, or close your mind to other things, and especially other people."

"And then, there's the last couple months. On the one hand, like I mentioned earlier, I've learned a lot from people who didn't have the breaks I had. But on the other hand, I've come to realize how engrained and accepted some toxic beliefs are, as with those Nazis we've run into."

"And that can lead people to do horrible things; but listen, forgive me for steering us away from this beautiful scenery. So let's get back to what we came here for."

"That's fine, I like it. But enough philosophizing and solving society's problems. Let's bask in the moment. I just want to gaze into those twinkling, Irish blue eyes of yours."

"Back at ya, and once again, who's the romantic one, Mister Wagner," she breathed deeply, as she drew him closer.

Over the next ninety minutes, the couple would shift between joining their friends, hitting the dance floor, or sneaking off for a private moment at their spot along the rail; yet all the while, they were constantly under the scrutiny of probing eyes.

Eventually, the city light grew brighter, as the ship neared its destination. Soon, out of the darkness, one could make out the first glimmer of harbor lights, signaling the approach to the port. Having made the trip a number of times in preparation for this night, Braun knew how much time was left before they reached the pier. With that, the ringleader made his move.

As the music blared in the background, Braun sent Kurt and Eric on their mission. Afterwards, he dispatched the others, Hans, Britta, and Martin, towards a small group of Jewish men standing near the other end of the stage.

Once the incendiaries inched their way next to their targets, Britta let out a hair-raising scream, "You grabbed me!" Martin followed with, "I saw that, you fuckin' k**e," before Krueger launched a haymaker at one of the stunned Jews.

As Britta continued to cry for help, a trio of off-duty firemen rushed towards the bogus victim, while a group of Jewish classmates sped to the aid of their friends, now fully under attack. Soon, the dance floor was transformed into a roiling mass of bedlam.

Meanwhile, Kurt and Eric waited at the stern of the ship, watching as the chaos exploded. When it did, Alex instructed the ladies to stand back, before rushing forward in a vain attempt to restrain his Jewish friends; yet, no sooner had he reached the scene of the action, than he spotted Krueger grab Lou's friend from behind and hammer him to the ground.

Seeing their opening as passengers raced about in panic, Kurt and Eric headed straight towards their prey, who seeking refuge, was pressed against the promenade railing alongside her friends. Just as he passed the frightened women, Kurt let loose a powerful heave that sent Maureen skyward. It was only through the quick action of her friend Molly, a one-time Captain of Mercy's basketball team, that prevented disaster. Reaching out, she grabbed her, before she tumbled into the churning waters below.

Unable to move forward, Alex turned back only to see what happened to Maureen. After fighting through the crowd, he pulled her into his arms, and tried to comfort her as best he could. At the same time, two of her girlfriends were screaming out to stop the fleeing attackers, but to no avail, as the pair had blended into the mayhem.

In an effort to restore order, the crew had sealed off the stairs, but not before the Nazis had fled to the safety of the main deck, where they had secured a state room a week earlier. With the music shut down, guards began the arduous task of separating combatants, blind to the fact that the instigators were long gone. Aware of the melee down below, the Canadiana's Captain radioed ahead for police support. Losing no time, he steamed towards the dock where, a lone squad car had been dispatched for its arrival.

Satisfied that peace had been restored, security allowed passengers to begin the process of filing out in an orderly fashion. Instead, chaos once more prevailed, as people rushed forward. Engulfed by a surging tide that seemed to carry them down the grand staircase, Alex desperately fought to catch sight of Maureen's assailants. After frantically scanning the crowd as he approached the main deck, he spotted the bald-headed man who attacked her. He was in the company of Krueger, Britta, and the scarred attacker of Jake Bloom. Finally, he recognized Braun, the machinist from Alpine, who was on the Curtiss tour, along with the fat man who fled Maureen's attack. He instantly knew this was the gang he'd been chasing. Turning, he pointed out the group to Maureen, who quickly confirmed his belief. Likewise, his friend Lou, who had made his way back, confirmed that the man matching Krueger, was the instigator of the fight; however, separated by a mass of bodies, Alex knew any attempt to move forward was virtually impossible. Still, he hoped he could grab one of the gang's stragglers.

Anxious to avoid disaster as the crowd pushed forward, stewards dropped the gangways the moment the last of the mooring lines were secured. They were barely able to unhook the gates before the surging throng spilled through. Soon, mobs of people were scattering past the two policemen awkwardly standing vigil.

Despite fighting his way through the crowd, no sooner had Alex reached land, than he realized any hope for capture was doomed. He watched helplessly as the gang scrambled into their getaway car, parked conveniently at the front of the lot. From there, they sped toward the exit, but were stymied by some cars waiting at the light. Seeing an opening, Alex turned back towards the cops.

"Hey, officers, see that beige Chrysler, n, one, four, eight, eight, they're the ones who started that riot on board, and…"

"Hold it. So, how many of these fine citizens do you want me plow through, to get to those arch criminals, ya think ya saw," he smirked, as the getaway car shot through the light.

Despite the rebuff and escape, Alex realized he may have cracked the case. Knowing this, he rushed back to meet Maureen. Although excited at the prospect of romance at his place, he was just as eager to get back to her house, and share these developments with the old man.

XX

By now, most of the workers had left the friendly confines of the Swannie Tavern for their homes in the First Ward neighborhood that bordered Buffalo's waterfront. What remained were a smattering of cops, reporters and lawyers who frequented what was still an Irish barroom oasis. For decades, it was a favorite haunt of dockside workingmen who soothed their dust-clogged throats with an array of local beers, and quenched their appetites on a menu featuring daily fish fries and the "Beef-on-Weck," Buffalo's signature sandwich, consisting of carved layers of meat, piled high onto a kosher salt, and caraway-seeded roll.

The old man sat at a table looking out toward a scene of bustling, industrial energy. Yards away, scores of "scoopers," armed with their ubiquitous shovels, rushed about the flood-lit deck of a lake freighter, off-loading its cargo of grain onto elevators feeding one of the massive silos of the General Mills plant.

Hugh Costello was in the company of his long time police comrade, Captain Kevin Duggan, awaiting the arrival of Alex Wagner and his granddaughter, Maureen. No sooner had he seen Alex's car pulling into a spot alongside the slip housing the fireboat, Gratton, than he was greeted by a youthful voice coming from behind his shoulder.

"Commissioner Costello, my grandfather told me you wanted to see me."

"I called your office, but the secretary said you were out."

"Yes, Agent-in-Charge Perry had me running errands all day, important ones," the fledgling agent added sheepishly.

"It's an official matter, Agent Higgins. Your boss said I could call on you if needed. Did he mention that to you?"

"Yes, he did mention it… but… ah…" he stumbled, as he eyed Duggan suspiciously.

"That's all right, Agent, Captain Duggan is a trusted associate of mine."

"And I'm friends with your granddad too," Duggan broke in.

"Of course, sir, but between you and me, since you're both friends with grandpa, Agent Perry told me not to let it interfere with my other duties."

"That's all right, son, this is important business, and we want someone from your office involved. If need be, I'll take it up with Agent Perry," Duggan said with an air of reassurance.

Suddenly, the door swung open as Alex and Maureen came in, along with the din of the industrial clatter from outside. After a quick round of introductions, Little Brick cut to the chase, "If you haven't already heard, Lisa Mangini has improved to the point that she can recall her attacker, and Jim Jefferson wasn't involved."

"We know," Maureen happily responded. "Gram called work and the foreman got word to us down on the line. We knew all along he couldn't have done it," she smiled at Alex.

"And Victor Lange told me when I got back to the office. Great News!"

"So when are they dropping the charges?" Maureen asked.

"The fellas on the case went down to the D-A's Office," Duggan replied, "and he got out late this morning."

"And was she able to describe the actual attacker, Captain?"

"Only in general terms, Maureen."

"Maybe some of the information we uncovered can help with that," Alex stated.

"I agree, so let's take up why we're here, the matter of this outlaw Nazi gang that we've been looking into. This afternoon, Captain Duggan and I have been going over what we know up to now, and we're convinced urgent law enforcement action is needed. But first, Alex, why don't you go over—especially for Agent Higgins who's new to all this—what have you come up with so far?"

After describing his paper's investigative series on the Bund, Alex chronicled all the gang's activities, starting with the attack on Bloom and the suspicious gathering at Camp Reichsadler, through the assault at Richardson's and the riot on the Canadiana. For the sake of Higgins, he spent additional time outlining the possibility of espionage at Curtiss.

With the background review complete, Alex and the others went into greater detail about the Nazi suspects.

"And with a lotta diggin' around, we've been able to link specific individuals to these incidents," Little Brick added.

"Right, there's the couple Hugh told me about this afternoon," Duggan said, as he flipped through his notepad, "Britta Voight, the singer and girl from Barnstormer's, and this fella, Hans Krueger, the gymnast and photographer. And as I told ya before, Alex, he's a former wheelman and strong-arm for the old Mitch Murphy gang."

"Yeah, my source at Reichsadler I-D'd her as being at that clandestine Nazi ceremony I mentioned, and said one of the group of Nazis was an athlete, which I didn't make the connection til recently; and remember, Krueger, the gymnast, threatened me when I tried to interview her at the Sangerfest competition…"

"And then, there's the big bald headed guy who tried to flip me over the side of the Canadiana," Maureen interrupted.

"Indeed, the mysterious bald guy who keeps poppin' up. Jim Jefferson unmasked him at Bloom's, and thinks he was the same bald-headed guy who was part of the gang that attacked him at Richardson's. Anyway, I remembered my source at Reichsadler saying she heard one of Britta's suspicious acting friends—a bald-headed guy—was a musician or singer. So, today, I headed over to the Sangerbund Club, and borrowed a picture of last year's Sangerfest Champs…"

"And sure enough, when he showed it to me in the car today, I spotted my assailant in an instant. I'll never forget that hate-filled face, and I'm sure my friend, Molly who was there, will I-D him too. They musta recognized me from the Bloom attack."

"So we swung back to the club office where the treasurer—who I asked to keep it under his hat—identified him as Kurt Metzger, from over on Sherman Street."

"Kevin, I want you to haul in that bastard, at the first chance," Little Brick uncharacteristically snarled.

"Don't worry, Hugh! I'll have my boys on it!"

"Captain, aren't Great Lakes waters under federal jurisdiction," the young agent asked.

"Yes, son, but local authority reaches out to the border, just like on dry land. This came up a few years ago. Hugh, you remember that, when that Bannon fella shot his wife on his sailboat, and dumped her overboard. We investigated, and he was prosecuted in state court."

"Getting back to the Sangerbund photo, Britta was in it too," the reporter interrupted.

"What about her boyfriend?" Duggan asked. "Anything positive?"

"Not in that photo, but realizing one was staring me right in the face, I dropped by the Turners Club. Fortunately, Krueger wasn't there, so I was able to get a Champion's picture of him."

"And you saw him fighting on the ship," the Captain continued.

"Yeah, I saw him drop a friend of my buddy, Lou Cohen who was right in the thick of it. So, I headed over to where they're fixin' up his family's business, the Starlite Grille, that I told you about. He immediately recognized both Krueger and Britta from the two pictures I had. Apparently, she started the fisticuffs by yellin' out that one of Lou's friends grabbed her, which Lou insisted wasn't true. He then saw Krueger and his pals jump some people, before scampering off in the middle of the bedlam. No doubt, it was an anti-semitic attack."

"Well, if this checks out, we'll bring this Krueger in too, as quickly as possible."

"And get this, according to Lou, one of 'im had a long scar down his face."

"Didn't you say the man you unmasked at the news shanty had a scar down his cheek," Higgins asked.

"Yep, and I'll get to him in a minute, but in the meantime, Lou told me that he thinks Krueger could be linked to the fire at the Club. Since the fight, he's been tryin' to figure out where he might have seen him before. Then, after seeing the picture, he thinks he saw him and another fella— who he also thinks was involved in the Canadiana fight—were hangin' out at the club before the fire."

"How can he be sure, that's a pretty popular place?" Duggan asked.

"Well, what made him remember was that he never saw them at the club before, and he thought something didn't fit... he thought they weren't hep."

"Hep?" the old commissioner asked.

"Sorry, jazz lingo, old fashioned, awkward, and he said they didn't seem to appreciate the music, like all the other regulars, and they seemed to be nosing around. And he thinks he recognizes the other guy who was with Krueger in the club. See that fella down in the bottom left of the Sangerbund group photo..."

"I see, rather ordinary, except for his beady-eyed, sneaky look," Hugh observed.

"We gotta share these photos with your source at Reichsadler," Duggan added.

"And we have to show them to Jim Jefferson and Lisa in light of what happened at Richardson's, especially Lisa. Any of 'em could've been her attacker, the rotten bastards," Maureen seethed.

"Don't worry, honey, that's at the top of our list, if she's ready."

"And both Alex and I recognized that little fella in the Sangerbund photo."

"How's that," Duggan asked.

"We saw him with the others fleeing from the Canadiana, and we both spotted 'im on a Curtiss plant tour earlier this summer. That should be of special interest to you, Agent Higgins."

"Didn't you already bring this up with Special Agent Perry?"

"We thought we had a strong case, but we developed more information since then. That plant tour I spoke about was part of a press conference announcing subcontracts for a new Hawk fighter. It's so innovative that the plane was kept under wraps throughout the program. That little guy in the photo was there as part of a group from Alpine machine, one of the subcontractors, which incidentally my family owns. I was there for the *Advocate*, and I remember during the tour of the production lines, he was constantly asking about operations and machinery…"

"Wouldn't that be reasonable since he worked at Alpine?" Higgins asked.

"Maybe, but as you'll see, I later found out he's a machinist and besides, he was asking about suppliers and operations, subjects outside his responsibilities."

"I was at the assembly, lined up with my coworkers next to the stage, and I noticed this guy seated in the crowd acting real nervous and constantly looking around—real odd! And he'd always turn his attention back to Alex, like he knew him or something. It was so weird, that I brought it up to Alex afterward."

"Maybe he recognized you from your family's business," Higgins observed.

"Or, perhaps he remembered Alex from the attack at the newsstand," Little Brick, countered.

"I pretty much forgot about it until I saw him at the Sangerfest competition. He was with a few singers talking to my brother. Later, I asked Freddy, who's the plant G-M, if he worked for us. At first he didn't recall him, but when I described him, he remembered that although he didn't know him, he was a master machinist at the company, and that his name is Karl Braun."

"Remember, it seems clear that this Braun fella is part of this Nazi gang," Maureen said.

"So armed with this latest information, I went down to the Alpine plant this afternoon to see what I could dig up. I know Mister Connors the chief guard…"

"Oh, yeah, Ken Connors, former desk lieutenant over at thirteen; good man," Little Brick noted before asking, "You didn't make contact with this Braun, did you?"

"No, he wasn't in, but that doesn't surprise me, since I'm sure he knew I spotted him take off from the Canadiana."

"Lucky coincidence, or he knows he's been compromised and flew the coop," Duggan observed.

"Knowing I was working with Commissioner Costello on an investigative article, Mister Connors promised me his confidence, and I used the Sangerfest cover story for the secretary in the security office."

"Good, no use tippin'im off, and of course, you can trust Ken Connors."

"He showed me Braun's company photo, which further nails his I-D and places him at the Canadiana, the Sangerfest and the Curtiss tour. And now, I can place him at the Bloom attack."

"How's that? I thought you said they all had masks except for Metzger and the guy with the scar," Higgins asked

"But somebody was driving the getaway car, and his Alpine file showed he registered a thirty-six, beige Chrysler Airflow for a company parking pass. It's the same make and color of the car seen escaping the scene of the newsstand attack, and the same type Britta's friend at Barnstormers saw picking her up. I'm sure its the same one I saw speeding off from the Canadiana riot. Too bad I couldn't write down the plate number I spotted."

"I hear what you say about this guy being part of a criminal gang, But being weird and nosy during a plant tour doesn't necessarily make you a spy." Higgins responded.

"But being in a Nazi criminal gang who's loyalties lie with a hostile foreign power that's rearming, can make you a spy, especially when it comes to motive. And I should add that on a night, shortly after the tour, my friend Lisa spotted someone spying down at the Hawk line from a skylight, maybe with a camera. Remember, Krueger's a photographer. Did your boss mention that?"

"He mentioned your grandpa's suspicions, but didn't go into it much."

With that, Alex and the old man went over details about Meyer, including specifics about the pedophile photos and blackmail note, along with evidence of his new found wealth, and the suicide note.

"And we even discovered the stationary used in the blackmail note may have come from the Sangerbund Society where at least four of the gang belonged," Hugh added.

"That's all pretty convincing, but I don't know how Agent Perry will feel about this. Still, since he's given me the latitude, I'll try to help you as much as I can on this."

"Well, like I said," Duggan continued, "I'll have my boys haul in this Metzger fella. Besides nailin'im on Maureen's assault, we'll grill him and any others on the newsstand attack, and the Richardson fight, along with squeezin' 'em to spill the beans on their fellow playmates and their antics."

"Oh, and yeah, as I mentioned before, I've got more on that scarfaced man. I'm pretty sure I got a positive I-D on him."

"How's that?" Duggan asked.

"When I was at the Alpine Guardhouse, despite my trying to keep things on the Q-T, Mister Connors let slip the name of Braun. No sooner did it escape outta his mouth than his secretary blurted out that Karl Braun is a cheap piker. Trying not to arouse her suspicions, and keeping it easy goin', I asked why. She went on to describe how one night, her and other members of the plant's ladies' bowling team ran into some co-workers at a downtown bar. One of them was Karl Braun. Later on, he suggested some of 'em head to a little diner down the street for some late-night chow. It seems even though Braun was a regular at this place, Ollie's, he tried to skip out on the bill. But get this, shortly after they got there, a buddy of Braun's showed up after his shift at Greco Gears. This secretary was immediately taken by how handsome he was, except…"

"Lemme guess, except for a big scar down his face," Duggan interrupted.

"Right, and although apparently nothing came of it, she did remember his name, Martin Hoffman… And before I forget, Jim Jefferson I-D'd a scar-faced man as being one of the Nazis trying to recruit with the KKK at the hobo camp."

"Good, we'll get him down at Greco tomorrow and you can I-D'im in a line up for the Jew's attack."

"That's good, but wait a minute, what was the name of that diner?" Little Brick asked.

"Ollie's, down on Mohawk Street, why do you ask, Gramps?"

"Yeah, Ollie's. A lotta folks go there late at night, after evening shifts, or after a night at the bars," Duggan recalled as his friend, Hugh, leafed through his notes.

"Sure, now I remember," the old man shot back. "When I was at Meyer's apartment after they found the body, I was downstairs with the coroner taking notes, when he pointed out the deceased musta been sitting down on a nearby bench havin' a smoke, before he got up and hung himself. The butt was still in the ashtray, along with a pack of Luckys and a matchbox. The matchbox was from Ollie's on Mohawk Street. I didn't make much of it at the time, but I just wrote everything down outta habit."

"This could be the link to the gang," Maureen blurted out.

"Absolutely," Higgins agreed.

"If we could show photos of Braun and Meyer to waitresses or whoever at Ollie's, maybe they'd remember them together, especially, since Braun's a regular," Alex noted.

"Kevin, you give Kane a call to meet us at Curtiss. We need a picture of Meyer. You explain the situation to him. He may still have a bug up his ass about me bringing up this espionage business."

"Sure, I understand. We're good pals, and he owes me big time for some favors."

"Maureen, you go with Alex. I know better than to think you're not coming," the old man chuckled, before adding, "young Higgins and I will ride with Kevin. And remember, when we get to Ollie's, it's just badges doing the talking."

Meanwhile, separated by a phalanx of grain elevators lining the Buffalo River, a far different gathering was taking shape. With darkness now settling over the landscape, a lone car was making its way down a dusty utility road, bordered on one side by the City Ship Canal and on the other by Times Beach. The beach was named after a local newspaper that promoted its creation a decade earlier. In the intervening years, the urban beach had lost much of its luster, in part due to the oftentimes acrid condition of the shoreline waters.

The car slowly eased into a spot near a swath of beach far removed from the south end, long preferred for its wide and deep cover of sand. There, the last stragglers of beach-goers were packing up their gear and heading to their cars. Despite its proximity to the heart of the city, locals typically abandoned the park at night, even at the height of summer, given its island-like isolation, and dark setting. Still, there were the occasional fishermen, or those romantics seeking a starlight view of the lakeshore waters.

As the occupants piled out of the car, they walked toward a wide patch of trees and overgrown brush that hugged a stretch of rocky shoreline. A pair of decrepit, abandoned shacks stood at the edge of the desolate scrubland, the last vestiges of a once thriving squatters village built along an old harbor break-wall. That was before the railroad decided it wanted the surrounding land for an access track to the adjacent ship canal. It didn't take long for city leaders to forcibly evict the threadbare residents, many of whose families went back generations. Nearby, a dilapidated dock jutted out into the inlet waters, where at one time, village fishermen would launch their tiny skiffs, and later sell their catch to harbor-side markets.

By now, Braun was barking out orders, as his gang set up camp at the fringes of the woods. All the gang was there except for Eric Bachmann, who feigned illness in order to hide his fear for what he saw as creepy things on the beach. As his comrades were unpacking the likes of Kerosene, binoculars and flares, Martin Hoffman was collecting driftwood for a campfire. Once lit, the otherwise innocuous looking bonfire was meant to be a navigational signal for accomplices out on the water.

"See, like I said, this is perfect. We'd sometimes use this spot when running booze for Mitch Murphy and Jimmy Gatzke."

"Indeed! And it must be a stark reminder of your criminal past, before finding meaning in our noble cause," Braun said as he surveyed the landscape.

In light of his unwavering commitment to the cause, Krueger felt stung by his leader's condescending tone. For his part, he took pride in his two-fisted gangster past. In fact, he viewed it as a manly pursuit, in line with his Nazi beliefs of Aryan virility. Still, he was unwilling to disturb the gang's camaraderie by calling out Braun. Instead, he chose to further proclaim his loyalty. "Yeah, I was prepared to go to jail, to make my smuggling money, but I'm happy to die for our blood and our Fuhrer. Sure, I was a gangster but I had the guts to put my balls on the line. The real criminals are those Jew bankers, and all those rich big-shots and their communist, New Deal allies."

"And their elite henchmen, like those know-it-all lawyers, doctors and businessmen we see at the Sangerbund, who think their shit don't stink," Metzger snarled as he poured the kerosene onto the wood and lit a match.

"Yeah, those communists and their union pals. Fuck, my brother Dirk tried to get a job at Seneca Brewing. He's a steamfitter but couldn't get in. Instead, they were taking Polacks and Dagos but not him! For C****t's sake, what's next, n*****s and s***s," Martin added, as he and the others took seats around the fire, looking no more menacing than typical nighttime beach-goers.

"I hate them all, especially all those fancy pants, smart-alecks. They went to college, so what! Can they make a cam shaft? *Scheisse*, they think we came from apes, but can't see that n*****s are monkeys," Braun sneered.

"They all think they're better," Britta chimed in.

"They'll fall into line or be crushed," Braun seethed as he looked over his shoulder to check on the car.

"And we gotta take care of those n****rs …" Metzger growled, before Braun reminded him to keep it down. "Because they want our women!"

"Right on that," Martin added. "In high school I had a crush on this pretty blond, Ilsa, a Dutch girl. Anyway, before I could ask her out, I heard she was seein' some c**n star of the football team. Once I found out, I wouldn't spit on her!"

"She shoulda been shot, and will be in time!" Kurt snorted.

"Women, " Braun scoffed. "You wouldn't see Aryan men do that, except maybe for some race traitors!"

"What about those plantation owners who fathered all those mulatto pickaninnies," Britta said.

"They were just tryin' to make smarter slaves," Metzger snickered.

"I wouldn't spoil my seed," Braun growled. "But women are a problem. They think they're equal to men, and more and more of them want to work."

"They should be raising children and keeping up the home, and most of all, obeying their men," Krueger smirked at Britta, who showed the last traces of a bruise near her eye.

"The time of the White Christian man is coming," Kurt nodded.

"No, White men, period," Braun asserted. "Maybe a White nationalist church of some sort. The Fuhrer has no use for religion, especially that, 'all god's children,' bullshit. He's creating that right now in the fatherland."

"Say, we better watch the time," Hans cautioned.

"Right, it's almost eight fifteen. They're supposed to be here after nine. Martin, grab the flares and the other stuff, and head over to the rocks above the dock like we planned," Braun dictated, before turning to Britta and ordering her to add more wood to the fire.

"You double checked on all the material?" Krueger whispered, once the others were out of earshot, sticking with their plan to keep them in the dark about some of the details.

"All accounted for. I'm keepin' 'em in the trunk. I'll go over and get 'em once we spot the boat. Although, I'm half tempted to hold back some of the prints for leverage."

"What! You can't be serious, Karl."

"Of course not, but it still boils my ass about all this Boss business."

"Yeah, I know. We do all the work, take all the risks, and he gets all the glory!"

"Even now, he's only supplying the boat, tonight."

"Gunter's piloting it, right, along with his aide at the Tourist Office, Weber, I think."

"Yeah, Fritz Weber. And I have no bone to pick with Gunter, he's a good contact and go-between. I believe him when he says he sings our praises to the Abwehr in Berlin. But this high and mighty, big shot over here, who provides some support, and gets all the credit! *Quatsch*, we do all the work, and come up with the tactics! That's not right, that's not how its supposed to be in the New Order."

"Didn't Gunter say the guy has power and standing here."

"Gunter says they're cultivating him for his connections, and they got plans, but that's so typical for the elites, who still get their special treatment; but in the Reich, it's supposed to be different. Fuck, our Fuhrer rose from the people, the masses."

"And like we've vowed, we've been bold, like Hitler."

"And it's our asses that get cooked, if things go sour. As it is, I haven't gone back to Alpine. I'm gonna quit. I'm sure that traitorous bastard Wagner spotted me on the Canadiana."

"That fuckin' *scheißkerl*! But you'll land on your feet. You're a great machinist."

"*Danke, mein freund*! But that's just another reason why I gotta suggest, one more time, that they send me to Berlin, so they can hear straight from us, about our efforts, our tactics. Maybe they can use it as a plan for other groups like us. Damnit, Gunter's the head of the Tourist Office. He outta be able to book me on the Hamburg Line, for C****'s sake!"

"But if they don't let you go, forget about it. Above all we're loyal, and we'll have our time. Hell, one day we'll get our version of the 'Blood Order,' like the veterans of the Beer Hall Putsch."

"I know. We know our value to the cause, and that's enough. Foot soldiers, not generals, like our Fuhrer was."

Meanwhile, Kurt and Britta dropped a load of wood on the fire, sending a plume of sparks high into the night air. Within moments, Martin started to wave his flares, upon spotting a navigation light bobbing on the water, as the boat made its way toward the shore. This brought Hans and the others rushing to the dock, while Braun headed to the car.

Nearby, a squad car slowed to a crawl as it approached the old Chinese lighthouse that sat at the tip of Kelly Island, the misnamed peninsula that was home to Times Beach. The cops were there to check out complaints of railroad vandalism, along with reports of night-time, cross-border smuggling.

No sooner had the '34 Ford V-8 turned onto the utility road, than its driver spotted sparks billowing above the north end of the beach. After easing their way behind a Chrysler parked beside a stretch of trees, the cops got out and surveyed the scene. While the driver began to take down the plate number, his sergeant scrambled up the nearby break-wall. By the time he reached the crest, he was met by the sight of Braun on his way to the car.

Upon seeing the cop, he turned and yelled to the others, "*Abbrechen! Abbrechen!*"

Hearing the command to abort, Martin snapped out his lighter and fired up the roman candles propped next to the dock, sending streams of glowing balls into the sky. Out on the water, the approaching boat cut its lights, before abruptly turning, and racing out into the darkness of the lake.

While keeping his eyes on the shadowy figure, the cop yelled out, "Sully, get your ass up here! And you, stop right there! And don't move!"

With the arrival of his partner, the old sergeant whispered, "Get down to the beach, and make sure there ain't no strays wonderin' off, and see that they ain't packing. Then sit 'em down and get their stories, each one separately. Go on, son." He then made his way to the stranger, careful to keep the others in view. "So what's goin' on here? A little old for a teenage beer party, huh."

"Yeah, we're all of age. We can show proof," he chuckled awkwardly.

"I ain't laughing, just answer the question."

Having previously rehearsed an alibi with the others, Braun was quick to reply, "Sure, sorry officer, we're here for a little celebration. Two of our friends got engaged. We picked up a case of Iroquois, and are toasting our friends and enjoying a beautiful night."

"Uh huh, and what were you yelling to your friend just now?"

"Yeah… ah, just to hold off on the fireworks. We wanted to surprise the couple with it."

"Didn't seem to work, did it?"

"Well, let's just say he ain't the sharpest knife in the cupboard," he again chuckled, sheepishly.

Still stone faced, the cop asked, "So what were ya doin' before ya spotted me? Goin' back to the car? Is it yours?"

"Right, heading back to the car… ah, is everything all right officer. Did we do something wrong?"

"Just answer the question, Mister…"

"Ah, Braun, Karl Braun, Here, I got my license and…"

"We'll get to that later. Like I said," his voice rising, "just answer the question."

"Yeah, it's mine and I was just going back for a bottle opener, stupid me."

"Ah, we all forget," he said, relaxing his tone before continuing, "But, hey, don't let me spoil the party. Lemme walk ya over to the car, Mister Braun."

Once at the car, the cop kept up with the exchange, "Chrysler, right? New one, too, huh."

"Yeah, thirty-six Airflow; great car"

"And gotta cost a pretty penny. So whaddah do for a livin,' Mister Braun?"

"I'm a senior machinist, at a machine works."

"Oh, really, which one? My older brother works at Ford."

"Ah, Alpine Machine."

"Nice. Still, a new Chrysler Airflow? Pretty fancy tin can for some Joe packin' a lunch bucket. Say, how'd ya do it, a second job?"

"Just watch my spending. My mother was a widow. Taught me how to stretch a buck."

"Sure… and hey, don't let me hold you up lookin' for your church key."

With that, Braun went through the motions of digging through the glove compartment, knowing he inexcusably failed to bring a key component of their cover story.

"C****t, I was sure I put one in there."

"That can happen. Check your trunk. Ya don't wanna let down your friends."

"Naw, I wouldn't put it in there. Listen, I don't want to waste your time any more," he replied, hoping to throw the bloodhound off his scent.

"That's all right, I insist."

"Knowing the incriminating nature of its contents, Braun tried his best to steady his hands as he turned the key and opened the lid. Losing no time, the cop started poking around the items in the well. "So what's in the box, he asked as he shined the flashlight on the object. Not waiting for the man to act, the cop unlatched the top. "What in the world… looks like a bunch of metal shavings."

"Yeah, like I mentioned," he said as he fought to hide the tension in his voice, "I'm a master machinist, and I was testing some equipment at a distributor for my employer. I saved some of the shavings. They can tell you a lot about a machine."

"Huh; makes sense, I suppose. Mind if I take a look at them folders," the cop said as he went on to grab the files. Braun helplessly looked on, knowing any complaint on his part would only further incite the policeman.

"What's the low-down on this gibberish? Some sorta foreign language?"

"Ah… yeah," Braun stammered as he tried to come up with a cover story for his notes on Britta's efforts at Barnstormers, and the report on his conversations with Meyer. He could only thank his lucky stars that the Abwehr required them in German. "Sure, I'm the secretary for the Sangerbund Club, a German American choral society. It's a report on our activities like competitions and performances and such and the …"

"Spit it out! I ain't got all day!"

"Yes …ah… and the The National German American Choral Arts Association requires an annual report that they use to certify us, and they want it in German."

"Geez, can't you people tone down all this German shit. You're fuckin' Americans! My little brother got killed at Belleau Wood to keep us from speakin' German here."

"I understand, and sorry for your brother, sir," he replied, while thinking the cop would rue those words someday.

"And what's in here," he snorted, as he snapped up the folder containing schematics for the Hawk's landing gear that were subcontracted to Alpine.

"Oh, thats just the blueprint for the part we were testing on the new machine. It goes with the shavings."

"And what's with that tube tucked in the back there. Get in there and pull it out," the cop barked as he stepped back and watched with caution.

As Braun leaned into the dark recess, he could feel the beads of sweat rolling down his back, knowing the tube contained rolled up blueprints of the complete Hawk, that even the dullest of laymen could make out, not to mention photos of the plane taken from the skylight at Curtiss.

Emerging from the trunk, he played his hand as best he could. Flipping open the lid, he pulled out the tip of a drawing, exposing a blue background and a series of arcs and lines. "See, same thing as the folder. More prints of parts we were testing at the machine vendor."

By now, he could almost hear his heart racing as he waited for the cop to respond. A demand for a closer look could result in a trip to the station, where further scrutiny would no doubt wreck their mission and land them in jail.

"Okay, you can put it back."

Braun could feel the pressure in his chest ease before asking, "So, is everything all right, officer? Like I said, we're just having a little celebration."

"We're gonna head back to where your pals are. I got more questions, and you better not be involved in any trouble here. Ya wouldn't wanna fuck up that nice job ya got."

With the rest of the gang safely seated around the fire, young Sullivan rushed up to greet the pair as they approached. "Sergeant Burke…"

Before he could blurt out another syllable, the old cop barked, "Hold on! You, Braun, plant your ass next to your buddies, and keep your yap shut!"

Keeping a steady eye on Braun as he walked towards the others, Burke continued, "So what did they tell ya, son?"

"Well, like you told me, I took each one off to…"

"Just what did they say."

"Well, each one to a man… er, including the girl, said they were celebrating the engagement of one of the guys and the girl…"

"Pretty convenient; almost like it was rehearsed, but go on, son."

"They had a crate of beer, but it only had a few bottles in it."

"Some party. A bunch a nuns woulda had more. Ya kiddin' me!"

"Whaddya think, Sarge?"

"Something sure as shit is goin' on here. So who's the so-called lucky couple?"

No sooner had the young patrolman pointed out the pair, than Burke bellowed out," Hold it right there… and follow me, kid."

Burke made a beeline to the couple in the corner, "Well, well, fancy runnin' into my old friend, Hans Krueger at this fine spot!"

"Yeah, it's been a while. Good to see ya, Officer Burke," he smirked.

"Right, seems like old times when you and your ah… business associates spent many a night here pickin' up your ah… product, before Revenuers and the Department caught on; say, but where are my manners. Patrolman, come over here, I wanna introduce Hans Krueger, former chief wheelman and sometime strong arm for the old Mitch Murphy rum runnin' gang; and then, after Mitch's unfortunate demise, for Jimmy Gatzke's crew.

"That was a while back, Sergeant. I'm a clean liver now."

"But do ya remember takin' a pot shot at me and my partner when ya left us in the dust with that souped-up truck of yours?"

"I never carried a roscoe, Sarge. That musta been another driver."

"Well, no doubt you're a fine law abidin' citizen now; which reminds me, I suppose I should be congratulatin' ya on your betrothal. And is this the fair young lady?"

"Yeah," Britta snapped barely able to contain her disdain.

"And that's why we're here tonight," Krueger interrupted, "celebrating our good fortune!"

"Sure, and Hans here musta got ya a fine ring, you bein' so pretty, eh, Miss? Can I see it?"

"Unfortunately, we can't afford one right now," Hans broke-in.

"Cut the fuckin' bullshit, Krueger! If this was legit, ya woulda paid a buck at Kresge's for a fuckin' ring. The whole thing's bullshit! You with the scar, wavin' the flares…"

"I was just celebrating our friends…"

"Shut your yap, before I bust up the other side of that lyin' face of yours! Do you think we're idiots! You were signalin'' that boat. And then this fella Braun here yellin' something at ya and you settin' off the fireworks and the next thing ya know, that boat's high tailin' it outta here. So, Krueger, just a coincidence you being down here? I don't think so. I figure you and your pals are up to no good."

"Like I said, just celebrating our engagement," Krueger smirked.

"Oh, so your hostin' a bridal shower, Missy," Burke mocked, as a look of rage crossed Krueger's face. "And you, sister," he growled as he shined a flashlight on Britta's face. "So, lo and behold, ya can't cover up that old shiner, can ya! Part of your engagement present, huh?"

"Mind your own business, I bumped into a kitchen cabinet."

"Funny how clumsy girls get when they take up with fine citizens like Krueger here— unless you're here for other reasons with these fellas here."

"Shove it up your ass, copper!"

"Watch your whorin' mouth, or I'll be haulin' your ass downtown on suspicion of hookin.' And you with the bald head. Yeah, who do ya think I mean, Grandpa? What's your story?"

"Just with friends, sir."

"And you with the car, Braun, you got anything to add?"

"Just what I told you before, officer," he pleaded.

"Well, ya can do your lyin' down at the station. We'll let the fellas in the suits check out your story."

"You can't do that. We haven't broken any laws," Braun protested.

"Can't ya read. The beach closes at dusk, but don't go pullin' that innocent act with me!"

"You got nothin', " Hans snarled.

"Well, I got a known smuggler showin' up at an old rum runners spot, when there's reports of French whores bein' smuggled down from Montreal."

"That's crap, we all got jobs," Britta shot back.

"So what! You can explain what you're doin' with four men, down at the precinct."

With that, Burke instructed his young partner to pick up the spent fireworks before rounding up the gang and dousing the fire. Once back at the road, they crammed the four male suspects into the back of the cruiser. With that, the sergeant turned to Britta, "I'll cut ya a break and treat ya like a lady, and not toss ya in the back with them crumbs. So slide in between us two."

She lost no time in shooting back a look of pure disdain.

"Don't press your luck, dolly," Burke snarled as she slowly complied with his order.

By the time the patrol car pulled into the downtown precinct, Duggan's sedan was crossing the nearby Church Street intersection, followed by Alex's Chevy. The cars' occupants had just secured a statement from Bennie, the nighttime cook at Ollie's. He identified Braun as being in the company of Pete Meyer, the night the Bisons clinched the pennant, some two weeks prior. More importantly, a night shift trucker and regular patron, after overhearing the cop's questions, volunteered that on that night, he recognized Meyer from his church. In addition, he recounted an uneasy encounter with a man called Hans. Finally, he was able to identify Braun and Krueger from the photos he was shown.

As the little caravan turned down Delaware Avenue, everyone in the cars was in a celebratory mood.

XXI

The sharp banging on the door jolted him from the nightmare of Nazi hordes surging through the streets. Shooting straight up, he panted furiously, fearing that gunfire had at last reached his home. Finally orienting himself to the reality of his surroundings, he jumped up from the bed, and began groping for his robe. As he struggled to shake off the last vestiges of sleep, he yelled out that he was on his way. Sliding into his slippers, he felt like he had just laid down his head, after a late-night strategy session to bring down the Nazi gang; yet, outside the window, it was still dark. Squeezing open the door until the chain snapped taut, he was greeted by the sight of Hugh Costello.

"Open up and get dressed, son. We gotta move fast."

As Alex threw on his clothes, the old man sat on a chair in the dinette, delivering his news through the door, "A lot happened last night that affects our case against the gang. It seems a couple of cops on patrol near Times Beach came across our favorite gang down where they used to smuggle booze during prohibition. The cops were there because of reports of smuggling prostitutes from Montreal. The two of 'em were checking things out when they saw what seemed to be a guy signalin' a boat off-shore. Once they approached, he shot off a warning flare that sent the boat skedaddling. That, along with cagey responses, raised suspicions. So, they took 'em down to the headquarters, so the boys from Vice could question 'em further…"

"Wow! How'd ya get word of this?" Alex yelled from the bathroom as he dried his face.

"My grandson who works outta HQ, heard about it at the end of his shift. Unfortunately, Vice had just let 'em go, after they stuck to their story that they were celebrating an engagement."

"What?"

"Yeah, Britta and Krueger. And that's what set-off Ernie Burke. He was the sergeant on patrol, a good cop. He remembered Hans Krueger from when he was a wheelman and strong arm for Mitch Murphy's rum runnin' gang."

"Sure, a shady bum like him; but did they come up with anything that could help us with the case?"

"The Vice guys, no; but hang on, it gets better. Danny, as you know, knows about our work and grabbed Ernie before he left. In the course of telling what happened, he mentions goin' through the driver's trunk…"

"Lemme guess, a beige Chrysler."

"Exactly, and he goes on to describe how the guy, named Braun—surprise—had all sorts of stuff from his work as a machinist, blueprints and metal shaving, along with German reports from his singing club…"

"Singing club, my ass! Blueprints, shavings, and German language reports, all that stuff gotta be related to the Hawk!"

"Right, sounds like they interrupted an attempt to hand-off sensitive military information."

"Dammit! How could they let 'em go!"

"They didn't know what we know, son, but they did get all the vital data: names, addresses, all that. And listen, Rick Fitzgerald—he's a patrolman who grew up in the neighborhood—anyway, while he's workin' the desk, he hears what Danny and Burke were talking about, and comes over. He goes on to tell 'em how he pulled over Braun and Krueger one night earlier this summer, when he was checking out complaints of homosexual activity on his beat. He recognized Krueger from gymnastic meets. Rick competes for the 'Y'."

"What's with that? Did anything come outta it?"

"They checked out, and knowing Krueger, he let 'em go; nonetheless, they were acting suspiciously down at the end of Kingsley Street."

"Something about Kingsley Street?"

"Yeah, I once captained that district, and there were always reports of kids hopping the fence and breaking into the rail cars. But get this, it's also an overgrown dead end that now butts up against the Curtiss plant property."

"Of course, Maureen's face in the skylight, earlier this summer! And, as we figured, Krueger, the gymnast and photographer, took pictures."

"Right! And remember, Maureen said it was right before an army inspection. Now, this new information would seem to place them at the scene! And young Fitzgerald told Danny he'd check his logs for a date"

"Bingo!"

"That's why we gotta move fast. It looks like they're moving their stuff."

Jumping into Alex's Chevy parked out front, the old man lost little time further filling in the blanks. "Duggan got his boys to pick up Hoffman, and he's on his way to Metzger's"

"That leaves the other three."

"Yeah, they all listed the same address on Krettner, around the corner of Broadway. Danny's meetin' us there."

"I know it's over near Saint Anne's. A lotta big ol' doubles down there."

Within minutes, they arrived outside a big American Foursquare. Although old, it looked well-kept. Fastened across the porch banister was a large sign proclaiming, "Rooms." No sooner had they pulled to the curb, than Danny bound out of the car that rolled up behind them.

Wasting no time, they rushed up the front stairs where they were greeted by a placard affixed next to the door, listing accommodations, rates and house rules. Stretched out across it, was a banner emblazoned with the word, "full."

A press of the buzzer was quickly followed by the appearance of a world-weary matron, no doubt, long up, and working hard. Peering through the space limited by the chain lock, she barked out, "What's your business. Can't ya see we're full?"

Her inquiry was met by Danny's I-D, and shield. "Buffalo Police, ma'am. Detective Costello."

Looking stunned, she swung open the door, "What's wrong, officer?"

"We wanna talk to three of your boarders…"

"Listen, we run a clean place here," she nervously broke-in. "We saved every penny and used my husband's bonus money from the War to buy this place. We ain't gonna risk it. Any funny business and your out!"

"It's nothing like that, Missus," Little Brick re-assured her.

"And who are you? A little old to be breakin' down doors and chasin' crooks…"

"I'm the former Police Commissioner and now a consultant."

"So what's up, the Lindbergh kidnappin'?" she snapped, regaining her spunk.

"No, and forgive me, what's your name, ma'am," Danny smiled.

"Schiller, Greta Schiller."

"Thank you, Missus Schiller, we just want to question, Karl Braun, Hans Krueger, and Britta Voight on some things."

"Ya just missed the two fellas. They took off in a cab,—one of 'em carryin' a bag—not two minutes before ya buzzed. I thought you was them commin' back for something."

"Do you know where they were going," Danny asked.

"Naw, I was out there sweepin', but they didn't say nothin'. Them two are sneaky and quiet. Although quiet ain't bad in this business."

"Which cab company?" Hugh jumped in.

"I dunno. All I remember was it's white."

"Gotta be Iroquois Cab. Missus Schiller, can we use your phone?" As the woman welcomed them in, the old man turned to Danny, "Call Iroquois' dispatcher. Find out where that fare was going."

"What about the girl," Alex asked, while holding back from identifying himself.

"She's round back in Room One, behind our flat. She's nice, not like the other two, and hard workin'. A good egg!"

Just then the sound of the buzzer rang through the hall, sending the woman back to the door, where she showed in Duggan and his partner.

"What's up here? I grabbed Quinn here and a squad car after leaving Metzger's over on Monroe Street. He wasn't there and his old lady clammed up."

"Braun and Krueger flew the coop in a cab a few minutes before we got here. Danny's checkin' with dispatch right now. We're on our way to question the girl in the back."

After ordering his partner to search the men's rooms, he joined Hugh and Alex as they rushed to the rear of the house. Rapping on the door of room one, Duggan yelled out, "Open up, police!"

"Go away! I didn't do nothin'!"

"Open up, or we're bangin' down the door!"

The door slowly eased open, revealing a robed figure that quickly turned away from the light in the hall. Once they followed her into the kitchenette, the reason became clear. Despite her attempt to avoid eye contact, she couldn't hide the fresh bruises and swelling on her face.

"Who the hell did this to you," Little Brick urged as he took her by the arm and lead her to a chair.

"Nobody, I tripped and fell."

"Please! Miss Voight! This is a crime, and we can help," the old man continued.

With that, the girl broke down and began to sob, as she tried to get out the words. Just then, Danny arrived and took the others aside. "They're headed to the Central Terminal."

"Danny, get over to the call box across the street, and let 'em know what's up," Duggan ordered. "Tell 'em I want 'em to send a couple cops from six down to the terminal, pronto. Have 'em alert Central's security as well. Give 'em a description of these jokers as best you can and grab some of those photostat pictures of these bums in the back of my car. I had one of my boys run 'em off at the County Clerks office last night."

By now, the dam had burst, and although barely able to speak through her split lip, Britta began to lash out at her tormentor, "He's a no good animal! He did this to me!"

"Who?" Duggan barked.

"You know who! Then why are ya here? Come on, Krueger, Hans Krueger!"

"So what happened? Does it have to do with that information they're takin' to the terminal," Hugh broke-in.

"Yeah, that stuff on the pla… " she said before suddenly catching herself. "Ah, listen, all I know is that they're seein' some guy down at the terminal."

"Right, the plane! Make it easy on yourself," Duggan snapped. "Who's the guy and what's his name!"

"Those two don't tell me crap. Just some guy they call 'The Boss.' But I ain't sayin' no more. I wanna see a doctor."

Taking the others aside, Little Brick whispered, "We gotta get to the terminal. Kevin, before you head out, can ya get Quinny down here and have him call an ambulance; and see if he can get any more outta her before it comes. Remember, these types like to brag to their girlfriends… Alex, you got your pictures, so head to the terminal. Once Danny is done with his call, we'll take his car along with those photostats of Braun and Krueger and get to the terminal A-S-A-P."

Just as they were turning down the hall, Britta looked up and yelled, "Hey, you! What are you doin' here?"

Knowing he was caught, Alex turned and faced the suspect, "Just checking out a report of a disturbance for my paper…"

"Bullshit! This is your fault! Sticking your nose where it don't belong!"

"Like I said, Miss, just doin' my job."

"Hope it's worth it! He knows who you are, and he'll make it hurt! He don't wait."

Unwilling to take it up with her, Alex followed the others as they rushed down the hall. Once outside, Danny was already waiting. Wasting no time, they jumped into their cars and raced toward the train station.

Flying past the tidy worker cottages that lined the approach to Lindbergh Drive, their pursuit came to an abrupt halt, the result of a crash three blocks ahead. The reason for the traffic jam was clearly evident as the front wheel of a bread truck was resting atop the marble balustrade surrounding Paderewski Circle, a rusty jalopy smashed into its side. Outside, the trucker was wildly waving his arms, no doubt trying to explain his version of events to the newly arrived motorcycle cop.

The circle stood at the entrance to a vast plaza that slowly rose some three hundred yards to the majestic Arte Deco railroad temple. Stopping his car, Alex hopped atop its running board, and surveyed the terrain in an effort to spot his quarry. His quest was rewarded upon seeing a white Iroquois taxi slowly approaching the scene of the vehicular mayhem.

After pulling to the curb, Alex got out and rushed back to his comrades, where he described the situation at hand. Knowing any delay could jeopardize their mission, they decided to split up, so that at least one of them could arrive on time to intercept the Nazis. While Alex took to his feet and ran towards the station, Danny flipped on his siren and sped down a one-way street in the wrong direction, hoping to get to the rear entrance as quickly as possible.

By now the cab had maneuvered past the logjam and was approaching the taxi portal just as Alex neared the crest of the promenade. Surprised by his dormant speed, he kept a close eye on his targets as they got out and headed toward the door. Much to his relief, the landlady's testimony proved right, as he could clearly see Braun carrying a briefcase of some sort.

Spurred on by the hunt, Alex carved his way through the people and traffic before arriving at the entrance canopy that stood beneath the Terminal's majestic tower. After passing into an elaborate, brass trimmed foyer that housed an assortment of shops, he turned into the cavernous main hall.

He was met by a vast expanses of soaring arches covered with Guastavino tiles, and at each end, towering walls of glass that sent streams of light cascading onto a polished terrazzo floor. Its adjacent four hundred foot train concourse fed fourteen tracks and seven covered platforms that could service over two hundred trains a day. For a moment, he was struck motionless, as he surveyed the imposing scene before him.

Looking to his right, past a bank of ticket counters, Alex was greeted by a granite archway engraved with the words, "Baggage Check;" yet no sign of Braun or Krueger. Just then, he spotted Little Brick and his grandson rushing up from the rear exit. As they approached, he could see Danny carrying a fistful of photostats.

Showing no effects of old age, Hugh greeted his young partner, "See anything yet?"

"Watched 'em as they came in, but lost 'em in the crowd."

"Danny's been lookin' around, while I stopped off at the security office. Gave 'em a bunch of these pictures of the two of 'em. Kevin Duggan had just arrived along with the cops from six, and young Higgins got there a little later. Everybody's fanning out."

"We'll get 'em unless they got lucky, and already boarded a train," Danny added.

"Gee, there's gotta be a dozen tracks here, and I see from the schedule board, there's gotta be a dozen of 'em leavin' in the next hour," Alex said.

"Don't forget, they may be here to met somebody, so it doesn't mean they're takin' off. Odds are it could be a handoff," the old man said.

With that, they agreed to split up and sweep the hall. The old commissioner, armed with his cache of pictures, headed to the information booth sitting beneath the four-sided clock tower.

Feeling the pressure of time, Alex scanned the landscape before spotting a janitor wielding his mop outside the Western Union Office. Figuring the man couldn't help but observe the comings and goings around him, he rushed to his side. Barely catching his breath, he asked, "Hey, my friend, did you happen to see a couple of guys, one of 'em carrying a brief case?"

"Mister, this IS a train station, you know," he chuckled wryly.

"Of course," he smiled back. "Did ya see either of these two," he asked as he showed copies of their photos.

"Hmm," he noted as he slowly looked over the photostats. "I think I saw that fella with the beady eyes headin' towards the restaurants. I remember 'cause he looked sneaky, like a pickpocket. I even checked my wallet," he laughed.

"Thanks," Alex yelled as he hurried toward the dining complex. Passing the closed lunch counter located at its center, he took aim for the coffee shop to the right. After turning the corner his heart sank as neither of the pair were anywhere in sight. Just in case, he walked over and stuck his head in the john, but to no avail. Continuing his quest, he made his way to the 'Deco D'Arte' supper club, at the other side of the diner. Expecting a deserted scene, he pushed his way through the smoky glass doors etched with art deco images of dancing couples.

After waiting for his eyes to adjust to the murky conditions, he was shocked to see his Uncle Max, as he sat in a booth, finishing off a plate of food, and looking quite satisfied and relaxed with a freshly folded copy of the New York Times on the edge of the table. Two other booths had people in them, but none were Krueger or Braun. Walking up to the table he blurted out, "Uncle Max, what are you doing here?"

Momentarily stunned, Max quickly collected himself. "Why having my breakfast before my train. You don't think I'd be eating at a greasy spoon like across the way before I travel," he chuckled. "Tim Williams, the owner, keeps this place open for his friends and regulars," he said with his usual aplomb before adding, "I suppose I should be asking you the same question."

"It's a long story, but it's part of the series I'm doing for the paper."

"Ah, that again. Haven't you had enough of that?"

"Well, hopefully this will do it. But listen, I gotta hurry, but where you going, Uncle Max?"

"On a buying trip to Thyssen Machine, in Munich. That's where your great grandpa started. I love to stay at our family place outside of town, breath that pure mountain air; recharge the batteries."

"That sounds great, Uncle Max. And good luck on that buying mission!"

"And if I'm going to pull off that mission, I better get going, myself. I don't want to miss my train," he said before getting up and embracing Alex with a hug and a good-bye.

"Oh, and just by chance, you didn't happen to notice somebody come in here over the last few minutes, actually, a fella who works for us, a master machinist named Karl Braun…"

This time, an awkward look descended upon his uncle's face before he snapped off a reply, "No, can't say I did. I was too busy enjoying a wonderful omelet that Tim's chef cooked up for me. As for the fella you mentioned, he doesn't ring a bell. Remember, we have over six hundred employees. But what's this all about, that story of your's again?"

"Yeah, like I said, long story. I just wanna talk to the guy."

"And like I said, don't get caught up in all that craziness; but listen. .. I got to run; come and walk me out."

Anxious to resume the chase, and as before, check out the restroom, Alex feigned nature's calling. "I gotta head to the head, Uncle Max. But safe travels. Love ya!"

After Max returned the farewell, Alex rushed to the men's room where he quickly looked beneath each stall door; but without success. Once finished, he noticed Max had left his newspaper on the table. Eager to catch up, he grabbed the paper, only to see an envelope drop to the floor, scattering its contents. Retrieving the pieces, he saw that it was a ticket packet from the German Travel Office, not his family's usual agent. More importantly, in making sure he got all the vouchers, he noticed that the railroad pass out of Bremen Harbor was for Berlin, and not for Munich, as Max had mentioned. Although wondering why the inconsistency, Alex quickly brushed it aside, as he rushed to the exit, eager to intercept his uncle.

Scanning the landscape, he saw Max standing near a row of benches at the center of the hall, frantically checking his pockets. It also caught his eye that resting at his feet was a cheap, battered looking briefcase. This was in stark contrast to Max's well-known penchant for expensive Louis Vuitton luggage, recognizable for its signature look. Also, upon looking at the newspaper in his hand, it was obvious that it had never been opened, unlike Max's remark that he had been reading the news while eating. Had it been a signal, lying on the edge of the table?

Suddenly, Alex was seized by an engulfing sense of horror upon remembering Little Brick's words about a hand-off. His sense of shock was interrupted by a voice coming from behind his shoulder. "Any luck so far," Hugh asked, as Danny stood at his side.

For an instant, Alex was tempted to rationalize and conceal what he observed, yet some inner voice told him otherwise. No sooner had he somehow managed to describe his suspicions about his uncle, than he spotted Krueger, Metzger and Braun—minus the briefcase—walking toward the far end of the great hall.

"There's the three of 'em," Alex blurted out.

"You two go get 'em. And give me the tickets, I'll talk to your uncle."

Sensing the presence of a posse, Braun suddenly looked back, spotting Alex and Danny in hot pursuit. Splitting up, Krueger bolted toward the exit, while Metzger and Braun ran into the train concourse with Alex on their heels. Danny raced after Krueger, who by now, was already out the door. Consumed with the chase, Alex was able to ignore the gut retching pain over his uncle.

Entering into the vast corridor, he didn't see his targets near any of dozen stairwells leading to the tracks. Rolling the dice, he headed for the first ramp. No sooner had he turned the corner, than he was confronted by a snarling Metzger standing sentry at the top of the steps. Snorting like a bull in the ring, the former wrestler lowered his shoulder and charged his opponent, smashing Alex into the opposite wall.

Gasping for breath, he somehow rallied his strength as Metzger wound up to deliver a haymaker. Instead, Alex launched an uppercut that lifted his tormentor off his feet.

Shaking off the cobwebs, while ignoring the blood dripping from his chin, the mad beast flashed a menacing grin as he got up and pressed forward. "Your ass is mine, college boy!" Yet his bravado proved fleeting as Alex followed with a right cross that snapped his head backwards. As his legs turned to rubber and his eyes spun like tops, Metzger stumbled to the floor, where he let out a meager groan before slumping against the wall.

With any bystanders scared off by his violent response, Alex flew down the staircase and onto the platform, where he saw Braun scampering across the tracks. Fearing capture, the Nazi turned around, only to be greeted by the looming presence of his nemesis. As a locomotive horn blared in the background, Braun struck a Nazi salute before leaping into the path of an onrushing express train. With screams of horror echoing across the platforms, Alex felt himself grabbed from behind by security personnel.

The security officers eventually led Alex and his groggy opponent to the main hall, where they were met by Danny Costello flashing his badge. "Hold that one for booking and let this one go," he said as he took Alex aside.

"Geez, you okay? Heard somebody got run over by a train. I got worried about you."

"I'm fine, Metzger wanted to tussle, but as you can see, I got the best of him. Then I chased down Braun, but when he spotted me, rather than face the music, he took a dive in front of a train. Unbelievable!"

"Ugh! Crazy fanatic, huh?"

"Guess so. And what about Krueger?"

"Lost 'im in the yard out back. That bastard can fly! But don't worry, we'll get 'im. I already called an A-P-B on 'im."

Alex paused to collect himself, before asking, "And what about my uncle?"

"Yeah… unfortunately, my friend, your hunch was right. The goods were in the valise, all right. Gramps took me aside and told me. I caught him, Captain Duggan and Higgins leadin' 'im in, when I was leaving the security office."

Catching his voice cracking, Alex continued, "Ah… did he say anything?"

"All he's saying is that it wasn't his and he was looking for the owner, and he wanted to see his lawyer, Al Fraser. Good luck on making this stick… er… sorry, Alex. Maybe there is an explanation."

"I sure hope so, but let the chips fall where they may," he said, feeling unconvinced by his own words.

"Well, lemme say it took a lotta guts to do what you did. I dunno if I could've done the same."

"Musta been listening to my better angels. Scant relief for how I feel right now. But do you think I can talk to him?"

"I can't see why not, considering all you've done; but it's Higgins' call, since it looks like the material in the bag is a federal rap."

Arriving outside the tower elevator lobby where the security office was located, Alex saw Little Brick at the door talking to Duggan and Higgins. Catching sight of Alex and his grandson, the old man came walking over.

"Danny told me what's going on. I want to see him"

"It's young Higgins' call until Perry gets here, but I understand. Let me talk to him."

After reassuring the young agent, he came walking back. "Yeah, no problem, Alex. I know how tough this is on you; yet, you showed great integrity. We'll let the justice system sort things out from here, so go ahead, but watch what ya say, and your time. Perry's on the way over, and no tellin' how he'll grandstand, or gum things up. Your uncle's in the first room to the right."

As he approached the door, Alex could feel his head spin, trying to absorb it all. By now, the excitement of the chase had been replaced by the cold reality of what lay before him. At the other side of the door sat one of the commanding figures of his life, accused of betraying his country.

Up to now, Alex's was a tight-knit world, defined by his family, a family whose oversized influence in their community was now threatened. Despite his desire to set his own path, he never doubted their love and support, or failed to take great pride in their standing.

Although his uncle could be tough, overly confident, and often-times enigmatic, Alex never doubted his greatness. To think that these charges could be his fate—and by extension, his family's—was incomprehensible. Still, values, hard work and most of all faith in God, were central to his family, and at the moment, this was the thought that was sustaining him.

Looking through the door window, he was surprised to see his uncle sitting on a bench, appearing unfazed by the controversy swirling around him. After steeling himself, he eased his way through the door. "Uncle Max, what's going on?"

"Don't Worry! We'll have this cleared up shortly, when Al Fraser, my lawyer shows up here. I've got a ship to catch tomorrow."

"But I mean, how did you find yourself in this mess? You couldn't have done anything wrong, right?"

Suddenly, Max's lively blue eyes turned stone cold. "Really! Weren't you the one who told that doddering old fool, Costello that that briefcase wasn't mine!"

"Well I know you love Louis Vut…"

"That's right! Of course it wasn't mine! I wouldn't be caught dead with crap like that. Somebody left it in the lounge. I was looking for its owner!"

Alex felt some hope in his uncle's innocence before suddenly remembering worrisome inconsistencies. "But I thought you didn't see anybody come into the restaurant when I asked."

"And I didn't know that guy you mentioned from Adam, and yeah, I was preoccupied with my meal and newspaper, so I didn't make eye contact with anyone. Still, I did hear some comings and goings outside my field of vision, so I suppose somebody could've come in, that I wasn't aware of. And by the way, you may have noticed some other customers in a booth across the way."

"But your ticket is to Berlin, not Munich…"

"Forgive me, I wanted to visit Berlin before heading to Munich. Should I have run that by you? And what's going on here! Are you my nephew, my brother's child who I treated like a son; or are you an accuser out to get me. You stand there and tell me!"

By now, Alex's emotions were in tumult as he wavered between belief and doubt. Seeking refuge in his uncle's innocence, he pleaded, "I just wanna know you're not part of this!"

"What, part of some crazy spy ring? Stealing away with some supposed sensitive material? Ridiculous! You should be ashamed of yourself just thinking that about me!"

"I'm sorry, if you're feeling betrayed…"

"I love this country! For C***t's sake, I'm a veteran."

Remembering the towering portrait of George Washington that flanked the stage at the Bund rally, Alex couldn't help but be reminded of their twisted sense of nationalism; yet more out of a hope to clear Max, than in advancing the probe, he pressed forward, "I know you're a proud American, but I gotta know you couldn't embrace this Hitler Nazism like over there? Right?"

Although he continued to eye Alex cautiously, Max once more felt certain that he held his nephew's allegiance. As such, summoning up his inherent sense of superiority, he couldn't resist the urge to expound, "I have to say I'm not happy with you right now, but I've been trying to set you straight for a while. Still, I know how much our family means to you, and that you don't want to disappoint us further…" Confident he struck a chord, he didn't wait for a response as Alex wrestled with his thoughts. "In any case, I'll explain things in a way that will help you see things better. First of all, let's just say this idea of me being some sort of Nazi… I'm no naive follower of some ideology," he chuckled dismissively, as he looked Alex squarely in the eye.

While hoping to hear something that would provide some relief, Alex was stung by his uncle's dismissive manner. As such, he sat back and held his tongue.

"But I understand when a man whose nature defines him as a leader, who takes up the challenge and pursues his destiny, is frustrated by what he sees: The inability to take crucial actions; to forge events! For Christ's sake, we've been through a disastrous World War and a depression that brought this country to the edge of utter collapse—and we're still not out of the woods on that. What these times demand is strong, decisive leadership that can get things done!"

"You mean, like FDR," Alex said, unable to resist defending a man he came to admire and follow.

"Please, the New Deal is falling apart. The Supreme Court is tearing it up, and now the Republicans and Dixiecrats are foiling his plans. He can't deal with it. How does he galvanize the people, with fireside chats? Come on! For god's sake, he's a cripple. How does he inspire strength and action?"

Stunned by his uncle's sudden lack of empathy, Alex shot back, "I thought you admired the man… but what does all this have to do with you being here."

Brushing aside his remarks, Max continued on with his manifesto, "We need more! And I want you to know my thoughts before they start up with me. Liberal democracy can't respond boldly enough, it isn't working anymore. Do you think Main Street Republicans, Segregationist Democrats and New Dealers can come up with solutions together? It's governmental paralysis. Leadership reflects the needs and will of the people.

Today people want their nation's interest first. None of this one-world, League of Nations nonsense! This nationalism is sweeping Europe, not just in Germany and Italy, but now in Spain. And the movement is gaining momentum in other countries too. It's a wave that cannot be stopped, but a true leader can harness it. A real leader knows how to exploit the system and inspire… no, take the people and lead them on his mission!"

Although stunned by what he heard and still somehow grasping for the best, Alex couldn't help but see another, hidden side to his uncle. "That's not leading, that's ruling. It's an authoritarian argument that could have been spoken by any true fascist."

"Please, my ideology is efficiency, results, like our family's business—successful!"

"With a healthy dose of Max Wagner thrown in, I suspect."

"Somebody will have to do it. I'm not saying it's me, but someone like me, who has support not only here and in the state, but around the country and overseas. Someone like me, who after the War, spent years doing business in Europe."

"You have to know foreign financial support is illegal."

"Of course, but just for argument's sake, don't be so naive as to think every campaign doesn't rely on shady sources of funding. Believe me, they all do."

"Under the table money from some tycoon is one thing, but from the likes of Hitler's Germany…"

"Who said anything about Hitler. Once the military and the industrialists over there have their fill of him, they'll show the door to that former paper-hanger, corporal."

"I've come to doubt that!"

"Still, whether it's Hitler, or eventually some other strong nationalist like Admiral Canaris, or Alfred Krupp, the steel magnate, America needs a strong leader to deal with such strong men, certainly not Roosevelt. And let's not forget, this new Germany hasn't done anything against this country."

"Other than inspiring fifth-column insurrectionists like those Bundist..." Alex said, unable to bring himself to even broach the subject of stealing military secrets.

"Oh come on, they're nothing. They're just frustrated, like a lot of other people as they see this country drifting toward socialism."

"Anyone promoting race purity, dictatorship and violence are hardy 'nothing.' They're dangerous."

"Well, there's always a fringe element on any side; but there's a huge number of good people who want a real leader who puts America first."

"Uncle Max, do you hear yourself? This is the last thing you should be thinking about."

"Like I said, when Al gets here, he'll swat all this away like some bothersome gnat."

"I think they're looking at this very seriously. At the very least, you better lay off talk like this during questioning."

"Listen, I won't be cowered! I'm innocent of this spying nonsense!"

"I don't necessarily share your confidence about just slapping this away."

"Hell, I almost wish they do charge me! No jury in the country will convict me. I'll show how they're coming after me because I'm a non-interventionist like Lindbergh, or Henry Ford, who they're also going after. No, I'll be seen as a stand-up guy with power, who is willing to take on the establishment. Something the average Joe can't do."

"Well, I hope it doesn't come to that, and that everything comes out okay when they question you," Alex said, unable to hide his skeptical tone.

"I can tell by your manner that you have your doubts," Max responded, somewhat bewildered. "Is this what I get for trying to help you all your life!"

"It's not about loyalty. It's about truth and what's right. Still, I want you to be innocent."

"Unfortunately, despite all my efforts, I hear that same mealy-mouthed response that I've come to expect from you lately."

Although once more stung by his uncle's comments, Alex refused to falter. Suddenly, all the nuns, coaches, and most of all his parents, were at his ear. "There's nothing mealy-mouthed about it; but I'm torn. I have my values, that I mainly got from my family and you're an important part of that. Still, I won't abandon that, even to please you."

"This will sound harsh, but I want the best for you. I can see now, that you're going to have to learn the hard way; but I hope that eventually you'll see the light. You see, it ultimately boils down to this, Alex: There's lions and there's sheep. I choose to be a lion. I suggest you think long and hard about joining the herds of sheep."

Once more gathering his nerve in the face of his uncle, Alex shot back, "That's an easy choice, Uncle Max, if holding to my values, and listening to my better angels means joining the sheep, I'm all in. It's better than ruling over, and exploiting others."

"All I can say is you better smarten up, and put aside any childish inclinations of yours."

"I'm not the one sitting here waiting to be grilled by the cops; but maybe you're right, maybe I should give up some of my childish inclinations, like putting my uncle on a pedestal."

"And I'll talk to the police, and still make it to New York for a nice dinner tonight."

"You're probably right. You'll always be the smartest guy in the room, Uncle Max. Still, you can't anticipate what you don't know. You can never really know what's around the corner. Commissioner Costello taught me there's no such thing as a perfect crime. There's always some unforeseen detail that trips things up."

"Of course, the genius police always get their man. So that's who you're listening to, that old fool, who's long past his best days, and who's filling your head with stories of spies and Nazi boogie men."

"Yes, him along with my family, teachers, and mentors like Victor

Lange. And then there's my experiences these last months, whether it be my series on the Nazis, meeting Jim Jefferson, or falling for Maureen."

"I notice I'm no longer among your pantheon of heroes,"

"You'll always be an important part of my life."

"Well, Fraser should be here any minute now. Besides, I want to get this nonsense over with as quickly as possible. And yeah, we'll be all right, you and me."

Alex desperately clung to his belief that Max was good at his core, but somehow became lost. Yet, as he looked down at his uncle, he saw a reduced, smaller man. While hoping it was some crazy mistake, and that Max's alibi would prove true, he couldn't ignore the evidence. He couldn't escape the thought that Max was the victim of his own ego; that he forgot to recognize evil for what it was; that he failed to realize that colluding with the forces of darkness could only serve to ease its spread; that attempting to "manage" Hitler would only feed the beast, and that rationalizing deals with the likes of the Nazis, could only come at the expense of one's soul.

"Sure thing," he said as he managed a wistful smile, before he left his uncle in his isolation. Alex slowly stumbled out of the office, stunned by the abrupt turn of events. Brushing past a crowd waiting in the foyer for the elevator, he was lost in his thoughts. Finally, he spotted Commissioner Costello holding court with the others at the far end of the room.

Sensing his young partner was too hurt to join in, the old man took him aside, where he offered his sympathy, while praising his skill and irreplaceable hard work in helping to crack the case. After asking him to convey his appreciation to the others, Alex headed to the door.

Once outside, he was met by the sight of a glowering Kurt Metzger handcuffed between two cops while standing beside a police cruiser. Just as they began to shove him into the back seat, he turned and snarled with a maniacal grin, "Revenge is sweet, you fuckin' traitor!"

Watching as the squad car carried its unrepentant cargo to a Headquarters booking, Alex brushed off his threat as nothing more than toothless bravado. Yet, as he approached his abandoned car at the entrance to the plaza, he suddenly remembered Britta's warning about Krueger. Suddenly, he was struck with horror upon realizing that the Nazi strong-arm was still at large, with a head start.

Maureen no doubt was still at home and had already been a target of the gang's wrath. For an instant, he stood paralyzed, wondering if he should run back to the office. Instead, knowing every second counted, he jumped into his car and sped to her rescue.

XXII

"**Y**oo Hoo, is anybody there…" The opening catchphrase of the popular daytime soap opera, "The Goldbergs," rang through the parlor, as Missus Costello brought out a tray from the kitchen.

"Honey, will you get the radio. I forgot it was on."

"Just a sec Gram, I'm finishing stirring the stew."

No sooner had the old lady started setting the coffee table than Maureen walked in and turned off the console. "I call it Kenna's ethnic hour, first 'The Goldbergs,' then 'The O'Neills,' followed by the ever-wise Mother Moran, of 'Today's Children.'"

"You don't have to tell me," Lisa Mangini said, as she shifted her position on the old divan, "I spend most of my time listenin' to the soaps since I got home."

"Well, that's good, you need the rest, dear. And do you need a pillow? Are you comfy?"

"I'm just fine. You're just like my Nana, always tryin' to spoil me."

"Well, you deserve it, all you've been through. And between you and me, I have to admit the soaps are my guilty pleasure. That Molly

Goldberg is a hoot, and Mary Moran, she's just so kind and caring, always fixing things for her family."

"Oh, and I just love 'Backstage Wife!' Imagine, a small town girl goes to New York and marries a movie star," Lisa cooed, as she held a hand over her heart. "So romantic! Really gets my heart pumpin' and my imagination goin.' if ya know what I mean!" she giggled mischievously.

"I see you're getting back to normal," Maureen smiled wryly.

"Ya got that right! The doctors say my noggin's coming along just fine. I still forget some things but they say it's just a matter of time before I'm back to where I was."

"Well, you sure look good, my friend," Maureen gushed as she gave her a big hug before helping her grandmother cut the soda bread and apply the butter.

"I'm just weak from bein' in the hospital so long; but my brother Dom's buddy, who's a gym teacher, comes over every other night and shows me exercises to build me up."

"Just take your time, you have to heal," Kenna cautioned.

"I know, but the doctors say I gotta push myself a little. You know, go out and get some fresh air and sunshine. Besides, I gotta get back to work pretty soon. I got a lotta hospital bills comin' up."

"Well, Sam Reed from the Hell Diver line is organizing a fund raising dance for you. And Mister Reagan told me when you come back, he's going to put you in the front office answering phones at your regular pay, until you're a hundred percent back on your feet."

"Yeah, Tim called about that the other day, and I appreciate it. The company's been good, sent me over some grocery money a couple times since I got out. And yeah, Sam's a sweetie, too. I miss all the guys. I figure they gotta be broken hearted, me not bein' around 'n all," she said with a frisky wink.

"All kidding aside, we all miss you a lot, my plucky pal."

"And you better believe I'm gonna make that dance!"

"You have a lot of people pullin' for you, dear," Kenna said before getting up to tend to her stew and start the coffee.

"Thanks, Missus C, and especially my family, who've been there all along takin' care of me. And along with you, Mo!"

"Aw, that's sweet. You know, every time I'm over there has been a joy. And you've really come a long way!"

"Just seeing friends helps so much. And speakin' of friends, I've been bitin' my tongue to surprise ya, but guess what …" before Maureen had a chance to ask, Lisa announced, "Jim Jefferson called me yesterday morning, as soon as he got outta jail. He asked how I was doin', and thanked me for gettin' 'im off the hook."

"Oh my gosh, how nice!"

"Yeah, and me bein' itchin' to get out, he was glad to meet me over at Delaware Park. I didn't want the neighborhood punks who live near my house hasslin' 'im."

"Geez, every neighborhood has those idiots. But I hope it wasn't too much for you."

"Naw, like I said, I gotta push myself a little bit each day. So I had my sister, Magdalena, drive me over there. It's so peaceful there, with the boats on the lake, and the people strollin' by."

"So how was it?"

"Real nice. We just sat on a bench and had a nice talk. The first thing I said, was how sorry I was that he got dragged into all this."

"It sure wasn't your fault …"

"Sure, and he said the same thing. Still, he didn't hold back about the cops who pinned it on 'im."

"People make mistakes, but it seems like lazy police work at best; or, maybe just plain 'ol bigotry, once they heard mention of a Negro man."

"Disgusting what he went through! Thrown in jail; his reputation dragged through the mud; losin' his jobs …"

"And not the first time he's been the victim of injustice; but listen, there may be a silver lining to some of this. Alex was so certain that Jim was innocent, that he got a promise from his father to hire him at Alpine Machine, once he was released. He got the same assurance from his friend, Sid Cohen, over at the Starlite, once it reopens, and he got a commitment from Dan Richardson, too."

"That's great! You'll have to tell 'im yourselves. He said he wanted to talk to you guys, too. Maybe he can get an apartment he's been dreamin' about, and maybe even a car."

Just then, Kenna popped her head through the kitchen doorway. "I'm just getting the coffee ready, and Lisa dear, did you try the soda bread? I baked it early this morning, after Gramps left."

"Why so early? Isn't today when he has his weekly breakfast with his buddies from the K of C?"

"He didn't want me to tell you he was picking up Alex and meeting Danny on that case."

"What!"

"He thought things might get a little dicey."

"Something must have come up. I betcha it was Danny, and I don't like it! I'm no hot house orchid!"

"I know honey, you can do anything. But, it was probably just Danny playing big brother; and being retired, Gramps deferred to him. And besides, you would never have called off our visit with Lisa."

Meanwhile, across the street, the man sitting behind the wheel of a freshly pinched Dodge had little doubt as to whom was home at the Costello house. Hans Krueger had just rolled up when Lisa was dropped off at the porch, where she was warmly greeted by Wagner's girlfriend. His adrenalin was still pumped up for having somehow evaded capture. It only served to excite his resolve to exact revenge on his gang's race-traitor tormentor. He went on to feel a sense of satisfaction for having the foresight to trail the couple earlier that summer.

After scanning the terrain for any nosy neighbors, he spotted a telephone line leading into the house. This only served to reenforce his desire to move fast, in case the old cop got wise, and alerted his prey.

He made one last check of his avenue of escape before patting his pocket for his pistol, a prized possession from his rum running days. Stepping from the car, he felt a sense of rapture as he approached the porch.

"And we have you all morning," Maureen bubbled.

"So what time is your brother returning to pick you up," Kenna asked.

"After lunch, Missus C. He's stopping by Aunt Tina's near Saint Lucy's, then he's swingin' by the Elk Street Market, before he picks me up."

"He'll to have to have some of Grandma's lamb stew. It's her specialty!"

Just then, their conversation was interrupted by a knock on the door.

"That must be Kelly the iceman. He's here early," Kenna yelled from her kitchen command post.

"I'll hold the door. I don't know how he does it at his age, lugging all those blocks of ice."

No sooner had she snapped open the lock and turned the knob than she was grabbed by her hair and spun around in a deft move worthy of a gymnast. Lisa's scream brought Keena rushing into the living room, where she stopped in her tracks upon seeing Maureen with a hand across her mouth, and a gun pressed against her temple.

After kicking the door shut with his heel, Krueger barked out, "Sit down and shut up."

Seeing the terror in her granddaughter's eyes, Kenna quickly complied. She pulled Lisa to her side as she slid onto the couch; but not before the terrified girl managed to blurt out, "It's… it's him," as a look of horror flashed across her face.

The Nazi was initially taken aback at being recognized, yet, he quickly realized it didn't matter. Her being there would only leave bigger headlines. "I guess you're not scrambled in the head, like the papers say. But yeah, we did share some intimate moments, didn't we," he sarcastically crooned, before shoving Maureen onto a nearby chair. Keeping his gun pointed at his captives, he slid over, and ripped the phone from the wall. He then quickly turned and snapped the door lock. "Move a muscle, and I'll put one in your girlfriend's head, and then in the old lady's."

"Funny, I do remember your pecker bein' so small ya couldn't find it," Lisa sneered.

"I wouldn't touch that stinkin' hole that takes in n****r cocks!"

"Watch your mouth, Mister," Keena shot back.

"Listen, ya old hag, take that napkin and gag the girl if ya don't want me to finish the job on her. Then do the same with the redhead."

Trying to buy time, she did as ordered and gaged Lisa, but as slowly and loosely as possible.

"Don't play games sister. Tighten it up and hurry; and when you're done, grab those two curtain sashes,"

Using the order as a pretext to stall on her granddaughter, Keena moved to the curtain where she tried to appease him, "What do you want, money? I'll show you where we hide the cash, and my gold jewelry. Just let the girls go."

"That can wait for now," Krueger sneered.

Knowing that he wasn't about to let them leave there alive, she tried her best to gather her wits. She knew that any distraction was their only hope, and that once bound, they were as good as dead.

Maureen quickly arrived at the same conclusion, and she was equally swift at forging a plan. "Everybody knows who you are Krueger, and both you and I know you wouldn't be here if your plans didn't fail, and your gang of Nazi freaks wasn't broken up." She pressed on, seeing the hatred fill his eyes, "Your best option is to grab the money and take off before it's too late."

"Maybe I can have the old man and your punk boyfriend join our little get-together, here, and still get the money." Turning back to Keena he snapped, "And get on with tyin 'em up."

Maureen knew he wasn't about to risk that. Eyeing the slicing knife on the table, she decided to goad him into a mistake. Betting he had a problem with strong women, she shot back, "I might even fuck you, if you let them go…"

"Nice to see your little girl bein' a whore like the other one, huh," he cackled at Keena as she began to bind Lisa's hands.

"Ah, just as I thought, you can't handle a real woman! Can you?" Maureen smirked.

Krueger rushed up, ready to pistol whip her, yet he somehow managed to catch himself as he reared back. "Oh, you're askin' for it, all right!" he seethed as he stepped back to collect himself.

With Krueger distracted in his anger, Keena lifted Maureen's arms behind her back, before barely looping the sash around her wrists. Once she was sure he regained his focus, she tightly tied the gag. "Don't worry, honey, everything will be fine," she said before adding the Irish words for "take the knife," "*tóg an scian.*"

"Hey, what was that foreign gibberish?"

"Oh, *tòg an scian.* It's just the Irish term for 'the Saints be with you,'" Keena said, confident that her granddaughter remembered the Irish household terms that she taught her as a child.

"You and your saints and fairies! No wonder your people were under the British boot forever," he chuckled.

As he stood there deciding how to deal with the old lady, he looked down and spotted the soda bread on the coffee table. Grabbing a fistful, he stuffed it in his mouth.

Seeing her opening, Keena shot back, "I don't want my kitchen burnin' down. So, if ya know what's good for ya, ya better let me tend to the coffee brewin' out there."

"Okay… " he mumbled between gulps. "But I'll be watchin' ya all the way. So, no funny business!"

Krueger slowly backpedaled to the kitchen doorway, where he watched the old woman turn off the range beneath the percolator, before she put the coffee grinder back in the cabinet. All the while, he repeatedly glanced toward the parlor, keeping a wary eye on his two captives.

Satisfied all was in order, he barked out one more command, "And pour me a cup—black. And make it snappy!"

Keena appeared to tepidly carry the cup back to the table. She no doubt was trying to spare a stain on the carpet, Krueger laughed to himself.

After all, it was a moot exercise, since by now, he had decided to kill her first. Then it would be the "d***'s" turn, so that the "red-haired bitch" could watch the slaughter before her time was up. Eager to get things started, he turned to demand that the old lady sit down.

Instead, a searing pain and blinding light engulfed his eyes, as Keena tossed the boiling coffee into his face. Dropping his gun, Krueger frantically clawed at his eyes in a furious effort to find relief. Keena wasted no time in rearing back and smashing the stoneware mug against his head, leaving the Nazi teetering on his feet. Clutching the broken handle, she yelled out, "Kill these girls, will ya!"

As if on cue, Maureen threw herself at the table and with a wide swipe slashed the back of his hamstring. The already wounded gangster now lost control of his leg, sending him crumbling to the floor. Unable to focus his sight, and dragging his bloody limb across the carpet, he desperately groped for his pistol. He finally made out the object of his salvation, but not before Keena kicked it beneath a nearby cabinet.

Keena wasn't about to take any chances as she shouted, "Help Lisa, and get over to Smitty's bar!"

By now, Krueger had begun to rally. Relying on his prowess as a gymnast, he lifted himself up, ready to pounce on the old woman.

The sound of snapping wood and exploding glass filled the air, as Alex came crashing through the door. He quickly got up, and seeing the terrified women and bloody mayhem, threw himself toward Krueger. The stunned Nazi offered little resistance as Alex drove him onto the floor. As he drew back, ready to launch the finishing blow, Keena yelled, "Stop, he's bleeding out!"

"Anybody hurt," Alex blurted out.

"We're all okay," Maureen gasped, as she pulled off her gag and finished untying Lisa.

"Grab that tassel on the table and tourniquet his leg," the old lady said, before falling into the arms of her granddaughter.

"I'll flag a car for help, as if ya deserve it, you animal," Lisa spit out, in digust.

"Leave me alone. I wanna die like a soldier," Krueger groaned, as Alex brought over the sash.

"You're no soldier, you're just a bloodthirsty thug. Besides, you don't get to make that call. We value lives and mercy in my house."

"Typical socialist drivel. Let's all hold hands," Krueger snarled, regaining his bravado.

"Maybe you'll see the light, once you pay for your crimes in jail."

"And I'll come out stronger, old lady, because our cause can't be stopped," Krueger winced through his teeth, as his leg began to throb.

"People are too smart for that," Maureen shot back.

"You're the fools! You refuse to see the dangers of the Jews, or the mongrelizing of society by the n*****s, and the rest of the scum!"

"I pity you, believing all the lies, scapegoating, and hate, and following that… that… person like a god," Keena said, shaking her head.

"Don't worry, the Aryan people will win. We will own you!"

Just then, Little Brick and Danny came rushing through the shattered door.   Captain Duggan followed, as he helped walk Lisa back from the street. Ignoring the wreckage around him, the old man scooped his wife and granddaughter into his arms, and showered them with kisses.

"How did you know about…" Alex stammered.

"Not long after you left, we got a call from Downtown, sayin' Britta finally spilled her guts. She told 'em Krueger knew your girlfriend's address, and she was in danger. We flew over as fast as we could… I see they didn't get through," Duggan said, nodding towards the phone on the floor.

"Heil Hitler," Krueger grinned in an effort to taunt his captors.

"Shut your trap, Mister Master Race," Duggan snapped, before turning to Alex. "Leave the tourniquet to me. You go over and hug your girlfriend. You did good, kid."

"Thanks, Captain but it was the ladies who did it." Taking up Duggan's suggestion, Alex joined Maureen before pulling her into his arms. After he went over all that happened with the others, including his uncle, the couple headed to the privacy of the kitchen.

There, Alex once more drew her close. "God, I was so worried you were hurt, or worse! I couldn't imagine…"

"Well, he was no match for me, Lisa and Gramma; or, a boyfriend who wouldn't be stopped by a locked door," she smiled.

"Sorry about that, but I would've smashed through a brick wall for you! And lemme say, you and your Gram are amazing."

"Thank you, my sweetheart. And I'm so proud of what you've accomplished. It all started with your series…"

"What we accomplished! Me, you, your Gram and Gramps, Victor, Jim, Lisa, Captain Duggan, Jake Bloom and folks like Marsha Andrews, the waitress from the camp, and that cook from Ollie's. I've learned so much from so many people. And I think I found my calling, the newspaper business!"

"I'm so happy! You really made a difference!"

"I hope so… but there's a hole in my heart with Uncle Max. I love him and he's been such a presence in my life. I can only hope for the best, but…"

"I know. However it goes, he deserves our prayers."

"God, I just can't imagine Max being part of that, but whatever the case, having you makes things better."

"Same here! I'm so happy we're together."

Raising his face after a passionate kiss, he smiled, "We've come a long way since the night at the Al Hambra."

"We've found each other and faced evil and overcame it. I'd say that's awfully good."

"I'm afraid to say that sort of evil isn't going away; it's not about to rest. But we do have each other, and yes, that's very good."

ACKNOWLEDGEMENTS

Special thanks to Patricia Tutuska and Paul Murphy for their help.

A proud Buffalonian, John Grandits formerly served with the US Department of the Treasury, and the Department of Homeland Security. Among his works are the novels, *Wayfarer's Passage*, a political mystery, and *Canalside Tale*, the story of a detective's redemptive quest for justice, set against a backdrop of powerful elites and struggling masses in 1880's Buffalo.

www.ingramcontent.com/pod-product-compliance
Lightning Source LLC
Chambersburg PA
CBHW070745160726
48004CB00001B/66